Racer's Fiancée

A Moretti Racing Family Saga

by

James Herbert Harrison

ISBN: 979-8-9896936-2-7 (Paperback)
ISBN: 979-8-9896936-3-4 (Hardcover)

Copyright © 2024 by James Herbert Harrison

All rights reserved.

No portion of this book may be reproduced in any form without written permission from the author, except as permitted by U.S. copyright law.

Previous Releases by James Herbert Harrison

Based largely on actual events, Miracle From Ukraine is a tale of international romance, intrigue, and heaven sent destiny set in the pre-war period of Eastern Ukraine.

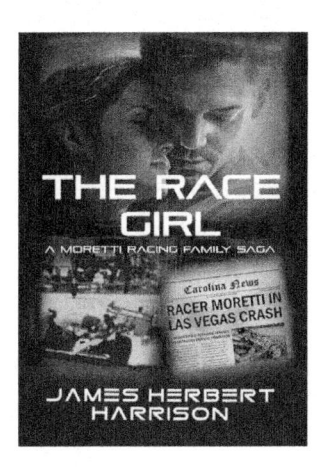

The first novel in the Moretti Racing Family Saga series, The Race Girl is a tale of two prominent families entangled when their two youngest engage in a forbidden romance, setting in motion the emotional intrigue of court room drama and high speed thrill of international motor racing.

Preface

Racer's Fiancée, the sequel to The Race Girl, is the second volume in The Moretti Racing Family Saga. The story was written to entertain those who enjoy a romantic sports yarn and intrigue readers who favor an organized crime drama. I make a tacit attempt to familiarize the casual fan with the immense challenges and rewards of modern big-time motor racing, requiring an indelible human spirit to overcome and succeed.

The story does draw attention to the serious worldwide problem of human trafficking, a crime that in many ways has no equal in sheer wickedness, and one that could someday touch the lives of anyone.

As a lifelong fan of the Andrettis, The Moretti Racing Family Saga series was largely inspired by their storied history in motor racing as well as the sport in general, the series, the teams, the drivers, and the family challenges behind the loud engines and roar of the crowds.

—James Herbert Harrison

Prologue

She sat on the pit stand with interest, getting used to her new station on the team as the lead driver's better half. Amanda asked a lot of questions and was welcomed with open arms by the other drivers' spouses and girlfriends, a close-knit group the series had always enjoyed. She wasn't sure if she was supposed to do much and her future father-in-law, team principal Andy Moretti, insisted that she could assist his youngest son Alex and the crew in any way she wished. She was enjoying the novelty of being able to chit-chat with her fiancé through his in-car radio as they casually discussed an upcoming trip to the mountains she had planned for them.

The series only had one female driver and Amanda had become friendly with Evelyn Stevens, her fiancé's former teammate and live-in girlfriend. Realizing that any lingering feelings of jealousy were comfortably in the past, the budding friendship was fueled by the fact that Amanda had taken much of the media attention away from Stevens, a scenario the Brit didn't mind in the least.

The fact that Stevens wanted to re-join Moretti Motorsport the following season, now the worst kept secret in the series' paddock, was now looked upon favorably by young Amanda and her newly rekindled relationships with Evelyn and Alex's sister-in-law, Crissy, were quite a contrast from Amanda's now toxic relationship with her own sister, Allison.

"Why are the cars so much slower here?" Amanda asked Andy. "Ninety-seven miles per hour doesn't seem that good, is it?"

Andy chuckled. "That's an average for the whole lap, Amanda. This circuit has some very slow turns, unlike Indianapolis. Alex will approach a hundred-ninety on the backstretch here."

Looking around at the track, which was run on actual city streets with temporally constructed barriers, fences, and spectator stands, she wondered why the series didn't simply schedule races at places like Charlotte which already had a ready-made speedway, not on the scale of Indy but much more so than this.

"We're kind of a hybrid between NASCAR and Formula One," Crissy explained. "That is the series' identity, cars that run on any type of circuit from one week to the next. You do like Long Beach, don't you?"

"Oh yes. I love that place," Amanda replied smiling. The famous California LA suburb had served as a backdrop where both of the young women had fallen for their prospective Moretti racing brothers.

She looked to the on-track action with a growing curiosity as the pre-race qualifications were much different from the format at Indy. The cars were all split into two groups, each running around the street circuit for a brief period, not racing each other but each driver looking for that lowest elapsed time on one fast lap. Qualification had moved eventually to the *Fast Six*, a final round where the fastest half dozen drivers from the earlier sessions ran in timed laps to compete for the Pole. Alex had been fast all day and roared past the pits passing Alex Palou, who patiently allowed Moretti some distance to set himself up for his best shot the next lap around.

Amanda was shown how to use the stopwatch feature on her iPhone to monitor lap times and cheered loudly when Alex passed the flag stand with a Pole-leading time of just a click over one minute, an average of ninety-eight miles per hour. Of course, the track's high-tech timing systems would monitor the official speeds, although Andy insisted that Amanda learn some things the old-fashioned way to give her a better grounding in their sport.

She thought briefly of how her future sister-in-law now coped with the dark side of the sport. The whole family was still recovering from Tony Moretti's life-threatening crash at Indy, one that had claimed the life of a young rookie named George Halbert, who was killed instantly. Amanda had a few passing thoughts on whether she herself had the strength to deal with such a trauma.

She watched with interest as Alex had dropped to third fastest in the session and prepared for one last fast lap before time expired. Suddenly, a tremendous crash was heard coming from the far side of the circuit. Amanda could quickly see from the reaction of the crew and their expressions toward her it involved Alex, and it was very bad. She froze momentarily and then looked behind at a track monitor displaying the replay of the accident. The number "5" Amoco-sponsored car had come upon a slower car which braked early before a tight turn. Alex had slammed on his brakes but couldn't avoid contact, his left front tire climbing over the right rear of the slower car, initiating a terrifying crash. Moretti's car flipped over and hit the concrete barrier hard, causing the car to nearly break in two.

"Oh my god! No!.. Alex,... No!... No!" She was screaming hysterically. The two had endured a year of clandestine romance, a life-threatening Las Vegas crash, another two years of dealing with the South Carolinian criminal justice system, and now that the skies had finally cleared for the two of them, this.

Her screams gradually declined as she wept uncontrollably when suddenly she was jolted, feeling some strong hands grip her shoulders. "Amanda!... Amanda!... Wake up baby," Alex yelled at her. "Amanda! You're having a bad dream."

Chapter 1

Indy Celebration

The world's largest sports stadium slowly emptied, as some 350,000 fans were treated to a race for the ages, two former teammates and romantics starting from the last row and fighting it out on the last laps for the most coveted trophy in racing. When the race winner, Alex Moretti, gave the crowd an added bonus by proposing marriage to his newly rekindled girlfriend, Amanda Cook, all right up on the victory podium, the crowd all knew it would go down as perhaps the most memorable 500 ever. The spot would go hyper-viral and become the most-viewed social media video in world history.

Among the few dry eyes in the place were those of none other than Amanda's own father, Byron Cook, and his secret mistress, Carolyn Tyler. Cook had experienced a long-running feud with Alex Moretti and his team-owner father, indeed a conflict launched two years earlier over Alex and Amanda's hidden romance, one that had nearly put Alex behind bars and all but destroyed the Cook family in the process.

Experiencing the surprising event unfolding before her very eyes, Amanda's mother, Sarah Cook, saw it as a miracle that could finally mend the rift at home and end the fierce dispute between the aspiring couple's fathers.

Although most of the Unibank dignitaries were as amazed and gleeful as was the crowd generally, Sarah was disappointed in her husband as Byron could barely force a smile, and when Sarah insisted that he stay over a day or two and take part in the celebration, he would have no part of it, explaining to his wife of twenty-two years that he would fly out on the corporate jet the next morning as originally planned, not even bothering to question Sarah about her own nor Amanda's extended lodging plans.

Following the many congratulatory hugs, backslaps, and handshakes, Alex and Amanda took an extra victory lap around the famous track in a new Camaro convertible. Afterward, the Moretti Motorsport contingent all gathered at the team buses in preparation for the post-victory party that evening. The immediate family members, including Amanda, would first pay a visit to the hospital where Tony Moretti was still recovering from the serious crash suffered a few days earlier.

Amanda expected a somber atmosphere in Tony's room but was surprised to see the entire family upbeat, although Amanda's expectant brother-in-law was still seriously injured and could hardly move in the bed. She learned that he had miraculously awakened just at the end of the race, able to watch the live feed of his little brother making history. She blushed while clutching her new fiancé's arm, seeing herself on the ESPN highlight reel accepting the ring before a worldwide audience. *Such a close-knit family,* she observed. *If only my own could have such tranquility.*

⚑✕⚑

Sarah and Amanda had surprised everyone earlier that Sunday morning by driving up to the race overnight following her high school graduation ceremony, all for the initial purpose of supporting the Moretti family as the older driving son remained in critical condition in a hospital IC unit.

Following a strange series of events where Amanda had gone from being estranged from Alex for months to suddenly his fiancée, Sarah felt it parentally prudent to stay close to her youngest daughter for a few days since Amanda wanted no part of leaving him again as the whole Moretti team would just travel up the road to race a few days later in Detroit.

When Sarah persisted that Byron reconsider, even suggesting that he accompany her to the motor city, he rejected it out-of-hand and kept with his plans to head back to Charlotte the next morning. If Sarah thought the surprising engagement would put an end to the long-running Hatfields and McCoys style feud between the two budding fathers-in-law, at least on the part of her husband, she was quite mistaken and disappointed.

She also had not forgotten about the rift that continued between the Cooks and the Williams family over seriously unpleasant revelations from Amanda's testimony in her future husband's trial. Lisa Williams had been Sarah's best friend since the two were kids together. They had both been maids of honor at each other's weddings, along with their husbands, who had served each other in the male capacity. The families had been extremely close for many years, making this rift, which had now gone on for over four months, especially painful. *Now is not the time to sulk about such things,* Sarah pondered. *That personal turf war will still be there when I return home.*

Uncomfortable was a word insufficient to describe the atmosphere around the Sunday evening dinner table at the upscale downtown Indianapolis restaurant. From a first-class Unibank VIP suite view, they had all seen a thrilling Indy 500 finish just hours before, a shootout between two drivers starting from the last row. The Unibank-sponsored car driven by Evelyn Stevens seemed to be heading toward a historic win when her car coughed and lost power with the checkered flag in clear sight, allowing her erstwhile lover, Alex Moretti, to pounce and take the victory in a photo finish.

Byron sat at the head of the table, extremely on edge out of fear his wife would sense he was cheating with Carolyn Tyler, his clandestine mistress, who was sitting right there with them.

Meanwhile, Sarah sat beside him opposite Tyler, naively unsuspecting, and could hardly hide her glee as a first-hand witness just hours earlier to the victory and marriage proposal. She had never shared her husband's anger toward the Morettis, accepting the serious Vegas accident just over two years prior as just that, an accident.

Their older daughter, Allison, tried to hide her immense anger as her background efforts to help her father bankrupt the Moretti family's race team had blown up in her face while her shy little sister, one who had spent her whole life in the older sibling's shadow, had suddenly become universally beloved and world-famous right before their very eyes.

The parents were all too aware their two daughters were at loggerheads with each other and thus believed this to be the reason Amanda would not be joining them for the evening. In reality, the eighteen-year-old was still starry-eyed over the events at the great race just hours earlier, a moment to be the stories of legend for generations to come. Separated from her new fiancé for the past three-plus months, Amanda was of a mindset not to let him out of her sight anytime soon, and the two declined her mother's dinner invitation, knowing her father would likely need some time to accept things.

Tyler was perhaps the most uncomfortable of the four, as this was the first time she had broken bread with Byron Cook and his wife, Sarah, all present together in an intimate setting since their affair had begun nearly two years prior. The tension between Byron and Sarah was slightly less than toxic over the race result, and now every time Sarah looked over at Tyler the mistress would feel her skin crawl.

The entire month of May had provided tremendous exposure for the corporate brand with the immense drama of their Unibank-sponsored star Evelyn Stevens' last-second qualifying run, and then her coming within an eyelash of actually winning from the last row. However, at Allison's suggestion and Byron's direction, Carolyn had orchestrated the removal of the Unibank livery from Alex Moretti's winning car, a serious chance error that ceded the paid dividends in advertising to BP's Amoco brand for many months to come.

Allison herself was planning her own summer wedding with Aaron Williams, although the grandeur and pomp surrounding a marriage involving two of South Carolina's most prominent families was suddenly shoved off the front page, not to mention the fact the two families were not speaking.

"The news about Louis Newberry is such a shock," Allison stated, wanting to break some uncomfortable silence. "I suppose Adam Herrera will take over as Evelyn's agent." *I know father will not like the thought of that.*

Herrera, the former Unibank Senior Vice President of Marketing, had been the driving force responsible for the banking giant's entry into motor racing originally. The California transplant had left months earlier when the Unibank CEO had stripped him of handling the Moretti Motorsport contract in favor of Carolyn Tyler, his closet mistress. Herrera had thus resigned and, given his known popularity in the racing paddocks, started his own agency representing teams and drivers.

"No, Carolyn will let it be known that would not be acceptable to us," Byron responded, eyeing his mistress with a neutral expression and feeling the pressure of his guilt. "As it appears that we're into this racing money pit for the duration, why don't you approach Stevens about becoming her agent yourself, Allison?"

Trying to appear surprised, Allison gave everyone a wide-eyed stare to gauge their reaction. This had been her plan all along, to start her post-college career as the exclusive agent for the world's most sought-after photo model while plugging herself right into the heart of the international racing scene. In addition to the commissions on Stevens' team compensation, the potential for advertising contracts worldwide would potentially rival major sports superstars like Patrick Mahomes and Ronaldo Christiano.

"Since I have suspended the contentious issues on her contract for now, there should be no rush considering such a tragic loss," Tyler exclaimed, in no way excited about the prospect of her lover's daughter getting so closely involved in their business, believing Allison to be a shrewd and cunning opportunist, one who would likely see right through her own part involving her father's infidelity.

"Evelyn was about to dump Newberry anyway," Allison added, better at suppressing her own guilt than her naturally straight-laced father.

"Allison! The young man just died of an overdose!" Sarah scolded. "Can we at least allow him a Christian burial before we speak of his shortcomings?"

"I'm surprised he didn't succumb to some sort of sexually transmitted disease. I heard speak that he'd slept with every whore in Charlotte," Byron added, a bit too casually to suit Sarah.

Allison just hesitated and felt a huge gulp in her throat.

⚑✕⚑

Sarah felt awkward on Memorial Day morning in seeing her husband off with the rest of the Unibank VIP entourage, including Wally and Mary Jane Remington, a couple the Cooks had long been close to. While Byron struggled to keep a straight face and Carolyn Tyler worked to look all business, Sarah and Mary Jane embraced each other on the tarmac as though the two could sense something was not quite right.

She had chosen to stay close to Amanda as the Moretti Motorsport team, along with all the rest of the series contingent, would remain in town for the Indy 500 winner's banquet dinner at the JW Marriott hotel on Monday evening. As race winner, Alex would be the evening's honored participant, but Amanda had captured the hearts of everyone as his new fiancée and the event had taken on an additional festive atmosphere in her honor.

The Moretti family's featured table was absent a few placings as Crissy Moretti stayed on station at the hospital beside a recovering husband while his grandmother, Matilde, and Aunt Marie agreed to watch the little ones. Tony was just starting to sit up in bed and speak openly, although other motions had yet to come.

Sarah sat beaming at the smile on her daughter's face, proudly showing off her new diamond ring after living through months of despair, when it seemed as though all had been lost between her and the only young man she had ever loved. Her mom was so happy for the two of them, a warm feeling that temporarily supplanted the stress that surely awaited her at home.

Coming from an old-fashioned southern culture, she felt somewhat self-conscious about being at this upscale formal dinner without her husband. As she observed all of the awards and listened to all the various speedway dignitaries and team personnel entertain with their speeches, her mind wandered as she looked back on her adult life, trying to recall if this had ever happened. The fact that Alex's father was unmarried nor appeared to be attached gave off the strange appearance that she was his "date" for the affair, as the seating arrangements had them both together at the head table with Alex and Amanda.

Calm yourself, Sarah Cook, her thoughts kept running. *You're the only person in this hall who worries about such things.* Yet she couldn't stop thinking about Andy, how he seemed to harbor no ill will toward her husband. *A stark difference,* she observed. Sarah couldn't help from being a little curious about his personal life, a man in upper-middle age now and still quite handsome. *Why doesn't he have anyone?* Sarah kept thinking. *His two boys both seem so romantic.*

Her thoughts returned to Byron and her disappointment that he hadn't stayed for this. The two hadn't shared intimacy since Amanda's accident and Sarah had hopes that their daughter's engagement with Alex Moretti would serve to bury the hatchet between the two patriarchs, perhaps giving the Cook family a new beginning. *Over two years...I need to start the process of rekindling what we had,* Sarah kept telling herself. *After so much time, so much bitterness. And now with Allison feuding with Amanda and the rift with their closest friends, the Williams, or former closest friends, it will be hard.... Very hard.*

The crowd was totally silent in anticipation as Alex took to the podium to accept the famous trophy from *The Captain,* Roger

Penske. A young man historically comfortable in front of a crowd, he began to choke up as he spoke.

"As you all know, the trip to Indianapolis started for me on such an ominous note. I got the call on Tuesday that Tony had been in a serious crash and was fighting for his life. When I first saw him there in the ICU, the first thoughts I had were how unfair it all was. I was always the careless one, the reckless driver who often pushed the car over the edge. But somehow the lord works in mysterious ways and I was brought here. I got in an IndyCar for the first time in nearly three years, just wanting to do the family proud,... and do it for Tony. Then, just as the race is about to start, I hear Dad over my headset telling me that Amanda was here, a girl that I had not seen or barely spoken to since Daytona. All throughout the race I drove my best and at the end, it just seemed that it was all meant to be. How many people ever go through life having their two most thrilling and emotional moments happen at the same time, indeed within minutes of each other? I am truly the luckiest man alive today.

I heard later that Evelyn Stevens had called Amanda on my behalf to encourage her to come and support me. Evelyn will long regret that call, as it may have given me that little bit of extra boost, just enough to travel 500 miles a second or two faster..."

The crowd roared with laughter at Evelyn Stevens' expense, one who forced a smile as she was still saddened by the news that her longtime agent, Louis Newberry, had just died on Saturday night of an apparent overdose. Even though they had fallen out in recent months and she had serious thoughts of dumping him, Louie had been with her from the start. Evelyn had missed becoming the first female to win the famous race but was yet thrilled for her former teammate, boyfriend, and his new bride-to-be, not to mention Andy Moretti, whose last-minute overture in sending his technical staff to assist her crew had played a huge role in her making the show period.

Later that night, the four gathered in the hotel's main lounge after the congratulatory post-banquet crowd finally dispersed. Andy and Sarah traded questions with the celebrated couple regarding summer plans, a wedding, etc. The lounge waitress was ever so apologetic toward Amanda for serving her a Sprite as the drinking age in Indiana was still twenty-one. Amanda was also getting her first taste of genuine celebrity, as more than a few patrons couldn't resist asking her *and* Alex for their autographs. At just past 11:00, the two wished to excuse themselves and departed for their room.

Andy and Sarah remained for a few moments as Amanda's mom was still adjusting to the reality of her little girl growing up.

"We could have arranged for them to have separate rooms for now, Sarah," Andy stated, seeing that she was still a bit uncomfortable.

"Oh, Andy. I just have to get used to it. I was barely sixteen when Byron and I married," Sarah replied smiling, not mentioning that she was pregnant with their first child.

"She's with a good man," Andy replied as he was getting accustomed to calling his youngest boy a man. "You know, Sarah. Alex had always been the carefree spirit of my two boys. As I look back on it now, ever since he met Amanda back in Long Beach three years ago, he's changed. I didn't pick up on it at first, but now I know it."

"I'm just glad to see Amanda so happy."

"How are you now, Sarah? I mean, I suppose Byron and I still have some fences to mend."

Sarah just stared at her wine glass momentarily before finishing off the last few sips. "You don't seem that bitter, do you? Byron really wanted to destroy you."

"Yes, well he didn't succeed," he answered, knowing Sarah was never in concert with her husband, something he recalled from the trial months earlier. "We'll all learn from it, hopefully."

"We've been married for twenty-two years, Andy. It feels strange that he left without me this morning. Other than a few out-of-town business meetings over the years, we haven't experienced that all that much," she said. Sarah didn't add that Byron didn't seem all that upset about heading home without her or that she would be away another full week, sentiments that bothered her. "Well, I suppose I had better head up to bed."

"I'll walk you up."

The two left the elevator and strolled together down the hall toward room 821, reserved for Sarah and Amanda. Sarah dug the keycard out of her purse and slid it through the lock mechanism.

"Andy, thank you for all of your kindness and hospitality you've shown me, having Maria take care of all my arrangements, the dinner banquet. Everything has been so nice," she said as she looked up at him smiling.

"It's the least I could do for,... one of my sponsors." Andy wished to say different words, but Sarah got his true meaning. "Good night, Sarah."

Meanwhile, Alex and Amanda couldn't get enough of each other. It seemed the long saga of being apart during the legal process and their dust-up following Daytona had now made them closer than ever.

By 2:00 AM, the two were ready to crash when Amanda gave her beau a serious look. "I'm thinking about Crissy, Alex. She's like become the soul sister I've never had. Do you think Tony will ever fully recover?" She didn't wish to say, but wondered how they would be, as a family, as a couple.

"We can only hope for the best for him, babe."

"And pray."

"Yes, that, too."

Crissy greeted the two the following morning as they entered the semi-private room. Despite it being barely a week since Tony's near-fatal accident, she appeared as a woman looking tired beyond her years. She embraced Amanda who became immediately emotional and felt the strength of her future sister-in-law seemed without equal. As much as Amanda had been through over the past two years, indeed a lot for any teenage girl to endure, she suddenly compared that to Crissy's saga and felt almost ashamed.

Ten days earlier, Tony had displayed a triumphant return to Indy following a year away while competing in Formula One. When he won the coveted Pole Position for the third time, Tony was tagged as a favorite to win the 500 in a very talent-laden international field. Three days later he struck another car in practice that had lost control and smashed hard into the turn four wall before veering right into Tony's path. Rookie driver George Halbert was killed instantly when the Pole sitter T-boned his car at over 220 miles per hour. Tony's injuries also appeared critical, and his survival had been very much in doubt.

Amanda was in tears while thinking about how fate had somehow played such a role in her life. She and Alex hadn't seen or even spoken to each other for months. If Tony had not crashed, Crissy would not have called her, and she would not have driven all night from Rock

Hill to Indianapolis with her mother, all of which set the stage for an event that would pass down for generations as legend.

The good news was that Tony had survived, had awakened, and was slowly making progress. He would be cleared for travel, and although the doctors preferred that he return to his Lake Norman home outside of Charlotte for several weeks of healing, he insisted that he rejoin the team in Detroit.

"Let's leave the boys to talk shop for a few, Amanda. I need a break and some coffee."

Alex gave his bride-to-be a supportive nod and watched as the two girls departed. The two passed by the numerous visitors and hospital staff, all of whom recognized Amanda from the many social media posts over the past forty-eight hours.

"I heard the Awards Banquet was quite a rush, Amanda."

"Oh, it was, Crissy. I'm so sorry you couldn't be there. Everyone was so nice, going out of their way to congratulate me like I was the one getting that big trophy."

"Yes, the paddock group here is so close-knit. I didn't realize that as much until I was no longer a part of it," Crissy stated.

"I don't understand, Crissy."

"When Tony left for Formula One last year, it was a huge adjustment. The paddock there is very high-pressure and just doesn't have this *we're all family* feeling that exists here."

"Hmm, I see,... I guess," Amanda responded, still not fully grasping Crissy's meaning. "What's it like being married to a racing driver? Like, I remember when Alex crashed at the start of the Indy three years ago. We barely knew each other yet, but I nearly fell apart."

"You can't dwell on the danger, Amanda. It will destroy you. You just have to keep praying and keep smiling. Your man cannot worry about what you think. When he's in that racecar, all of his concentration is necessary. One small lapse could mean just one mistake, and mistakes at 200 miles per hour are not good. So, have you two set a date yet?"

"No, we haven't. I know my mom wants a big wedding."

"Do I see a *but* in that next sentence?"

"It's kind of complicated, Crissy."

"It's your dad, isn't it?"

The two pushed their service tray toward the hospital cafeteria's cashier while Amanda began to blush, as it seemed everyone there; staff, patients, and visitors, seemed to pay extra attention to her presence. Crissy could see her being self-conscious about it. They migrated toward a relatively secluded corner table and sat down.

"My father really wanted Alex convicted," Amanda stated. "He knew I would be hurt badly if that happened, but it seemed he didn't care. I don't know if I'll ever have a good relationship with him again. And then there's my sister. We're like not on speaking terms, either."

Crissy passed on commenting about Allison, recalling that she had never so much as sent her husband a *"Get Well"* text. "If you choose to just have a small ceremony, Tony and I will happily stand up for you. You and Alex can always repeat your vows in a more formal setting later."

"I would be down for that in a heartbeat, Crissy. I just don't want to hurt Mom. She'll be extremely disappointed. I know that may seem flakey, Crissy, but my mom has, like, always been there for me, even when Dad wanted a rope around Alex's neck."

"Sarah is such a special lady. You're fortunate to have that support in your life." Crissy gave Amanda the short version of her own story, one of a broken home, alcohol, and drug abuse, with drifters sleeping with her mother at random. A father she never knew.

"You seem to fit in well with Tony's family," Amanda stated, a bit curious for the reply.

"Oh yes. When I met Tony, it was like I was reborn. The whole family, Matilde, Marie,... they treat me like a princess."

"And Tony's father?"

"Andy is great. He's always very serious about the business, so we don't spend a ton of time together."

"He doesn't have a woman in his life?"

"No, not so much," Crissy answered. "I think Andy is lonely, though. I can sense it. Tony's mother is talking to us about flying in from Europe for a visit. It took her a few days, but she heard about Tony's accident. Neither he nor Alex have seen her in years."

"Oh? Have you met her?" Amanda was genuinely curious about this news.

"Yes, one time. She came here when Tony and I first got married."

"So she hasn't seen her grandkids?"

"Not yet," Crissy answered while looking away, in her own mind thinking Tony's mother reminded her of her own.

"How do Andy and his ex-wife get along?"

Crissy gave her a look while shaking her head. "It's kinda weird, Amanda. They try to act normal around each other, but I can tell there is friction. Sabetha is still a striking woman for her age. She was a model, you know. The two of them took a weekend trip to Key West together back then. The family had all sorts of opinions on whether it meant something. But they returned and things didn't seem any different between them. She went back to Europe and went years without us having any contact with her."

"They must have been a hot couple when they met back in the day," Amanda added.

"Oh yes, she was quite famous and I'm sure Andy was a dashing Grand Prix star. Like you and Alex," Crissy replied, smiling.

"Like you and Tony."

"Thank you, sis. Flattery will get you everywhere."

Amanda blushed slightly, a warm feeling coming over her at Crissy Moretti referring to her that way. She could tell the two of them were going to be close.

※

Within minutes after Tony had regained his clarity, his thoughts migrated to the challenge of Moretti Motorsport's Formula 1 team, just starting to move up in the pecking order before his choice to run at Indy. Still a question of whether he himself would ever drive again, the older of the second-generation drivers began to lobby his younger sibling on taking his place.

"I'm just getting back into the Dallara," Alex stated, referring to his long exile from IndyCars. "Maybe next year, brother. We can arm wrestle over who will be number one."

"I may never drive again. You know that, Alex. I remember that test in the McLaren we did three years ago in England. You were a click faster than me then and I wasn't holding anything back. With some good practice, I think you're ready," Tony stated. "The team is in serious trouble now. I know Dad's worried stiff."

Prior to his accident, Tony had been doing very well, out-qualifying and consistently finishing three to four places ahead of Moretti's second driver, Geoff Leland. There had even been rumors of Ferrari and Mercedes' interest in pursuing his services. The news that Monaco had been canceled had been received enthusiastically in the Moretti household. Tony had the last two weekends in May off, anxious to get back for another chance at winning Indy, and Crissy was thrilled to be back in the States for a few weeks.

But fate had struck and Tony was nearly killed, while his brother reluctantly climbed into his pole-winning car and won the race despite a last row start. The Moretti family had endured the extremes of emotions and now Tony, happy to just be alive, struggled to stand on his own. While not a man to drown in self-pity, he knew his future driving a race car was looking questionable, to put it optimistically. He was also one to consider the ongoing fortunes of the family team over his own considerations, always of the belief that in the long term, both would go hand in hand.

"I remember Daytona all too well, Tony. Amanda and I endured a forced absence for two whole years and then immediately after the trial ended and the charges were dropped, I go tracing off to Daytona and another race. That whole episode nearly destroyed us, and I don't want a repeat of it."

"Amanda could travel with you," Tony replied expectantly.

"You know it wouldn't be the same, Tony. She's only been to a few races and always as a guest. Formula One has a bit too much,... what's the right word? *Glitz*. You know Amanda is not like her older sister. She's not as comfortable in the limelight."

"Well, it appears you've put her there, brother. And after your time with Evelyn, I know you appreciate how that can affect someone," Tony added.

Prior to meeting Amanda, Alex had a lengthy romance with Evelyn Stevens, the boys' teammate and the sport's adopted model celebrity. While the two shared a strong intimate bond, her commercial demands fueled by her overzealous business agent were the reason Alex sought romance elsewhere. "You're right. I do."

"If rumor has it, she'll be back with the team next year. How will Amanda feel about that?"

"I think she'll be all right. You do know that Evelyn called Amanda and asked her to call me before the race."

"Yes, and you know who put her up to it," Tony replied with a slight smirk.

"Yes, Crissy. But Evelyn did call her and the rest is history," Alex added, the two pausing their conversation as the station nurse came in to check on him.

"You always did have a flare for the dramatic, little brother. But I will be able to tell my grandkids that their grandmother had a hand in it."

As did you, Tony, Alex knew, seeing no need to revisit the horrors of his brother's accident.

On Wednesday morning, Alex, Amanda, and Sarah piled into Amanda's Mustang and headed north for Detroit. Sarah fancied herself as a kid again, the wind blowing her hair all around as her future son-in-law insisted they drive with the top down. It seemed as though every other passing vehicle, particularly the trucks, were honking at them, many of them truckers but a goodly number who simply knew who they were now.

Alex offered to ride in one of the cramped rear seats, but Sarah would have no part of it, feeling she was perhaps over-parenting as it was. It was a lot to consume as just a few days earlier she was attending her youngest daughter's high school graduation and now having to adjust to the idea of her suddenly being engaged to be married. She was still feeling exhilarated by the thrilling race victory, the dramatic proposal to Amanda by Alex in front of a worldwide audience, and her VIP treatment at the victory banquet.

Sarah still had to face the emotional challenges at home, but suppressed the thought for now, hoping to just enjoy the upcoming weekend. The family problems with her husband, older daughter, and the Williams would still be there when she returned. *I can't change that,* she pondered as she waved at the next horn-blaring semi-truck they passed.

The three stopped for fuel just outside Fort Wayne and the girls hit the restroom.

"Amanda, don't you think it bothers Alex, all those honks and catcalls along the highway?" Sarah asked, blushing.

"No. It gives him a sense of pride, I think. And Mom, are you like, blind? They were not all honking and yelling at me."

Alex finished fueling and entered the store to purchase some drinks and snacks. Amanda and Sarah joined him at the register when the young woman behind the counter became most animated.

"Oh, my lord! You're Alex Moretti and is this Amanda? Could I please get your autographs?"

Alex looked around, not wanting to attract too much attention as Amanda turned beet red. "Sure, do you have something we could sign?"

The woman frantically looked around, finally producing an Indianapolis Motor Speedway Museum flyer and digging out a flair marker. "Just sign it *Alex and Amanda Moretti,* please."

Alex smiled and quickly signed his full name with an "and" sign after it, and Amanda looked sheepishly at Sarah while simply signing as "Amanda", all to the delight of the cashier.

The three gathered themselves and retreated back to the red Mustang when Sarah requested they ride with the top back on, amused but having enough of all the loud horns and colorful sign language, much less the wind.

"I'm not sure I'll change my last name," Amanda declared, mostly to give Alex a rise. "Why can we not become Alex and Amanda Cook?"

Alex accelerated down the entry ramp back on I-69 and glanced through the rearview mirror for Sarah's reaction, who gave him a quick grin and rolled her eyes.

"We'd have to contact the speedway staff and have them change the Borg-Warner Trophy. I'm not sure that would go over real well, Amanda. I thought you liked my last name!"

"Oh, she does," Sarah responded quickly. "Don't let her fool you."

Amanda smiled inwardly while glancing away as they passed through Fort Wayne. She briefly thought back to their first encounter in Long Beach, California, over three years prior. She had thought the dashing young race driver was the hottest-looking guy she'd ever met, and at the time she wasn't even old enough to drive a car. Even though he was dating the popular British driver, Evelyn Stevens, Amanda could see her older sister being aggressive toward him despite her own serious engagement to Aaron Williams. It was all in vain on Allison's part, as Alex rejected her outright. Amanda had fallen for him that very night, a love affair that hadn't seemed to be made in heaven. But the two had endured and were engaged to be married, not to mention now world famous. *Amanda Moretti. It has a nice ring to it, I think.*

Andy and his younger sister, Alex's Aunt Marie, joined the three for dinner at their Detroit hotel, where they would lodge through Saturday night and head back south to the Carolinas right after Sunday's event. Sarah and Amanda quickly learned the post-race celebrations for the Grand Prix in Detroit, as with most of the rest of the season's events, would lack the huge media pomp, awards banquet, etc. of the 500 in Indy, a scenario not altogether unwelcome. Sarah needed rest and the coziness of her own bed, while Amanda wanted some privacy with her race man for a few days.

Marie was Andy's younger sister and handled all the company's travel and guest arrangements. She was completely falling for Amanda like everyone else, not to mention a fondness for her mother. Marie had only known Sarah in the past as Byron Cook's wife, his being the figure who attempted to financially destroy the Moretti family. The two soon got along splendidly and following dinner, Alex suggested that he and Amanda had to catch up on some "personal business" and departed for their top-floor suite, a special arrangement approved by Andy himself, with Sarah having a private suite right down the hall.

Marie escorted Sarah to the lounge where the two soon-to-be middle-aged gals enjoyed some fine wine and chatted away into the long hours. Sarah had been curious why Maria, one who appeared to have been quite the beauty in her own right, had no family of her own. Maria shared that she had been married once to one of Andy's former Ferrari teammates, a young Austrian she left after learning of his infidelity. Efforts for reconciliation were not to be, however, with Maria suffering further heartbreak as he was killed shortly thereafter in a 1000-kilometer sports car race in Barcelona.

They shared toasts, laughed, and talked as though they had known each other for years. Sarah had long missed the friendly comradery she had with Lisa Williams, as the two lifelong friends had not spoken in months. For her part, Maria had become so consumed with helping to run the family race team, she had little time of her own for personal friends, male or female, and thus enjoyed the time with Sarah immensely.

They spoke at length about the clandestine romance between Alex and Amanda, not to mention the long-running feud that ran in concert between their two fathers.

"Is Byron having a hard time dealing with this new arrangement?" Maria asked, as she felt it quite odd that both of Amanda's parents had not stayed over for the 500 post-race festivities, which was quite an event, especially when one of your own wins.

"I'm afraid so, Maria. Byron can be a hard man. He always had this strange dream that both of our girls would marry into the Williams family. I've been telling him for years the Old South's days of arranged marriages were over. I think he always saw Aaron and Kyle Williams as the two sons he never had. As fate would have it, Allison is planning to marry Bud and Lisa's oldest son."

Sarah didn't add her long-held view that the two were not quite right for each other, but she had always hoped for the best. She also knew that Maria was in that courtroom when Amanda testified that she had been sexually assaulted by Kyle Williams, but thought better of discussing it, while Maria obliged by not commenting or asking about it, either.

"I know Andy is certainly glad it's over, at least the legal part of it," Maria stated chuckling.

"What's funny, Maria?"

"Can you keep a secret?"

Sarah hesitated, wondering what dramatic revelation could possibly be disclosed that would surprise her, following the events of the past week. "Of course, Maria. Girl Scouts honor."

Andy's younger sister was one who seldom spoke out of turn but it had been a while since she had been this tipsy. "Did you know the details of why the lawsuits were dropped?"

"Byron just told me the lawyers had finally settled out of court."

"Ha!" Maria shouted before downing one last gulp of the Chardonnay. "I guess that would be a true statement."

She had Sarah's attention. "And?"

Maria looked around in an animated way as though she was about to disclose issues of national security. "Well, correct me if I'm wrong, but Byron felt he had pulled off quite a coup last fall when Evelyn Stevens left us and signed back on with Roberto Santos."

"Yes, I recall that. So?"

"You know, Sarah, IndyCar is much different than Formula One or even NASCAR. Most of the sponsors' bang for the buck comes from the big race at Indy. There is no bigger blow to a team and their sponsors than not even qualifying for the race. And you know that Evelyn was at risk of just that going into Bump Day."

"Bump Day?" Sarah asked, a slightly bit embarrassed that she was unfamiliar with the term.

"Yes, the final day of qualifying. Pole Day is on Saturday and Bump Day Sunday. There are always one or two too many cars and drivers for the starting grid. It's much the same at other big races but much more visible at Indy. To not qualify for the race at all is a death knell for most teams. Adam Herrera approached all the concerned, Evelyn, Andy, and Byron, with a proposition late on Saturday. Roberto Santos couldn't be reached, but they all had a conference call without him. Adam's plan involved Andy's top techs and engineers helping the IndyWest guys in getting Evelyn's car ready to qualify the next day, all on the condition that Byron have Unibank drop any and all lawsuits pending against Moretti Motorsport and our family members. Byron wanted Andy to guarantee that Evelyn would qualify as a condition, but Andy refused, informing Byron they would do their best but there are never any guarantees like that in racing. Byron reluctantly agreed they all would issue a press release first thing Monday morning, Evelyn did qualify on Sunday, Byron held to his word, and the rest is history."

"What a great story! But honestly, Maria, after Alex's trial ended as it did, Byron had little confidence in the outcome of the years-long lawsuit, anyway. Had Evelyn failed to qualify, Byron would have been in hot water with the bank board members, so all's well that ends well."

"Maybe I shouldn't tell you this, Sarah, but I suppose it matters little now. At the very minute Adam Herrera was on the phone trying to get Byron and Andy on the call, the team's best engineers were already in the Santos garage working with Evelyn's team to improve the car for her last chance run."

Sarah was wide-eyed. "Oh, my god! Did Andy know about this?"

Maria could only smile. "Of course. As all of his own drivers were comfortably in the field, the team had the rest of Saturday night off. A couple of the guys knew Evelyn was in dire straits and volunteered to help her out."

"And Andy gave them permission to do that?"

"Permission? My brother suggested it," Maria stated.

Sarah just looked ahead as if in deep thought. *I had best never let Byron know this. His bitterness would only deepen. That was very generous on Alex's father's part. Quite virtuous, indeed.*

⚑⚑

Alex and Amanda enjoyed a couple of hours of intimacy, both still feeling as though lost time had need to be recovered. The two still hadn't fully gotten their minds around the fact they could actually be together now without constantly having to look over their shoulders. Amanda was still getting used to her newfound stardom and for his part, Alex hoped against hope she wouldn't get too used to it. She had already received three offers from press agents and was yet to be comfortable signing autographs.

Their relationship had certainly come full circle after spending over two years in a state of romantic exile from each other. In the back of his mind, Alex's conversation with Tony was bringing on new challenges to his mental energy. As much as he was thrilled to be back behind the wheel of an IndyCar, the lure of Formula One was there. How his shy southern belle would adapt to that scene in Europe and other continents was a question yet to be answered. *Of course, she would be excited initially,* he figured. *But over time?*

Allison Cook's disguise had been flawless right up to and including the blonde wig, huge sunglasses, and overstuffed brassiere, reflecting a woman with a well-endowed bosom. The security camera files would reflect a likely prostitute in case the police suspected foul play, which was doubtful. She had called Newberry a few minutes early on the throw-away phone, instructing him that she would just meet him in his room, thus skipping the previously arranged hotel lounge thing.

Louis Newberry was Evelyn Stevens' long-time agent and had been harassing her for not paying the bonus she had promised when he delivered on an agreement of Stevens leaving Moretti Motorsport and returning to Roberto Santos' IndyWest Team, a likely career step backward, notwithstanding the extra retainer she would earn in the coming season.

Knowing that Louie had made out like a bandit on the new contract anyway, Allison had continuously procrastinated on paying him the twenty-five grand, knowing full well the arrogant slob could hardly disclose her involvement to any of the key participants. He couldn't tell her father, bank CEO Byron Cook, that he had accepted a bribe from his daughter, nor could he disclose their arrangement to Stevens, who was nearly at her wit's end with Newberry over the fine print in the new contract.

When he had sent her some compromising audio and video files of the two of them having sex together during their earlier Charlotte hotel meeting, Allison went ballistic over the pompous Newberry pulling such a stunt, predicating the recruitment of a resourceful US Navy Intelligence officer for help, conveniently being a man she was cheating on her husband with. Lieutenant Jordan promised her that if he got possession of Newberry's phone and computers, the compromising data could be wiped clean.

"I am so sorry, Louie. I had some complications with Aaron and his family, forcing me to lay low for a bit," Allison offered as she retrieved two hundred-fifty-one hundred-dollar bills from her large purse, watching him skim through the stack while wearing that disgusting smile of his.

"And just to celebrate our little reunion," she added while producing two small champagne bottles, handing him one while she kept his attention by starting to unzip her dress.

Standing before him now and nearly naked, she smiled inwardly at his look of lust. "A toast, to our success and to Evelyn's winning tomorrow."

His head began to spin and his eyesight blurred. His bottle, which he had devoured in two big gulps, was spiked with 200 milligrams of Fentanyl. He struggled to stand and move toward her, knowing she had drugged him. His smirk turned quickly to one of shock and anger before he collapsed to the floor.

She made quick work to gather his Samsung phone, Dell notebook computer, and a couple of USB flash drives. Jordan instructed her on conducting a thorough search to find Louie's video and audio recording devices, in case the buffoon was attempting more blackmailing shenanigans. Finding none, she retrieved the twenty-five grand, packed everything up in the empty suitcase she had brought, and departed casually through the hotel lobby. An Uber driver happily accepted cash to drop her off a few blocks away where she would stroll casually into the Hyatt Hotel. She shared a moment of nervous exasperation when joined in the elevator by a contingent of Unibank executives, including her own father and Carolyn Tyler, the very woman who had botched the Stevens contract.

Keeping her face down as if heavily engaged in something on her phone, Allison's worries regarding her being recognized quickly dissolved as the bank executives were full from plenty of downtown Indy partying and paid her little notice. She did see her father was a little too consumed with Tyler as both appeared to be much too cozy than mere business acquaintances. Despite a natural inclination to feel sorry for her mother, she was quite aware that her parents had shared little intimacy since Amanda's accident over two years prior, and being "Daddy's little girl" from birth, Allison could never find fault with her father. She would have to keep a keen watch on Carolyn Tyler, however, a woman she perceived as nothing more than a gold-digging bimbo.

The police engaged in a cursory investigation following a 911 call received late on the morning of the famous race by the hotel staff. While the case was assumed to be one of a common drug overdose, there was an examination of the hotel's security camera footage. An Uber driver was questioned regarding the female who had been filmed in the hallway outside of the victim's room and leaving the hotel in the Uber driver's vehicle. Although the woman appeared overdressed in a leather jacket and large hat for a warm and humid evening, the Uber driver could not recall her vividly and stated that she did pay in cash. A follow-up check of his phone data revealed that her call for pickup came from a number registered to a prepaid phone.

More investigation further revealed the phone was purchased at a Walmart store and a study of some store videos was inconclusive as the large-breasted woman in large sunglasses and wide-brimmed hat could not provide any positive identification. The coroner later certified the death as an overdose of fentanyl, and the case was then closed.

⚑✕⚑

Allison would make an appearance at the IndyWest hospitality area on race day morning playing the social butterfly, particularly toward Evelyn Stevens, who would soon need a new agent. The buzz regarding Stevens' miraculous qualifying display the previous Sunday was still the talk of the team and their guests, as the famous British girl had taken to the speedway in the abhorrent weather to qualify for a place in the field just as the clock expired and the skies opened.

⚑✕⚑

Over nine hours southeast in a Charlotte area trailer park, Remi Dalton cracked an eye open as her phone buzzed for a third time.

She reached for it, knocking it off her nightstand. Picking it up off the floor, she saw the missed calls, hesitated, and dialed.

"Good morning, my lovely! So glad you gave me the pleasure of a callback."

"Don't give me that bullshit, Cotton. What the hell do you want this early?"

Eugene "Cotton" James had a long soft spot for Dalton, a woman he had met years earlier while plying her trade as a stripper and prostitute. "Have you read the Observer this morning?"

"Read the Observer!?" Remi barked at him. "I haven't had my first smoke or coffee yet, you ass. What about it?"

"Oh, you'll be interested in this. I'll text you the link. After you've read it, call me back. But take a Midol first," he instructed and disconnected.

Remi rolled back over, barely awake, and chose to get out of bed, heading to the kitchen to start the coffee pot. "Midol my ass," she mumbled when clicking around on her phone for the Charlotte Observer page. She was jolted when she read the online article.

Evelyn Stevens' Agent Found Dead in Downtown Indy Hotel

Her heart sank. She had the sleazy PR agent on the ropes for his part in a contract conspiracy against his own client, and now the SOB was dead of apparent suicide. She read the details of the story and called James back. "What do you make of this?"

"You know this slug better than I do. What do you think? An overdose?"

"I'm drained now, Cotton. Louie was a drinker, not so much a druggy, and never one to partake in that shit alone."

"And right on the eve of the biggest event in his business... Doesn't pass the smell test. It's a good thing I helped you set up that dark web account. With the transfers he sent you these past few weeks, you wouldn't want questions. We've lost a target now, though."

"We? Have you cut yourself in now, Cotton James?"

"You need a partner, Remi. You're in over your head. Besides, I miss you."

"Okay, Romeo, what difference does it make now? We can't squeeze blood out of a turnip."

"I think the Cook girl bumped him off. She's the mark."

"And you have proof of that, Cotton!"

"Not yet. I think we should rattle the cage a bit, but I want in for half," he replied slyly.

"Half! I did all the work, you shit!" Dalton was wide awake now.

"Trust me, Remi. The real work hasn't started. If we play this right, it can be huge."

Cotton would know best about this kind of chicanery, she considered. "Now that Louie's at room temperature, how do we proceed? He's been my main source of income lately."

"How about I stop by later and we'll work out a plan together?"

"No, the last time you stopped by, I couldn't get your ass to leave," Remi replied in retort.

"No need for sweet talk, my long-lost love. I'll be up there in a couple hours."

"Make it three. And you're not staying over, Cotton!" Remi yelled as she hung up on him.

Remi Dalton, once a ravishing beauty, had become battle-worn over the years with an access of drugs, alcohol, and a three-packs-per-day smoking habit. Her occupation as a stripper and freelance prostitute had given way to that of becoming a paparazzi reporter.

The gig started to pay off when she developed an arrangement with one of her "customers", a sleazy sports business agent, Louis Newberry, who had as his only client, Evelyn Stevens, who happened to be the world's most popular female racing driver. A media frenzy went into overdrive when Stevens began a romantic relationship a few years back with Alex Moretti, the handsome youngest son of legend, Andy Moretti, owner of Moretti Motorsport and his two sons' boss. Newberry would tip Dalton off as to where the sports' first couple would be, all for a nominal fee, of course. Then ole Louie got greedy and the fees became untenable, all for naught when Stevens and her racing boyfriend suddenly broke up.

Dalton then chose to spy on Newberry himself, uncovering an amazing if shocking discovery. The slob had conspired with Allison Cook to have Stevens resign from Moretti Motorsport and drive for Roberto Santos' IndyWest team, a deal all tied to her lucrative Unibank sponsorship. Cook's father, the banking giant CEO, had engaged in a long-running vendetta to destroy team owner Andy Moretti and his son, a vengeance resulting from a secret romance between Stevens' former beau and the youngest Cook daughter, a teen girl nearly killed in a serious car accident. What began as a devious financial stunt had turned quite sinister, and Remi had a front-row seat to the entire show, secretly recording it all. The best part was that Allison Cook's dad was a super-rich banker and her fiancé's pop was a huge car dealer.

Even though Cotton James had been one of her best customers, he was never more than just that, a customer. She had long given up on having a serious relationship with any man and, in a certain way, had given up on society. Remi Dalton was a hard woman, always believing she had to stick it to the man before the man stuck it to her. Cotton James was no exception. Now his little come-ons meant only one thing. He saw dollar signs.

Following three strong cups of coffee and two smokes, she began to straighten up the small trailer. Perhaps she would even shower and apply some make-up. But upon reflection, she thought better of it. *No, not for Cotton James I won't.*

⚑×⚑

James arrived, himself clean-shaven and sporting a clean Lynyrd Skynyrd tee shirt and fresh-washed jeans along with his signature cowboy hat and boots. Without so much as a "hello" or "come in", Remi just opened the door in her well-worn bathrobe and then disappeared as he stepped in. He heard the toilet flush just prior to her re-appearing.

"So, now that Louie is dead, what's the plan, Cotton?"

"I'm glad you're so emotional about his demise," he answered with his typical sarcasm, a trait that Remi despised about him.

"He was always an asshole and just used me, like someone else I know."

"All right, Remi. Let's dispense with the niceties and talk business. If this Louis Newberry's death is what I think it is, we may be sitting on a goldmine here... If we play it just right, that is."

Remi chose to forgo the dispute regarding the terms of Cotton's proposed partnership. Despite her certain disdain for the man, she knew she was completely out of her league. This was no routine shakedown of someone cheating on their spouse. No, if Cotton was right, this was now murder. His background as a former army ranger in Iraq, police detective, and private investigator, was much better suited for the task at hand. She already had the cards. He would deal them. They discussed at length the various options, precautions, and alternate plans should something go array.

"What if it turns out this Cook broad didn't do it, or that we can't prove any of it? We're screwed, Cotton."

"We can still fall back on the original mark, her part in conning Stevens on her contract. We'll need to bait her a bit on the serious part. If she bites, we'll know she waxed Ole Louie."

"She's a rich bitch, I know that," Remi added. "Don't screw me on this, Cotton."

"You know me better than that, honey britches."

"Oh yeah, I know you, Cotton James." *And I'm not your honey britches.*

Chapter 2
Late Visitor

The two were exhausted and consumed in sweat after another afternoon of illicit sex. She had been having an affair with the young naval intelligence officer for just over seven weeks now and he was following a familiar pattern of becoming attached to her. He had carried on the ruse of being one of Aaron's best friends, which made the deceit all the more iniquitous.

"How long are you going to stay with him, babe?" Jordan asked. "This having to sneak around undercover is getting a little crazy."

She gave him a sly smile, not admitting that the forbidden part of their liaison was what gave her excitement. "Our families have been close for years, Eric. It would break my mom and dad's heart if I left him now. We're supposed to get married. Come on."

The young lieutenant lacked the monetary wealth to capture her hand, something Aaron Williams had through his father, the largest car dealer in South Carolina. Between his family and her own, Allison aspired to be one of the richest women in the South, determined to make her mark regardless of who she had to step on or sleep with in the process.

Right now, that progress was being impeded by one Amanda Cook, her younger sister who was grabbing all the headlines. "That little bitch. She is ruining my life. All because of her, my future in-laws don't trust me. Her damned lies! Her lies about me, about

Aaron's little brother! I would be Evelyn Steven's agent right this minute if it was not for her! I wish Amanda would just disappear."

"That could happen," Jordan stated, a tone lacking in insincerity as he continued to massage her toned backside.

"Yes, so you do magic now, do you?"

"Listen, baby. Enough power and money can make anything happen," he answered.

That would be nice, wouldn't it? Allison pondered, giving her clandestine lover a devious smile. "When I return from Hilton Head, you can further explain your little David Copperfield theatrics to me."

🏁✕🏁

The atmosphere was frigid. Lisa Williams made a tacit attempt toward kindness toward her future daughter-in-law, despite the cold shoulder her husband was displaying toward her. Aaron Williams, ever so much the family diplomat, struggled to manage his father's vitriol toward his future bride and the Cook family in general.

For her part, Allison's disdain toward the Moretti family, which would soon include her own younger sister, had given her some common ground with her planned in-laws, happy as she was for small victories. Despite the feuds involving two of the state's more prominent families, she had little or no fear of Aaron breaking off their engagement. His younger brother was the alpha male of the two, as Aaron tended to follow and not lead. He had always been overly susceptible to his father's wishes, a trait Allison had hoped to use to her advantage.

Despite his shortcomings, Aaron did worship the ground she walked on, a feeling that was far from mutual. Allison was never in love with Aaron Williams, but his dad had become rich in the car business and was very influential in state and national politics. Someday his two sons would inherit his vast automotive empire and it had often been mentioned that Aaron would run for office,... high office. This had been the driving push toward Aaron attending The Citadel and establishing a career as a military officer. This path played less an important role in national politics in recent years but was still a strong badge of honor in his southern conservative state of South Carolina.

Aaron had gone with his father and brother for an afternoon golf outing, a party that included the Lieutenant Governor, Stuart Helmann, while Allison and Aaron's mother, Lisa, went shopping.

Their relationship had taken a rather odd turn since the trial, as Allison knew that Lisa had always seen her sister, Amanda, as her favorite for as long as the two families were close. The long game plan had been for the two very prominent families and lifelong friends to get closer with the two Williams boys each taking one of the very beautiful Cook daughters as brides. This had blown up when Amanda became a defense witness for her chosen boyfriend, Alex Moretti. Amanda Cook's testimony that she had been raped three and a half years earlier by none other than Aaron Williams' younger brother, Kyle, had shocked the whole town of Rock Hill and, indeed both of the Carolina states as well.

In the aftermath, Amanda declined to press charges but refused to back off from her claim that Allison's future brother-in-law had drugged and sexually assaulted her. Five months past the explosive courtroom trial, the red-shirt Clemson quarterback, a young man primed for superstardom, had a huge and damaging stain on his reputation.

A statement by Alex Moretti in the trial, acknowledging Amanda's claim that her sister desired to sleep with him, had caused further consternation as an angry Aaron Williams had bolted from his seat in the second row of the courtroom and attempted to physically assault Moretti on the witness stand. He was restrained by the bailiff and a deputy sheriff and charged with Assault and Contempt of Court. The Williams' expensive attorney managed to get the assault charge dropped while Aaron pleaded guilty to the contempt charge, paying a lofty fine and being sentenced to six-month probation.

The two sat comfortably in a corner booth at the Harbour Bakery and Cafe, taking in a late breakfast and some quite tasty coffee. Lisa struggled at being comfortable around Allison, not only because of what had happened in that York County Courthouse months earlier, but had certain reservations about Allison generally, a young woman she had known since birth. Lisa and Allison's mother, Sarah, had been inseparable as best friends since youth and both had been godmother to each other's children. It had been five months now and the two had barely spoken. Lisa had universally adored Sarah and had always been struck by the fact that her two girls were such close mirror images of her. But Lisa had always felt her best friend's daughters were completely different personalities. Amanda seemed to be so much like her mom, having that innocent kindness, never a coarse word about anyone. But Allison seldom came off as innocent of anything, a person who was quite good-looking and knew it, a very ambitious girl who would go places in her life, even if the ride to get there often involved unpleasantness.

"When will Sarah be back home?" Lisa asked nonchalantly, making conversation.

"I think after the Detroit Grand Prix. She didn't want Amanda to be up there alone," Allison replied quickly. "It's just me and Dad holding down the fort until she gets back."

"And what about when Amanda returns home?" Lisa asked, having learned about the falling out there and Allison telling both

Byron and Sarah that she would never step foot on the property again so long as Amanda resided there.

"I'm not too sure Amanda will come home anytime soon, Lisa. She may just follow the Moretti Motorsport clan around like a gypsy all summer and not step foot back in Rock Hill."

"And how is Sarah taking all of this?" Lisa asked, herself still disgruntled at Sarah for her longtime friend's lack of empathy for her two sons.

"I don't know," Allison replied. "That whole trial took something out of her, Lisa."

Yes, hasn't it taken a toll on all of us, Aaron's mother thought to herself. She had avoided a lengthy dialog regarding his Contempt of Court conviction, despite a lingering thought in the back of her mind regarding the stinging court testimony from Alex Moretti. His stating that he believed the woman her son planned to marry, indeed the very young woman she was hosting this holiday, desired to sleep with him was disturbing for all the Williams. It had all but made her husband's blood boil.

"You know that Kyle is having a very difficult time with this, Allison. He's tagged to be third string this fall. His father is convinced it's all about Amanda's testimony. He's afraid a great future for Kyle in the NFL is in jeopardy," Lisa stated.

Allison held a hidden anger that she was somehow being targeted as the one at fault. Admitting guilt or responsibility for anything negative was not in her DNA. "I don't know what got into Amanda, Lisa. God knows she and I are no longer speaking."

The two had been close since college. While in his capacity as Chairman of the York County Planning Commission, Helmann had been instrumental in fast-tracking a goodly number of regulatory obstacles when Bud built his first dealership. Stuart played a similar role in William's expansion before moving up the political ladder. In return, his old college pal had contributed generously to his campaigns for office, soon to include a U.S. Senate run.

The two rode together in their golf cart to the fifth tee-off. "So, what did Coach Fairchild have to say, Stuart?" Bud asked after he felt enough small talk had passed.

"I can tell you, Gabe is not a happy camper on this," Helmann replied. "He's gone from a man seeing your boy as the key to another national title to an albatross around his neck. He knows his locker room in the upcoming season will have a black cloud over it. Kyle may be better served at another school, perhaps for a year or two, until this story dies down." The Lieutenant Governor did not dwell on the fact his good friend and Clemson football coach had all but mentally moved on from seeing a future on the school gridiron with Kyle Williams at quarterback."

"So, what's Kyle supposed to do, Stuart? The Cook girl declined to press charges. What happened to innocent until proven guilty?"

"I know she declined to press charges. But she didn't... Well, a retraction on her part would be the best, Bud."

⚑⚑

The atmosphere at the Williams' evening dinner table was quite tense. The family patriarch could hardly look at Allison without visions of the trial constantly haunting him. He had worked all his life to build up an empire of car dealerships, now numbering twenty-three. He was a man who had the governor and state party chairman's private cell phones on speed dial, but for all of that couldn't seem to get his youngest son on the football field.

Allison couldn't keep from noticing Kyle appearing quite upset and unable to keep from staring at her. The subject of Aaron and Allison's soon-to-be wedding was not even being mentioned.

"So, how was the Lieutenant Governor's game?" Lisa asked in an attempt to break the ice.

"Dad and I smoked them," Aaron offered, not getting so much as a nod or a look from his father.

"I choked on the sixteenth," Kyle added.

"We should finalize the wedding plans," Lisa added. "We haven't much time and I have so many invitations to get out."

Everyone was now waiting quietly for the head of the table to add his voice. "Helmann suggested this wedding be postponed," Bud stated, breaking his silence.

The family, along with their week-long guest of honor, Allison, were all stunned but sat still while awaiting his further comment.

"He believes as I do that this wedding needs to be delayed after some time passes, allowing this stigma with Kyle to subside. The Clemson coaching staff strongly believes the press is still too hot on this and wants to avoid the media circus. Stuart even suggested a transfer to another school may be in order for Kyle, but even that is unlikely this year."

"Dad! What's done is done!" Aaron responded. "There's nothing we can do about what happened in that trial. Allison and I want to get married."

"Your father may be right, Aaron," Allison spoke while she reached under the tablecloth and squeezed his hand. "Let's give it some time." She was quite motivated to get back on her would-be father-in-law's good side. As such, being in a hurry to change her last name was secondary. *We're both in San Diego living together anyway, so what's the big deal?* She pondered, careful not to show Aaron her lack of disappointment.

"Amanda has already stated that she will not file a complaint. I think this wedding will serve as a start to heal these wounds, don't you think, honey?" Lisa added.

"Her not filing a complaint isn't good enough," Bud responded quickly. "There are no criminal complaints filed in most of these types of cases. Hellman suggested that Amanda needs to come forward with a public statement that the whole episode involving her and Kyle was just a misunderstanding," Bud stated, staring at Allison as he spoke. "Do you think that's possible on her part, Allison?"

The would-be daughter-in-law, feeling a bit under siege, studied momentarily for the right words. "After the lies she yelled out about me, we're not even talking. I doubt we will be anytime soon, Bud."

"Well then, I had better have a talk with your dad then, right there in his office."

The significance of Bud Williams' statement rang clear on the implications. He and Amanda's father, the CEO and President of Unibank, had conducted millions of dollars worth of business dating back nearly a generation. But Williams had not planned nor requested a meeting in the downtown Charlotte corporate tower in over fifteen years.

Later that evening, Aaron and Allison strolled hand in hand along the beach, with the bride-to-be acting most distraught.

"How about we just elope, baby?" Aaron asked, always wanting to please her.

"No, Aaron! I want a big, extravagant wedding. It's my dream!"

"At the end of the day, we'll be married. That's all that matters, Allison."

No, what matters is the publicity, Aaron, you wimp, she thought. "I know that, honey. But do you have any idea how crushed our mothers would be? We cannot do that to them," she added while wearing her contrived sad face look.

⚐⚐

Andy had a full plate now as the team motored into Detroit for the downtown street race. His whole life picture, both personally and professionally, had taken a different direction in the brief span of just two weeks. The secession of legal hostilities between the team and Unibank had cleared a huge black cloud over the enterprise and opened the door for his youngest son, Alex, to be reinstated to the team again after a two-year hiatus. Of course, with Alex winning the big one and becoming simultaneously engaged, he and his fiancée were certainly the flavor of the month as the IndyCar series entered its busy summer schedule.

Tony's injury and obvious lengthy recovery had opened a huge new challenge for the Formula One squad. Team manager, Ian Miles, had come to terms with former F1 pilot, James Robinson, to fill the seat in Tony's absence, a period they all knew could likely mean the rest of the season. Robinson had achieved limited results in his brief Formula One career, but the Excel-X team had never run as high as mid-pack and the Brit had always felt he had performed to the limit of the team and equipment provided, a sentiment universally felt by most former drivers in the world's most high-pressured sport.

"He's been spending night and day on the simulator, Andy," Miles stated. "But he needs track time. I miss the old days when we could test as much as we bloody wanted."

"Let's just do the best we can and get through this, Ian. It is what it is."

Andy disconnected with Miles, his internal stress meter climbing. Both men were very worried about the team's performance, as they should be. While Tony had gradually improved his results since the beginning of the previous season, the second team driver, Geoff Leland, had regressed to becoming a mere backmarker, a total disappointment in the veteran after the team made a decision to pick up the option on him for another season.

Adding to his mental overload, his former wife called and wanted to fly over from Europe for a visit to meet her soon-to-be daughter-in-law, not to mention her two grandchildren, neither of whom she had ever seen or held. Andy had mixed emotions at seeing her as he drove southwest toward the Detroit-Wayne International Airport. His mother, Matilde, had convinced him to go and pick Sabetha up personally, just a thought in starting this family greeting off on the right foot. His strong reluctance was overcome by his mother agreeing to tag along, herself.

He had not been up close and personal with his ex in almost five years. She had flown into LA for Tony's wedding, escorted by her boyfriend, Andre, the son of a wealthy French industrialist whose arrogance impressed no one. At the time, Andy was not in a romantic relationship with anyone, which seemed to make Andre uneasy, the man having the troubling habit of always checking his watch, as though always pressed to be somewhere else.

Sabetha, you always pick some winners, he thought, shaking his head. She was visiting alone this time, had not mentioned anything about her current intimate status, and Andy hadn't bothered to ask.

He was stuck in traffic on I-94 while his phone jingled. Sabetha had arrived.

She'll be an hour getting through customs, he thought before answering. "I'm stuck in traffic. Probably 30-40 minutes out."

"Andy, I'm here in the passenger pickup lane," Sabetha replied with an edge of aggravation in her voice.

Great, Andy thought. *You were never one for patience, were you, Sabetha?* "I'm driving a tan Lincoln Navigator with North Carolina license plates. We'll get there as quick as I can," he stated and disconnected, knowing she would never bother to wave down a vehicle, expecting him or anyone else in her celebrity orbit to recognize her.

"How are you feeling about this? It's been what, five or six years?" Matilde asked.

"I'm mixed on it, Mamma," Andy responded neutrally. "With so much going on, I've been too busy to even think about it."

"Well, I for one am looking forward to seeing Sabetha again."

"You always were one for the high road, Mamma. Does that mean you'll be in charge of the welcoming committee?" Andy recoiled sarcastically.

"I suppose I will be, Andy. Since no one else wants to volunteer."

"I haven't dealt with this level of media frenzy in years. I just hope her visit is brief."

⚑✕⚑

While the rest of the Moretti family expressed no rancor when learning of Sabetha's sudden decision to visit, neither Tony nor Alex expressed much enthusiasm. Her oldest son did recall some fond memories of her from their time in Genoa, but Alex had none as by the time he was of age to start remembering his mother was gone and the boys were raised by their grandmother. As much as the family matriarch had preached the virtue of forgiveness, Alex would carry the knowledge his whole life that his natural mother had abandoned him as a child.

They pulled up to the passenger pick-up lane curb to Sabetha, wearing an extremely short skirt as though it was still the 1990s. Andy and Matilde both quickly got out of the car with the two women initiating a welcoming.

"Sabetha, it is so good to see you," Matilde declared as she embraced her former daughter-in-law.

While the two women greeted each other heartily, Andy quickly grabbed his ex-wife's luggage and tossed the three bags in the back of their vehicle, already concerned at the sheer volume for someone here on a brief visit. The two parents of the now-famous third-generation Moretti racing brothers approached each other with mixed expressions while a myriad of emotions set in.

Andy had fallen in love with the former professional model while driving for Frank Williams' Formula One team nearly thirty years earlier. Following a torrid romance played out on the backdrop of the Grand Prix season all across Europe, they were soon married and it was a cheerful time at first. Andy was a rising star on the Formula One circuit, Sabetha gave birth to their first child, and life seemed as though it couldn't be better.

After two stellar seasons, Andy became embroiled in a contract dispute with Williams and appeared to be heading to McLaren as the marquee's team manager, Ron Dennis, had his eyes on the dashing young charger for some time. Things fell apart on all fronts and just when it appeared that Andy Moretti could be without a ride totally, a fatal crash taking the life of Ferrari's lead driver, Marco Santora, gave him an opening. This was not the best of times for *The Prancing*

Horse competitively, however, and Andy's career seemed to take a dive. Sabetha had an affair with a billionaire financier and the two separated.

The couple spent the next few years in a sort of marital limbo, crossing intimate paths intermittently, and kept delaying a final divorce when a second son was born. Sabetha seemed to gradually despise the whole family thing and Andy's racing woes hadn't helped matters. The couple finally terminated the marriage while young Alessandro was yet two years of age. The act of abandoning her offspring didn't sit well with the Moretti family lineage, particularly in Andy's eyes, and nearly all communications regarding Sabetha's two sons had come through Matilde's social media.

Although still an attractive woman by most measures at forty-seven, Andy believed time had not done Sabetha any favors. Her years of alcohol and drug abuse had taken its toll and no amount of Botox or breast implants could hide it.

"Sabetha, you're looking well," Andy stated, trying to disguise his insincerity. "You must be tired after that flight."

"Don't concern about it, Andy. I just want to see my grandchildren."

"I had Maria arrange for a room on the top floor of the hotel, right across from her and Mamma."

Sabetha had a passing thought that Andy would want to sleep with her, an arrangement that had been discarded.

There was also some long-term friction between Andy's ex-wife and sister, as the very woman whom Maria's ex-husband had cheated with was a very close friend of Sabetha's. Thus, Maria had long harbored a resentment that her sister-in-law had done little to stop it, and indeed may have even had a hand in orchestrating the adultery. But with Maria having her mother's personality, she wouldn't display such animosity, which had dampened with the passage of time.

The drive back into downtown Detroit was long in the traffic, making an uncomfortable reunion even more so. Matilde engaged in a smattering of small talk to avoid the obvious discomfort between her only son and his former bride, as Sabetha hadn't been seen or rarely heard from since Tony had gotten married several years earlier. *How will the whole of my family receive her?* Matilde pondered.

The former French super-model had gone through two brief marriages and untold other relationships since she and Andy had finally divorced. Spending her life in the fast lane, she was used to getting whatever she wanted without recognizing that she was just often being used.

In the back of her mind, Sabetha always had this strange if conceited feeling that she could always go back to Andy, fueled by the knowledge that he had not re-married in all those years, nor had any serious relationships. They had last seen each other briefly at London Heathrow a couple of years earlier, but only in passing. She was with someone and he was into running his race team, as always.

Though his head of hair had added some gray and he had gained a few pounds, Sabetha thought Andy had changed little. As he drove on, he spent the majority of time on his mobile phone with various race team members. She did overhear him talking to his right-hand man, Bob Ward, about the weekend's Formula One race in Barcelona, curious that he wasn't there. In her mind, a European Grand Prix carried much more prestige and importance than this American urban street race, and downtown Detroit wasn't exactly Monte Carlo.

The greeting of Sabetha was very emotional for the whole family, all of whom were at the Moretti hospitality bus in the paddock. The noise and crowd of a race weekend was certainly routine for Sabetha, but getting reacquainted with the family after such a long absence was not.

Three-year-old Adrian was uncomfortable in her grasp, a child with a mischievous nature and seeing his grandmother as a stranger. The baby was another matter, as young David relished everyone's attention.

The buzz under the team hospitality canopy suddenly caught a bit of silence as Alex walked in with two women, neither of whom had ever met Sabetha, and one who carried quite a legend thanks to the robust efforts of the paparazzi. With some obvious reserve, Alex embraced his mother, recognizing her change in appearance.

"So, Alex. This beautiful mademoiselle must be your fiancée?" Sabetha asked assumingly.

"Yes, Mother. This is Amanda."

Amanda held out her hand as her natural shyness set in. Alex had spoken little of his mother in the three-plus years she had known him. The few bits of information she did pick up on were quick and to the point, having him state that she left when he was too young to remember her. "Hello, Mrs. Moretti. It's a pleasure to meet you."

"And bonjour, Mademoiselle Amanda. You are as lovely as advertised. And please, just call me Sabetha," she politely demanded. "And this must be Allison, your older sister, I assume?" She asked as Sarah appeared.

They all laughed a bit at Sabetha's expense. "Not quite, Mother," Alex replied. "This is Sarah Cook, Amanda's mother."

Sabetha was taken aback by the surprisingly fit and attractive forthcoming in-law, decked out in her short denim shorts and oversized Moretti Motorsport tee shirt. "How charming. I see where Amanda gets her lovely smile. I am Sabetha Moretti. Pleased to meet you, Madame Cook."

"The pleasure is all mine, I'm sure," Sarah replied in her friendly southern accent, smiling while thinking it strange herself that Amanda's future mother-in-law had not appeared in the time she had known Alex and his family, three years that were indeed quite tumultuous for her youngest offspring.

Sabetha observed that Sarah seemed to be very acquainted with the family, particularly her apparent close relationship with Maria and her own former mother-in-law, Matilde. It was almost as though she had taken up some sort of special station around the paddock. This came as quite a surprise as it was no secret that her husband and Andy had been at odds personally for well over two years, despite the recent press release that all of their litigation had been resolved. "And when will I see Monsieur Cook? I'm sure he is quite excited about this engagement," she asked.

"Oh, Byron is still reeling from the surprise," Sarah responded while stealing a quick glance toward Amanda. "He had to return to Charlotte right away. You know, business."

"I see, Madam. Funny I have never been to that place," Sabetha added, knowing the entire Moretti family had relocated there. "And when will you be returning? I'm sure your husband has missed you."

"Oh, I will be flying back home after the race on Sunday," Sarah replied, the question a bit bold for someone who barely knew her or her husband.

"Splendid. Perhaps we may get to spend some more time then," Sabetha replied, causing more than one eye to be raised as she had not announced any plans for an extended stay in America, nor what her near future plans for lodging entailed.

She struggled to hold back the tears as she leaned over to embrace him. Sabetha had thrived on the high-speed dangerous world of motor racing, always being attracted to the very best drivers in the world while risking injury or death every time they sat behind the wheel. Now the dark side of the sport had hit home. Here was her firstborn, relegated to a wheelchair, at least for now, and uncertain if he would ever be able to stand on his own again, much less ever drive a race car.

"He's improved mightily these last few days, Sabetha," Crissy stated, still uncertain if her mother-in-law should be addressed by her first name, or *Mom, Mother,* or *Madam Moretti,* as Sabetha had chosen to keep her first married name, one well-known worldwide.

"He looks quite *Bev*, as the Brits like to say," Sabetha replied, hiding her true feelings.

"Waking up and seeing Alex on that podium, and his proposing to Amanda, was one of the happiest days of my life, Mother," Tony stated, still a bit chalky in his speech. "Other than my own bride saying yes, of course."

"And your sons being born!" Crissy came back heartily, a quick change of expression presenting a reminder that Sabetha had not bothered to cross the *pond* and meet either of her newborn grandsons.

The girls were jumping with excitement as the laps wound down. The race had been exciting with multiple crashes and lead changes. With eight laps remaining, Alex found himself chasing the wily Scott Dixon, who by all calculations would have to pit for a quick splash of fuel unless yet another caution occurred, which by this point in this race seemed likely. It had been Alex's first street circuit race in an IndyCar in almost three years, but he took to it like a fish in water.

He had stalked Dixon skillfully lap after lap with Andy constantly on the radio, encouraging him to be patient. "He's short on fuel," he kept saying. "Get on his tail in turn two and take him on the backstretch next lap."

Alex was right on Dixon's gearbox as they passed the pit lane entering the first turn. This was it, his moment. As he closed on the orange and blue car braking into turn two, the car's yellow light flashed on. A car had hit the wall going into the last turn. "Damn it!" Alex yelled. "I had him!"

Just keep your head, Alex," Andy cackled over the comm. "Stay on him and when he makes a mistake, pounce," the legend would say. But he knew that Dixon, his own former teammate and the series' winningest active driver, making a mistake was most unlikely.

Following three laps of caution, the race would end with a two-lap shootout. But now Dixon would be on it full throttle himself as fuel conservation was no longer a concern. Although Alex mercilessly chased the cagey veteran, both chassis and engines were identical. The superbly set up Chip Ganassi entry driven by the six-time series champion would not be denied and beat the Moretti Motorsport entry to the flag by just over half a second.

"Oh no!" Amanda yelled from her perch atop the canopy-covered VIP box that overlooked pit lane.

Matilde smiled heartily. "Our boys can't win every time, girls."

Sarah was quite exhilarated herself and embraced her daughter. The attitude of Alex's grandmother and all of those around them painted a distinct picture. Finishing a close second at Detroit was nowhere near the letdown of a similar result at the Indy 500. Unlike the big race, Alex would join the victor on the podium along with Kyle Kirkwood, the third-place finisher.

Less emotional was a rather stoic Sabetha, a woman no longer prone to these emotional displays, even in the case of her own son. She forced a smile while popping two pills.

Amanda made her way down toward the Moretti pit box to comfort her race man, expecting him to be quite down. Alex was relatively content with his second-place finish, noting that he certainly wasn't the first to share the podium as runner-up to Dixon, and likely wouldn't be the last. The pit reporter, Gretchen David, was delighted to get both him and Amanda in on the post-race interview.

Back up under their VIP canopy, Sarah and Sabetha took in the post-race activity.

"This is nothing like last weekend at Indianapolis." Sarah observed.

"No, it isn't. I'm accustomed to the races in Formula One, which are all huge celebrations. I'm not sure why Andy is still here," the French woman added, all with an apparent air of disrespect toward the American open-wheel series.

"Perhaps it's because of Tony," Sarah responded, thinking this French woman should know that.

"Indeed, dear. Tony's absence in Europe is why Andy should be there. I'm here to look after my son."

Sarah could not respond and just looked away while thinking, *Somehow, Madam Moretti, you just don't seem to fit the mold of the all-caring mother. Besides, Madam, your son has a very strong and loving wife, in case you haven't noticed.*

The Detroit Grand Prix was in the books. Despite having only competed in two races, by virtue of his victory at Indy and another second-place tally, Alex Moretti suddenly found himself a very respectable eighth in the championship points race.

The Moretti clan would all pack up everything and head south to Charlotte for a few days' break before heading back up north to Wisconsin for the next race. Alex would reflect and consider how much better his Lake Norman condo would feel since the last time he left it just over two weeks before, when his personal and professional life was in shambles. He felt largely on top of the world now, other than the still reeling from the aftershock of his brother's injuries.

He and Amanda would drop Sarah off at the airport as she preferred a first-class plane ticket to another several hundred miles in her daughter's Mustang. As she sat in the terminal waiting to board, her thoughts were of her husband, a man who had been difficult for over two years, but one whom she wanted back. As both of their girls would be off and married soon, she hoped the two of them could rebuild their relationship and perhaps do some traveling together.

Something or someone at her gate caused Sarah's thoughts to shift toward Sabetha Moretti, a woman that caused Sarah some strange reservations. *How could she have never seen her grandkids before? It surely doesn't appear to be an issue of affordability. And suddenly she shows up because of her older son's racing accident? That happened two weeks ago!*

Sarah boarded the plane and was seated in the front row, her mind still wandering. *What a turbulent two weeks this has been.* She was, of course, thrilled with Amanda's engagement and she herself had thoroughly enjoyed being around the Morettis again. So far as this Sabetha, Sarah kept telling herself the woman's estranged dispositions were really none of her business. But whether because of her protective nature toward Amanda or something else, she couldn't shake the strange feeling of wishing Sabetha Moretti would shorten her stay and head back to whatever life she had in Europe.

***

"I'm just not comfortable with it, Matilde. Our place isn't that big, anyway."

"Well, Crissy. You know Tony's summer schedule, and thus yours, has changed now. He will need a lot of support. And then there's Adrian and David."

"We have always had all the support we needed, Matilde," Crissy answered. "Andy has a much bigger place. Why can't Sabetha stay with you for a few days while she's here?"

Matilde knew her granddaughter-in-law was right, and that she was uncomfortable around Tony's mother. She was the type of person who always strived to see the good in everyone, but even Matilde could see there was something out of character about Sabetha's visit. Andy's mother also didn't know how her son would react to his estranged ex-wife staying under his roof for any length of time. It wasn't as though he had a relationship to consider. Matilde wished he would get involved instead of being so married to his race teams all the time. *Isn't natural,* she often considered. *Perhaps he and Sabetha could reconcile?* Matilde just slowly shook her head. *Fat chance of that. I lived through their separations and divorce... And neither one of them has changed a bit.*

***

Andy had flown directly from Detroit to London as he and Ian Miles needed to stave off disaster with the performance of the Moretti Formula One team. Geoff Leland had suddenly been cast as the number one team driver, a position he claimed he always wanted and deserved.

"The bloke has put on a good thirty to forty kilograms since last season," Miles stated.

Formula 1's strict weight restrictions predicated that many drivers now resembled horse jockeys. Such a subtle change, seen on the surface as insufficient, was magnified when hundreds of a second on the race track was critical.

The journeyman driver had been wining behind the scenes that the boss's son, Tony, had been getting all the best equipment and personnel, a claim that Andy felt was ludicrous. *Well mate,* he thought of the Aussie. *Now put up or shut up.*

Their second driver, newly promoted Robinson, was having the devil's day coming to grips with the car on the circuit in Barcelona, crashing twice and causing substantial damage to two cars, an act that would rob Andy and Ian Miles of some precious hours of sleep.

The team had found themselves in jeopardy of not making the starting grid for the Spanish Grand Prix because of the FIA's 107% rule, which mandated that all cars qualifying time be less than seven percent over pole time. They had shown tremendous progress after just two seasons but now much of that success was being credited to Tony's driving prowess and not so much the quality of their cars. This was also causing quite a lot of anxiety with Ford, their engine supplier, as lack of performance in the back of the grid in any racing venue would reflect badly on the OEM manufacturer. In the case of Formula One and its massive worldwide exposure, such slumps were magnified many times over.

Andy hadn't been getting too much pressure from the team's sponsors, at least yet. In light of Tony's life-threatening injuries, the BP execs were still quiet. But he had been in this game for a long time. The renaissance he enjoyed from the Indianapolis 500 no longer played long in the Formula One paddock or press. He knew that pressure was coming and would come hard if his F1 squad faltered.

"She's what!?" Andy yelled into his phone. Many of the engineers and technicians stopped work briefly, quickly looking up toward the big boss as it appeared he was dealing with some sort of catastrophe.

"What was I supposed to do, Andy? Have Maria get her a nearby hotel?" Matilde replied innocently.

"I'm sure Maria would relish that," Andy replied. "How long does she plan to be there?"

"She hasn't said, Andy. You're not around that often, anyway. Does her presence bother you that much?" *It's not as though she's interfering with your love life.*

"Not sure on the answer to that, yet, Mamma. It's just strange, that's all. After all this time, Sabetha suddenly cares about her kids and grandkids?"

"She is Tony and Alex's mother, Andy. And Adrian and David's grandmother. Have a heart, will you?"

"I have to go. See you on Thursday," Andy responded and disconnected. *I did give her my heart once, Mamma... And she broke it.*

While Alex and Amanda enjoyed a post-engagement trip to Gatlinburg, Tennessee, Andy and Tony conversed regularly. Still working on his physicality, Tony seemed to have his full mental devices in order and had Crissy drive him to the team facility in Huntersville daily. While still a long way from being behind the wheel, if ever, Tony wanted to be involved and worried about losing the gains the team had made in Formula One. Even when at home, he couldn't just relax and enjoy a quiet convalescence, spending every spare minute studying technical data, rules, regulations, and practice lap times.

Tony had long revered the great Formula 1 drivers in history, Stewart, Senna, and others. He wondered if his father could have matched their records in Formula One had he been fortunate to be with the great teams at the right time. He knew that was the key.

Of course, his father had enjoyed a distinguished career combining his Formula One exploits and IndyCar. His numbers had almost mirrored the great Emerson Fittipaldi in that respect.

Tony had certain human traits that were different than many drivers. Less a dreamer and somewhat more pragmatic than most, he was a man who knew he may never drive again but would be content being remembered as a man like Adrian Newey, a designer/engineer more responsible for team and driver championships than any other in the history of Formula 1. He planned to be at the head of Moretti Motorsport someday, and wanted the marque to be at the forefront, at least spoken in the same conversation with the likes of Ferrari or McLaren.

Getting a bit depressed that he could yet fully get around and enjoy his young boys, Crissy could see her husband missing the action, the team comradery, and the pressure of competing. She would have a talk with her father-in-law about it when he returned.

Matilde would arrive with Sabetha each day for a lengthy visit and Crissy became annoyed that her mother-in-law would step outside to smoke at least once every hour, returning with that odor that didn't mix well with her expensive perfume. There was something else about her that would become readily apparent by the end of their visit. Crissy had seen plenty of it during her younger days in Southern California... *She's doping.*

Byron had been uneasy at the thought of having Carolyn as a weekend "guest", but knowing he could have the run of his place alone, he was tired of sneaking around to her downtown apartment. While still at Indy, he discussed with Allison the possibility of her coming home for a visit the following weekend, but she was committed to spending the whole week with Aaron and his family in Hilton Head.

He was still somewhat blitzed that Sarah had even entertained staying away from him for two whole weeks, something the two had never experienced in all their time being married. But that was more of a male chauvinist thing with Byron Cook, and since his spouse was going to be away on holiday, he would take advantage of it.

He had initially suggested that he and Carolyn get away for the weekend, perhaps to Sanibel Island or Key West. But his mistress complained of needing a break from the travel and truly wanted to spend a weekend in *his house,*... and *in his bed.*

Byron gave their housekeeper a paid weekend off and he and Tyler would have his large mansion on the lake all to themselves. The two would have to use caution while milling around outside, as he was always leery of the prying eyes of nosey neighbors, many of whom were very accustomed to seeing Sarah out and about. He had some comfort in the fact the Cook estate encompassed three plus acres and was relatively private due to a tall privacy fence, actually a brick and mortar wall, which surrounded the property on all sides down to the lakeshore.

Tyler was subtly ratcheting up the pressure on Byron to fish or cut bait with his marriage, a step he had never come to terms with emotionally. She had been his lover for nearly two years, an arrangement that had grown all the more uncomfortable and increasingly difficult to keep under wraps around the corporate office, as once a secret is known by two individuals, it's no longer a secret.

Adding to the burden was Byron's increasing inability to manage Tyler, particularly since her detailed work in handling Unibank's motorsport program had been close to a disaster. He had chosen to deflect some suspicion by placing her under the charge of his longtime friend and ally, Wally Remington, who was now Unibank's Chief Financial Officer. Wally was Byron Cook's most staunch supporter on the Board, but had strongly suspected the CEO's affair for months and was somewhat annoyed that Cook had not taken him into his confidence about it.

Tyler had basically replaced Adam Herrera in managing the huge motorsport sponsorship department, but the former Vice President of Marketing's position had not officially been filled, a promotion she fully expected.

"Remington mentioned to me that he was looking at outside talent for the position, Byron. Tell me you're not going to hire a new boss for me after all the hard work I've put into this," she demanded.

"I'll have a talk with him," Byron lied. He and Wally had been discussing the issue of replacing Herrera for weeks as the CFO was of the strong opinion that Tyler was in way over her head, and that he had too much on his plate to constantly have to overlook what she was doing.

"You need to take care of your woman, Byron," she responded, smiling as she moved down toward his midsection.

He heard his phone buzz and reluctantly reached over to the nightstand to check it. "It's Sarah. It's past eleven PM. I better answer it."

Tyler listened and could see Byron was suddenly rattled about something.

"Why didn't you call and tell me this earlier, Sarah? I'm already in bed.....Oh, I must have missed it.....Uh, huh.....No, don't take a shuttle. I'll get dressed and be there within the hour.....I'll call you when I'm close." He disconnected.

"Damn it, Carolyn! She decided to catch a plane and come home early. And she's already landed at Douglas International. Let's get dressed and gather your things."

He had planned an early Monday morning quiet trip to drop his mistress off at her apartment before heading to the office. Byron's nerves were severely frayed as he thought of the consequences of just allowing the late-night call to go to voicemail. Sarah would have taken a shuttle taxi home and to what, her husband in bed in their own home and in her own bed with another woman!? The BMW sedan sped toward downtown Charlotte at eighty-five as Byron would have to drop Tyler off several hours earlier than planned before doubling back to pick up Sarah at the airport.

"Are you sure you gathered up all of your personal belongings, Carolyn?" Byron asked one last time, knowing they were in a rush to get out the door.

"Yes, Byron. Stop worrying." She really wanted him to appreciate her commitment to him in the relationship. After all, it was Sarah who declined to come back home with her husband, not her.

He pulled in front of her building, just a few short blocks from the Unibank tower. If she expected him to park and walk her to her door, she would be disappointed. They shared a brief kiss and she could tell he was stressed, wanting to head out right away.

If Carolyn Tyler wasn't a gold digger before hooking up with the big boss, he certainly had contributed in making her one now. She walked hurriedly to the ground floor elevator with her bag in tow, reflecting on how she had become emotionally attached to the President and CEO of the huge banking conglomerate she had worked for several years. It had been nearly two years that she and some friends were having a few cocktails at the downtown hotel lounge when she recognized him, a man whom she had never met formally despite working together in the same building for nearly a decade. Of course, like everyone else, she had been well aware of the tragic accident a year earlier involving his teenage daughter, Amanda, and his ongoing disdain for all things motor racing, especially the name Moretti.

After a few drinks, the class barrier between the two dissolved and they were sharing life stories together, culminating in the two having sex in her apartment. A couple days passed afterward with no communication and Tyler began to think of it as just two ships passing in the night. But on the third day, he rang her extension, asking if she would care to meet him again, that afternoon even. Their torrid affair had begun.

Within six months Tyler was moved into the bank's department overseeing corporate marketing contracts, and she familiarized herself with Unibank's motorsports advertising. It wasn't long before she and Byron's time together became more than simply satisfying each other's physical needs. He needed a female to provide moral support for him in his mission to destroy the Morettis, and his wife had not provided either. When Tyler shared with him her observations regarding loopholes in the Unibank-Moretti Motorsport contract, namely regarding the star British female driver, Evelyn Stevens, the boss was all ears.

During the lengthy trial in which Alex Moretti's charges of Statutory Rape were dismissed, Tyler had sold him on letting her manage the motor racing program, as he thought this would be the last year for it. The unforeseen circumstances at Indy of Andy Moretti helping Stevens to qualify, his oldest son having a serious crash after winning the Pole, and a final shock, Alex Moretti winning by a car length over Unibank's star, Stevens, and proposing marriage to Byron's daughter right there on the victory podium, had all struck the illicit couple like a bolt of lightning.

Returning from Detroit, Amanda had announced plans for her and Alex to take off in her Mustang for a week-long excursion where she had reserved a private cabin in the Smoky Mountains. Her folks, Byron and Sarah Cook, were not at all content with their youngest girl venturing off on this trip so soon with her new fiancé, albeit for two polarizing reasons.

Byron was still reeling from the two-year running feud with the Morettis, a clan that was soon to be connected to them by marriage.

It was his bank's decision to involve themselves in sponsoring Moretti Motorsport that had set the stage for Amanda's connection with Alex Moretti in the first place.

Sarah had not been away from Amanda for this length of time since she last went to Gatlinburg with her best friend and her family two summers before. At eighteen, seeing her youngest take off like this was hard on Sarah, a loving mother having to accept the offspring leaving the nest.

Although it had been months now since the trial had ended, the tension in the Cook's household had not receded, and Byron was still very bitter over all of it, especially since the relationship with their lifelong friends, the Williams family, had not thawed in the least.

Sarah sat alone up in bed while Byron feigned doing business in his den. He would enter their master bedroom, always first hitting the bathroom, and she could hear him swashing with mouthwash repeatedly before coming to bed. He would still reek with the smell of whiskey and she would always roll over and act asleep, avoiding any conversation she knew would be difficult.

Byron had felt betrayed by his wife of twenty-two years ever since that fateful day in Las Vegas. While Amanda lay in that hospital and the whole family came to grips with the news of her nearly two-month pregnancy, he had been hellbent on exacting revenge on the Morettis, young Alex who had violated their precious belle, and his father and team owner who must have had tacit approval of it. Sarah had never supported him with her all-sympathetic, all-forgiving attitude.

They had not been intimate in bed since that day before in Las Vegas. Soon to be forty-four years of age, Byron had found such satisfaction at the corporate office in the person of a middle manager, Carolyn Tyler. That chance encounter at a hotel bar in downtown

Charlotte, resulting in his ongoing illicit affair, was an act that an overly naïve Sarah had never suspected.

⚑✕⚑

Sarah was exhausted and slept late the next morning. Following a quick cup of coffee and some texts to Allison and Amanda, both of whom were vacationing with their beaus, she opted for a shower before leaving for some shopping.

Reaching in to adjust the showerhead, she suddenly spied something foreign, a small blue bottle of shampoo which she grabbed to examine. *KÉRASTASE, Paris? Who uses this? Not Byron... Juanita, the housekeeper? No, and she would never shower in here, anyway... Allison? Possibly. But what would she be doing in our bathroom?*

Sarah stored away the thought and finished. She grabbed her phone and pecked in the shampoo brand name. *Forty-two dollars for a small bottle!...* She had planned to present a long overdue romantic evening for her and Byron, even donning some sexy lingerie that she hadn't worn in years. But this little mystery had now given Sarah Cook pause.

⚑✕⚑

Juanita showed up for work on Tuesday morning, thanking Sarah for the long weekend off with pay, an act that didn't ring familiar with Byron Cook and triggered more questions. Sarah asked her about the errant shampoo bottle left in the master bathroom shower.

"I cleaned it thoroughly on Friday, Mrs. Cook. I don't recall seeing that, but I could be mistaken. You wouldn't wish for me to discard something like that, would you?"

"No, I suppose not, Juanita."

The housekeeper departed and Sarah sat on the edge of the bed, staring down at the floor as if in deep thought. She then chose to make a call.

"Allison! How are you, honey?"

"Just peachy, Mother. And you?"

"I'm tired from all the travel and decided to fly home last night. Have you, by chance, been home to see your father since Indianapolis?" Sarah asked anxiously.

"Oh no. I've been down here at Hilton Head the whole time. I have fences to mend here," Allison stated with an edge, wanting to remind her mother that Amanda had still put her in a bad light with her future in-laws. "Why? Is Daddy okay?"

"Yes, yes. No worries. Other than the tension following the trial, how are Bud and Lisa doing?"

"Mom! What kind of question is that!? The post-trial tension *is* how they are doing."

"When can you come home, Allison?" Sarah asked with a degree of desperation in her voice. "I want to see you."

"When will Amanda be back?"

"She and Alex will be in Gatlinburg until Saturday. I think."

"Well, Mom. Like I said, I won't set foot there again while she is there."

"Oh, honey, what would it take for you two to bury the hatchet? This unpleasantness must stop.."

Allison was quick to reply. "I'll tell you what it would take, Mother. Amanda needs to make a public statement that she was wrong about what happened between her and Kyle."

Sarah briefly closed her eyes and shook her head. "That would amount to her admitting to perjuring herself on the witness stand!"

"No, she would just have to admit that what happened back then was a big misunderstanding, that's all. Things will never be right between me and Aaron's family until that happens. Will you talk to her, Mom?"

"Allison, your sister says she was sexually assaulted!"

"It was three and a half years ago, Mom. I was there. We were all drunk. Should Kyle Williams have his whole life ruined because of one foolish incident that happened when he was a minor?"

"Why don't you suggest to her that Kyle may apologize? Amanda has already come out and said she wants no more pain with this."

"I'll come visit and we'll talk about it later this week, Mom," Allison stated, shaking her head. *Amanda and I are not talking, remember, Mother?*

"Oh, that will be great," Sarah replied and, following a few more minutes of small talk, the two disconnected.

⚑⚑

She sat impatiently half a block away, waiting, and kept looking at the time. Byron generally got home before 6:30 and it was nearly 6:00 now. Sarah looked around while thinking she had led such a sheltered life in an upscale, exclusive lakeside subdivision. She couldn't recall the last time she had driven into the heart of Charlotte on her own, despite its proximity.

Finally, his BMW pulled out of the apartment parking garage and headed south just past her new Cadillac Escalade SUV. Byron appeared to be busy checking phone messages, seemingly oblivious to her presence parked on the opposite side of the street. Sarah was overcome with a combination of fear, anger, and sorrow as she struggled to hold back her tears. *What do I do now? Like I'm going to just walk into that building and start knocking on every door, thinking I'll recognize someone.*

Sarah pulled away and headed toward the expressway, crushed emotionally. She knew her husband was having an affair but didn't know with whom. *How long has this been going on? Is it someone I know?*

She drove south on I-77 toward the Tega Cay exit, trying to remain calm. *How should I act when I get home? Should I confront him now or wait until I know more?* Sarah's nerves were frayed as she found herself slowing down as if not really wanting to deal with this crisis.

Chapter 3

South Metro Shockwave

Byron pulled into the driveway, surprised when he hit the garage door opener and saw that Sarah's SUV was not there. A creature of habit, she was always there to meet him, and after their brief greeting every weekday evening, he would rest assured his secret was secure. He hung his suit coat on the stairway banister and loosened his tie as he entered the den to pour himself a bourbon. He wondered how his marriage had gotten this far off track. His wife was beautiful, moral, and faithful, but she had not backed him up in protecting their daughter. Even now he was vexed at what kind of life Amanda would have, marrying a race driver. *And Sarah is totally giddy about it!*

He constantly attempted to mentally justify his indiscretion, but deep down Byron truly wanted things to return to the way things were, but he was in deep with Tyler now. She expected much from him and had him in a box. *How long can we go on like this or how could I even exit the relationship?* He constantly agonized over it. He heard the garage door opening. Sarah had come home.

She walked in and headed straight upstairs, not bothering to greet him. *A bad sign.* She approached after a bit with the sad eyes of a woman who had been crying.

"What is it, Sarah?"

She struggled to look up, trying to gather the courage to confront him,... but she wasn't quite there. "My family is falling apart, Byron."

"What's going on now?" he asked sheepishly. "I thought Amanda's new engagement had you overjoyed."

Sarah looked at him, fighting to find the right words. It shouldn't be that difficult. They hadn't been close for over two years now. But she hesitated. She had to know more. "Allison is still refusing to be in this house with her sister, Byron. The Williams want Amanda to make a public statement, denying what happened between her and Kyle."

Byron shook his head in mild disgust. "I suppose that would be out of the question right now."

"Of course it would!" Sarah barked back. Unable to say any more, she shook her head, walked briskly away, and up to their room.

On Thursday afternoon, Allison returned to the home she grew up in. She had thundered out the door months earlier, swearing to never return so long as Amanda was there. Now that her despised sister was getting married, she felt the moratorium on visiting her parents' home could be eased upon. It was largely an act on her part, as she knew all of Amanda's claims in that rape trial were true, but in Allison's world a confession displayed weakness, an everlasting barrier to the quest for power, and in her mind she had all the tools necessary to gain that power, sex appeal and access to money.

Sarah and her firstborn shared some brief small talk regarding Detroit, Hilton Head, and local gossip. Allison was intrigued about the news that Alex's long-estranged mother was visiting and could tell by her tone that her own mother didn't care much for her. *But something else is severely bothering you, Mother. That cheerful mood that had always lifted everyone's spirits here is missing. Is it all about Amanda and I, Mother? Or something else?*

"Mom, don't let this rift between Amanda and I ruin your life. We're both moving out anyway. Things have a way of working out."

"I'm so glad you feel that way, honey," Sarah replied, surprised and pleased at Allison's apparent change of heart. "I have something upsetting to tell you. I believe your father is having an affair."

Allison froze for a moment, thinking about the right response. "Mom, how do you know?"

Sarah stepped away toward the front door and grabbed her purse, reaching inside and pulling out the mysterious shampoo bottle. "Have you ever seen or heard of this stuff before?"

Allison took it from her, examining it thoroughly. "No, it like doesn't look familiar."

"I found it in our master bedroom shower when I got up Monday morning."

Allison gave her a stern look. "Mom, you can't condemn my daddy over a bottle of shampoo. Did you ask him about it?"

"Not yet. But he's spent a couple of late afternoon hours in an apartment a few blocks away from the office these last three days. He had always told me he was working late."

"Mother! You had him followed?"

"No, nothing so dramatic as that, girl. You do recall that Byron had that GPS locator app installed on all our phones a few years ago. He wanted to always know your whereabouts."

"I had forgotten about that," Allison stated, vividly remembering that she had promptly disabled the app when she found out about it.

"Well, I turned it on and saw his location there, always after 4:30 PM. I drove there and saw him leave just after six. I know it must be another woman, Allison," Sarah said, becoming misty-eyed.

No stranger to such indiscretions herself, Allison feigned shock and embraced Sarah, the all-caring daughter sharing tears with her stricken mother. "When are you going to confront him, Mom?"

"I don't know... I feel like such a fool. I guess I shouldn't be so shocked. We haven't been close since the accident in Vegas."

"Should I stick around until Daddy gets home?"

"No, honey. We have had enough grief in this family already. I'm going to wait until I know for certain who the other woman is. Plus, I don't wish to pull you and Amanda into our mess," Sarah relayed with a sad seriousness. "But you can do one thing for me. Reconcile your issues with her, please."

Allison left for the condo in Rock Hill, a vacation rental that she and Aaron would use when back in town. As she drove out of Tega Cay, her mind was racing. Given her own promiscuous attitude toward marital infidelity, Allison Cook saw opportunity in every crisis, personal and professional. She also knew with little doubt who her father's lover would be and didn't like it, not so much because of the trauma inflicted on her mother, but for quite another concern—Carolyn Tyler's access to her father's money.

She had been fabricating a plan to secure her goal as Evelyn Stevens' agent, a daunting task but not beyond Allison Cook, a woman with no limits to her scheming repertoire. Stevens had an open concern, given her goal to return to the Moretti Motorsport stable next season and Allison's on-going personal rift with her sister, who would soon be a Moretti herself. As such, Allison was working to mend fences with Amanda, at least superficially. She now had a cause to disguise the ruse, their rallying together to provide their mother some emotional support.

Allison had been keeping in close touch with Evelyn, presenting her concern and offering help to mediate the lingering contractual conflicts between her and Carolyn Tyler. The Brit seemed to be in fairly good spirits following her loss at Indy, if one would consider finishing less than half a second behind the winner in second and collecting a cool million bucks in the process as a loss. This was all despite the somber news of losing her longtime business agent to an overdose and dealing with her friend and former teammate, Tony Moretti's severe injuries.

Stevens held a hidden suspicion of Allison Cook, seeing her as a woman who had strong ambitions and the will to walk all over anyone or anything that posed a threat to those. The female racing star was a realist, however, knowing Allison was the daughter of the man who funded her paycheck and had to admit the young woman had become a positive force in easing her contract demands.

Prior to confronting her father, Allison had to know for sure that Carolyn Tyler was indeed his mistress. To accomplish this, she simply inquired through an old high schoolmate, a young woman who Allison had socialized with at Aaron's high school reunion months earlier. She learned that Mary Jo Nelson was by chance employed at Unibank's corporate tower as a middle manager in personnel. Since Allison Cook was the headman's daughter, the young woman didn't hesitate to gain some brownie points by providing Carolyn Tyler's home address, along with all the other pertinent data in her file, information that matched the address Allison's mother had given her to the letter.

He worked to clear away some final documents while he kept an eye on the clock. Whether it was simply habit or subtle pressure from Tyler that he stop in at her apartment near daily, Byron had a nervous feeling on this day due to last evening's interaction with Sarah. Certainly, the personal animosity between their two girls was upsetting, but it wasn't anything new. No, something else was on her mind, he knew, intensely worried that since they were all in such proximity at the Indy VIP suite, his extra-marital affair would be impossible to disguise. It would be simple if he could just break it off with Tyler and proceed as though it had never happened. *But no, she would never go for that now.* She was an employee and he was the CEO. Bad karma.

Just as he prepared to depart, his desk phone buzzed. "Mr. Cook, your daughter, Allison, is here to see you."

Not waiting for another prompt, Allison abruptly headed for his office door and entered, closing the door behind her and sitting down to face a father, a man wearing a blank if surprising look.

"Daddy, I think you had best just tell me about it."

He hesitated, taken aback and having difficulty facing his daughter with the typical denial. "How did you find out?" A man not prone to tears, he struggled as his eyes began to show worry and stress.

"Mom knows, Daddy. She is really hurt. This is bad."

Byron leaned back in his executive rocking office chair, temporarily looking away toward the west wall. "I never meant to hurt your mother. It has—"

"I know, Daddy. You haven't made love together in over two years. I don't fully blame you. I hate this for Mom but don't blame you. But Daddy, Carolyn Tyler? A middle manager in this building? Hello!"

"I don't know what to say, Allison. It just happened."

She wasn't buying it. In Allison's mind, nothing just happened. *It may have just happened with you, Daddy. But not Tyler. You're the perfect mark. She just happened to be in the right place at the right time. Yeah, right.* "How long have you been seeing her?"

"It was probably six, maybe eight months after the Vegas accident... You know I was in a fit of rage over that and your mother—"

"I know, Daddy. She didn't back you." *And you were pumping Tyler for more than a year before you handed her Adam Herrera's job, a woman with zero qualifications in marketing.* "What's important is that you have yourself a real mess now. This will come to light, Daddy. The dust-up with the Board over Evelyn Stevens' contract dispute hasn't been totally resolved. You know what will happen when Forsythe finds out you've been screwing the very woman who botched that whole contract. You'll be forced to resign."

Byron placed a hand on his forehead as if massaging an on-coming headache. "Maybe I should just resign."

"No!" Allison nearly screamed. "Use your head, Daddy. You have to help me clear up this mess with Evelyn Steven's contract now, before the shit hits the fan."

"How am I going to do that? The damn lawyers would take a month to work on it."

Allison was momentarily ashamed of him. She had always admired her father, a man who had risen to be one of the most influential and powerful bankers in the world, and all by early middle age. "Are you not the President and CEO? Do these attorneys not work for you?... Now listen. I want to be Evelyn Stevens' agent. If I can get this cleaned up, it'll happen. I have the proposed amended documents right here. You just have to push Tyler to cooperate."

He contemplated how the next couple of days would play out, dreading the confrontation with Sarah. "Are you going to be at the house when I get there?"

"No, I won't. You must face that music on your own, Daddy. And I broke confidence with Mother by coming here. It would be best if you didn't mention that."

"Yes, of course."

He was running nearly forty minutes late when she saw her phone ring. *Byron*. She started to have a nauseating feeling and answered.

"Sarah knows about us."

Tyler took a deep breath. "I can't believe it took this long, Byron. What did she say?"

"I haven't talked to her yet, Carolyn. Allison informed me. I'm already ten minutes from our exit."

"You knew this day would come, Byron. What are you going to do?"

"Let me call you later."

He pulled up to their security gate and hit the remote, waiting for the white steel barrier to slide open, strangely wanting it to slow down. Sarah could hear the garage door open and prepared for what was coming. She had spent nearly all day going over what she would say to him.

A simple web search made for less anxiety of an extended investigation into her husband's mistress identity. When she typed in the address on North Davidson Street, several names appeared through the popular "find anyone" website, including one Carolyn Diane Tyler. Strangely, Sarah didn't feel anger toward the woman and by then, her feeling of rancor toward Byron had become more of an aching numbness.

Sarah had chosen not to contact Amanda just yet. *Why ruin her holiday with Alex? It wouldn't change anything. I'll break it to her when they return.*

Byron walked stoically in and headed for the den, dropping his briefcase and losing the sport coat. Sarah soon appeared in the open French doors and the two stood facing each other in the home office for some uncomfortable moments.

He looked resigned. "How long have you known?"

"Since Monday morning. Your lover managed to leave this in our shower," she replied sternly and tossed the blue shampoo tube at him.

"Sarah, I know you have reason—"

"Spare me, Byron. I don't need your excuses. I don't need to hear about my being cold all these months. I don't need to hear how I didn't stand by your side while you endeavored to destroy the Morettis and ruin Amanda's life. I would say I'm mostly upset about the charade you and Tyler pulled right in front of our daughters in Indianapolis."

Byron made a futile effort to embrace her, but Sarah quickly backed away. "Don't touch me, Byron… I want to end this. I'm suing for a divorce."

He was stunned. As much as he knew that such a demand was likely, he held out a pittance of hope for a reconciliation. "Sarah, I know you're upset. We shouldn't make any important decisions while we're emotional. I suggest we let things stew for a couple days and revisit—"

"No, Byron! Of course, I'm emotional. I've been emotional for two years while you had no empathy whatsoever for what Amanda wanted or cared less about her being raped by Kyle Williams. I should have realized months ago that I have never really known you."

He slowly slid down into his den office chair, just staring down at the floor and without words. He had been in denial that somehow his affair with Tyler could simply be terminated and that he and Sarah could get back to where they were. But in Carolyn Tyler's mind, his getting anything less than a full divorce wouldn't do. She had him by the balls and could, and indeed would, ruin him.

"I'll contact James Edmunds tomorrow morning and set up a meeting."

"I will hire my own lawyer, Byron. For now, I would like for you to pack some things and leave me in peace tonight. I know you have an apartment in downtown Charlotte where you'll be welcome."

Before he could look up and respond, she had left the room.

🏁

"What the fuck is this, Eric!? You promised me this was taken care of," Allison screamed.

The naval intelligence officer nearly flinched at her vitriol, seeing a side of her for the first time he hadn't experienced. *Such language from a cultured southern girl.* He slowly shook his head as he re-read the email a few more times.

I have the goods on you and Louie, audio and video that not only Evelyn Stevens would be interested in, but also the Indianapolis Police Department.

To guarantee my confidentiality, you will wire $50,000 into my private Swiss bank account CH930076201162383423 no later than July 1st.

Hot Lips

"*Hot Lips*, huh? This is a dark web email, hard to trace."

"Hard to trace!? You're the expert, Eric! Dammit, find out who this bitch is!"

"You're assuming it's a she, Allison. Whoever this is, they were clever enough to record you and that Louie character in the act of—"

"Don't remind me, asshole! How long will it take you to find this,...whoever in hell he or she is!?"

"Hard to tell. Do you think this *Hot Lips* was working with Louie to shake you down?"

"Who the fuck knows! The pig is dead, Eric. What difference does it make? You just find out who sent me this! July 1st is less than three weeks away! You have their Swiss bank account number!"

"Whooh, Allison. I can't just hack into a Swiss bank to pull IDs on accounts." The junior naval intelligence officer began a concern that he had oversold this babe on his abilities to emulate James Bond.

"You're Naval Intelligence for the United States Government, aren't you? I'm counting on you, Eric."

"And if I do find out who it is, then what?"

"Just get me a name and location. We'll go from there. Do it!" She yelled before giving him an about-face and slamming the door behind her.

I guess no sex today, the devious Eric pondered, this being the first time Allison Cook had left his apartment without it. *This has potential Court Martial written all over it. I love ya, Allison Cook, but I don't love ya that much.*

Carolyn Tyler sat in his executive office, confronted with the proposed changes to the Evelyn Stevens contract.

"I have to get all of this cleaned up before my divorce proceeding becomes public, Carolyn," Byron explained. "Not to mention our relationship."

Tyler continued to review the draft he had handed her. Her initial thoughts were that her immediate boss, Unibank CFO Wally Remington, had come up with it until he himself had questioned her about it. *Byron wouldn't fabricate something like this on his own. He would consider working on such details beneath him. But who, then?... Allison!* "Since Louis Newberry is no longer among us, Byron. Who put this together?"

He hesitated, knowing she and his oldest daughter had never been that comfortable around each other, a condition that bothered him greatly. "My daughter, Allison, has become quite close to Evelyn Stevens. She may likely become her business agent."

"Oh, that's just great, Byron. The party we're to negotiate with on a multi-million dollar contract will be none other than your own daughter? How do you think the Board will react to that?"

With everything else going on right at that moment, Byron hadn't even considered it.

"Seriously, Byron, are you and Sarah really going through with this?"

He wasn't prepared to answer Tyler's direct questions. "It appears so, Carolyn. She has already retained Randi Huntoon as counsel."

"Randi Huntoon, huh?" *As a divorce lawyer, a real warrior. He doesn't appear to be taking this news well. Is it the upcoming battle in court?... Or something else? Time to press.* "Byron, what does the future for us look like now?"

Another question he was unprepared for. "Let me get through this first, Carolyn."

Tyler knew that her affair with Byron Cook would soon come out and could end up in many different ways, so far as she was concerned. *Right now, while he's feeling vulnerable, I need to get that commitment that he has always been elusive about.* "Byron, you know I'm going to be seen as the *Wicked Witch of the South* now. Are you planning on marrying me, or not?"

He looked at her, struggling to smile. He had never thought that far. The truth was, he had wished for months that somehow he and Sarah would get close again and Tyler would just fade away. But he had carried things way too far for that. *After spending two years on a vendetta over Amanda's forbidden romance, how will I look now? Like a damned hypocrite. If I refuse to marry her, what will she do? If I don't commit to her personally, she'll demand that Marketing VP promotion. The Board will never go for it.* He knew that even Wally, his closest ally on the Board would never support such a thing. *She could destroy me professionally.* "Let's not go public for a bit, Carolyn. But yes, we'll marry."

Alex would take off early on his morning mountain hike. The cozy log cabin nestled on the hilly dead-end road was just far enough from Gatlinburg to be free from the tourist traffic noise and other typical urban sounds the newly engaged couple was accustomed to. He had been to several mountain ski resorts before, mostly as a young boy in Europe, but this place did have a certain unique charm about it.

What a whirlwind the past few weeks had been as Amanda had gone from total sadness over her estranged boyfriend, to a tacit reconciliation, to accepting his proposal, and now experiencing her first-ever full-blown vacation with the man in her life. Add to that, her beau was the newly crowned Indy 500 champion and suddenly both of them had changed their international celebrity status from key figures in the trial of the century to becoming motorsport's royal couple.

The thrill of the attention quickly ran its course with Amanda on a personal level, however, and she was all too happy to see that Alex was enjoying their privacy himself, a trait in him she had not known for certain as all of their previous adventures had been forbidden and cloaked in secrecy. In effect, they couldn't even think about going public until now.

She heard the back door open announcing Alex's return, and she chose a quick game of possum, pretending to still be asleep. Alex wasn't fooled as he ran and jumped on top of her, grabbing her around the waist as the two giggled and rollicked back and forth over the width of the king-sized bed.

"Don't you ever stop, race man1?" Amanda yelled as the two prepared for yet another intimate moment, their laughter interrupted by the buzzing of her phone. She held Alex back with one hand, leaning over to check it. *Allison?... Why in the world would she be calling me?* "Wait, race man. I better answer this."

They drove down from the scenic mountains east on Highway 74 toward the Charlotte metropolitan area, their pre-honeymoon vacation cut short by a couple of days as Amanda wanted to get home to comfort her mother. Allison's overture regarding the two sisters putting differences aside seemed like a good idea under the circumstances. All lingering hesitation with Alex showing up at the Cook estate seemed inconsequential now, as Amanda's father had taken up temporary residence in town with his mistress, anyway.

Amanda drove while Alex spent much of the trip on his phone catching up with social media, a skill his good friend and competitor Pato O'Ward had taught him well. It worked out as Amanda wasn't much in the mood for conversation.

For her part, Amanda knew that her forbidden romance and engagement to Alex had played some part in causing her parent's problems, knowing that Allison would certainly play that up for all it was worth, despite her sudden suggestion of letting bye-gones be bye-gones between them. Although concerned that her dad had left her mom abruptly in Indy two weeks earlier, Amanda had at least seen flashes of her mother's smile and happiness in Indy and Detroit that had been missing for far too long.

Amanda had noticed the past week that Alex had barely mentioned his own mother, a woman who still had a mystique about her. She wondered how long Sabetha would stay in America. *Perhaps this is an opportunity for Mom to spend a bit of time with her and the rest of Alex's family. Take some edge off the situation between her and Dad.*

During the following few weeks, Allison was very forward in playing the sad, sympathetic daughter to both of her parents, her big fear still being Carolyn Tyler and her sway over her daddy's financial decisions, like backing his oldest daughter in a major business venture or even someday running for office.

Amanda was much less outspoken, still barely speaking to her father and not pushing her mother. She was still basking in the glow of her engagement to Alex while not totally surprised about her parents' issues. The latest revelation that her dad had cheated on her mother had served to push Amanda even farther away from him.

Sarah was anxious as this was the first time that she, her two girls, and her soon-to-be ex-husband were in their home together since Alex Moretti's trial several months earlier, not to mention that both Byron and his despised future son-in-law were together in the same room. Sarah had encouraged Allison to bring her fiancé, Aaron Williams, but the young Marine officer had duties. The five muddled through a few uncomfortable pleasantries prior to the serious call to order.

Byron had agreed to Sarah's demands and the terms of the special cutout in their divorce settlement, a massive trust account with the two daughters assigned as beneficiaries.

"Allison, Amanda, it is our wish that you two will bury your differences and remember that we are still your mother and father, and it is my hope that your future husbands may someday bury their animosities toward each other as well," Sarah opened while giving Alex a focused smile.

Byron sat beside her solemnly, appearing all in concert until she mentioned their future sons-in-law part, which produced a blank expression on his part.

"Your father and I are setting up a special trust account for the two of you, currently valued at forty million dollars, accessible by you both upon Amanda turning twenty-one."

"I have arranged for an attorney in our legal department to act as executor," Byron added. "The fund will be invested in various stocks and securities until Amanda comes of age when you two will jointly take over the decision on how the fund is managed."

"It is our wish that you will both continue that partnership three years hence," Sarah interrupted. "But the funds will be open to you both at that time to withdraw or invest at your leisure, split 50-50 between you for the trust value at that time."

Allison and Amanda shared looks, neutral in expression but both stunned in mindset, albeit from far different perspectives. Both girls had known they would eventually be heirs to the Cook's vast wealth as an inheritance but were surprised at this staggering amount happening right at this time.

Allison struggled to remain neutral as she was blitzed at not having access to her share for almost three years, all due to Amanda's age, and the mere thought of having to split it with the one person she held responsible for all the family's troubles, *despicable*.

Indisposed to caring little about money, Amanda stole a glance toward Allison while squeezing Alex's hand.

"Do either of you have any questions for us?" Sarah asked, in a tone that radiated calm and somewhat irritated Byron, a man still in some denial that this was actually taking place.

Never one to hide her emotions, the girls both got the feeling that Sarah had gotten past the stress and trauma of her marriage to their father ending, even to the point of optimism and relief.

Alex was quite stunned, realizing for the first time the immense wealth he would be marrying into. Never one who had been attracted to Amanda for such reasons, he had always wanted to make his own legend and in certain ways looked upon the trust as a negative. After all, now Amanda would have close and serious dealings with her sister, a woman Alex still viewed with extreme mistrust.

⚑⚑

Matilde noticed Sabetha would spend an inordinate amount of time sitting out at the pool just clicking around on her iPhone. Her guise of an abrupt visit to look after Tony was obviously a thinly veiled ruse. Even when Crissy would drop Adrian and David off, Sabetha would pay them little attention, and she and Maria were gradually getting fed up with her. *It is time to pry,* Matilde was thinking as she fixed her a latte and strolled outside, taking up station next to her former daughter-in-law in a poolside lounger.

"Would you like one of these, Sabetha?"

"No, thank you, Mamma. I'm fine."

She hasn't called me Mamma in years. "Tell me, Sabetha. What's going on in your life?"

The tall, former super-model hesitated. She had known Matilde for a very long time, a woman who had instincts like no other person she had ever met.

"You haven't spent much time with Tony or the kids. Something is bothering you, Sabetha. Kindly share it with me."

Sabetha knew Matilde would get around to being direct, eventually. "I'm sorry, Mamma. I'm in some trouble. My boyfriend, Anton, is being investigated by Interpol for dealing in narcotics."

"Have you been involved in this, Sabetha?"

"No, I have not. But I may be questioned as a potential witness."

"I see." Matilde wanted to scold Sabetha, a woman prone to this sort of thing. "So, just give a statement that you don't know anything."

Her eyes began to fill with tears. As much as Sabetha wanted to avoid disclosing her personal issues, she knew the one person on Earth who would be sympathetic and offer help was Matilde Moretti, the kindest woman she had ever known. "I'm addicted myself, Mamma. I didn't know what to do or where to turn."

A normal woman would get angry at this, but not Matilde. "You poor child. Have you thought about a rehab center?"

"I'm working on getting off in my own way, Mamma. If I could just have a little time, I know I can beat this."

Matilde was skeptical. "Where are you getting this stuff, Sabetha?"

"I brought some with me, in prescription bottles. I am working hard to take less each day, believe me."

"I see."

"Mom, can we keep this between the two of us? I am embarrassed," Sabetha asked expectantly.

"My lips are sealed for now, Sabetha. I'll take you at your word that you will get clean, girl. How long will this take?"

"Two to three weeks, I hope. Maybe four."

Sabetha, you never told us you may be here for a month! Andy will flip out if he hears that. "So, your drug problem aside, how does it feel living under the same roof with Andy after all these years?"

"Oh, Mamma. This place is like a resort hotel. But it's not like we're sharing a bed together."

"No, I know that."

"Just out of curiosity, does Andy have any love interest? Other than his race cars, that is."

"Not so much. I do sense a loneliness there, though. What about you? Are you serious with this Anton?"

"No. We just connected at a party in Paris several months ago. He's just a sixty-year-old playboy with an ego."

"I think you're getting a bit old, yourself, for that sort of thing, Sabetha."

I've been thinking that for years, Matilde. "Do you think things could ever be right for Andy and me?"

Oh, Sabetha, one step at a time. "Hard to say. I would suggest you seriously rid yourself of your drug addiction. After that, God only knows what the future holds," Matilde stated. "I would encourage you to get closer to your children and grandchildren. And your boys have taken up with two wonderful girls. Get close to them, too."

Andy's race team was becoming a tale of contrasts during the summer heat and busiest part of the schedule. The NASCAR team's lead driver, Alan Allison, had won four more races following the marque victory in the Daytona 500, adding to his five other top-five finishes. Under the old NASCAR points system, Allison would be running away with the Cup Championship merely halfway through the season.

The IMSA sports prototype team had top-three finishes in Daytona and Sebring prior to winning in Long Beach. A disappointing Lemans, where both team cars were involved in racing crashes, was followed up with a stellar one-two finish at Watkins Glen, New York a week later. Jon David Hill, who had struggled to reach stardom in the IndyCars, took the checkered flag with the best drive of his career.

Alex had injected new optimism in the Moretti IndyCar camp by winning at Indy, finishing a close second at Detroit, and winning again at Road America in Elkhart Lake, Wisconsin.

Following Sarah's two turbulent weeks at home, Allison sent Amanda a text, suggesting they invite their mother out to California for the IndyCar race in Monterey, giving her a break from the pending divorce proceeding. Allison's true motivation was the opportunity to have Evelyn Stevens see both Cook girls interacting in relative harmony as a basis to further lobby her for the business agent job. Amanda was not fooled by this but could hardly object, as spending a few days in the scenic area around the Laguna Seca race track seemed appealing.

To her contentment, Amanda learned that Alex didn't expect her to hang around the paddock 24/7 during a race weekend. "I know you need a little space and a break from it," he had told her. She had actually relished being on the pit stand during qualifying and the race itself, but wished to spend some time driving down the rugged California coast highway in her Mustang with her mom, recalling that nearly all of their family travels in the past were so "structured" as managed by her father. It also gave her an opportunity to get a break from Alex's mother, a woman who made Amanda just plain nervous.

By this time, Sabetha had been visiting for over two weeks and had seemed to take up residence in Andy's Lake Norman lakeside home, which had spurred all kinds of speculation.

Amanda and Crissy would talk multiple times per day with both in concert regarding their discomfort with Andy's former spouse. "How long does your mother plan on staying?" Amanda had asked Alex, to which he replied, "I have no idea."

Andy arrived back in the States late the following Wednesday, not thrilled that his ex-wife had not only made her way to North Carolina, but had extended her stay indefinitely. His mood was sour anyway, as the Spanish Grand Prix had been a catastrophe for the team. Geoff Leland had qualified on the seventh row but crashed into a Williams on the first turn, taking both cars out of the race. Worse, Robinson had failed to meet the 107 percent cutoff and had just managed to get the FIA officials to let him start dead last due to a decent showing in the morning warm-up. As luck would have it the entire session was run with a great equalizer - rain. Lady Luck would run out for Robinson during the race, however, as the car lost its two lower gears and the rookie driver managed to burn out the clutch in the process, resulting in a DNF. The motorsport media had given the team somewhat of a break over Tony's serious injury, but were now criticizing them as no longer ready for prime time. In the high-pressure world of Formula One, things could get quite cold in a hurry.

⚑⚑

Prodded by Amanda, Sarah reached out to Sabetha and reluctantly offered to host Alex's mother for a day. With Alex spending most weekdays at the race shop, Amanda planned a visit with her longtime best friend, Trisha Shyree, and offered to drive Sabetha down to the Tega Cay estate. Although still having reservations about the woman, Sarah was committed to showing the European some southern hospitality.

Entering the same dining establishment for lunch the Cooks and Williams had frequented so many times during the trial, Sabetha tensed up with a creepy feeling that everyone in the place had frozen and were staring at her, as though all these strangers knew her history.

"Don't worry your pretty self, Sabetha. Everyone in here knows me," Sarah stated, herself a bit self-conscious of all the stares. "My divorce has been the talk of the town."

The two chatted over lunch, mostly about their children's lives, with Sarah doing most of the talking. She did want to pry a bit and learn how this woman could wait years to spend any time with her kids and grandkids. Sarah found herself questioning how this woman would leave a life with Andy Moretti, a guy who appeared to be such a great provider and family man.

"You chose to keep the last name. How did your subsequent husbands feel about that?"

"I choose what my last name will be," the French woman replied rather sternly, given as a slight toward Sarah's old-fashioned culture. "You were quite committed to your husband in every way, it seems, and what did it get you?"

Sarah suppressed a wave of hidden anger, believing that if any woman was going to school her on a woman's role in a marriage, it certainly wasn't going to be Sabetha, but she chose to let it pass. "How do you think Amanda will handle being married to a race driver?"

"I suppose I should say that I hope she can. It can be difficult, you know."

"Well, Sabetha. She's endured more drama in these past three years than most women deal with in a lifetime. I know she's truly committed. He's the only guy she has ever loved."

"She's only eighteen, Sarah. And she is beautiful."

"And?" Sarah replied, now getting offended.

"I'm sorry, did not mean to imply—"

"Forget it," Sarah cut her off, raising a hand to call for the check.

Sabetha appeared rather nervous and excused herself to hit the ladies' room. Sarah sat patiently while a couple of locals approached to pass along regards. She knew the two were just being nosey and she reveled in the opportunity to tell them,... nothing.

There's something going on with Alex's mother, Sarah thought to herself. She was making the effort to forge a good relationship with her, for Amanda's sake, but she was finding it challenging, as she didn't quite think the feeling was mutual on Sabetha Moretti's part. *The woman acts like she is trying to be nice to me,* Sarah considered. *Somehow, she seems so fake.*

Sabetha returned and the two departed the restaurant. She declined Sarah's invitation for a game of tennis and the two headed back to the Cook residence, where the guest preferred to simply pass the rest of the afternoon outside at their pool.

"It's much more private here than at Andy's place," Sabetha observed.

"Oh?"

"Yes, the big privacy wall is all around."

Sarah departed briefly and returned with two fruity cocktails from the house. "Why do you think Andy never married again?"

Sabetha quickly looked up, thinking it a very subtle question. "I don't know. You don't know him. He's married to his race team."

"That bad, huh?"

"Oh yes. The Moretti family has always been like that. Matilde would tell me she only had a life with Andy's father if she traveled to the races, which was all the time, of course."

"And you didn't know this before you married her son?"

Sabetha paused, simply staring out at the pool water for a few moments. "Andy was every girl's dream in the paddock back then. He was so handsome."

"And still is," Sarah blurted out, almost before thinking.

Sabetha paused a brief moment, reading much into this American woman's comment. "Things were really good for a bit," Sabetha reflected while she stared down into her glass, as in deep thought.

"So, what happened?"

"Everything changed when he went to Ferrari," Sabetha answered.

"Was he unfaithful to you?"

"Unfaithful?" Sarah's guest for the day simply looked up at her, slowly shaking her head. "No, he was never unfaithful to me, that I'm aware." *No, I was the unfaithful one.*

Following the disaster in Barcelona, Andy quickly replaced Robinson by hiring Wolf Von Prinze, who had a forced retirement from the Sauber team after a mediocre last season, replaced by the Formula 3 champion, Max Boyle.

Wolf had not kept himself in shape over the several-month retirement, and his limited time in the car resulted in his also failing to qualify under the 107% rule in his first race. Due to his past Formula One experience, the stewards waved the rule and allowed Von Prinze to race in Montreal, but he ran as basically a backmarker, continuing to cause Andy's struggling F1 squad immense embarrassment. Some snide remarks began to surface in the European press, the same voices that were critical of Moretti Motorsport being allowed to enter Formula One in the first place. These were loudly squashed by Andy's supporters in the F1 paddock, given the circumstances of Tony's tragic injuries. Nevertheless, the team was in dire need of a better pilot to stand in for him until their injured star could return. Many were questioning, albeit silently, whether he would ever recover and drive again given the seriousness of his injuries, as Tony could barely even stand and walk on his own without help.

Having plenty of idle time on his hands, Tony dove headlong into studying all the technical aspects of the team's cars, getting ample support from the engineers in allowing their popular wounded warrior program access, Q&A, etc. While Tony had always been technically astute as a driver, he now wished to study and know everything - every spec, every adjustment, and every algorithm.

He was also lobbying Ian and his dad for an important move, that of putting his little brother in their Formula One car.

Allison's nerves were frayed. It had been over a week and Jordan had come up with nothing. She began to think the unthinkable, that she may have to come up with the cash and just pay the fifty grand to this *Hot Lips. But what then? How long before the bitch demands another fifty,... or more?*

She was in a box while studying in detail the fine print of the trust fund the parents had set up for her and Amanda. *This bullshit about Amanda having to turn twenty-one before either of us have access to our money! That just absolutely sucks!*

Meanwhile, former Unibank Marketing VP, Adam Herrera, was racking up race team clients in droves, making his decision to step down and go freelance appear brilliant. Allison knew this was all due to her suggesting to her father the idea of Evelyn Stevens leaving Moretti Motorsport for the IndyWest outfit, a move designed to harm Moretti Motorsport that had blown up in their faces. She would move in as Stevens' agent and deal with Herrera, a sharp executive who would know he himself was negotiating with his former boss's daughter. It had been set up perfectly until Allison's father started screwing a mid-level bank manager. *That gold-digging bitch left that shampoo bottle there on purpose. She'll have to be dealt with.*

For a woman who seemed to live her entire life in conflict, Allison Cook now found herself dealing with three different crises at once. In addition to this blackmailing *Hot Lips,* she now had the issue of her parents' divorce, adding to the lack of support from Aaron's parents, whose prestige and and finance were paramount to her future plans.

She barged into the trustee's office unannounced and demanded an audience. For years, nearly everyone who worked in the Unibank office tower knew when Byron Cook said jump, they would ask how high, and that status now extended to the CEO's very arrogant and demanding daughter. The surprised attorney was a longtime Unibank stalwart agreed upon by both Byron and Sarah.

"Let me ask you, Mr. Stanfield. What happens should either of us need that money, say, in case of emergency?" Allison asked, wearing her best innocent Southern belle expression.

"There are provisions to change the terms toward beneficiaries in the Trust. For the next two and a half years, Byron and Sarah would have to agree to any alterations."

"Should Mom or Dad remarry within the next couple of years, could either of their spouses of change the terms?"

"Only if either were granted Power of Attorney to act on Byron or Sarah's own behalf, Allison. This is typical in cases involving serious disability, mostly with the elderly."

"And what about my sister and I? What if one of us were to be severely injured or die in an accident, God forbid?"

"Well, in such an unfortunate scenario, when one or both of the beneficiaries become unavailable to exercise their duties and obligations under the terms of the trust, nor effectively assign their own Power of Attorney, the entire fund would forward to the surviving beneficiary. Now, in Amanda's case, she would have to reach twenty-one years of age. If both of you should happen to meet an unfortunate demise and pass or become disabled to the point of cognitive incompetency, the entire fund would be awarded in equal amounts to four selected charities, a stipulation insisted upon by your mother. A kind woman, if I must say.

"Yes, kind she is," Allison responded... *And foolish.*

Andy seemed to stroll around the facility at a hundred miles per hour, his phone growing out of his ear and the stress obvious. Miles was putting all the more pressure on the engineering staff, and while none offered an opinion out loud, most were of the belief their drivers were just not up to the task.

After years of planning, lobbying, and endless effort to get into the world's top motor racing discipline, Moretti Motorsport had steadily gained ground in Formula One. Because of the danger factor, very few Formula One drivers took advantage of taking a shot at Indy, and many were prohibited from doing so contractually. It was, however, quite unexpected for the worst possibility to happen to Tony Moretti, still considered an IndyCar favorite and veteran.

Team Moretti had been riding a worldwide high with media and fans alike due to what occurred at the Indy 500, but with the *What have you done lately?* mentality, rumblings from that often hostile media and its effect on sponsors were imminent.

"He's just getting back into racing, Tony!" Andy yelled into his iPhone.

"Yeah. So, what's your point, Dad? Do you remember that test in Britain that Zak Brown set up for us? Alex was faster than I was, as much as I hate to admit it."

"I don't want to push him, Tony. He's doing really well now and might even compete for the championship this year. He's not clamoring to jump into Formula One, anyway."

Both father and son knew Alex's driving career was currently being guided by his newly rekindled romance with Amanda, at eighteen perhaps not prepared to engage in globetrotting with the international jet-setting F1 crowd.

"At least consider my taking over as Chief Mechanic for Wolf. Straus just doesn't seem to be on the same page with the man," Tony suggested.

"Where did you come up with that?"

"I'm still close to our entire engineering department, Dad."

"What's that supposed to mean?"

"I can tell by the tone of their texts. Owen especially is not onboard with the general consensus that Von Prinze is the entire problem."

"Well, I've got a call I have to take. We'll talk more, Tony. Just take care of yourself." Andy disconnected and would make it a point to have a word with Stuart Owen, the team's sharpest engineer, about his conversations with Tony. There was always tension within a race team when it wasn't winning, as Andy knew as well as anyone. He'd been thinking about his dream of Moretti Motorsport being a top-tier Formula One team with his two sons driving. He also knew there was a strong possibility that Tony may never grace the cockpit of a racecar again.

I don't know, Andy pondered, obviously conflicted. Alex had come back to the team big, and his enthusiasm had reignited the IndyCar squad as Andy had not seen since Tony moved to F1 a couple of years prior. *I don't want Alex to suffer a fall by going into Formula One too soon.*

The stress was written all over Miles' face. The F1 team manager missed the days when he and the boss had good things to talk about, namely the gains they had made in their last race and what they would do to move up even further at the next Grand Prix. Now, the whole team had suddenly become a backmarker and that term *107 percent rule* was dominating much of their conversation. "We just have to admit it, Andy. Tony was just a bloody fast driver, despite the shortcomings of the car. We'll just have to do the best we can and concentrate on developing a better package for next season."

"BP may pull the plug on us, Miles. We have to give them something they can hang their hat on, and that means soon."

"I can't take a bloody cow and turn it into a horse, Andy!"

"What do you think about putting Alex in the car?" the team principal asked, genuinely wanting to gauge Miles' reaction.

"I'm sure that will be the plan sooner or later. He'll need some time in the car first. Lots of time. You know that."

"Yes, you're probably right. Tony is actually pushing me on it. I think this recovery is hard on him. He's not used to being boxed in at home during the heat of the summer racing season."

"Well, Andy. If you think Alex is bloody up to it, send him over here."

The pilot announced the pending landing as Andy glanced out the window at Charlotte International Speedway below, reflecting on how often he was flying back and forth from the team's headquarters in Huntersville and the F1 facility in England. He had always seemed to be of a mindset that his presence at Silverstone was direly needed as the team overall had the most to lose with its performance in Formula One. After all, the annual budget dwarfed that of all of the other Moretti teams combined.

Now with his oldest son nearly losing his life and his younger boy getting married, not to mention his missing his two grandsons, Andy was more and more inclined to believe that his F1 team manager should require less maintenance.

He was greeted at the airport in Concord by Alex and Amanda. After a stressful few days in England, seeing the smiling faces of his youngest son and future daughter-in-law served as a quick breath of fresh air for the Moretti family patriarch.

Amanda was mostly quiet while Andy and Alex engaged in shop talk related to the team, both domestic and abroad. She gathered that Alex's father had a lot on his mind, as she had yet to fully grasp the pressure of being in Formula One. *Could this be because of Alex's mother being here?* Amanda thought.

"How are things with your family?" Andy asked, not wanting Amanda to feel cut out of the conversation.

"As well as can be expected, sir," she replied. "My mom spent the day yesterday hosting Sabetha down at our club."

"Oh, really?" Andy quickly replied, stealing a glance toward Alex to check his reaction.

"Looks like she's planning an extended stay, Dad."

Andy glanced out the right window, momentarily saying nothing. Amanda said little herself, wanting to observe the two Moretti men to gauge their mood. She had somewhat reserved judgment on Sabetha's visit, always of the belief that siblings should be close to their parents, although understanding from her own experience how challenging that could be. She could tell her future father-in-law seemed in no way enthused about seeing more of his ex-wife.

⚑⚑

Marie greeted them at the door, not knowing how her brother would take his ex-wife still being in residence. His mood seemed subdued, which told her that Alex and Amanda had already broken the news. Andy looked past her, not sure of how his next words would come. He thought briefly about confronting Sabetha head-on but thought better of it as Matilde entered the foyer to greet him.

"Hello Mamma," Andy expressed while embracing her. "I understand we still have an extended guest."

"Yes, Sabetha would like to stay a few more days. I told her it would be fine with us." Matilde would often assert herself as the head housemaster since Andy was away most of the time.

"Not like her. What's going on?"

"Maybe she likes seeing her sons and grandchildren, Andy," Matilde replied while her son just looked at her as if considering his response.

"You think so?" he answered dubiously.

⚑⚑

Aaron looked uneasy as he could tell Allison wanted something. His nature predicated that he allow her to open the conversation.

"Honey, I need your help in raising some funding," she stated, while putting her arms around him.

"Funding? Funding for what?"

"I need the money to start the business, honey. I need seventy grand."

"I assume you have some sort of business plan for this."

"Of course," she replied, slightly put off that he seemed to be questioning her, something he had never done in the past.

"I can help you, but not the full amount, Allison," Aaron responded. "You don't really need to lease an office for something like that. You'll be traveling a lot, anyway."

The conversation wasn't going the way Allison had hoped. She knew Aaron, still a lieutenant in the Marine Corps, would have to get his money from his parents, which really meant his father, a man who didn't currently support his son marrying a Cook, at least yet. She had most of the fifty grand on her credit cards but that would tap out her credit lines and then what would happen? She hated the idea of having to pay this *Hot Lips* as the due date approached. *Damn you, Eric Jordan! It's been over two weeks and you have nothing!*

Waiting for Aaron to retire to bed, she sent Jordan a text message. *"I'm running out of time. I need something, Eric!"*

He didn't respond until the next morning.

⁂

"Ten grand my ass, Eric! Admit it, you don't have the kahunas you always claimed!"

Her illicit lover knew she was right. He was a snake and a braggart, a young man who had said anything to get Allison into bed. He had made a few token attempts to identify this *Hot Lips* and had come up empty. More advanced attempts on his part would have brought on immense scrutiny and real potential problems which he would not risk. Jordan did have an ego, however, and would not be quick to admit failure.

"We may have to bargain with her to buy more time," he stated, slyly implying they were both a team now.

"What!? Bargain? How?" Allison was obviously beginning to panic, not a natural act for her.

"I just need a bit more time."

"Bullshit, Jordan! This is serious! My whole life is at risk here."

"I told you before, Allison. Money can buy you anything."

"Oh, now you are shaking me down, you bastard!"

"Hold on there, girl. I may need to take this off-site. That costs money. Do you want my help or not?"

"I guess I have little choice, do I?'

"Perhaps not.... We'll send *Hot Lips* an email claiming we need more time," Jordan claimed.

"And what if the bitch won't play along? What if she just forwards the stuff out of spite? I cannot chance that, Eric."

"She,... or he, won't do that. These types play for money, not vengeance. Besides, the more dialog you have with her, the better chance I have to identify her."

Using a dark web email Jordan set up for her, Allison sent *Hot Lips* a message stating she needed another thirty days to raise the fifty grand. Following another half hour of fulfilling Jordan's physical needs, she departed his place, now questioning her decision to disclose the full details of her predicament, as she had an epiphany that Eric needed to know what she was capable of. But it was now hitting her that his knowing too much about her could be dangerous.

Chapter 4

Desperate Measures

Adam Herrera had quickly created a lucrative business for himself. Since leaving his senior management position at Unibank on less than congenial terms months earlier, he had set up shop as the commercial agent for some of motor racing's top North American teams and was quickly gaining a reputation as a mover and shaker in the industry.

He did face a major hurdle, however, with his first Formula One client, Andy Moretti. Since his son Tony's serious accident at the Indianapolis Motor Speedway, the Moretti Formula One team's performance had gone straight into the tank. Herrera's overtures to the team's sponsors regarding renewal contracts for the next season and beyond were not going well. Having a corporate logo pasted on the side pods of any Formula One car at an international Grand Prix had value, but that exposure was greatly diminished when those banners were on slow backmarkers only seen by the legions of the F1 worldwide audience when the lead drivers would pass and lap them.

"At least BP is stepping up with the Amoco brand in NASCAR and IndyCar, Andy. I'm working on a strong co-sponsor, a Danish investor, Van Boden, one whom Harrington at BP referred. But they're holding back, waiting to see what BP does, and I know they're talking to another team."

"What's it going to take to nail them down, Adam?"

"After scoring no points at Silverstone, we need a good showing in Budapest, Andy. You know how the game is played. The lower our performance, the less we can demand. I know Tony has been pushing the idea of putting Alex in the "28" car. What about it?"

Andy just slowly shook his head. "You know Alex is just getting back into the game, Adam."

"Just getting back into the game? Winning the Indy 500 and winning two out of three IndyCar races since then? I'd say right now Alex is the game, Andy."

"Yes, he's doing great and I'm so proud of him. But he hasn't been in the cockpit of a Formula One car for over two years, and that was just a test in a year-old McLaren."

"Yes, and Tony reminded me that Alex was consistently two-tenths faster that day than he was. We need to shake things up, Andy. Just the media buzz that Alex will be driving in a Grand Prix. That would be huge."

"You do know that he values his time off with Amanda, Adam. They do have a lot of lost time to make up for."

"Of course! But she can go with him."

"That would cause a full-blown media circus." Andy's tone sounded neutral, which Herrera took as a yes.

That's music to my ears, Adam thought enthusiastically. "This presents us with a huge opportunity, Andy."

"I'm not too sure Amanda is into all that just yet, nor Alex, either. It was the media demand that came between him and Evelyn. And despite missing the first four races, Alex could possibly win the IndyCar championship. That would be huge for him and the team as a whole."

Andy digested Adam's remaining input. The man had always been loyal and had never steered him wrong on anything before. "You may be right about that. I'll talk to him. We could announce that Alex will be driving at COTA. That way, the IndyCar season will be several weeks in arrears and Alex would have at least some time to prepare."

"Waiting until the US Grand Prix in Austin is way too long, Andy. Look, IndyCar will have a three-week break soon. Alex could drive in the Hungarian Grand Prix. And if that goes well, even Spa."

"We don't have a good car right now, Adam. And driving a slow car in a two-hour race, knowing you don't have a chance in hell of winning, can ruin a driver's morale, and in some cases their whole career."

"The car wasn't that bad earlier in the season, Andy. And only one thing has changed since, that being a Moretti behind the wheel."

The two disconnected and Herrera was optimistic. *At least I have him thinking.*

Sabetha had been visiting for a month now and her plan to keep her stay incognito was short-lived as a social media post on Amanda's Facebook showing Sabetha at the Moretti hospitality bus in Detroit was spreading like wildfire, along with all sorts of rumors speculating that Andy and Sabetha had gotten back together after so many years.

Andy had himself been cordial but somewhat distant toward his ex-wife the whole time, made less awkward by his busy schedule and little time spent at home. It was no secret in the Moretti family that the F1 team was really struggling in Tony's absence, to the extent the financial viability of the whole operation may be at risk. To that extent, the family patriarch didn't want to be bothered with these petty issues.

The middle-aged former French model seemed to be content with hanging out at the Moretti home and continued to spend most daytime hours lounging out by the pool. Both Matilde and Marie felt awkward and found themselves checking on her multiple times per day with trays of food and drink.

It was late afternoon and Marie approached through the veranda, carrying a pair of binoculars, scanning the vast expanse of Lake Norman out toward the far shoreline.

"What are you looking for, Marie?"

"There's a boat out there, Sab. A cigarette cruiser that has been there every day this week."

Andy's estate sat atop a large wooded bluff overlooking the lake in a way that onlookers from the water could not view the home near the shore right below and any efforts to do so would have to be from quite a way out in the channel.

"There are always boats out there, Marie."

"Sure there are. But this one is anchored in the same area near the far shore pretty much every day from late morning until sundown. We had those when we first moved down here when Alex and Evelyn were still together, the paparazzi. But they stopped after Alex got his own place down around the bend. I thought no one knew you were here."

"You assume they are spying on me?" Sabetha asked defensively.

"I can't prove that boat has anything to do with you or this house, Sab, But again, does anyone outside the family know you're here?"

"No! At least not that I'm aware!"

"Okay then. Calm yourself, Sabetha," Marie replied while again raising her binoculars for more examination. "Oh, now it's speeding away."

Marie departed the pool area, leaving the binoculars. Sabetha grabbed them and began to scan the lake herself, a woman now quite nervous, and moved to another pool lounger where the branches of a large pine partially obstructed the view from the lake. *Anton knows I'm here now.*

⁂

"I'm just not ready for that, brother. I'm taking Amanda to the beach that week. She needs a break from all the racing and the media. You know how it is."

I suppose I really don't, Tony reflected. "I haven't led a life with as many headlines as you, little brother. So, I suppose I wouldn't know. But I do know this. The F1 team needs to show something good, and soon. The team needs you."

"I was thinking maybe next year, Tony. I haven't been in the cockpit of an F1 car since that test in England, what three years ago? I'm still getting used to driving on road circuits."

"Get real, Alex. You've won two out of three times in the past month. Would have been three in Detroit had it not been for that late race yellow. You could be the best driver in the world right now," Tony added, wanting to pump his younger sibling up.

"I'll think about it, brother, but I'll have to talk with Amanda about it," Alex responded, recalling the last time he had canceled last-minute plans for them to go off racing. *I can't have a repeat of what happened over Daytona.*

"Let's just go to Silverstone for a few days. You can at least get some sim time. Perhaps prepare for a drive at COTA after you win the Astor Cup. How about that?"

⁂

"Come on, race man," Amanda responded. "With all that's going on, I can't leave my mom right now."

For the first time since their emotional reunion, Alex didn't really want Amanda to make this brief trip to England with him. He and Tony would be super busy at the facility and Amanda would be couped up there during the day, likely bored stiff. "I'll only be a few days, baby. They want me to get some prep for the US Grand Prix in Austin."

"Austin, Texas? Oh, that place is a hoot. When will that be?" Amanda asked.

"It's not until well after the IndyCar season is over."

"Why do you have to go over there? I thought the team headquarters was here?"

"It is, but the Formula One shop is in the UK, the epicenter of F1. I'll spend most of my time in the simulator and we don't have an F1 sim here."

Amanda knew she was getting spoiled, having Alex's near undivided attention non-stop since Indy. She didn't want to turn into a younger version of his mother. "Okay, but don't forget. You promised me after Toronto we're going to the beach."

Tony was still recovering and relegated mostly to his wheelchair, but thrilled to make the trip to England for a few days with his brother, allowing the two to spend time with the Formula One team and allow Alex to get some practice on the team's F1 simulator, his only avenue to get a feel for an F1 car as the FIA had strict limitations on the teams' live track testing. The Moretti team had already pushed the mid-season limit.

A natural behind the wheel, Alex took to the simulator like a rock star on stage. The extremely expensive machines were generally used for tweaking performance engineering-wise, but the simulated lap times were not taken too seriously as they related to a real car on a live circuit. It couldn't be ignored, however, that in short order, Alex's numbers were far better than either of the current drivers.

By mid-morning the second day, Ian Miles was on the phone with his boss. "Andy, I think we should plug Alex in as number one and relegate Leland to number two."

"What? Just because of his time in the simulator? Am I talking to the same Ian Miles I last spoke to? You know, the old-school chap who always scoffed at taking too much stock in those. What did you call them?... Bloody toys, I believe."

"Andy, it's not just Alex entertaining himself," Miles added. "Yes, Leland is complaining about him taking up valuable sim time, but I tell you, Andy, just Alex being here has energized this whole building, unlike anything I've seen since I was at Ferrari when Schumacher came over from Benetton."

That's Alex. Ever the bubbly entertainer, Andy smiled to himself. "When he gets back, I'll discuss it more with him. I'm not sure he and Strauss would work well together."

"My thoughts exactly, Andy. I was thinking about pairing him up with Tony as Chief Mechanic."

"Tony, Chief Mechanic!?" How did you come up with that, Ian?" *As if I don't know.*

"You know Tony and I talk every day and usually multiple times. You know he's smart, Andy. He wants in and he knows he may never drive again. But Tony's a bloody racer. He's a Moretti and needs to be in the game. You would know that better than anyone."

Andy was starting to become sold. Ian had always been a supporter of Mason Strauss, a veteran Chief Mechanic, the term F1 uses regarding a Crew Chief. He also realized Miles was protecting himself from being the scapegoat for a failed F1 team, a pressure that would be somewhat relieved if his boss okayed putting his own sons in control of one of their cars.

"Ian, you keep this conversation between us. Got it?

"Of course, Andy."

The two disconnected, and Miles was smiling. He would take the two Moretti boys to dinner and discuss a plan to move forward, believing he now had their father sold.

Cotton was flabbergasted at this latest message. *"The bitch wants another thirty days!"*

He quickly pecked out a reply. *"We had better talk. Usual place, 9:00 AM tomorrow."*

Eugene "Cotton" James was a man who always lived on the edge, a man of little wealth, one who could never work on the clock, and never wanted accountability. As one who never possessed good looks, the only woman who had a soft spot in his heart was a paparazzi-tired female, Rebecca "Remi" Dalton. Always one to look over his shoulder, he would not tread likely for tomorrow morning's visit.

He waited in his truck behind the cafe, checking to see if she was being followed. Her plan for shaking down the Cook woman for fifty grand upfront and whatever came afterward was bold and potentially lucrative, but not without risks. At just past 9:00, Remi pulled her tired-looking Subaru into the lot and parked.

She sat at the end booth as he approached and sat down, a man wearing a serious expression. The waitress took an order for two coffees and walked away smiling.

"What did I tell you, Remi, about sending me text messages through your own phone?"

"Cut the bullshit, Cotton. What should we do?"

"It's not bullshit, Remi! I gave you that *burner* phone for a reason. Stop being stupid!"

"When you're through, Cotton, tell me what we should fuckin' do about this?"

"First of all, tell me you have not replied."

"No."

"Cook wants to stall, obviously. Could be her raising that amount of cash. Could be she wants more time so she can find you. Probably both."

"Yeah, yeah, blah, blah."

"Don't be a fool, Remi. Send a reply that gives her another two weeks with a ten grand advanced bonus now."

"And if the bitch doesn't play along?"

"Just add a teaser to get her attention. I made some clips and this one should serve the purpose."

Dalton pulled up the dark website Cotton had set up for her and sent out her reply, including a video clip of Allison Cook on her knees servicing the late Louie Newbury. The image of Allison's fave was blurred for effect. The two sat anxiously for several minutes, wanting or hoping Allison Cook would quickly reply.

"Why not have me over for the weekend?" James asked. "The A/C on my trailer is out and I'm getting hot, just the way you like me."

"I'm broke, Cotton. Have to work. If the bitch sends me the ten grand, I'll owe you one."

Allison was seething with anger at this latest email from *Hot Lips*. The text was quite to the point.

Don't fuck with me. A day late or a dollar short will cause this clip unblurred to be sent to aaron.williams@williamsbuick-gmc.com. Ten grand by midnight tomorrow will buy you two weeks. The ten grand is not a partial payment! It's an interest payment for all of my charitable patience.

Chow,
Hot Lips

"Did you get that, Eric?"
"Yes, I got it. It's up to you, but you need to keep up the conversation. I got an interesting hit on something."
"Tell me."
My source caught a text message that read, *"The bitch wants another thirty days."*
"That's it?"
"That's it. Could be nothing. But it originated from a cell tower in of all places, Charlotte."
"Charlotte!?" Allison yelled. "Who is it, Eric!?"

"Hey, calm down! We haven't gotten that far, yet. You need to keep up the exchanges and we'll see where this goes."

"Don't tell me to fuckin' calm down! It's my ass on the line here, Eric!"

Jordan held his phone away from his ear, which was burning. "Okay, it's your ass. What are you going to do?"

"I don't know. I need my money's worth. Find out who this bitch is," Allison yelled as she disconnected. She had handed Eric Jordan a couple grand to pay a "source" at the NSA in Washington to find the identity of this Hot Lips. *I now have two assholes shaking me down... Chow? What a bitch.*

The four sat in Andy's office, knowing the topic of discussion in advance. Tony and Ian had convinced Andy to make a mid-season change and put Alex in the Moretti Formula One car as their number one driver. Now Alex himself had to be sold.

"You did very well on the simulator," Andy began. "Of course, it's not the live car, but as close as we could get. Do you think you're ready for Formula One?"

"I still want to win the IndyCar Championship, Dad. How will that work?"

"There are only three dates in conflict," Tony interjected. That would leave seven Grands Prix you could run, even if we had Von Prince drive those three."

"You're basically taking away nearly every weekend I would have until mid-December," Alex responded.

Andy gave Tony a look, as weekends for a Moretti meant racing, but he knew what Alex was thinking. "Have you had this conversation with her?"

"Nothing to this extent."

"Well?"

"She's my fiancée. God knows she has been through a lot for me, Dad. More than any girl should have to. And she plans to start college this fall in Charlotte. This started out talking about one race several weeks after the IndyCar season was over."

"It's your call, Alex."

"You know she and I have a lot to make up for. I was thinking maybe plan for next season."

"Things change, son. Tony being out has really hurt the team," Andy responded.

Seeing the issue was truly a burden, Tony made a suggestion. "Could we just commit to two races, Hungary and Spa? Those will both be during the long IndyCar break and before Amanda's semester begins. Then we can see how it goes and better decide what happens after that."

"How about inviting Sarah, too?" Alex asked.

Tony and Ian looked at Andy for a reaction.

"I have no problem with that."

Tony and Alex shared a look of acknowledgment that their father appeared more than simply agreeable.

"Oh, come on, race man! With everything going on right now, I hate to run off on Mom like that."

Alex enjoyed it when Amanda referred to him with her favorite pet name. "Why not just bring Sarah along? She could probably use a break from all the local drama herself."

"I'll talk to her," Amanda stated. "But I'm not sure Mom will want to be around your mother for that amount of time."

"I don't think my mother will be there," he replied. "Dad certainly hasn't invited her."

Hmm, Amanda thought. "Well, it may like appear somewhat awkward, your mom being banned while mine is invited?"

Alex thought Amanda's choice of words was quite forward. *But banned isn't that far from being right on,* Alex considered. "Dad didn't seem to have any objections with your mom being there, not at all."

"Oh?" *Isn't that interesting?*

Alex was pleased with Amanda's excitement. "Can I assume your Passport is in order?"

"Well, like, I don't know," she replied, concerned.

"We'll have to check on that. We could spend some off days at a place in Croatia I remember from the Rally. You'd love it."

"Oh, so we wouldn't be coming back between races?" Amanda asked. "I don't know if Mom can be away that long. Not right now with everything going on."

"Well, I guess we could return after Budapest, if that would make you feel better."

"Let me talk to her. If it doesn't work out and you have to go without me, I'll just like have to deal with it."

"No. I don't want to go without you, Amanda. I've done that enough times over the past two years."

The world motorsport media was in a frenzy again regarding Alex Moretti and his fiancée, Amanda Cook. The press announcement that he would be driving for his father's struggling team in the Hungarian Grand Prix went viral and Adam Herrera was now giddy about his next meetings with British Petroleum and the Van Boden Financial Group.

Despite the tension still under the roof at the Moretti lakeside home over Sabetha's stay, the whole family seemed quite upbeat now in high hopes for the plug Alex would inject into the F1 team's season woes. Even though Alex was only slated for two races, Herrera now felt positive about securing a favorable sponsor package for the following season, including Amoco branding for all of Andy's North American-based teams.

The only silly season drama left for Adam appeared to be Evelyn Stevens' renewal with Unibank, connected to her planned move back to Moretti Motorsport for the following IndyCar season. As much as Byron Cook wanted Unibank out of motor racing, Stevens had become the international face of the Charlotte-based financial giant and to drop her would hand prospective competitors a coup of epidemic proportions. The world's preeminent female racing driver's only obstacle to courting Herrera as her own agent was his representing her would-be new boss, Andy Moretti, still in an adversarial relationship with Cook, even though their legal challenges had been settled.

All-in-all, Andy chose to have a summer mid-week barbeque to celebrate the developments for all of the local team personnel, family, and friends. Many were surprised at meeting Andy's ex-wife, a woman whose international legend had preceded her. Sabetha played up the attention for all to see, upbeat for a change and perhaps overzealous, presenting herself as a sort of guest of honor.

An unexpected guest arrived also in the form of Alex Moretti's future mother-in-law, Sarah Cook, one who still shared an uneasy presence near Sabetha Moretti.

Andy stood after the guests were all amply served and proposed a toast. "Here is to our number one Grand Prix driver in Hungary and Spa-Francorchamps, Alex Moretti! It's been quite a year!"

All stood and yelled, glasses clicking all around as the buzz seemed contagious.

"And I just got word today that Miles has arranged for two three-day live testing sessions at Brands Hatch, England, between races. Alex will be in last year's car, but the seat time will be invaluable to his success."

Suddenly the excitement was diminished, at least in one quarter. Amanda was not expecting this news about Alex having to spend time in England between races, although she made her best effort to hide her disappointment. *It is his huge opportunity, girl. Like, deal with it.*

At near sundown, the crowd began to disperse, with only the immediate family gathering around. Sabetha had become quite animated due to her many cocktails and other *effects* that only Matilde supposedly knew about, to the point of appearing cozy around Andy.

Amanda semi-joked that her mom would worry about her, having yet to mention that she could make the trip to Hungary with them.

"Don't worry about her, my dear," Sabetha bloated out. "Perhaps Madam Sarah and I can spend more time together while you are all off on your European holiday."

"Amanda, why not invite Sarah to join you?" Andy interjected, causing a quiet stir, not to mention a discerning stare from Sabetha, who had no such invitation herself. She would have declined at any rate, in no way prepared for a return to Europe just yet, but it made for an awkward setting, nonetheless.

Amanda gave her mother a questioning grin, knowing that Alex would support it.

"Oh, I don't know," Sarah reacted. "I know the race team has a lot going on there. I wouldn't wish to be a burden."

"No burden at all, Sarah," Andy added. "I know you would be uneasy with Amanda being over there."

Sabetha's festive mood had now diminished.

⚑⚑

Later in the evening, Sarah prepared to depart as Alex and Amanda escorted her out to her SUV, after she had declined an invitation to just stay over.

"I hope they don't think I'm becoming high maintenance," Sarah declared seriously.

"Oh, Mom. Don't be ridiculous," Amanda replied, looking toward Alex for his comment.

"You all enjoyed Monterrey, didn't you? Some of those places over there are quite adventurous. Time permitting, my grandmother might even wish to show Sarah her home in Italy." Alex added, himself pleased that Amanda would have her mother's company while the team demanded his attention span.

Amanda gave her that innocent, shy grin that Sarah so cherished. "Well, Mom. What do you think?"

"We'll see, honey. Let me sleep on it."

⚑⚑

Allison's panic was getting worse by the day. She had tagged a credit card for ten grand and sent it to *Hot Lips* as Jordan had not come up with anything else on her *or his* identity. Now Eric wanted more funding for his so-called connection in Washington. *What an asshole, Eric!* She was completely wired as she struggled to retain a neutral persona around her fiancé.

"What's wrong, baby?"

"Nothing. I'm just tired."

Aaron sat up in bed. "You've been tired all week, Allison. What?"

"Things are just a mess, Aaron. My parents' marriage is breaking up, I can't seem to get my business off the ground, and your family doesn't want us to marry," she replied, feigning crocodile tears.

"What can I do?"

"I need you to support me."

"Okay, how?"

"Help me set up a credit line at another bank."

"What? Your dad is the CEO of one of the largest banks in North America. Why on earth would you want to do business with another bank?"

"See. Aaron! After all this time, you still don't even know me. I want to make my own mark. I want us to succeed together, not just because we're rich kids."

Aaron put his arms around her. "You know I would give you the world if I could. Just tell me what I need to do."

Her back up against him, Allison couldn't help but break a devious smile. She then changed back to her sad facade, rolled over to face him, and subtly slid her hand down.

Andy entered the kitchen at just past dawn, casually greeting his mother who was already there preparing coffee, as she had always done early before Marie and other house guests awakened. Matilde could tell something significant was on her only son's mind.

"What's going on with you, my son?"

"Nothing, Mamma. I just have a lot on my mind."

"You always have a lot on your mind. And I am your mother," she reacted. "Tell me what is bothering you."

Andy stirred briefly, willing himself to move his early shop agenda forward and defer these domestic issues for another day. "Has Sabetha given you any indication as to when she's going back home?"

"Not specifically," she responded, feeling guilty for withholding information from him.

"What do you think about Alex driving in Europe for a couple of races?" Andy asked, wanting to change the subject, at least for now.

"Not much, Andy. We've run all over the world to race cars our whole lives. It's not like he's never been over there. I just hope it doesn't disturb his relationship with Amanda, but I assume you've already considered that... That kind of caught everyone off guard, you inviting Sarah. And I do mean everyone."

"Sabetha paid me a visit late last night, right after our guests had left and you and Marie retired."

"Oh?"

"Yes. She was drunk. And that's not all. Did you know about her drug addiction?"

"She told you that?"

"No. I saw the needle marks all over her arms, Mamma. I suspected it from the time she arrived in Detroit. But I didn't know how bad it was until last night."

"I was aware she was taking pills quite often," Matilde replied. "So, you two slept together?"

"No, and she got ugly when things didn't go too well in that regard. I'm telling you, Mamma, that woman is totally deranged. Now she's accusing me of having something going on with Amanda's mother!"

"Oh, my!" Matilde responded, acting surprised. "Sabetha is probably just embarrassed, Andy. She's been so used to being the most beautiful woman in the room her whole life... And Sarah? Well, we all know full and well where those girls get their vanity, don't we?"

"Mamma, stop! Sarah's husband tried to throw my son in prison and bankrupt this family!"

"Yes, and Sarah was never a party to any of that. I know on good authority that Sarah and Byron Cook's marital problems are largely a result of his vendetta, which she did not support. And if you're worried about appearances, you haven't exactly been avoiding her... You do find Sarah attractive, don't you?"

"I suppose I do. But after all we've been through since meeting the Cook family, how would that look, Sarah and I dating? The press would wear us out, Mamma!"

"That didn't seem to bother you at the 500 awards inner, or in Detroit, or in Monterey... Just saying."

Andy just looked at her momentarily, finished his coffee, and checked his phone for messages. "I don't know why we're even engaged in such chatter, Mamma. I've got to get going," he said, hastily getting up to gather himself for the half-hour commute to the shop. "And do me a favor, Mamma. Please don't start any rumor mill."

"Wait, Andy! What about Sabetha? Are you going to demand she leave, or what?"

He hesitated and looked around, assuring no one else was within earshot. "It needs to be soon."

"Go make some bread for the family," Matilde stood and stated, giving him a hug goodbye just prior to his heading out the door.

Shortly thereafter, Marie entered for her own morning caffeine fix. "Good morning, Mamma!"

"Good morning."

"Has Andy left already?"

"He has... A lot on his mind."

"Oh, Andy always has a lot on his mind."

"Oh, yes... And now your brother is in love again," Matilde stated, smiling offhandedly.

Marie almost spilled her coffee. "What!? Is Sabetha staying here?"

"No, definitely not."

"Then what are you talking about, Mamma?"

"How many guesses do you need, daughter?"

Aaron Williams was a young Marine officer dealing with his own stress issues. Allison Cook had been his sweetheart since they were toddlers, literally the love of his life.

He had a solid future with his father, Bud Williams, being one of the largest car dealers in the South. That empire would be handed to Aaron and his younger brother, Kyle, someday. The move to attend college at The Citadel, the historic military academy in Charleston, was all part of a plan promoted by his father to pave the way for Aaron to enter politics. As such, Aaron cared little about Allison's career path interests. His father saw her as one of the South's most eloquent belles, the daughter of the highly respected and prestigious Cook family, another key to promote the proper Williams' image. The families had all sought the same arrangement for Aaron's younger brother and Allison's younger sister, Amanda, which had simply gone array.

Aaron was still uncomfortable with the whole idea of this alternate bank account, as Allison should have had unlimited resources from Charlotte-based Unibank. After all, her father was the President and CEO. Her desire to make her own mark out from under her father's shadow didn't fit with her somehow. But now he was co-signing for her exploits, and if that made her happy, all the better.

Allison just needed this California bank account to cover transactions, which hopefully would be few, between her and this Hot Lips, as well as Eric Jordan, whom she had to pay another two grand. He had bragged about all his talents and resourcefulness related to intelligence gathering, all as a ploy to get in her pants, a scenario she knew from the get-go and endeavored to take advantage of it. Now push came to shove with him demanding expense money to tighten up a *friend* at the NSA. It was bothering her more and more, the growing number of those who had information about her *problem*.

She completed the documentation for her LLC company so she and Aaron could set up the new account with a $150,000 line of credit. Shortly after the two left the bank, she saw another email notification from *Hot Lips*. As she speedily drove through the San Diego traffic, she sat on pins and needles, wanting to get rid of Aaron and deal with it.

"Allison, slow down! What's your hurry?"

"Oh, Honey. I'm just wired now, so excited to get started."

"Enough business for now. I'm off for a few days. How about we get home, gather up some things, and take off for a few days? Maybe head up to San Francisco?"

"Oh, Aaron. That sounds good, but my period is getting ready to start. How about a rain check?"

Aaron was silent and just stared out at the surrounding traffic. *How can my beautiful fiancée be the only female on the planet with two or three menstrual cycles a month?*

"You fucking bitch!" Allison yelled. She sat alone after sending Aaron out to pick up some groceries, anything to get him out of her hair for a few minutes.

Hot Lips had sent her a new message that she had missed the deadline and included a screen mockup of a Facebook page, the sultry image of Allison kneeling on the floor servicing the disgusting Louis Newbury. Her face was no longer ghosted out, and a message was added with a notification that read:

This is a warning, Rock Hill Bitch. Next email will be to the Indianapolis Police Department. Don't fuck with me!

"Oooooh!" Allison became unhinged, taking a few minutes to compose herself before blasting out a reply.

You'll have the money in two days. My new account will have the funds by tomorrow at midnight.

In less than a minute, she received a response.

I want the payment in full – NOW!

An exasperated Allison replied.

Day after tomorrow, Hot Lips. Promise. PS: How do I know you won't take my money and just come back for more?

Hot Lips quickly replied:

You're just going to have to trust me!

Sarah was upbeat while she spent a day shopping with Amanda, the two buying some clothing and other items in preparation for their upcoming trip to Europe. They would be traveling to Budapest, Hungary, on Wednesday for a stay through the Grand Prix on Sunday, followed by another week in England, a trip to Belgium for the Grand Prix there, and back home.

Amanda chose to stay with her mom in Alex's absence since the news became public regarding her parents' pending divorce and the two settled in for a quiet evening together, mother and daughter.

"How would you feel about Allison accompanying us to Budapest, Amanda?"

Amanda hesitated, not saying anything for a bit, which told Sarah she wasn't hip on the idea.

"It's really important to your father and I that you two bury the hatchet... Please."

"Mom, what happened years ago is over. I don't wish to relive it. I'm excited to travel to Hungary and see my future husband race in his first Formula One Grand Prix. I'm happy that you will enjoy that with me. I know Allison wants to be Evelyn Stevens' agent, so like, whatever."

"I wish there was some way to reconcile things with the Williams," Sarah added, knowing she would be hitting a sensitive nerve.

"I will not make a public statement or sign any kind of affidavit that I lied on the witness stand, Mom... I did not lie."

"Oh, honey. I believe you. I just wish there was some sort of way to compromise on this."

"I know you miss your time with Lisa, Mom."

"Yes dearly. But make no mistake, my family comes first. I just want my girls and I to all be close again."

Amanda sighed. *Your girls haven't been close for years, Mom, through no fault of your own.* "I'll get along with Allison, for your sake, Mom."

"You really didn't have to suggest to Alex's father that he invite me next week, Amanda. I don't want to be seen as the mother-in-law from hell, you know."

"Mom, I was as surprised as you were. And I asked Alex about it, too. He told me his dad just came up with that on his own."

"Really? Hmm... Well, I honestly didn't relish spending any more time around Sabetha. She just makes me feel uncomfortable."

"Mom, Alex's mother isn't going."

"I just feel kind of funny about that."

"I just know that Alex said his father was emphatic that she was not traveling with the team, period," Amanda advised. "He thinks his dad is as uncomfortable around his mom as everyone else is."

Sarah appeared pleasantly stunned. "Seems bizarre." *Then why is she still at his house?*

Allison was bitchy as she meandered from one concourse to another at the Hartsfield International terminal for her connecting flight to Budapest. She had spent much of her life with access to travel on a Unibank corporate commuter jet without the hassle of being treated like a coach-class consumer.

She was shaky and wasn't sure it had hit her. She had paid this Hot Lips $60,000, rolling the dice that Jordan would identify the bitch before the blackmail got worse. He almost knocked her down when he proposed this latest scheme, horribly expensive and fraught with risks, but a cure for many of her problems. When her boarding time approached, Allison got up and stepped out away from the crowd to make one more call.

"Eric, are you positive everything is set up right?"

"Yes, baby. Just text me the exact time you'll be there."

"And you definitely told them I would be wearing a light-colored baseball cap, right?"

"Allison, calm down. Yes, just make sure you have that hat on. Everything will be fine. Trust me."

"I have to go," she closed and disconnected. *Trust me,... yeah right. I don't trust anybody, Eric Jordan.*

The paddock was buzzing during the early practice session. The championship fight was tight between the four top-tier teams, Ferrari, Red Bull, McLaren, and Mercedes. Most of the media, however, were focused on the Moretti team and particularly Alex and his fiancée, Amanda, the couple who had captured the imagination of the entire planet just two months prior. Even Sarah had her share of media attention as the mass of journalists pushed to get in whatever sound bites they could muster.

One bombastic podcaster stepped over the line, shoving a microphone in Sarah's face and asking if the long saga with her daughter's romance had contributed to her own marital problems.

"Why, I beg your pardon. I don't believe that's any of your business. Now if you'll excuse me."

The team was cautiously optimistic in the first session as Leland was fifteenth fastest, followed right behind by Alex at seventeenth fastest, not spectacular, but at least the 107 percent rule was not in play. Tony was acting as assistant to the Chief Mechanic, Mason Strauss, a man who would announce his plans to retire within the month. Official titles aside, Tony would be running the show regarding his brother's race strategy.

Despite her best effort in disguise, everyone could sense that Allison Cook, a late unexpected addition to the Moretti hospitality contingent, seemed uneasy, as if preoccupied. She had claimed that she was disappointed that Evelyn Stevens was not in attendance, learning late that none other than Carolyn Tyler had arranged a promotional appearance for her on behalf of Unibank at a world banking conference in New York.

The Moretti family and all of their guests were staying at the Corinthia Hotel in downtown Budapest, planning dinner a short walk down the boulevard at a well-known dining establishment, Caviar and Bulls. It was a hot day in late July and they all looked forward to freshening up prior to dinner.

It was understood that Andy and his sons would be a couple of hours later in departing the track as the team would gather to go over the data from the session, discussing plans for adjustments before tomorrow's opening qualifying session. Andy and Adam Herrera would both pay close attention to their sponsors, British Petroleum and next year's secondary sponsor, Van Boden Financial, whose attending contingent was overwhelmingly positive about the Indy 500 winner, Alex Moretti, and his now famous fiancée being on hand, consuming much of the media attention generally reserved for the championship point leaders.

Allison nudged Amanda on the bus, quietly suggesting the two break away from the hotel briefly and shop for a present for their mother, perhaps stop in at a sports bar next door for a cocktail. Amanda remained apprehensive about being close to her sister, a female who always had an ulterior motive, but chose to play along to get along.

The two agreed to meet back in the hotel lobby after checking into their rooms, losing their backpacks, etc. Allison entered her room and sent out a text message. *"We'll be on the street in twenty minutes."*

Eleven time zones away, Eric Jordan received the message and replied, *"Stay close, just you two."*

Allison stepped off the elevator and swallowed hard. "Amanda! What's with the hat?"

"It belongs to Alex. You said we're going to a sports bar, right?"

"You just never wear hats, that's all," Alison replied abruptly.

"Is everything okay, Allison?"

"Sure. Let's hit it."

The girls headed south on the boulevard in search of a boutique. Amanda wondered what kind of gift Allison had in mind for their mother, a woman whose wardrobe seemed to have no vacancy.

Allison was beside herself, not recalling Amanda ever wearing a baseball-type hat until now. She tried to appear casual while she pecked out a follow-up message to Jordan. *"We both have hats on! Better abort!"*

🏁

A block north, Burim Basha sucked on his thirtieth cigarette of the day while his ten-year-old Citroen minivan idled impatiently at the curb. "I think that must be them up ahead, Armend."

Armend Cazacu had become a trusted subordinate, a young gangster who saw Burim as his ticket to rise up in the organization. This was a first for Dominik Markovic, who was new and unproven.

The underboss stopped several meters ahead and prompted his two *Brigăzi* soldiers to get ready. "Are you awake back there, Dominik?"

The Hungarian teen had his EarPods blaring and didn't answer.

Burim reached backward and slapped the young gangster upside his head. "Hey, asshole! Are you ready!?"

Markovic tensed up, giving Basha a stern look, but said nothing as he removed the pods and snapped to attention.

Allison fidgeted, waiting for Jordan to reply to her text, grabbing Amanda by the shoulder as she turned to approach a boutique window. "Amanda, wait for me."

Amanda turned and gave her older sister a questioning look when suddenly she noticed two rough-looking young males approaching.

While the girls were accustomed to drawing attention, these two were staring in a menacing way as one quickly made a call on his phone.

"Burim! Both of them have on light colored baseball caps!" Cazacu declared. "What the fuck should we do?"

Basha was pissed. "Just wait."

Markovik was impressed with this new pair, beautiful beyond belief. "Let's just grab these two bitches and keep them for ourselves, Armend,"

"Leave them!" Basha ordered, and pulled up to the curb and tooted the horn.

The two intimidating males gave the girls a last look before making their way to the van, with Cazacu having to grab a salivating Markovik, before speeding away.

"What the fuck, Burim!?"

"The American called us off," Basha replied. "And Dominik, keep your ugly fucking mug away from the glass!" *The young fool has much to learn*, he thought.

⚑✕⚑

That was like creepy," Amanda declared.

Allison sighed. "Let's get a drink."

"Are you sure I'm old enough here?"

"It's eighteen, Amanda."

The two entered the establishment, noticing most of the many large TV monitors were featuring coverage from the Hungaroring racing circuit. Amanda's mood brightened when a paddock journalist was interviewing Alex.

Allison bit her lip, suddenly appearing pissed at someone or something. "So, how do you feel about Dad's mistress?" Allison asked, as if to sour Amanda's enthusiasm.

Amanda replied without looking away from the sports coverage. "Like, what should I think? It's our dad and our mom. It sucks."

Wanting to strike out at her sister and blame her for their parents' divorce, Allison held her tongue. "Yes, it does. This Carolyn Tyler is nothing but a gold digger."

Amanda chose not to reply. *You would know what that looks like, Allison.*

⚑×⚑

Jordan was pissed at having to call off this asshole, Basha, who in turn gave him an angry language-laced tongue lashing. He dialed up Allison immediately and got dumped into her voicemail. She finally called back nearly an hour later.

"Allison, what the hell are you doing!?"

"The little bitch showed up with a tan baseball cap of her own, Eric! She never does that."

"So, now what?"

"The four of us are all going out for coffee in the morning. I'll text you when and where and again when we're ready to head back out on the street."

"Allison, these aren't the kind of people to jerk around. Don't screw this up!"

The two disconnected and Jordan prepared to make another call he dreaded. Eduardo Blaku had left Bucharest and set up shop in Tijuana, Mexico four years earlier, the *Nasu*, the term for Romanian strongman, still controlled the mafia there. Jordan had met the man at a strip club just south of the border, started a relationship, and had traded a few favors back and forth. Blaku was thrilled to make the grab of the beautiful and well-known Amanda Cook, and was thus angry at learning about this aborted takedown.

"Mr. Jordan, you put my people at substantial risk with this stunt."

"I'm very sorry, Eduardo. Allison had specifically set this up with her wearing a light-colored baseball cap, stating her little sister never wore one. The two actually do look very much alike. It's not beyond anyone who does not know the two to get them mixed up."

Blaku sounded extremely unhappy. In the bigger scheme of everything his criminal empire had going, this miscue was truly insignificant, but the strongman would not show as much to this young American military officer. "I would like you to send me the locations of these two sisters and I will oversee this from here. I want to be in the loop on things."

Jordan didn't like the sound of that, as he knew he was about to lose control of things. He had built up his relationship with Aaron Williams and his family's close ties to the Cook family as key to being the agent for Eduardo Blaku in all negotiations, adding his impromptu ability to provide key inside intelligence information regarding the police, both domestically and internationally. Now he hoped his station would hold. When Blaku made a request, turning him down was not an option.

"Allison has insisted that all communications go through me, Eduardo."

"How much did she pay you to set up her own sister, Eric?"

Jordan was taken aback, not expecting such a straightforward inquiry. He would have a natural tendency to reply with "That's none of your business", but that would be a mistake with Eduardo Blaku. "Fifty thousand," he replied.

Blaku didn't believe the American for a minute. Jordan had paid him a twenty-five thousand dollar retainer with another twenty-five grand to be paid when the pickup was completed. Subsequently,

Jordan was to get a third of the booty obtained from the future sale on the dark web.

Jordan realized that he would have difficulty knowing exactly what that amount would be, as Blaku was to be trusted to disclose it fairly when the time came. Of course, Jordan gave Allison no knowledge of this arrangement, as she simply agreed to a flat hundred grand to make Amanda disappear.

"Well then, you will come out handsomely, no out-of-pocket initially and a generous commission soon after."

Jordan had himself been paid half of his hundred grand and like Blaku would be paid the remaining balance upon completion. Discussions had yet to occur regarding any adjustment or refund should the sanction not move forward with either party. Getting anything back from Blaku would be a challenge, he knew, the same for his paying any deposit back to Allison.

"The next event is this coming weekend at Spa-Francorchamps in Belgium. When I get the details on the when and where I will forward those to you then, and you will coordinate with your people on the ground," Jordan stated, trying to sound as though he was still in charge.

"I'm afraid a grab in Belgium is not on the table. It is out of bounds so far as my trade agreements. Looking at the schedule, it would appear Monza is the next date I could work with."

"That's over a month away!" Jordan replied in excited retort, knowing Allison wanted something immediate.

"We're not fucking stealing candy, here, Eric Jordan! You just get me the information in advance that we need! Am I clear!?"

Amanda laid her head across his chest as Alex struggled to get to sleep. Normally, a quick workout in the hotel gym followed by a hot shower and good sex would cause him to fall right off. But Alex was wired. His first day on the track in the Moretti Formula One car had been a disappointment, at least by his own standards.

He had matched the team regular, Geoff Leland, which had actually made the veteran Aussie pilot look bad considering it was Alex Moretti coming in out of the box. But Alex knew he was better and wanted to show it. He had informed Amanda that he wanted to get up early and head to the track, understanding that she may wish to sleep in and perhaps spend the bulk of the morning with the girls, meaning her mom, Allison, and Crissy.

He had been quite hesitant to accept the F1 drive, happily settled in again with the IndyCar team and even challenging for the coveted Astor Cup awarded to the IndyCar series champion, despite missing the season's first four races. His close friend, Alex Palou, would be hard to beat, as well as all the Penske drivers, but right now Alex entered every race feeling extremely confident.

He always figured he would be in Formula One eventually, maybe even as early as next season, but the family needed the help and Tony had worked tirelessly to sell him and their father on it. Alex could also see his older brother as a major force on the team, a man not sitting around feeling sorry for himself but indeed engaged as Alex's de facto Chief Mechanic. He was so thankful for how Amanda had supported him, never voicing much objection to his changing focus on a different series, one that would take him around the world. *God, how I love this girl,* he thought proudly.

Bud Williams had quite enough of watching his youngest boy shunned at the opening Clemson practice sessions. He had applied political pressure in every way imaginable, but the erasable coach, Gabe Fairchild, was not budging. A man who had led Clemson to the national championship game four times in the past seven years and winning twice was standing on solid ground.

Williams hadn't bothered to make an advanced appointment and simply called from his mobile phone on the expressway. He would have no part of the CEO's executive secretary's lip service that Byron Cook was unavailable, exiting the elevator on the top floor and standing before the uncomfortable woman's desk. "Inform Byron that I need a word."

Cook didn't appreciate the interruption but arose from his office and approached his old friend, knowing something was up for Williams to just barge in like this. The two men had been like brothers most of their lives but had rarely spoken and had not mingled socially since the trial several months prior. "Bud, why don't you come on into my office? Bernice, please bring us some coffee."

Williams entered and sat down, his tone speaking volumes of the seriousness of the setting. "So Byron, are you going to marry that mistress of yours?"

The President and CEO felt a hidden anger build up, not appreciative nor accustomed to being addressed in this way, but refrained from telling Williams to mind his own business. "Once my divorce is final, I'll choose what path to take in my personal life."

"What about Sarah? Is she seeing anyone?"

Again, Cook was taken aback at this forward question, realizing that his soon-to-be ex-wife would be among the most eligible and sought-after bachelorettes in the entire metro, *largely because she was still quite a stunning woman, but partly because of the wealth I have built.* "I don't know, Bud. Her business, I suppose."

"Well, Byron, let's get right to it. We've known each other far too long to waste time with petty bullshit. Aaron and Allison are waiting for our approval to get married. I'm hesitant to support that marriage, while my younger son's future as a potential star quarterback in the NFL is being ruined. Coach Fairchild won't let him play because of the stigma hanging over his head, all due to what came out in that so-called trial."

Williams paused momentarily to get Cook's reaction. To his chagrin, his long-time banker just stared back at him for a tense period before finally issuing a reply. "Yes, very disturbing revelations, they were."

"Byron, they were just kids! Okay, Kyle may have had too much to drink and things got out of hand that night. We can't punish my boy for the rest of his life because of one mistake. After all, no harm became of it."

"No harm, Bud? No harm? Amanda had worshipped the ground Kyle walked on, just as Allison felt about your older boy, Aaron. We were happy about it. You and Lisa were happy about it. But what happened that night did happen. It screwed up Amanda's brain and drove her into an ill-advised romance with a race driver! That has destroyed my marriage, Bud!"

The car dealer couldn't recall ever seeing Byron Cook speak with such emotion. The man had always been all business, a true ice man relating nearly everything to dollars and sense.

"Byron, I would like Amanda to issue a public statement regretting what happened all those years ago, that it was all a misunderstanding. All those kids got in your liquor cabinet, after all."

"Amanda has already stated that she wants no part of any charges being filed. She just wants to move on. I despise what she is moving on into, but she's eighteen now and no longer listens to anything I have to say. I do know she will not issue such a statement, Bud. That would be paramount to her admitting she lied on the witness stand in a court of law."

Williams was stunned. He believed that his personal needs as a major Unibank client would buy him some consideration. "Very well, Byron. I regret to say this, but Unibank is not the only financial institution out there. Your competitors are knocking on my door every day. I've been very loyal to you all these years. If that public statement is not issued by September 1st, I'll begin moving my banking business elsewhere."

Now it was Cook who was stunned as the man had suddenly become confronted with a cold reality, indeed a crossroads. His old and dearest friend was asking--no demanding--that he sell his youngest daughter's moral integrity in the name of business. The man had obviously come here fully expecting the bank CEO to fold like a cheap suit.

His analytical logic kicked in, turning the wheels upstairs on the monetary ramifications of what was happening here. Bud Williams was, at one time, Unibank's biggest client on nearly all metrics. Byron had taken the account that he had secured and used it to move up the corporate ladder, all the way to the top floor as President and CEO. Over the years, Cook had turned Unibank into an international banking giant with key acquisitions and adding multi-million dollar corporate customers, some in the billions. Losing Williams as a customer would be a setback, no doubt, but in the larger scheme of things, nothing like it would have been years earlier when Unibank, Carolina National Bank as it was formerly known, was more of a regional entity.

Cook stood up from his executive desk chair. "You do what you think you have to do, Bud. Now, if you will excuse me, I believe this meeting is concluded."

The excitement in the Moretti Motorsport hospitality area was electric. Alex had gradually moved forward in the first session, advancing to Q2, while teammate Geoff Leland had not made the cut, although his speed had improved to the point where the 107 percent rule was not a worry.

The year's Formula One driver's championship was the most competitive in decades and the lead drivers for Red Bull, Ferrari, Mercedes, and McLaren all had a mathematical chance, as well as three of the four battling for the coveted Constructors Championship. Team Moretti was on the outside looking in on all of that, but where they finished the season would have a profound effect on their share of the lucrative overall purse. Things were looking positive for a mid-level finish early in the season with Tony as their lead driver, but since he had gone down in May the team was staring at the real possibility of finishing dead last in the standings. Alex Moretti's rookie performance thus far had injected some new and sudden optimism, a boost the team direly needed.

The girls were ecstatic when Alex crossed the finish line with two minutes remaining in the second session, just two-tenths off the best time of Lewis Hamilton, which put the number "28' Moretti car sixth fastest and solidly in the mix for Q3 and the final run for the pole.

Even though she feigned excitement, Allison felt that both her mother's and sister's behavior in hollering and jumping up and down, along with Tony's wife, Crissy, was patently ridiculous. Sitting on pins and needles every time her phone would beep, she was extremely anxious to hear from Eric Jordan that he had identified this *Hot Lips*.

On another front, Allison was having second thoughts about the scheme trumped up by Jordan. She had looked hard into the stares of the three thugs from that white van, having recurring thoughts that even she was above participating in such a diabolical act, omitting the fact that she had indeed committed homicide just a couple of months before. Now, as she sat there among the throngs of cheering fans and the loud noise of the passing cars, the wheels were turning on possible alternatives to access that lucrative trust fund, ideally cutting Amanda out of it altogether.

"You're right on the edge, brother. If anything is to be gained, it will be in the second sector, turns six, seven, and eight," Tony directed. "Keep it tight. You're only a minuscule tap of the pedal or steering wheel away from putting the car in the sand. The McLarens and Ferraris corner better than us. We're right there with the Mercedes and Red Bull cars, who make up for it on the straights. Avoid following the top-tier cars like the plague. We'll bring you in and out to put some distance there for a fast run."

Alex was really getting into the interface between himself and his older brother, who would be calling the shots from the pit box. While both had a strong resume of success, the two were very different in style. Tony had always approached racing very analytically, striving to learn every aspect of a car technically and how to use the knowledge to his advantage, always fast but knowing when to strike while also knowing the car's limitations and willing to accept the second or third place points where necessary. He had always been compared in that respect to the legendary Niki Lauda.

Alex was much different in his approach. His style was to always drive to the front at any time during the race, much like another legend, Mario Andretti. He was harder on the equipment and tended to win few races by simply outlasting the competition. Alex was always considered a man to beat and quite often the results were black and white. He either wins or doesn't finish. The compliment of the two working together seemed a combination that promised future success.

By midway through the final qualifying session, Alex was running eighth fastest, disappointing in his mind but stellar for a team that hadn't seen a fourth row start in ages. He was a full two seconds a lap faster than his teammate and had even bested the effort of an icon, two-time world champion, Fernando Alonzo. Crossing the finish line with less than a minute remaining, Alex was hell-bent on putting forth his best effort. The entire team contingent stood frozen with their fingers crossed as they watched on the monitor their rookie driver maneuver the Moretti car in and out of the turns on the back side of the circuit, bringing it home with an amazing time of 1:18.324 seconds, good for fourth fastest overall, and just over a tenth of a second off of Max Verstappen's pole-winning time.

The entire paddock seemed electrified by Alex Moretti's performance. Team members, fans, and pundits alike had all but written off Moretti Motorsport as a viable team in Formula One. Now, Alex Moretti's personal story, along with his stellar out-of-box run, had the motorsport media spinning with a new headline.

Reporters and want-to-be-star podcasters hustled for anyone in the Moretti camp who would stand still for a recorded comment. While Alex and his fiancée, Amanda, garnered most of the attention, everyone within the family's inner circle was sought out for interviews, including some cases that became blatantly uncomfortable.

A prominent European sports commentator sought out and cornered Sarah Cook, taken by surprise to find herself before a camera before she could even think.

"This is Andrea Martinelli on-site at the Hungaroring and I have with me Alex Moretti's future mother-in-law, Sarah Cook. Sarah, I understand this is your first Formula One Grand Prix. How has the experience been for you?"

"Oh, this whole experience has been so exhilarating. The atmosphere reminds me of the Indianapolis 500. I'm truly enjoying my time with my daughters here."

"Sarah, the world knows you are divorcing your long-time husband, the prominent banker, Byron Cook. What has been his reaction to your personal relationship with Andy Moretti?"

Sarah froze, giving the journalist a blank stare and struggling to suppress a sudden anger. "I beg your pardon, I need to move on now."

Martinelli turned to face her cameraman as Sarah abruptly walked away. "That was Sarah Cook, obviously uncomfortable discussing her romantic relationship with Andy Moretti, the longtime bachelor, team principal of Moretti Motorsport, and her own daughter's future father-in-law."

In another quarter, Allison busied herself ad-nauseum to be the subject of as many personal interview sound bites as possible. Disappointed that Evelyn Stevens was not in attendance, she reminded every journalist who would listen that she was quite close to the famous Brit and hoped to be her future business agent. She spied the well-known French sports journalist, Sharice Moncet, and stood by impatiently as the Parisian personality was in the middle of interviewing McLaren CEO, Zak Brown. Upon conclusion, Allison feigned to accidentally bump into her.

"Oh, I'm sorry, Sharice. How clumsy of me."

The famous reporter, temporarily taken aback, composed herself quickly. "Oh my, you must be Mademoiselle Amanda Cook, Alex Moretti's fiancée."

She signaled her cameraman to focus. "You must be very proud and excited about Alex—"

"I'm sorry. I am Allison Cook, Amanda's older sister."

"I see, Mademoiselle. You girls surely do look alike... How excited you must be about your future brother-in-law's prospects this weekend?"

Allison suppressed a hidden anger. *Amanda, Alex, Amanda, and more Alex. Ohhh!* "I am here on behalf of Evelyn Stevens, who we hope will be rejoining Moretti Motorsport next season—"

Moncet seemed impatient at Allison's harangue, her personal vibes not lost on the Cook sister. "Mademoiselle Cook, perhaps you could assist me in arranging a lengthy personal interview with Alex Moretti and your sister, Amanda?"

"I may be able to do that, but now—"

"Merci, Mademoiselle. This is Sharice Moncet coming to you live from the Hungaroring, where Alex Moretti will attempt to make history by winning in his very first Grand Prix."

Allison stood steaming as the popular reporter and her cameraman left her standing to quickly advance to a more important Formula One personality. *Oh, you bitch! You want me to help you arrange an interview for you with my sister!? Like hell, I will!*

Chapter 5

In Broad Daylight

Burim sat at the back of the loud club in Budapest's red light district, sucking on a cigarette and working on a steady binge of cheap house liquor. Growing up in the slums of Bucharest, he was shunned by his father, choosing to make his way as a common street thug. His uncle Eduardo had brought his nephew into the organization as part of a long-term plan to have him manage the Eastern European operation. The syndicate had expanded and was heavily involved in narcotics, prostitution, and human trafficking.

The twenty-five-year-old was pushing his uncle, a man who had long since moved and operated out of Mexico, to give him more responsibility beyond his current limited position, a move that was slow in coming. The young man was paid fairly well but wanted that big score, knowing that his slice of the underworld pie was minuscule in the overall business model. He saw this latest gig, connected to some rich and powerful Americans, as his ticket out of the sleazy dives he managed. The directive to back off and just keep watch on the target was in his mind degrading, a waste of his many talents.

The bio was fascinating, a strikingly beautiful eighteen-year-old girl, daughter of a multi-millionaire, if not billionaire banker, and engaged to an international racing star. The strange thing was her sister, who had somehow been involved and was excluded, a sister who was equally as gorgeous and herself engaged to a wealthy American car dealer's son.

He was to just watch the girl at a safe distance and await orders. He sent yet another text to Armend, stationed in the bar at the hotel, demanding an update.

"Nothing to report," was the reply. "None of them have left the lounge."

Absolute bullshit, Burim pondered, a young man hungry for action.

Both Amanda and Crissy felt something was bothering Sarah during dinner, as she had declined the invitation to attend some popular Grand Prix parties. This suited Allison fine as she wanted to really lighten up, let her hair down to party, and in no way wished to have her mother along to pass judgment.

Sarah retreated to her room, not in the mood for socializing and feeling some melancholy that this trip may have been a mistake. While the idea of going to one of these nightclubs with her daughters had its appeal, as she had never done such a thing with the two as adult women, she was getting a dose of what it was like for Amanda to literally become a celebrity and now finding herself in the public eye, and subject to all the abuse that unrestricted social media could muster.

Her phone buzzed and she was surprised by the caller ID. She had rarely spoken to him in weeks as most of their communications were now channeled through attorneys. She adjusted her mindset before picking up. *Tyler will no doubt be sitting right there,* she thought, then realized the time change would still have it midafternoon there when she pressed the green button. "Yes, Byron."

"Really, Sarah? How long has this been going on?" Bryon barked.

"What are you talking about, Byron?"

"It's all over social media, Sarah. You and Andy Moretti!? And I'm the one made out as the guilty party in front of our daughters."

"Byron! There's nothing going on with me and Andy!"

"You've practically become part of that race team, Sarah. Even his ex-wife is quoted on—"

"Byron, you're not listening! I have not been involved with Alex Moretti's father! I have not been involved with anyone!"

"Sarah, I know we're going through an expensive and very public divorce. Let's agree to keep our personal lives private, and not embarrass each other. For the sake of our daughters, Sarah."

He had now struck a nerve. "For the sake of our daughters? If anyone is going to preach to me about setting a moral example for Allison and Amanda, it certainly wouldn't be you, Byron Cook! And by the way, whatever I do in my private life now, and whoever I do it with, is none of your business! And I see no good reason for this conversation to continue."

Byron Cook sat in his executive Unibank office staring down at a phone set on speaker, one that now played a constant and annoying dial tone.

⚑×⚑

Andy was furious. Here it was, the morning of the Hungarian Grand Prix, his BP-sponsored car in its best starting position ever, and now he had to deal with this personal bullshit. The three sat in the hotel coffee shop early, needing a private conversation before the buzz of the many guests stirring.

"I've been nice to her, Crissy," Andy stated defensively. "But I think I'm nice to everybody,"

"Have you even spoken to her about this, Dad?" Tony asked.

"Not since this video hit the fan. I wondered why Sarah seemed kind of distant over dinner late yesterday. I thought she was mad at me."

Tony and Crissy shared a look, his giving her a single nod as if to signal to his wife the okay to disclose something important.

"Andy, this Andrea Martinelli is a long-time friend of Sabetha," Crissy stated.

"And who is Andrea Martinelli?"

"She's the so-called journalist who cornered Sarah and posted the quick interview on YouTube, Facebook, and X."

Andy shook his head. He was getting ever more angry at his ex-wife but had always refrained from verbally trashing her in front of the family. After all, she was his boys' mother. Suddenly, all three froze and looked up as another early morning guest entered.

Sarah smiled neutrally and sat down with the three of them. "Good morning, everyone."

Following an awkward few moments where none of the four quite knew how to begin, Andy finally spoke up. "Sarah, I'm really sorry about all this unwarranted aggravation. I regret to say that I believe it was Sabetha who started this BS."

"Sabetha? Why would you say that?" Sarah asked with genuine curiosity.

"When I had that party a couple of weeks ago, she had way too much to drink. She came to my room after midnight and,... well, let's just say things didn't go as she had planned. In her intoxicated state and rancor, she accused me of having an affair with you."

Crissy and Sarah shared shocked expressions. "And that's it?" Crissy asked finally.

"Yes. I escorted her back down the hall to her room and went back to bed. I have no idea how or why she came up with such a crazy idea."

"We had best head up to the track, Dad," Tony interjected, looking at his watch. "We have a race to run and you'll just have to give Sarah a rain check on any additional socializing, I suppose."

The four just paused, digesting Tony's off-the-cuff comment before Crissy would lead a chorus of laughter. "That's what I like about you, honey. You're always so logical."

Andy and Tony both arose from their table, indeed planning to head to the track early, while Crissy and Sarah remained tending to their unfinished coffee and Danish pastries.

"So, Sarah. How are you feeling?"

"I don't know. I certainly never wanted to become a controversy and cause any more family problems for Andy," Sarah replied.

"Oh, Sarah, God knows you've had more of your share of family problems."

"Crissy, now that we're talking about it, what is your mother-in-law's disposition? I mean, is she residing at Andy's place now permanently?"

"Heavens no. Honestly, I hate to say it but we're all wishing Sabetha would pack up and go back home. I can't stand her chain smoking habit, and you know she's popping pills."

"How do the boys feel about that, Crissy? She is their mother."

"The same as her two grandkids. She has never been close to them. She's there because she has problems she needs to escape from."

"And what about Andy?"

"I'm not sure, Sarah," Crissy replied. "Andy is quite good-hearted. If he was at home every day, things may be different. But between everything going on here in Europe and a race every weekend somewhere, I think he's just busy and tolerates her for now."

"Yes, I can see that in him."

"My father-in-law does have a lot of good qualities, Sarah. He's an older version of my husband, after all."

Sarah was feeling that Amanda's future sister-in-law was promoting. "You know, Crissy, I don't think I'm the type to flirt. In fact, I think I've gone out of my way not to be. I can't imagine how Sabetha came up with this."

"She's intimidated, Sarah. Sabetha has been used to being the center of attention her whole life. And now? Well, coincidentally, you're a very attractive woman about to be divorced, and in her mind, seemingly always around."

"Oh my. Perhaps I should cut this trip short and head back home, then."

"No way, Sarah. Amanda would be crushed. You're practically part of the family now."

"Thank you for saying that. But with Andy having so much pressure on him, I wouldn't wish—"

"Sarah, trust me. Andy likes having you around."

"Oh, come on, Crissy. He's never given me any indication that—"

"I know Andy went through a lot with that long-running feud with your husband. He's not one to outwardly make waves. But I've seen him interact with many women over these last few years, many who have tried to get close to him. He looks at you differently, believe me. Even Tony has noticed. So don't think about going home. Like the line in that old Bonnie Raitt song, let's give them something to talk about."

※

The nerves were pumping. Alex glanced over to his right where the Ferrari piloted by Carlos Sainz sat third on the grid. The standing start of a Formula One race was among the most exhilarating of any sporting event in the world. Tony had stressed over and over for Alex to get off to a solid start and not try to win the race in the first turn.

Factually, qualifying position and getting a good start were more critical in Formula One than any other motor racing discipline, with the possible exception of drag racing. Andy had told his boys many times about the trials and tribulations of the great Michael Andretti's disastrous starts when driving for McLaren as a rookie in 1993.

The drivers behind him on the pace lap gathered to their starting positions as he waited for the starting lights to distinguish, signaling the start. He quickly had a flashing thought of Amanda, then of passing Evelyn to take the checkered at Indy just months before.

The cars all jumped forward, heading down the front straight toward the first right-hander. He had started solidly and entered the second turn in sixth position, losing a couple of places but staying out of trouble. He spent the first several laps getting comfortable, not pushing it but sufficiently fast to maintain position on a circuit known for passing being difficult.

Attending her first Formula One Grand Prix, Amanda found things exhilarating but not nearly as comfortable as the races back home that she was accustomed to, starting with the term *WAGS* attached to the Formula One wives and girlfriends. While a select few were openly friendly to her and genuinely curious regarding her and Alex Moretti's story, many saw her as some sort of threat to their status in gathering social media prowess.

And then there was the seating arrangement in the stands, as the *WAGS* were restricted from actually being in the pit area or the more prominent pit boxes, reserved for the Chief Mechanics, engineers, etc. But the robust crowd was huge and more reminiscent of the excitement at Indy than most of the other IndyCar races. She would come to learn that each country's Grand Prix was their own largest sporting event, drawing from fans worldwide.

On lap fifteen, Alex passed a Williams driver to take fifth place and then the very next lap drew a crowd roar when Alex out-braked George Russell into turn one, moving up to fourth place and just completing fastest lap of the race.

"Alex, take care of your tires! I want you to make it to lap forty-five!"

"I hear you, brother! But Russell is hard on my ass!"

"Stay on your lines, Alex! So long as you get a good run off the last turn, he won't be able to pass."

Alex's driving style found it very hard to manage tear wear. He was a charger, a driver who just wanted to race hard, pass the car in front of him, and lead. He came up quickly on Lewis Hamilton, who ducked into the pits on lap thirty-six right in front of him.

The girls in the stands, namely Amanda, Crissy, and Sarah, stood and screamed as Alex raced by them on the front straight in third place, less than ten seconds behind second-place Lando Norris and resetting fast lap. The announcers were actually discussing the probability of Moretti being on the podium and possibly even winning.

On the very next lap, both of the leaders pitted and Alex Moretti streaked down the front straight as a standing crowd went wild. "Oh my god!" Amanda yelled. "Come on, race man! You can win!"

Tony called for Alex to pit on the very next lap but his younger brother waved him off. "I got this, Bro."

"Alex, the tires! You need fresh tires!'

Alex crossed the line on lap fifty sixteen seconds ahead of second place Norris, but the McLaren was gaining nearly two seconds per lap as the lead Moretti driver finally entered the pits with just nineteen laps remaining. The crew made quick work of changing all four tires in less than three seconds, but with the in-and-out slower pace, Alex exited pit lane and found himself in fourth place. He would run right on the tail of third place Hamilton's Mercedes for the rest of the race, and that is where he would finish.

The rookie driver was showered with accolades upon entering pit lane for reasons he could not comprehend. The fact was his fourth place had equaled Tony's best-ever result from last season's rain-soaked Dutch Grand Prix, and many of the paddock reporters behaved as though he had won.

"Alex, could we surmise from this result that you will drive in all of this season's remaining Formula One events?" Paul Newkirk of BBC asked expectantly.

"Too soon to tell. But maybe."

"And I believe this young lady wants to get in here," Newkirk added, smiling, as Amanda had made her way down with a congratulatory kiss for her man. "Amanda, what would you like to tell our worldwide audience about your fiancé's performance today in his first Formula One Grand Prix?"

"He's my race man! He's the best!"

The entire Moretti Motorsport entourage was celebrating in earnest at the team hospitality trailer, with the lone exception of Tony, a man somewhat subdued. "We could have finished higher if he had pitted earlier," he informed his father, a man who didn't need to be told.

"I know. It's the boy's first race, Tony. And it is the best F1 finish we've ever had. Let's enjoy the moment."

The team overall was ecstatic. The combo of Tony as Chief Mechanic and young Alex driving had injected energy into a losing team unlike anything seen since Mario Andretti and Colin Chapman came together nearly half a century earlier. Even Geoff Leland had responded to the pressure and finished a respectable twelfth, up five positions from his average finish prior. Toasts were abound and the entire entourage could hardly contain themselves.

Amanda and Crissy made token efforts to cheer Sarah up, one who had suddenly had a complex in always believing someone was looking over her shoulder, while subconsciously going out of her way to avoid any eye contact with Andy, and asking herself why she should be feeling guilty about it.

The one person who looked totally out of character was Allison, a gal who normally relished a good party—the louder and wilder the better--and seemed to have a certain disdain for not being the center of attention. Her mood didn't improve when she saw an unwanted email pop up on her phone from none other than *Hot Lips. You bitch!* Allison thought as she digested the message.

You look like you're having a hot time over there, Cook. I always wanted to travel to Europe but need more funding for it. HA! Better watch your back! Hot Lips.

⚑×⚑

Nearly five thousand miles west, Cotton James worked on a 7-Eleven tuna sandwich as he sat watch on an unsavory insurance agent. The man's wife suspected him of cheating and had hired James to gather the goods on him. The job was time-consuming and boring but helped pay the bills for a man always behind on something. He had reluctantly agreed to work with Remi for a third of the take on her Allison Cook gig, hoping his generosity would help her open up to him more, a desire that had yet to bear fruit, plus the former prostitute had not paid him all of his third of that last transfer.

By coincidence, his phone buzzed. *Remi...Could this be an invite to dinner?*

"Yes, sugar twat!"

"Can you believe that bitch is in Hungary celebrating with those Morettis at this Grand Prix? She must have money to burn!"

Cotton was pissed and immediately hung up, grabbing another phone from his glove box and dialing the number of the burner phone he had given her.

"You asshole! Why did you hang up on me?"

"Remi, I told you never to discuss business with our personal phones!"

"I thought you wanted to have a personal relationship with me, Cotton James."

What a stupid cunt! "Remi, this is dangerous! This Cook woman committed murder. Do you think for a second she wouldn't put you on ice if given half a chance?"

"Oh, Cotton. She's already paid us sixty grand. I'm ready to squeeze her for more. Are you with me or not?"

"I'll be by tomorrow and we'll talk about it. Until then, don't do anything stupid!"

⚑⚑

On Monday morning, Team Moretti and their guests were all packing up, preparing for travel northwest to the team's European headquarters in England, preparing for the next race in two weeks at the famous Spa-Francorchamps Circuit in Belgium. Joining the supporting contingent was Evelyn Stevens, much to the delight of Allison Cook, who proposed the girls plan a week-long holiday in Paris together.

Amanda was hesitant, not wanting to leave Alex, but relented when it was obvious her mother was all in on the idea, and Crissy would be joining them, as well. Tony and Alex were on board as they would be working long hours at the shop and agreed to join them in Paris for two days over the weekend.

Sarah was still bothered by the phone call earlier from Byron, an emotion she could barely disguise.

"Oh, Mom. Don't worry about it!" Amanda stated in an effort to lighten her mother's mood. "It's social media. You can't let anything on there get to you."

"I can attest to that," Crissy added, chuckling. "When I was pregnant, Twitter was full of crap about how Alex's girlfriend was so much better looking than his brother's wife."

That got a quick rise from Stevens, who gave Crissy a look before the two of them laughed at each other.

"I don't see what the bloody problem is," the Brit added in jest. "They look like the perfect couple to me."

That remark did get a stunned silence from all, including a sour look from Allison.

"Oh, just kidding!" Stevens quickly added. "You bloody Yanks are so sensitive."

Crissy and Amanda, two who had become like true sisters, shared a questioning look that quickly turned into smiles toward Sarah, who avoided them and just looked out the window toward the quaint French countryside. But she now struggled to hide her own smile.

The luxury suburban home was eighteen kilometers east of the center of Paris in a very upscale and touristy area near the Disney Park. Originally built a century earlier, the four-bedroom property had been updated and included a large patio and pool, plus ample gardens, giving the place a private, cozy appeal.

Basha lay behind a hedgerow with his binoculars, studying the many movements within the house. Not sure why he was told not to move in Budapest, the Romanian had taken it upon himself to track the Cook sisters to Paris, his first endeavor out of his local domain. He was certain his forward-thinking ambition would impress his uncle in Mexico.

Thus far, there were five of them, all females who clung together. All of them appeared quite attractive and mostly young, a sportsman's paradise in his line of work. Thus far, no opportunity had presented itself, as in two days they had hired a taxi van which had pulled up in front of the house to take them places, returning late afternoon to early evening in similar fashion.

On the third day, Friday, Basha would gather his two cronies, Armend and Dominik, and follow them.

Alex never thought work could be so much fun as he was practically wearing out the shop simulator, joking that his dad should consider opening up tours to the public and charge for rides in it.

If Tony had any enormous challenge with his brother, it was keeping him serious. He did have to admire Alex's natural talent for driving fast without the concentration he was used to, almost as if he was enjoying a carnival ride. *Little brother, you could be the best ever if you would just listen to me a little bit,* Tony considered.

The two sat down in Andy's office along with two other engineers going over data sheets from Hungary. "See how your times fell off once you hit thirty-five laps on the tires? Had you come in when prompted and matched your times for thirty-five laps on the second set, you would have finished second, just three seconds behind Leclerc's Ferrari."

"I'd have passed him if I were that close."

"You would have had a shot at him, at least," Andy declared, sticking his head in the door.

"We're going to run a different strategy at Spa," Tony interjected. "We'll start you out on the softs, counting on you to run really quick laps and pull you in on lap twelve. We'll then run the harder compound and hopefully won't have to stop again."

"It's a whole different game there, Alex, compared to Hungary," Andy stated. "The Red Bulls and Mercedes will have an advantage on the straights. You'll have to make it up under braking and get a good run out of the corners. Just don't take the car places it's unwilling to go. When are you two heading out?"

"Right after lunch," Tony replied, as Andy's two sons were leaving for Paris to join their better halves for the weekend.

Andy was feeling better about things and impressed with the effort his two sons had put in. Prior to the race in Hungary, the team would have been happy just to finish a car in twelfth place. With Alex coming in fourth, and that after a miscue in pitting late, his team was starting to be in the conversation with top-tier teams now, a feat he figured would take at least two more years to accomplish.

He would have passing thoughts of what to do about Sabetha. This latest caper involving these absurd social media posts about him and Amanda's mother bothered him greatly. *Of course, I find Sarah attractive. What middle-to upper-middle-aged guy wouldn't?* But the relief he felt when the long lawsuit saga between him and Byron Cook was settled and the last thing he wanted to do was poke the bear. But he couldn't stop harking back to the feeling he had at the Indy 500 Awards dinner. Sarah sat beside him causing quite a stir, and as much as he strived to remain reserved, he was proud of her and liked her presence beside him. He would allow things to calm down and perhaps invite Sarah out to dinner at some point and see where that went. Of course, there would always be the possibility that she would connect with someone elsewhere. *After all, Sarah would be quite a catch,* a thought that admittedly concerned him. *Best I not fool around too long.*

⚑×⚑

Allison had gotten accustomed to feeling a pinched nerve, mentally, every time her phone buzzed announcing a new message or email. She checked it promptly, a message from Jordan. *"Call me ASAP."*

She stepped away from her friends and family entourage and dialed. "Talk to me."

"Good news! I believe we've found your *Hot Lips*."

"What!? Tell me, Eric! Who, where!?"

"We've isolated the calls to a house trailer in Pineville, North Carolina. I have people watching the place. Shall I have them deal with it?"

"Hell no! I want to be there! Just make sure she, *or he,* doesn't slip away, Eric."

"I've got people in top of it. When are you heading back?"

"First thing in the morning... I'm so proud of you!"

"I'm sure you'll show your appreciation when you return, Allison."

"Of course, count on it." She disconnected, her mood taking a one-hundred-eighty-degree turn for the better. *Pineville, huh? Someone I know? But who? I'll have to inform Aaron that I'm flying into Charlotte to stay with Mom for a few days. He won't be happy, but that's too bad, Aaron. You wanted to be a military officer.*

Cotton approached slowly in his well-worn GMC, knowing the two in the late model Hyundai four-door sedan looked out of place just up the lane from Remi's trailer. He passed slowly while avoiding eye contact and pulled around the corner, parking in front of another mobile home four pads down.

He then made his way up to the back door and knocked. Remi opened, looking like she had just gotten out of bed in her faded bathrobe.

"What are you doing back here—?"

"Shut up, Remi! Get dressed now. I'm getting you out of here!"

"Calm your ass down, Cotton James. I haven't even had my coffee fix yet."

James moved quickly past the frowning woman down the narrow hallway to her back bedroom, peering through the flimsy curtains to check the Hyundai for movement before grabbing Dalton sternly by the shoulders. "The Cook woman has fingered you, Remi. She's a killer. Do you understand? Now, get dressed."

Remi looked through the curtain herself at the strange car parked down the lane, one that indeed appeared unmatched in her trailer park. "Where are you taking me?"

"We'll talk about that after we leave. Leave your personal phone here and plugged into power. Now hurry."

"My phone!? I can't do without—"

"Remi, you stupid twit! That phone can get us both killed. Now shut up and let's go!"

The two departed through the trailer's back door unseen and headed to Cotton's pickup. He then fired it up and took the circle drive around the back way to the park exit, as to not pass by the Hyundai again.

The girls were enjoying the sights and sounds of Paris. All had been to the typical tourist attractions such as the Eiffel Tower, the Louvre, and the Arc de Triomphe in previous years, but enjoyed the shopping, the many street entertainers, and restaurants.

Amanda was already missing Alex, working to avoid sending too many texts, knowing he would be working hard with Tony and the staff at the Moretti facility, preparing for the upcoming race in Belgium.

Allison worked hard in strengthening her relationship with Evelyn Stevens, somewhat anxious that the British racing driver seemed to discount any conversation about hiring an agent. But Allison had suddenly become quite cheerful and the rest all wondered what had come over her.

The Le Chardenoux was a popular midtown cafe on Rue Jules Valles, a place where the female entourage enjoyed their last holiday together, as Sarah announced her decision to catch an early morning flight to head back home the next morning. Her announcement at the late lunch genuinely affected Amanda and Crissy, while Allison feigned sadness and abruptly announced that she would also be leaving with her mother.

Stevens was somewhat relieved, as she would be heading to London to visit with her own family the next morning. While she enjoyed the camaraderie of Amanda, Crissy, and even her former boyfriend Alex's future mother-in-law, the Brit was tired of Allison's constant attempts to talk about her contract when that was exactly what she hoped to escape from with these few days off in Europe.

The hired taxi van driver headed southeast on the Boulevard Voltaire before making a right turn on Rue de Charonre just a few short meters before another quick left on the Rue Jules Valles, a one-way street. Suddenly, a frantic youth ran out in front of him and the driver slammed on the brakes to keep from running him over. Before the bearded, overweight driver could jump out and give the careless youth fool a brisk French tongue-lashing, the passenger door quickly opened and the driver felt the cold steel of a pistol under his chin.

"Pull over!" was Burim's command, the last breathing thing the driver would ever hear.

The van pulled at the curb in front of the crowded bistro as Allison waved down their taxi and stepped forward, surprised at seeing the driver who looked familiar from,... *Budapest?*

Crissy served to accommodate a tourist who recognized Evelyn and wanted a photo with her in front of the cafe door. She heard Sarah scream as two young males grabbed both Allison and Amanda, shoving them into a taxi through the side door just before it sped off.

Alex and Tony entered French territory at Calais for the five-plus hour drive to Paris, both noting their phones were flooded with messages.

Tony quickly called Crissy, who sounded like a basket case.

"Why haven't you been answering your phone!?" she yelled.

"We've been in the Channel Tunnel, baby. What's up?"

"Oh my god, Tony. It's Amanda and Allison. They've been kidnapped!"

Tony froze, not believing what he was hearing. "Crissy, calm down and tell me what happened."

"I can't calm down! The police are here and Sarah is screaming. How long before you get here?"

Tony took in the rest of the story, informing his wife they were still nearly three hundred kilometers out. He disconnected, wishing he could drive the rest of the way himself. Informing Alex of the details, he grabbed the side of the passenger seat, knowing his brother would press the gas pedal down, and hard.

The *Commissariat de Police*, the term for police station, was a buzz with their normal activity adding to the explosive news the famous Amanda Cook, fiancée of racing driver, Alex Moretti, had been kidnapped in front of a prominent Paris bistro in broad daylight, along with her older sister, Allison.

A throng of media reporters began to gather outside in anticipation of a press conference, with each filling their waiting time discussing anything related to the saga of the American Cooks and Italian-American Morettis. The immense media fodder already in the public domain provided no shortage of stories about the Romeo and Juliet-style history of the feud between the Morettis and the Cooks, adding to boundless theories about who could have been behind the kidnapping.

With Sarah so upset she could hardly speak, Crissy filled Tony and Alex in as best she could on what happened. "We were all standing out in front of the bistro when our shuttle van pulled up. Two young men got out and quickly shoved Amanda and Allison through the side door and sped off before we could even react. Sarah started screaming and next thing I knew the police were showing up."

Alex escorted Tony along with Crissy and Sarah through the web of cameras as the two entered the building and were led to the office of a captain, who also had an officer from Interpol in attendance.

Brief introductions were exchanged as the law officers readily recognized the internationally famous racing brothers, while both waited anxiously for an update. Alex was, of course, most distraught and Tony did most of the talking.

"We've located the shuttle van in a basement parking garage located in Porte de La Chapelle, one of the undesirable sections of Paris," the captain began. "The driver had been shot in the head. Unfortunately, the three security cameras in the garage were inoperative at the time. Every tenant in the building has been questioned. Of course, Monsieur, the residents in La Chapelle are not noted for being cooperative with police."

Alex was not pleased. "What are the chances of Amanda and her sister being found, Captain?"

"We're doing what we can, Monsieur. This was a kidnapping well-planned out and by serious miscreants as noted by their open willingness to kill a taxi driver. We get young women kidnapped in Paris every week. Unfortunately, few are found unless the perpetrators make a mistake, which forces us to wait until we hear from them."

Lieutenant Meier from Interpol spoke up. "This may not be a typical human trafficking case. The fact these girls have extremely wealthy parents lends this to be a kidnap-for-ransom case."

"Well, which of you gentlemen is in charge of the case?" Alex asked, sounding somewhat exasperated.

"I am for now, Monsieur, Captain Le Fleur replied. Interpol will take charge if the hostages identify as being outside our jurisdiction."

"I just want my fiancée and her sister back unharmed," Alex replied, working to appear rational. "What can we do to help?"

"Just allow us to do our jobs. You will make statements to the media. We understand that. But please, do not engage in separate negotiations. We will want to have a meeting with all family members as soon as possible. Since the girls' father is in America, we will hold an online conference later today, Monsieur. It is important that everyone is on the same page.

※※

The tenement apartment building in the seedy section of Paris was the residence of a longtime Basha associate from Bucharest, one who cooperated in taking out the security cameras hours before the scheduled arrival and arranging the alternate two vehicles in waiting.

Three hours later, the silver Citroën CX-5 motored down the A6 expressway toward Dijon, just northeast of the Swiss border. The single male driver, fresh from a clean shave, would draw little attention at the border checkpoint. The two captives were both sedated in the rear of the vehicle, bound together and covered with blankets. Burim and Dominik, both also having a fresh shave and change of clothing, would follow twenty kilometers behind in a small white Volkswagen Polo GTI.

Both vehicles had been stolen with separate stolen plates which would be disposed of later the following morning. Burim smiled, confident this free-lance mission would rapidly elevate his station in the organization.

"Damn it, Sarah! How long have I been trying to disengage this family from this Moretti outfit!? Now look at what's happened!"

Sarah had been in a constant state of tears since it happened and lacked any current resolve to push back against her husband. "This isn't helpful, Byron. You can blame me, you can blame Andy Moretti, or you can blame anyone you want, but that won't bring our girls back. Now, please."

"Who will be on this Zoom call?"

"I don't know, Byron."

"I see no good reason for the Morettis to be involved now."

"Byron, Crissy Moretti was there, right beside me. Amanda is engaged to be married to Alex Moretti. Get a grip!"

Byron was angry, but forced himself to lower his temperature. "Allison sent me a text message that the two of you were flying home tomorrow morning. Are you still coming?"

"Oh no. My daughters are here. I can't leave, Byron. I think you should be here yourself."

Dalton saw the news alert on television. "Son-of-a-bitch, Cotton! Can you believe this shit!? Now what are we going to do?"

James had brought Remi to an old farm near the small town of Taxashaw, just south of the North and South Carolina line, owned by an old army buddy who let him hunt there.

"Well, at least we did get sixty grand out of her."

"Sixty grand? The bitch is a millionaire, Cotton! This was my big chance in life! I'm screwed!"

James kept wishing she would refer to things as *we*, but had learned disappointment had come with the territory when it came to his relationship with Remi Dalton. "Did I not tell you to never discuss her on your own phone? At least while she's somehow in captivity, you won't have to worry about her showing up to kill you, Remi."

"What about them assholes outside my trailer? They haven't been kidnapped!"

"I wouldn't worry about them as much. She's gone and they'll stop getting paid, so they'll disappear eventually."

"I wanted to shake the bitch down for more money, Cotton! Now there is no way."

"Oh, I don't know. I'll come up with something, so long as you're nice to me."

Interpol hosted the Zoom call early that evening. The guests included both the girl's parents and their fiancés, neither of whom shared pleasantries.

Interpol Captain Russo's main reason for wanting all the parties on was to stress the need to negotiate with the captors with one voice, in effect, coordinating everything through them.

"How long before we should expect to hear from these monsters?" Byron asked.

"I would expect in a day or so. They will get the number to call from the captives. As such, expect the call to come into your phone, Monsieur Cook, but it could come into any of you other three."

"What is your expectation?" Aaron Williams asked, a question that had been posed and answered multiple times during the previous afternoon hours.

"I expect a large monetary sum to be demanded in exchange for their release."

"What's the chances of these thugs demanding cash for the release of the girls separately?" Alex asked, recalling something he had seen on the news weeks ago regarding the conflict in Israel.

"Possible, oui Monsieur. But that would dramatically increase their risk. Thus, I am doubtful of that."

Byron scoffed. "Do you really think these animals care about risks, Captain?"

"I believe this crime was not committed by a few low-level street thugs. They knew who these young women were and where they would be. They know they have wealthy parents and prominent fiancés. This was planned and orchestrated in a way that suggests a higher level of organized crime organization. Like a major corporation, these syndicates seldom take these kinds of steps without considering the risk factor."

The session ended with the four guests discussing who would stand by in Paris with Sarah and Alex there now and Byron committing to fly in the next morning. Aaron would be on stand-by, subject to the Marine Corps granting him leave from duty in San Diego.

Byron arrived in Paris the following morning and both he and Sarah appeared at a press conference, making a public appeal for information on their daughter's whereabouts and for the captors to release them.

There was immediate friction between Byron and Alex Moretti, thus Alex made his own public comments separately so as not to cause any more consternation. He now had a constant state of nausea and had to take some strong sleeping pills just to get a few hours of shut-eye.

The police announced they made a positive identification of one of the perps caught on the bistro outside security camera. His name was Dominik Markovic, a twenty-year-old Serbian national with a rap sheet of car theft, sexual assault, and suspected involvement in prostitution and human trafficking. His image now appeared all over the world press, both main and social, giving the family at least some semblance of hope that progress was being made.

Eduardo was not happy. His nephew, long a young man with a rogue streak, had taken it upon himself to nab both Cook sisters, including the one who was to pay them through Eric Jordan, a young man now totally blitzed.

Blaku worried little about Jordan as there were always those out there who could be corrupted like him, but now he had two of his people out of Atlanta who traveled to Charlotte to stalk this blackmailer, and they had lost her.

The biggest problem was his nephew failing to complete the grab in Budapest and choosing on his own to travel to Paris, way out of their agreed jurisdiction. However, now that Burim did have both of these two girls in hand, the Romanian mafia kingpin saw big money to be made, the black market for two beautiful and relatively young sisters being quite robust. Add to the fact that the girl's father was one of the world's most prominent bankers, just added icing on the cake.

However, one of Burim's young gangsters being identified by the police was disturbing, as his mug was all over the newswires. If the fiery Markovic was arrested, the consequences for the organization were dire. That risk would have to take priority.

✦

The space was dark and dingy. The girls were both mentally and physically tired, scared, and hungry. Sore from being bound together and gagged throughout the long journey from Paris, neither had a clue where they were but knew it was a far cry from the comfortable surroundings they were accustomed to.

The two captive sisters examined their surroundings, a dusty cellar that had little in creature comforts. Two small windows, both filthy and having multiple bars over them, allowed some faint light in during the day. There were a few half-empty paint cans in one corner stacked on a rough wooden workbench and in another corner an old antique-looking cooking stove.

Allison was distraught in more ways than one. Her plan to rid herself of Amanda in Budapest had blown up in her face, all over something as folly as Amanda wearing a rare cap. She had not established any plan "B" with Eric Jordan and was shocked in Paris when the same mobsters had shown up and grabbed both her and her sister.

She did have the wits not to let on anything but shock and fear toward Amanda, refraining for now from screaming at the captors, which she was convinced would serve little purpose. Her thoughts of anger were directed toward Jordan instead. *That bastard sold me out! If I ever get out of here...*

"Where do you think we are?" Amanda whimpered.

"I haven't a clue, sister."

"What do you think will happen to us?"

Allison had the same thoughts but took her lead as the dominant sibling always had. "I assume they're after some sort of ransom. They know our parents are rich."

"Oh God, poor Mom. I can't imagine what she's going through," Amanda stated, while also thinking of Alex. *Where is my knight in shining armor?... He's a race driver, Amanda, not some super cop.*

They could hear activity on the upper floors but couldn't understand the language. It sounded like all males and not especially pleasant. Allison moved a couple of the old paint cans against the damp concrete wall and stood atop them on her tiptoes in an attempt a look out of one of the dusty windows.

"We're in a city and there are low-rent apartments across the street. Not a good neighborhood."

"Are we still in Paris?" Amanda asked anxiously.

"I can't tell. There are no signs that I can see."

Both froze as they heard the door at the top of the wooden steps open and some light show through. Footsteps were heard and a rough-looking tough approached with a paper plate including some black bread and sausages along with a single bottle of water.

The male appeared to be in his early to mid-twenties, stocky, and dark-completed, perhaps of Arab descent. He didn't speak as he set the plate on the floor, eyeing the two with a sinister lust.

"Where are we?" Allison asked boldly.

"You will eat," he responded coldly.

"I need to use the bathroom," Allison added.

The thug just grunted and turned to retreat back up the stairs, shutting the door behind him and restoring them to near darkness. An hour later, he returned carrying a large metal bucket which he sat under the steps. "You will shit in that."

"We will need some toilet paper," Allison replied angrily.

"What does this look like, American whore, a five-star hotel?"

⚑✕⚑

The Belgian Grand Prix was held under a cloud of darkness. Andy Moretti made a decision to withdraw his entire team and the overall enthusiasm surrounding the whole weekend was dampened as the worldwide news media was dominated by the kidnapping of the American young women, one of whom was the very popular fiancée of one of Formula One's rising stars.

Andy, Miles, and Adam Herrera were on hand to lend the PR effort for the sponsors, all of whom put on their best faces of support and sympathy. While they all acknowledged the seriousness of the crime perpetrated on Alex Moretti's fiancée and her sister, they also knew there were chances the young women may never be found. Andy had now withdrawn from one Grand Prix and faced what would happen next. Fortunately, they were entering a lengthy summer break for the F1 teams. They were all hoping and praying for the girls' quick release while planning for the real possibility of having to cover the Dutch Grand Prix without their new lead driver.

Byron and Sarah both spent ample time appearing on network news programs, pleading for their daughters' release. Sarah was quite annoyed by some of the journalists' questions regarding relations between Byron and Andy and/or whether he blamed his future in-laws for his daughters being kidnapped.

She was equally annoyed at some of his answers and broke into one question herself, declaring a kidnapping like this could have happened in any large city in the US as well. Off camera, there was obvious tension between the two as Byron had obviously not let go of his animosity toward the Morettis, going back to the trial.

"This is not helping, Byron."

"You know Allison and Amanda would both be alive and well back home if they would never have met these wops."

"Yes, Byron Cook. How many times are you going to tell me that?"

Burim sat at the small kitchen table consuming some sausage on a bun and downing his few beers. The boredom of waiting was setting in. Once advised of what his nephew had accomplished, his uncle had directed that he transport the captives to a safe house in Bucharest, wanting them on his own turf. The strongman had considered traveling to Romania to take charge of this prize himself but the risk of his being arrested when traveling back to Europe was too high, thus he sat back briefly to observe how Burim would handle this, the first significant undertaking he would have as underboss.

Dominik had been a challenge for Burim from the start but had been loyal to him in the two years since bringing him on. The directive received from Tijuana was somewhat unsettling. He would not let him out of his sight and the orders to stay inside were making both young Romanians quite edgy. While both had grabbed too many young women off the streets of the Balkan countries to count, the two sisters with their photo-model looks were a cut above what they were accustomed to, and the orders to leave them clean and unscathed were more taxing for young Markovic with every passing day.

"I want the mouthy one, Burim."

"You leave your stinking fuckin' hands off, Dominik. There's too much gold in these two."

"How long am I going to be stowed up in this fucking place?" Young Markovic was accustomed to frequenting one of their many strip clubs in Bucharest's red-light district and having his way with any of the young women he wished, mainly desiring the newly acquired.

"It shouldn't be long. Now take them some food and water."

⚑✖⚑

The two had not spoken in over three years when they met and agreed to a general framework to divide Europe, as not to compete and step on each other's toes. Anton was extremely angry that one of the captors had been identified as a young Romanian with a long record, a youth tied to the Blaku *Brigăzi,* the local term for Romanian mafia.

The Frenchman knew Eduardo would not be forthcoming in taking any responsibility for the stunt in Paris, and as such, these organized crime leaders had to establish concern and suspicion toward each other, mindsets that always served as a basis for their relations. While Laurent had no appetite for such actions involving high-profile targets, he believed Blaku to be quite the opposite, although the Romanian had no recent history of violating their agreed-upon boundaries.

"You do realize, Monsieur Blaku, this episode will place focus on all of our operations." Laurent found himself purposely addressing the Romanian in a condescending manner, feeling the man to be less of a threat since he had gone into exile in Mexico.

"I am offended by your tone, Senior Laurent." *Touché!*

"This happened on my turf, Eduardo. But the one identified perp is Romanian, I would call on you to help me identify them and deal with this effectively. Can we both agree on that?"

"Of course, Anton," Eduardo replied, and the two disconnected. *I hate that frog bastard!*

The case was still being officially handled by the police in Paris as no credible evidence had surfaced suggesting the Cook girls had been transferred out of the city. As this had become the most high-profile kidnapping in decades, the tip lines were flooded with false sightings and wild-goose chases which thus far had produced nothing.

Byron and Sarah had now passed their period of vindictiveness and settled into a very stressful game of waiting. Both had agreed to cooperate with the authorities fully in allowing them to handle all negotiations with the captors, at least for now, including having their personal phones tapped and recorded at police headquarters. With each passing day, their anxiety grew with the temptation to take action themselves. On the sixth day, the two made a joint announcement at a press conference that a one-hundred-thousand-dollar reward would be issued to anyone who provided credible information that would lead to the safe release of their daughters. While the police generally welcomed any action that would entice anyone to provide leads, this new reward offer would naturally add to a new flood of bogus incoming calls.

Alex was being prodded by the family to go ahead and fly back home, but he resisted as if somehow believing he needed to be right there at the scene of the crime. His relationship with Byron remained frigid, and the two would still never appear in front of the cameras together. One thing regarding Alex did appear obvious. All plans of driving for the young racing star were suspended for the time being.

※

Andy himself avoided confrontation with Byron and flew home to deal with race team matters while determined to table an issue with Sabetha, who appeared in no hurry to vacate his residence.

Matilde could tell by the look on Andy's face the day would not be business as usual. Following their traditional greetings, Andy was quick to speak his mind. "Mamma, we have faced more challenges than any one family ever deserves, and now this latest trauma with Amanda and her sister. You would think that Sabetha would have at least called, offer some solace to Alex,.. or something."

"I do know it's bothering her, Andy. She's become quite distant this last week, but I know it's bothering her."

"Well, it's time for a *Come-to-Jesus* meeting with her."

"She's out by the pool, Andy."

Sabetha Moretti was a very troubled woman. She knew her longtime boyfriend, Anton Philippe Laurent, was involved in all sorts of underworld activity. He did have his legitimate businesses, but she knew by the characters who he met and associated with that Anton had a very dark side and seemed he was always being investigated by Interpol. She had overheard a behind-closed-door conversation between him and his younger brother regarding the police wanting to question everyone in his personal and business orbit, including Sabetha herself. For that reason, she had sought temporary refuge in the States, all to Anton's approval. If push came to shove, the European authorities could have worked with the FBI and sought her out, or taken the more serious step of having her arrested and expedited. If it ever got to that point, she knew her life would be in imminent danger.

Andy strolled outside and sat down next to her on one of the poolside lounge chairs. "Sabetha, we need to talk."

"I know, Andy. I know it's high time for me to go back... I'm sorry about what I said about Madam Cook." Sabetha had tried to lure her ex-husband to bed and it backfired, a watershed moment in her life as no man had ever rejected her sexually. *Madam Sarah is so beautiful, so pure with her polite accent, and so kind. Why wouldn't he be attracted to her?*

Andy hesitated, caught a bit off guard. "You need help, Sabetha. You need rehab. We should check you into a local clinic before you leave."

"No, that's all right. I appreciate your hospitality, Andy. Anton is being investigated by Interpol and he wanted me out of sight for a while."

That's the kind of people you choose to attach yourself to? Andy thought but held back saying so. "So you think this Anton is behind this?"

"No, I do not. He knows my connection with Mademoiselle Amanda."

"Are you telling me your sugar daddy is too morally upstanding? Really, Sabetha?"

"I'm not telling you that. But I do know him and he likes to operate in the shadows. He would know this would dominate the news around Paris for weeks if not months. Anton has always been leery of too much publicity."

"You know the family is suffering over what happened. You could have at least called Alex."

"I know, Andy. It's obviously too late for me to be a good mother now."

"It's never too late, Sabetha. You should just call your sons every once in a while... I'm sorry is a good start."

"Noted, Andy." Sabetha was never one who took preaching well. "The girls were kidnapped for either ransom or being trafficked. Because their parents are multi-millionaires, it is likely the former. But it could be the latter... Or both."

"What are you saying, Sabetha?"

She looked over at him with tears forming. "Last year there was a young girl kidnapped in Amsterdam, the daughter of a well-to-do restaurateur. The criminals demanded ransom and while working with the police, her father paid them two hundred thousand pounds. Their daughter was never released despite the payment and has not been seen since."

"So you believe the girl was trafficked?"

"They could have held the girl and demanded more money," Sabetha explained. "Or she could have been sold on the black market."

"Or they could have just killed the girl."

"She was sold or forced into prostitution, Andy. A young and vibrant young woman would have no value to them dead."

Andy took a deep breath. His ex-wife seemed to be all too knowledgeable in such matters. "You can stay here until you get yourself cleaned out, Sabetha. But that does not mean indefinitely."

Chapter 6

The Price of Cotton

It had certainly been a season of highs and lows at Moretti Motorsport. The Formula One team had started respectable in the first six races with Tony consistently gaining mid-field finishes. Leland languished four to five places behind, knowing this would likely be his last tour in F1.

The IndyCar squad was a different story, entering the month of May with no top-five finishes. Andy had continued to be stressed out over the pending lawsuit unsettled with Byron Cook and Unibank, which was holding up bringing Alex back into the fold. However, things were looking up when Tony won the pole for the 500 as an F1 team "guest" and a miracle circumstance developed with former Moretti driver Evelyn Stevens that brought about an unlikely and quick settlement to the huge lawsuit on extremely favorable terms. Alex replaced injured brother Tony and promptly won the 500, going on to win three of the four next races, and lifting up the entire IndyCar squad.

While the IMSA and NASCAR divisions were holding their own, the F1 team had fallen into despair with their lead driver's injury until Tony convinced Andy to put Alex in the car. That had seemed to be high risk as most F1 pilots had undergone years of driving in all formulas including miles of testing in Formula One cars before even attempting to run in an actual race.

Alex, however, took to the car like he was born to it, nearly finishing on the podium in his first race despite a pit stop snafu related to tire wear. The whole European operation was fully pumped preparing for Spa when their new star took a personal gut punch and had not appeared in the Silverstone facility since.

A very emotional person, Alex had hit the bottle again and now struggled to even get out of bed, shower, or shave. Crissy and Tony paid him a visit at his Paris hotel, avoiding the entrenched throng of reporters out front.

"This is not what Amanda wants, Alex," Crissy began.

Alex looked up at her, speechless. He had somehow felt that his being there near the scene was important, as though the cops would slow their investigative efforts if he left. He was tired of visiting the police station every day and learning about the dozens of new leads that had come in and produced nothing, while dealing with the reporters asking the same questions and having to give the same answers.

"Your hanging out here in such a state is not solving anything, brother," Tony added. "Why don't you fly home and have Grandma feed and take care of you, if just for a few days? Amanda's parents are here. When some news pops up, you'll know about it immediately.

Alex didn't respond, which didn't mean no. "Give me an hour."

Crissy and Tony left Alex's suite and headed down to the lobby cafe, resisting the temptation to step outside because of the still mass of reporters and cameramen. Alex appeared just past 2:00 PM, looking quite sprite after several days of personal neglect.

Tony had avoided a tinder subject but wanted to table it before heading back to England. Crissy gave her husband a concerning look but he had held his tongue long enough. "Alex, I know this is awkward, but we need to discuss this. The team has gone into limp mode and needs direction. You need to announce something regarding your status."

"Give him a little time, honey," Crissy quickly added in defense of her traumatized brother-in-law.

"I'm not there yet, Tony," Alex replied. "How would that look, my just blowing off something as serious as my fiancée's kidnapping?"

"I wouldn't call it that."

"I think my being in Paris, speaking to the press every day, helps keep the pressure on the police."

Tony wanted to tell his brother it was wishful thinking on his part but refrained. "Well Alex, there should be some way to accomplish both."

The three flew the twin-engine jet to England, landing late afternoon at London's Luton International Airport, forty-five kilometers from Silverstone. Tony would head to the team facility there while his spouse and brother would both fly home, getting a much-needed break from an eventful and traumatic European trip.

Tony was met at the curb by Ian Miles, a man as stressed out as anyone over the past week. No one, including the Moretti Formula One team manager, dared to suggest that Alex should just get back to work.

"We need a plan for Zandvoort, Tony. You know I didn't agree with the withdrawal at Spa," Miles stated, a man always known as having an iceman persona.

"What about Wolf?"

"Is that a joke, Tony?"

"Ian, I don't believe that either Verstappen or Hamilton are available."

"Our sponsors are getting anxious. I have to have a plan for them."

"Let Adam Herrera handle the sponsors, Ian," Tony replied, knowing that as sharp as Miles was in all aspects of managing a race team, his social skills in public relations were not a strength. "How is Robinson doing on the simulator?"

Miles shook his head. "He does fine on the sim. It's when he's in the car that I worry about. At least we have another couple of bloody weeks to prepare for,... something. Assuming nothing develops with those two young women, what do you think of the chances of Alex coming back?"

You are a cold fish, aren't you, Ian? "I wouldn't count on that. My brother is an emotional wreck. I'm not sure he's in any state to drive a race car at three hundred kilometers per hour," Tony replied, but was thinking. *Perhaps that's exactly the therapy he needs right now.*

The flight across the Atlantic seemed to take forever, as Crissy could tell Alex felt guilty about leaving Paris. She regretted leaving Tony in England but dearly missed her boys, ever confident in leaving the two in the care of Tony's grandmother and aunt, but anxious about having the two around their own grandmother.

"You know Tony is preparing himself for the day when he will manage Moretti Motorsport and you will be the star driver," Crissy told him, feeling the need to make conversation and ease the stress of the issue regarding Amanda's kidnapping.

"So you really think his driving days are over, or is that wishful thinking on your part, Crissy?"

"You don't seem convinced yourself, Alex."

"I think he would resign himself to driving if you put enough pressure on him."

"Is that such a bad thing, Alex? Would you quit driving, for Amanda's sake?"

Alex stared out at the ocean waves below in serious reflection. *She has never asked me if I would ever stop. But that first time she saw me crash... It was three years ago at Indy. She barely knew me then, but that look in her eyes...*

"Well, Alex?"

"I'm sure that day could come... But Tony is at the peak of his career, on top of his game. He may have been the best in the world before Indy."

"He says that about you."

"I know better. Tony is so much smarter than I am. Always so much in control, never a false move in the car, like Dad used to say about Alain Prost. He would have been world champion, eventually. Zak Brown even joked about my brother jumping ship and driving a McLaren. It was one of those off-the-cuff comments designed to generate laughter, but to also start a buzz."

"How would that work if either of you were not driving for your dad?"

"Good question. You know we get paid nothing compared to the better drivers on top-tier teams. I know it's been mentioned that we would both become partial owners. Anyway, I'm sorry if I'm making you feel guilty. You're probably right. Tony's condition is resolute to where he is on the team now."

Now Crissy stared out the window, deep in her own thoughts. *Would her husband really think about getting in a race car again? I'm not sure he could handle it... I'm not sure that I could.*

Alex knew his father's real dream was that both boys would each win at Indy and that both would drive a Moretti in Formula One. He would sometimes compare us to teammates in the past, the example of McLaren in the mid-eighties when Niki Lauda would tutor Prost, the hard charger who would learn from the master, or when Michael Schumacher at the end of his career would impress Nico Rosberg. *We'll get there, brother.*

Alex received a text from Sarah, asking him to meet her at his father's home immediately. His mother had something important to share with them in private regarding the Cook girls. He and Crissy landed in Concord late at night and were greeted by Andy, who proceeded to drive them to his place, as Alex didn't wish to wait another minute to talk to his mother about Amanda's disappearance. Pulling up to the circle drive in front of the residence, Sarah's SUV was already there. The three walked in and were greeted cheerfully by Matilde and Maria, who escorted them to the family room where Sarah and Sabetha awaited.

Small talk was quickly discarded as Sarah spoke. "Sabetha, tell them what you just told me."

Andy's ex looked rough. Her normal signs of addiction were accented with hours of dried tears. "I have been in a bad relationship with Anton for a long time. He is very wealthy and has always given me whatever I wanted. He owns several businesses, mostly legitimate, but is also involved with other dark ventures."

"How do you know this, Mother?" Alex asked, wanting her story to get to the point as related to Amanda's disappearance.

"The characters who would constantly be around. Many were very strong, fit men and had guns. I was always told that Anton and I needed protection from the same type of people who kidnapped Amanda and her sister, but I knew that was not all of it. Quite often these men would come and meet behind locked doors. I would listen sometimes with my ear to the door. Anton had accounts with several banks in London, Frankfort, and Zurich. I often heard the names Herr Helmet Grether and Zurich International Bank, mostly when these private meetings were held.

Almost a year ago, an article appeared in the *Le Parisian* about Anton being investigated for illegal activities including narcotics, prostitution, and...," Sabetha paused, fighting back tears.

Sarah reached over and placed a hand on hers. "Please proceed, Sabetha."

The woman composed herself and continued. "And human trafficking."

The family all became silent and shared serious glances.

"So, what happened to the investigation?" Andy asked.

"I read where Interpol has dropped their case against him, but I did overhear Anton tell one of his bodyguards to keep a close eye on me. That was right after the news from Indianapolis. I told Anton I wanted to travel to Detroit to see my family."

"I'm surprised he let you out of his sight," Tony stated.

"He didn't. The whole time I was in Detroit, he had one of his thugs watching me. After Detroit, I was booked on a flight back, but chose to come down here instead."

"You placed this whole family in danger, Sabetha!" Andy yelled excitedly.

"Please, Andy. This is not helpful," Matilde interjected.

"Do you believe your life is in danger?" Crissy asked seriously.

"Not since the charges were dropped. Anton has people at Interpol bought and paid for."

"Then why the extended stay, Sab?" Marie asked, speaking for everyone.

"I've wanted to get away from Anton for a long time. When I got here, I saw such a family. My sons had met such good women. My husband had built such a great company, I had beautiful grandchildren, and things were so,... normal here." Sabetha chose not to share with the family that she didn't think Anton would ever let her leave him... Not alive, anyway.

"And you have another problem," Andy exclaimed.

"Yes, I have a heroin addiction. I want to cleanse myself of it and know I could never do that back there."

"Let's get back to Amanda's disappearance," Sarah spoke. "Do you think this Anton is behind Amanda and Allison's kidnapping?"

"No. Anton never wanted to engage in high-profile ventures. He would always fear such publicity."

"So, why would you think his banker, this Herr Grether, is somehow involved?"

"I have heard petite tips over time. Whenever anything was mentioned related to the dark business, his name would always come up. One of Anton's henchmen mentioned something about all of their competitors laundering their cash in Herr Grether's bank. He is the one who knows where all the skeletons are buried."

"You say you believe this Anton has the police in his pocket," Alex stated. "It sounds like you believe it would be a waste of time for us to talk to them about this Swiss banker."

"I don't know. Surely not every cop in Europe is on their payroll."

Sarah reluctantly chose to call Byron, deciding this latest revelation was quite important. "Byron, I am here on a speakerphone with Sabetha Moretti. She has something important to share with you."

"Monsieur Cook, I have some information that I believe may help you find your daughters."

Sabetha Moretti? Andy's ex-wife? We can't seem to ever get away from these Morettis! "I'm listening."

"There is a banker in Zurich. His name is Helmet Grether. He will know who can lead you to Amanda and her sister."

Byron was familiar with Helmut Grether, the two having met at a conference in Frankfort a couple of years earlier. "How would he know anything about this?" Byron asked skeptically.

"He knows all of the major players involved with human trafficking in Europe."

Byron was taken aback by what this French woman was saying. "Are you suggesting that Helmet Grether is a criminal? Do you have proof of this?"

"No, Monsieur. Please, just trust me that I know enough. If my daughters were kidnapped in Europe, Monsieur Grether would be the first place I would go for information. I wish I could offer more. I will trust in your confidence."

Byron and Sarah decided to have a personal conversation with the Swiss banker without involving the police, at least initially. Flying back to Paris to first get an update from the local police, they were not encouraged by the lack of progress. This Markovik character, who was identified at the scene, had seemed to disappear and all other leads that had come in had turned up nothing.

Grether hung up the phone, surprised at the call received by the American Byron Cook in requesting an audience that very day. He had recalled meeting Cook, the very progressive banker from America, and the whole world had now become acquainted with the Cook family over the tragic news of their daughters' kidnapping.

The brief flight from Paris to Zurich took an hour, a trip made rather uncomfortable because Carolyn Tyler had traveled to Paris with Byron as though she was already a step-parent. This made the flight seem awkward as barely three words were spoken between the three of them.

They took a shuttle from the airport and were dropped off in front of the historic bank building twenty minutes later.

"Carolyn, if you wouldn't mind waiting for us here," Byron instructed. "I think the two of us need to meet with Herr Grether alone."

The two women shared a brief uncomfortable look as Sarah didn't believe this to be something Byron's mistress should have to be told.

The executive secretary announced the guests' arrival, and the aged banker came out of his office to greet them. "Herr Cook, how pleasant to see you again," he stated while the two shook hands. "And your lovely wife, welcome to Zurich. I wish our meeting could be under better circumstances for you."

Sarah blushed slightly at the reference to her being the lovely wife as she sized up the man. Helmut Grether was a portly man near seventy with thin greying hair and a goatee beard, hardly the type of man she pictured as being involved criminally in anything related to human trafficking. But she also knew looks could be deceiving.

She had ample time to reflect on her thoughts about Andy Moretti's ex-wife. Despite her opinions about Sabetha, she didn't believe the woman would disclose something of this nature about such a distinguished figure for no reason. Struggling to discount any preconceived notions, she felt there must be something sinister about him.

Grether ushered the two into his office and shut the door behind them. "Could I offer you coffee, tea, or anything?"

Byron and Sarah shared a look as he shook his head. "We're fine, Herr Grether."

"I am so sorry for this news about your daughters, which has dominated the news media here. Has there been any positive development on that?"

"Thank you for your concern, Herr Grether. Unfortunately, nothing has changed."

"It has been, what, a week now? I would think the perpetrators would have reached out by now."

"Eight days," Sarah replied blankly. "Eight long days."

"Such a terrible world we live in now. How may I be of assistance?"

"Herr Grether, we are from North America, and other than a few prominent individuals in the financial world, we are not that familiar with the many movers and shakers in Europe. I was hoping you could give us some advice on who we should be talking to, someone who could lead us to our daughters' captors."

Grether leaned back in his comfortable executive leather chair, a defense mechanism as he was taken aback by such an inquiry. "Well, Herr Cook, I'm just a simple banker like yourself. I believe such questions are better directed toward Interpol. Of course, I know you have already been in close contact with them, no?"

"Yes," Byron replied quickly. "But they are, should I say, reluctant to name names without any solid proof of any impropriety. I thought you may know some of the players here, some who may know those who would engage in less than legal activity."

Grether's expression changed quickly. "I'm not at all certain what you are asking of me, Herr Cook."

Sarah chimed in before Byron collected his thoughts. "We were told by a confidential source that you would be the one who could lead us to the people who kidnapped our girls."

"A confidential source, you say?"

"Yes, sir. This person gave us the information in confidence," Sarah replied, taken as a bit of sarcasm.

Now Grether's eyes shot daggers at Sarah and then toward Byron. "Indeed, we Swiss bankers know well the meaning of confidentiality. Are you making some sort of accusation, Frau Cook?"

"Of course she is not," Byron answered quickly. "We are under much stress over our daughters' disappearance and just looking for answers anywhere we can get them."

"I have advised you to consult with Interpol on such matters," Grether sternly stated. "I know nothing of these criminals who kidnapped your daughters and have little else to offer you in that regard. Now, I am a very busy man, and if there is nothing else—"

The banker stood up as a signal for the two to depart, not offering a hand or anything but a rather distasteful expression. Byron and Sarah themselves stood and walked out, nodded to the banker's secretary, and entered the elevator.

Standing silent until the elevator doors closed, Byron lashed out. "Sarah! You don't come to a meeting with a man like Helmet Grether and talk to him like that!"

"He's lying."

"You don't know that," Byron stated, feeling exasperated. "You open yourself up to libel with that kind of talk."

"Don't be a wimp, Byron."

"Sarah, you can't keep going off half-cocked, throwing out accusations without proof!"

"You mean like the way you have behaved these past two years!?" Sarah barked. "I'm immune to fear of lawsuits by now, Byron... And I know he's lying."

Anton Philippe Laurent lounged on his sixty-two-foot yacht moored in Monte Carlo, enjoying a cigar following a mid-afternoon round of sex with two Swedish girls that were arranged the day before. The fifty-nine-year-old billionaire had an army of subordinates to manage his empire of investments that included shipping, electronics manufacturing, and real estate, all cover for his more illicit endeavors.

He had turned his phone beeper back on, checking the dozens of calls that had come in. Most he discarded, some he delegated to his right-hand man, and one he knew he should return.

"Herr Grether, I see you called earlier."

"Philippe, I trust you are well," the banker stated, always addressing the Frenchman by his middle name.

"Oui, Herr Grether." *I know you didn't call to check on my health.* "What can I do for you?"

"Is this phone secured?"

"You're insulting me. Of Course it is."

"I had a very unpleasant visit earlier today."

"Oui, go on."

"Herr Byron Cook and his wife paid me a visit."

"And?"

"Frau Cook stated she had a confidential source who informed her that I could somehow help them in getting their daughters released."

"And you believe this visit is somehow connected to me?" Anton replied in a tone to relay that offense was taken.

"I never stated as much. Philippe, tell me your fingerprints are nowhere near this."

"When did you get religion, Herr Grether? You of all people know our business is not all pristine. But no, my people had nothing to do with this. I would know, of course."

"And how is Sabetha? I assume she is still on holiday in the US?"

"Oui."

"She is this Alex Moretti's mother, the young man engaged to be married to the Cooks' youngest daughter. I can assume Sabetha and Frau Sarah Cook know each other."

"I don't know about that," Anton replied testily. He did know that his longtime girlfriend and Sarah Cook were indeed together in Detroit several weeks earlier and that Sarah had been staying at her ex-husband's home north of Charlotte since.

"I don't like this unpleasant exposure, Philippe."

"And you think I do? I will look into this and keep you informed should something significant develop."

"I know you will, Philippe." Grether closed as the two disconnected. He wanted to take the Frenchman at his word, believing that Laurent would not undertake anything so rash. One could never be fully certain, but Grether did know one or two other *clients* who likely would.

Laurent was both angry and troubled, advised earlier that Sabetha should be silenced to avoid any more worries with Interpol. He had kept his relationship with the famous French model mostly to stroke his ego, never believing she would betray him or that she knew anything that could damage him, anyway.

"Who else could have dropped Grether's name?" Dion asked. Laurent's right-hand man had been against allowing Sabetha's American holiday from day one. "I'm telling you, Anton. Sabetha knows more than you give her credit for."

"Why have we not learned who is behind all of this?"

"We're still shaking the whole city down, Anton. Thus far, nothing."

⚑⚑

Remi was getting bored. Hanging out on a run-down old hog farm was not her cup of tea. Cotton would leave to work on his sleazy cases early each morning and sometimes not return until after dark. He kept insisting that he was protecting her from danger, but she was seeing his cure as worse than the disease. *I will demand the bastard take me home when he gets in.*

She had a local Charlotte TV station on, casually watching a network game show. Suddenly, there was a break for a news alert. Allison Cook's mother, Sarah, appeared at an impromptu press conference along with Alex Moretti, the famous young race driver so well-known in the Carolinas because of his famous trial.

The two were back in the Charlotte area, making a joint announcement that they were personally increasing the reward for any information leading to the Cook girls' release to a full *million* dollars.

Strange that Byron Cook, the banker and girls' father, was not on the set or even mentioned, Remi felt.

⚑⚑

Byron was not a happy camper as Tyler replayed the press announcement on her phone for his consumption. He then dialed his soon-to-be ex-wife's number. "Sarah, your acting solo on this is not helpful. We need to always show a combined presence."

"What has our combined presence gotten us thus far, Byron? I want my daughters back!"

"Did the Morettis put you up to this?"

Sarah Cook was not a woman inclined to emotional outbursts, but he had struck a nerve. She had always been the subservient spouse, always in support of him, and seldom losing her temper. "Go screw yourself, Byron!" She clicked hard on the disconnect button. *I can't believe I just told him that...* She sighed briefly and consciously shook her head. *But it was about time.*

⚑⚑

Byron had discarded his many messages left at the bank as well as on his personal phone, and they were becoming annoying. *What does this two-bit private eye want now?*

He finally chose to call and put a stop to it. "James, what do you want!?"

"I want to help you find your daughters."

"Yeah, the last time I hired you, Cotton James, it blew up in my face. Now quit calling and leaving me these damned messages!" Click.

⚑⚑

The struggling private detective was dejected. His protected girlfriend, a term that James liked to use whether she agreed with it or not, was giving him hell each minute. He did have a plan, be it a longshot, to try and locate the Cook girls, but needed money and the richest banker in the South had just slammed the door in his face.

He watched a YouTube replay of Sarah Cook's press conference, with Alex Moretti appearing next to her and both taking questions. James knew that bad blood would still exist between Byron Cook and all of the Morettis, even recalling something on social media a few weeks back about a possible romantic connection between Andy Moretti and Sarah Cook. The pending divorce between the Cook girls' parents was still big news. He had an idea.

Alex agreed to meet this character just over a sandwich and beer at a popular bar and grill near the team headquarters facility in Huntersville. He thought he had seen him before, a man dressed like a hybrid between a rodeo bull rider and a Hells Angels biker, but couldn't place him.

James sat down and quickly ordered a draft, putting out a hand. "Cotton James, Alex."

"James," Alex acknowledged. "Have we met before?"

"No, but everyone knows who you are. You're famous, or infamous depending on who is asked."

"What can I do for you, Mr. James?"

"Just call me Cotton. And it's not what you can do for me, it's what I can do for you."

"You have about twenty minutes of my time."

"I'm an independent investigator. I would like to work on finding your fiancée."

Alex leaned back, thinking this cowboy must be a flake. "What, you surely don't think she's being held around here?"

James chuckled. "Not likely. I have a background in army intelligence and spent two tours in Iraq. I have a contact from Israel who works with me. We bagged a ton of terrorists and interdicted a major human trafficking ring once," the slippery P.I. claimed, which was slightly exaggerated. "We're uniquely qualified to find those young women."

"So you believe Amanda and Allison have been abducted by some human traffickers?" Alex thought of the words *sex slave* but couldn't bring himself to say it.

"Not necessarily. The girls' rich parents are the key to keeping them out of that sick privation. No, I'm sure the culprits have a huge ransom in mind."

Alex looked at this rag-tag guy, reminding himself how he must have looked when unbathed and unshaven for days on end. "Mr. James, Cotton if you will, you were in Iraq with this Israeli what, fifteen to twenty years ago. Don't you think the people, places, and things have changed since then?"

"Probably. But the techniques are the same."

"What is your proposal, then?"

"Well, you folks are offering a million-dollar reward, correct? I'll work for the million, but I will need some earnest money, for expenses. You can call it an advance."

Alex gulped his beer, staring forward for a moment. *What's the chance this clown is for real? He may just be some two-bit hustler who ran out of hurricane victims to shake down.* "When can we have a conversation with this Israeli partner of yours?"

"That won't be possible. People in that organization frown on having their identity disclosed."

"Do you have a card? I'll think about it."

"Alex, every day that goes by reduces the chances of your ever seeing Amanda alive again—"

Young Moretti snapped, quickly grabbing the mouthy James by the collar, predicating a quick reaction as James quickly grabbed his wrist, twisting his arm around his back. The bartender quickly signaled for help and a waitress immediately started to dial 911. James released Alex and gently patted him on the back, realizing the handsome young racing champion would be quite recognizable here and he would quickly be outnumbered.

Alex raised a hand, looking around to the many onlookers who had gathered. "It's okay. We're good."

"No offense, Alex. But you have little to lose... And the clock is ticking." James left a ten-dollar bill on the bar and prepared to leave.

"Hold up, James," Alex demanded. "What kind of advance are we talking about?"

Cotton pulled himself back up on the bar stool, looking around and waiting for the two to reacquire a semblance of privacy. "We'll need seventy-five grand to start."

Alex looked at him, actually expecting the sum to be higher. "I'll have to discuss this with Sarah."

"No problem. You know how to get hold of me."

꧁⚑✕⚑꧂

By day ten, both Amanda and Sarah were in dire need of a bath. They had prodded this Dominik character for days and he had only thus far reacted with a creepy contempt. Despite their dingy appearance, the young criminal had gathered some predatory thoughts.

He noticed the two did look very much alike, almost as twins as advertised. But they were different in personality, as one had always an expression of being fearful which was common for captives in his trade. The other one, slightly older, had a more sassy demeanor and one that triggered his twisted desires.

Switching on the single light fixture near the center of the cellar's joist ceiling, he brought down a plastic bucket full of soapy warm water and a sponge. Both girls looked at it with mild anticipation, thankful for anything they could use to wash themselves.

Dominik approached Allison. "Strip off your clothes. I will clean you."

She just stared at him a moment before speaking. "Just leave it. We will make do."

"I said strip off your fucking clothes... Now!"

Allison stepped forward and spit in his face.

"You Yankee bitch!" The angry young Romanian quickly backhanded the rebellious woman before grabbing her blouse and starting to tear it off of her as she fought back frantically by scratching and clawing at his face and neck.

He then reached up and grabbed her by the hair, forcing her head back when he felt a hard pain on the right side of his head. Amanda had jumped up on his back and bit down hard, taking a chunk out of his ear and causing it to bleed profusely.

Dominik hollered with pain, "You fucking American whore!" Now filled with rage, he withdrew a switchblade from his pocket and prepared to teach the younger one a lesson she would never forget. He approached as Amanda screamed, grabbing her by the hair and pulling her head back. "Now you little bitch, you want to know what real bleeding looks like?"

Amanda continued to scream as the blade brushed against her own right ear when a sudden gunshot was heard, causing Dominik to freeze, dropping the knife before falling forward, a pool of blood beginning to color the cold concrete floor beneath him.

Burim stepped forward, holding a German P-38 pistol in his hand, saying nothing. His uncle had directed that Dominik Markovic be eliminated in a timely fashion when his mug had been blasted all over the news media. His misbehavior had just made the task less difficult. *You overvalued yourself, Dominik.*

He then moved to face Amanda, a terrified girl expecting anything. Burim simply nodded and grunted. "You two will clean yourselves and then drag this piece of shit over there, under the steps."

"He will start to stink!" Allison barked, thinking she had to do or say something.

"Do not worry about it. I will bring some Lysol spray later." He then walked back up the steps, extinguishing the lone lightbulb and returning the damp cellar to near darkness.

Following the worst feeling of terror either had ever in their sheltered lives been through, the two sisters had reached a seminal moment. When under duress, Amanda had thrown caution to the wind and acted to protect her sister. When Amanda faced the terror of a knife-wielding attacker, Allison had frozen.

Flying into Tel Aviv was risky. Israel was basically at war with Iran and its proxy terrorist groups, Hezbollah, Hamas, and the Houthis. Cotton had sent his former comrade a message that he would travel to Israel the next day and wanted an audience. As all travelers into the country were closely watched, the former Mossad agent declined an airport pickup, directing James to catch a shuttle to a designated hotel where he would arrange their meeting.

The retired American Army Ranger had heard back from Alex Moretti just an hour and a half after their lunch encounter. Sarah had insisted she wanted to meet him and the three met later that same afternoon in a North Charlotte shopping mall parking lot. His tale about he and the Israeli having a working relationship was quite a stretch but had secured him some cash, and if the Israeli operative didn't want in on the gig, he could perhaps steer James in the right direction.

He checked into his hotel and entered his fourth-floor room, a simple two double-bed floor plan with a small table and comfortable chair in the corner. He would text the Israeli following a trip to the bathroom and prepare for their hookup. Cotton flipped on the light and was jolted. There was the former Mossad operative sitting there in the corner staring at him, a small pistol in hand.

"Whooo! Hang on, Arieh," Cotton stated while showing his empty hands. "That's no way to get reacquainted with old friends."

The former Mossad agent relaxed, placing the Jericho 941 handgun back in his vest pocket. "These are trying times we live in, Cotton. Cannot be too careful."

"Yes, I know. Especially now. I'm surprised you were so easily available." Cotton had not seen Ariel Levy since 2005 but had casually kept up from time to time on social media. The former Mossad officer had definitely aged, his black hair now almost white, and appeared to have lost some weight.

"I retired five years ago. Not that I couldn't be called up. If things get bad enough, we'll all be on the front line."

Cotton had always had a grudging respect for the IDF, realizing 99% of all Americans had no clue what life would be like when one's subdivision is literally fifteen or twenty miles from the battle line where your enemies wanted to kill you. "I appreciate your meeting me on such short notice."

"I know you wouldn't fly all the way over here just to buy me dinner, which I'll oblige you to do. And I know Israel is not high on you Americans' vacation list right now. So, why are you here?"

"I'm sure you have seen the news coverage of the American girls who were kidnapped in Paris."

"Yes, how could I not?"

"Exactly. I'm working for the family. They have hired me to find them."

"You? How did you manage that?" The Israeli would never have guessed this Cotton James would have such prowess or connections.

"These people are actually from my hometown, so let's just say I have a sentimental connection to this case." Cotton was bullshitting Levy, a man who wasn't fooled.

"And they'll pay you a lot if you succeed in returning their daughters to them."

"You always see things so clearly, Arieh."

"So, tell me what you know. Then tell me what you wish to see me about."

"Most of what I know is what has already been reported. The Cook girls were on holiday with their mother and two other young women. They were grabbed outside a popular Paris bistro. It was three men in a shuttle taxi van found abandoned in a rundown apartment parking garage. The taxi driver was found in the back shot in the head. One of the perps was identified as Dominik Markovic, a street thug originally from Bucharest. The captives nor Markovic have been seen or heard from since."

"Not much to go on. Have the captors contacted anyone?"

"No, not yet. But there is an interesting twist. The youngest girl is the fiancée of Alex Moretti, the famous racing driver."

"Yes, I saw the coverage of them at the Indianapolis 500. Quite a story. Because of him and the girls' parents being quite wealthy, I can see why they would be prime targets. And now they are offering a full million-dollar reward."

"Indeed, Arieh. There's more. Moretti's mother is a well-known model from Paris and has been on holiday in America for several weeks. She dropped the name of a prominent Swiss banker to the Moretti family and the girls' parents, claiming the banker could lead them to the captors. His name is Herr Helmet Grether."

"Grether, huh?"

"Sound familiar?"

"Oh yes, I'm familiar. He's the bagman for much of the human trafficking industry worldwide. But Grether is very well connected. Many of the European Union's politicians are in his pocket and more that are not are bought and paid for by his customers. He is very instrumental in setting up shell corporations for the mafia and is rewarded by their laundering massive amounts of cash in his Zurich bank."

"So you believe this Grether knows firsthand who kidnapped the girls?"

"I wouldn't go that far, at least yet. The challenge is proving it. You are not aware of the circumstances surrounding my retirement, are you?"

"How about you enlighten me, Arieh."

"I had an Al-Qaeda terrorist ring fingered to a safe house compound in Berat, Albania. My team wanted to take them alive, of course. We didn't know this was a holding station for dozens of teenage girls who had been kidnapped or entrapped from all over the Balkans. We were successful in busting a half dozen alive including the cowardly *captain*. They were all *persuaded* to sing like birds and we worked with Interpol to build a criminal case and bring down a few layers of their syndicate. This Herr Grether was strongly implicated. The case was suddenly and without cause shut down and I was offered an early retirement with no penalty. I learned that two members of our own Knesset were implicated as well as a prominent general in our own IDF."

"I suppose much has happened since we last worked together. Well, I don't know how lucrative your retirement is, Arieh, but if you'll work with me I will definitely make it worth your while."

"What does that mean?"

"I'll pay your expenses and if we get the girls back, we'll split the remaining amount of the reward, less the expenses, of course."

"Who else is on the team?"

"We're it."

"We'll need help."

"Once we get them fingered, we can bring in some local police."

"No, Cotton. You have no idea where this may lead us, and thus have no idea if local police can be trusted. And I'm not the man I used to be. I have a cancer."

James looked up at his old comrade-in-arms. "I never would have guessed. You look healthy as a horse. A bit thin, maybe, but good." James was attempting to make his old comrade feel better. "How bad is it?"

"It's in my stomach. I've refused treatment and I'm fighting it with an experimental diet, designed to starve the tumor to death."

"How is that going?"

"So far so good, I think. But it has affected my stamina. Again, I'm not what I was the last time you saw me."

"Hell, Arieh, neither am I. Okay, you say we need help, but I can't bankroll an army division. What do you recommend?"

"My younger brother, Alon, is available."

"Is he good?"

"Good enough. He's ten years younger than I am and very fit. Just retired as an Air Force Major, M-16 pilot. Of course, he is subject to being called up any day, but we can't plan for that."

"Okay, let's bring him on board, but you two will split your half of the reward."

"Make it $300,000 each including expenses. This could get dangerous and Alon has a family to support."

"You drive a hard bargain, Arieh... How should we proceed?"

"There are a lot of suspects in Paris, of course. We just have to shake them up... I'll call my brother now."

The call came in at 9:00 AM Paris time. Using an AI voice, the caller demanded that Byron pay five million US dollars in unmarked cash. There would be another call in forty-eight hours with specifics.

The police insisted that Byron keep the caller on so they could trace the call, which he couldn't control as the recorded message completed in twenty-seven seconds and clicked off. The call could not be isolated but had been pegged to a tower in Bucharest, Romania, covering an area with over seven hundred thousand population.

This development did predicate the investigation would be handled by Interpol, and plans were quick to move the case command center to Lyon, just over 450 kilometers south in France. Byron immediately got sideways with the lead investigator, who wanted his own negotiator to do all the talking with the captors. This didn't sit too well with a man like Byron because it was his daughters, his money, and he felt as a negotiator he was as good as it gets. The dispute thus far was all academic, as the captors, using this AI-recorded message format, had closed the door thus far to any back-and-forth negotiations.

No sooner than Sarah was notified by Byron about the call, she got off and contacted Cotton James, who in turn informed Arieh and Alon that there would be another call in forty-eight hours, instructions for paying the five million dollars in exchange for the Cook's daughters. They also learned the call came from Budapest's 10th District known as the Horror of Ho's, an area rife with poverty, corruption, and crime.

🏁

"That is a very bad element there, Cotton. One of the most dangerous in the world," Arieh declared. "But I think the call from Romania must be a diversion. The perps would have to be around Paris to arrange pickup of the cash. I doubt if anyone at that level would be foolish enough to place a call from a place where they were actually keeping the victims."

"We don't exactly have a *Sayeret Matkal* platoon to send in there and start knocking down doors in every seedy house of ill repute in Paris," Alon added, referring to an elite IDF special forces unit.

"And we don't have much time, fellas," Cotton added. "The clock is ticking."

🏁

As the Dutch Grand Prix approached, Miles' panic meter continued to climb. Geoff Leland had never done particularly well at Zandvoort, and the Moretti team manager feared their second car may not even qualify. He wanted to push Andy to encourage Alex's return, knowing it was a tender subject, but things for the team were dire.

His argument was that Amanda and her sister's kidnapping, while still dominating the headlines and social media, would subside eventually and the race team would need to survive. Miles was pushing Andy as hard as he felt possible, hoping the boss wouldn't blow a gasket.

"I can't put this on Alex right now, Ian. You just have to manage the team through it."

"How about we put Tony back in the car?"

"Come on, Ian. Get real."

"It worked for Scott Stoddard," Miles responded tongue-in-cheek.

Andy grunted. "We don't live in Hollywood, Ian." His manager's reference to an injured driver in the classic old racing film, *Grand Prix*, a scene depicting a badly injured driver being helped back into his car, was something that had crossed his mind. "The FIA would never go for that, anyway."

"The FIA would go for a lot of things right now, Andy. Amanda Moretti is still the international racing community's sweetheart."

"Her name is still Cook, but she will hopefully be my daughter-in-law someday. She's family, Ian. Stop thinking of her in terms of a marketing symbol for the team."

"I don't want Moretti Motorsport to be a footnote in history as a failed effort in Formula One."

"Nor do I, Ian." Andy knew that Tony would get back in a car again if he saw that as their only option. His oldest son knew he would be handed the leadership of Moretti Motorsport eventually. It was their family legacy, their family's support. To the Morettis, it was a way of life. But speaking of family, Andy knew what Crissy's reaction would be for even whispering a rumor about Tony driving again. *It would be one of hell to pay.*

Burim had received a stunning rebuke from his uncle. Eduardo would deny having any connection to the Paris incident, but as much as powerful men like himself and Anton Laurent worked to exercise control of their agreed boundaries, they couldn't manage everything, particularly an overzealous and greedy street thug gone rogue.

His nephew's delay in initiating the ransom call, and then making the call from Bucharest, had placed much of the Blaku syndicate operations right in the crosshairs. Burim had considered it a weakness to delegate the task of handling the calls and the ambitious young gangster didn't fully trust his locals to keep an eye on the captives while he traveled to Paris to make the calls himself. With pressure mounting after so many days, he had panicked and callously chose to make the call from the Romanian capital, over a twenty-four-hour commute from Paris, foolhardy on his part as he would travel to the French capital to grab the cash at any rate.

He felt the five million dollars would please his uncle and place him in the forefront to move up in the organization. Eduardo would look upon such a major intake favorably, but the exiled mobster worried he needed to keep his sister's only surviving son on a short leash.

Tony cringed as he broke the idea to his bride over the phone.

"Are you crazy, Tony!?" Crissy yelled back. "Does Andy know about this?"

"Not yet," Tony replied, not wanting his wife chewing his dad's butt out prematurely.

"You can barely walk! Get that stupid idea out of your head right now!"

"It's just a passing thought."

"Well, think about some other passing thoughts, like growing old enough to see your grandkids!"

"The team may fail if we don't do something."

"Then have your dad do something, just not something stupid! When are you coming home?"

"I should fly out late Saturday."

Crissy didn't like an ugly dispute over the phone and fought to lower her temperature. "I love you. But that doesn't mean I'm not pissed at you, Tony Moretti."

The second call came in just an hour and a half past the forty-eight hours. Again, an AI voice was used, only this time the call came in from Munich, a stopover by Basha on the long route back to Paris.

The call itself was disturbing to the point of being terrifying. The Cooks were directed to have the cash in a suitcase prepared in twenty-four hours and delivered to a location in the Paris Nord train station on the Rue de Dunkirk. A courier would meet the bag man and mention the pleasant weather. The transfer would be made and once the cash was in hand and verified, the girls would be released. If any police were seen or anything about the package compromised, such as having a GPS emitter, the girls would be found with their throats cut. The message, delivered through the artificial tone of AI itself, was extremely cold and to the point.

Both Byron and Sarah were shocked as they discussed this latest demand. As painful as it was to pay five million dollars for ransom, the whole idea of not exchanging the money for their daughters on the spot was horrifying. The mere fact they were dealing basically with a digitally recorded voice had negated any possibility of any fruitful negotiation.

Byron had taken the call from his office in Charlotte. "Captain Le Fleur is on the phone. Let me call you back, Sarah."

"No! I want to be on the call. I'll hold."

The three were connected and the Interpol officer insisted that they should not agree to leave any cash without seeing the girls and having an exchange on the spot.

"They could kill them, Captain!" Sarah screamed.

"Your daughters are worth nothing to these criminals dead, Madam. If you leave them cash without securing your daughters, you just invite further extortion."

"And what if you are wrong, Captain!?"

"I would advise that we have officers there as monitors but not have anyone show up with the money. They will call again and then a real negotiation can be made for the transfer. Trust me, Madam, we have dealt with situations like this many times."

The police captain disconnected as Byron and Sarah remained for an emotional and difficult discussion.

"Sarah, Le Fleur is just trying to do his job."

"Yes, Byron. His job is to apprehend criminals. If he succeeds, even if our girls are murdered, I'm sure he'll give us his condolences and pat himself on the back for catching the killers and preventing another kidnapping."

"What do you suggest then?"

"I don't know, Byron," Sarah replied as she broke down. "I just want my babies back."

"As do I, Sarah."
"I need to make another call."
"Alex Moretti is not part of this negotiation!"
"He is Amanda's fiancé, Byron!"
"Does that mean he's going to help with the five mil?"
"Get a life, Byron!"

Sarah informed Alex of the details of the call and the two agreed to jointly contact Cotton James, updating him. At this point, neither had much confidence in James producing anything soon and pretty well admitted the seventy-five grand they had given him was a waste of money. But in the big scheme of things, they agreed that amount of money was inconsequential and anything he came up with would be more than Interpol was accomplishing.

"Do you have anything to tell us, James?" Alex asked.

"Not yet, but we're working on it."

"Mr. James," Sarah added, pleading. "We don't have much time."

"We're shaking down every brothel and two-bit mobster hangout in Paris. It's slow and tedious work. Something will break."

"What can we do to help you, James?" Alex asked.

"Just keep me informed of any new developments on the spot, regardless of how insignificant you may think they are."

The call concluded. Cotton didn't mention they were getting no indication that anyone involved with the local human trafficking trade in Paris was behind the kidnapping.

Both Allison and Amanda had become almost numb to their surroundings. They had been nearly two weeks in captivity and mostly in near total darkness.

Allison's fear and feelings of helplessness were overshadowed by her extraordinary bitterness at being a part of the trauma she had initiated. Unable to discuss it with Amanda, of course, she tortured herself wondering who had stabbed her in the back. *Was it Eric Jordan? He took my money and set it up. Is he part of this cabal?* She was fueled by thoughts of what she would do to him if she ever survived this.

Adding to her natural anxiety of being a hostage, Amanda now felt extremely creepy coexisting in this dark cellar with a corpse, made all the worse by feeling filthy. This was causing her extreme insomnia, which would intermittently cause her to collapse to the floor in exhaustion.

Strangely, the bled-dry corpse just a few meters away affected Allison little, her mind constantly scheming of how they may escape, or how she may escape without Amanda and explain it, and how she would deal with Eric Jordan and this *Hot Lips* upon her return.

Neither had shaved since the morning before their kidnapping, shampooed their hair, or worn clean clothes. They hadn't had any hot food or so much as felt a drop of warm water.

The main captor who had shot their erstwhile attacker had departed for a time and left them with a new thug, an ugly overweight male who appeared in dire need of dental care. As disgusting as he appeared, the grunt at least hadn't attacked them and had even left the lone light on for a day, be it accidentally.

The new guy would bring them some food and water periodically but paid the two little mind, always appearing consumed by whatever was on his phone.

Allison moved close to Amanda, whispering in her ear as believing there would likely be bugs allowing their captors to listen to everything they said. "I have an idea, Amanda."

Amanda turned and stared at her sister, fearful of what could go wrong with Allison's plan, but agreeing that extreme measures had to be considered. She worried about her ability to pull her weight in the plan but worked to prepare herself, nonetheless. Her natural instinct to attack Markovic when he had threatened her sister had surprised even herself, an act that was playing a key part in Allison's thought process.

Chapter 7

Race For Amanda

The Unibank corporate jet arrived just before dawn and Byron was sour toward Alex, who met them in the hotel lobby. The CEO became annoyed that his mistress chose to engage in small talk with the young man, one who he blamed for every personal crisis he had experienced over the past two-plus years.

Sarah would have sympathized with his consternation hadn't the issue at hand been so traumatic. While she and Byron were committed to showing unity as emotional parents, Sarah had the strange feeling that Alex Moretti was more representative of her immediate family now.

Byron guarded the duffel bag full of cash as the four met with Captain Le Fleur and his accompanying officers. The four all rode into the city in a black armored Peugeot automobile, hoping against hope this would lead to their being reunited with Allison and Amanda again.

⚑✕⚑

Burim wore thick sunglasses, had a white wide-brim hat covering a wig over his shaved scalp, and full beard as he stood in the crowd watching for his mark. He consciously looked around for plain clothes police who themselves would be blending in, not identifying any, but knew they must be there. The Romanian knew that handling the pick-up himself was risky but wouldn't trust any of his subordinates, even his right-hand man, Armend, with that much cash. *They'll think I'm just a low-level grunt anyway, who wouldn't have any useful information if they did nail me.*

He saw the carrier approach, wearing a black baseball cap as instructed. The point of contact was the water fountain at the restrooms near the main ticket window. He confronted the suspected cop twenty meters before.

"Put the case down and head straight to your left toward the boarding ramp. Do nothing stupid unless you want two dead young women."

Burim picked up the bag, heading straight toward the exit and for the curb on Rue de Faubourg-Saint Denis, where he was picked him up in a yellow Renault. They drove away several kilometers when the Romanian retrieved a phone and dialed Byron Cook's number. "You call off these cops following me, including this helicopter overhead, or you get two dead daughters!"

"Wait!" Byron yelled. "You got your money! Now where—"

Burim cut him off, opened the passenger window, and tossed the burner phone out into a curbside drain.

His driver kept looking in the mirror. "I don't fucking see any cops."

"Me either, or the chopper. But that'll give the assholes something to talk about for a bit," the Romanian underboss commented, thinking himself quite clever. "Just drive."

Burim was dropped off twenty blocks to the east. He would stroll into a nondescript apartment building and out the rear exit where a commercial moving van awaited. He would pick his driver, Micah, up three blocks away before heading south and out of town. The two stopped at a fuel station where Burim lost the hat, wig, and beard.

Micah took over the driving chores while his boss finally clicked the latches on the suitcase to check its contents, smiling and taking a deep breath as he saw the bounds of cash.

The follow-up call to Byron's phone regarding some alleged pursuing police and a chopper had accomplished its desired effect, fermenting extreme mistrust now between the captives' parents and the police.

They all felt spent. Forty-eight hours had passed and no word on the girls. Nausea began to turn to anger as Captain La Fleur was giving them a passive version of "I told you so."

Byron had let three calls from Aaron Williams go to voicemail and finally took his fourth. "I have nothing to tell you, Aaron."

"We should never have agreed to drop that much cash without securing Allison and Amanda on the spot, Byron!"

"Must be something to it, Aaron. You're only about the four hundredth party to inform me of that." Byron bit at him, regretting it soon after. "We're all frustrated, Aaron. Maybe we should get our own people to apply some pressure, the State Department, the FBI, or something."

"We don't even know if Allison or Amanda are still alive, Byron."

"Can't lose hope, son. All we can do is just see this through."

Alex was not happy that he had agreed to go along with Sarah's choice not to disclose details of the ransom drop to Cotton James, fearing their interference may endanger the girls. He did contact the operative to check on their status and lamented the fact that James and his mercenary partner had thus far come up with nothing.

Arieh had his contacts in the Mossad watching out for any helpful communications picked up but was drawing blanks. The three had shaken down multiple suspected traffickers all over Paris, actually rescuing several teenage girls in the process, but had come up short on the Cook's daughters.

James kept telling Alex such investigations take time while Moretti snapped back at the private detective, reminding him that he hadn't related such low expectations when he was trying to get their seventy-five grand.

"If they want immediate results, we'll have to really stir the pot," Arieh stated, himself deflated at hearing this latest news.

"Meaning what, brother?" Alon asked.

"Meaning we need to head to Zurich, where we should have gone in the first place."

❧✖❧

Tony entered the Huntersville facility, warmly greeted by everyone there after spending some time in England. The Carolina team staff was happy that he seemed a bit more mobile, extracting himself from his car and moving fairly easily with a single cane.

Though not confronting such dire financial consequences as the F1 team, the IndyCar squad was deflated themselves since their new lead driver, Alex Moretti, had taken this self-imposed sabbatical, painful as it was, especially since he was solidly in contention for the championship. All told, they all knew their problems were minuscule considering what his fiancée Amanda was going through. After all,

Alex didn't even know for certain if she was still alive, though such observations were never uttered.

Crissy pulled into the driveway and was upset when she hit the garage door opener, seeing Tony's Ford GT was not there. She entered the kitchen realizing the kids were gone, as well. She kept calling Tony's phone and getting his voicemail. By now all the more angry, she finally called his Aunt Maria.

"Yes, honey. He dropped off the boys a couple of hours ago. I think he was just heading—"

"I know where he went, Maria."

Crissy was worried and about to bite a nail in two. Tony had not driven a vehicle himself since the accident and now his exotic Ford GT sports car, a vehicle not at all easy to get in and out of, was gone. *He thinks this proves something!*

Entering the facility thirty minutes later, Crissy appeared ready to extract a pound of flesh from the first person she ran into, including her father-in-law. To his fortune, Andy had left hours before and knew nothing of Tony being there.

She was initially greeted by Andy's General Manager, Bob Ward. "Good morning, Crissy."

"I'll take your word on it. Where is my husband?"

"Still in the back of the shop. In the simulator, I think."

"Simulator!? That shit!" She stormed through the facility, ignoring any and all of the restrictive measures in the building, as none of the staff wished to confront her.

There he was, enclosed in the large white machine which looked like some expensive carnival ride, shaking and bouncing up and down, forward and backward, and generating the all too familiar racket of a race car. Her anger subsided just a smidgen as she could see through the glass the father of her two boys was obviously having a ball for a change.

But her glee was quite temporary as she walked over to the rear of the machine and jerked down on the power cutoff switch. The machine froze in place as Tony pushed open the cover and prepared to exit, seeing his bride not looking all that lovely with her hands on her hips and breathing fire.

"Okay, baby. Don't say it."

"Don't give me that okay baby shit, Tony Moretti! What in hell are you doing!?"

"What's it look like?"

"No!"

"Look at me. I'm fine," he said as he struggled to extract himself from the simulator without his cane.

"Like hell you are! Miles is pushing you to drive again, isn't he? That British bastard is doing this to spite me, and I'm going to demand that your dad fire his ass!"

Half the building came to a standstill, having never witnessed Tony Moretti's lovely wife, Crissy, in such a state.

"I haven't made any decision to drive the Formula One car again."

"No!? Then why wait until I plan a shopping trip to sneak out in your car, drop the kids off at their grandmother's, and pull this shit!?"

Tony blushed as a kid caught in the cookie jar. "Because I knew you would stop me."

"Okay, now that you've pulled this childish prank, have you gotten it out of your system!?"

"I'm going to drive in St. Louis."

"You are going to do what?"

"The team needs a lift. I'm going to drive the oval in St Louis next weekend," Tony stated.

Crissy just stared at him. She had believed that his driving days were over following his near-death incident at Indy. Marco Andretti's wife, Marta, had warned her at the time. "They never get it out of their system."

"When does Andy get back?" she barked at Ward.

"I don't know. I could call him."

"Never mind, Mr. Ward. I'll give him an earful tonight," Crissy stated as she walked out.

Tony and the GM just stood and watched her backside. "Mr. Ward, Tony?" Ward asked, having always been on a first-name basis with Crissy Moretti. "Are you sure you're up to this?"

"It's just her way of saying she loves me, Bob. Let's check the sim results."

Back in Paris, Alex saw a text pop up on his phone, an eye-opener. *"Do you know about this?"* Crissy had attached a photo of Tony in the IndyCar simulator.

Brother, what's going on? Alex thought, shaking his head. Not wanting to get on his favorite sister-in-law's bad side, he replied. *"I had no clue, Crissy."*

He then had another call come in from Sarah. "We got another call, Alex. Meet me down in the lobby."

Sarah shared the call, saved as a recording on her phone. The message stated the Cooks had cheated him as there was not a full five million in the bag. Expect another call in forty-eight hours.

"Those bastards!" Alex claimed.

"My god, Alex," Sarah stated sadly as she embraced him. "Let's not lose hope."

"We need something to prove Amanda and Allison are still alive and well."

"We can't even have a conversation with these animals. Just these godforsaken recordings."

"Let's call for a press conference. They'll be watching those, whoever the sons-of-bitches are."

An hour later, Alex and Sarah joined together in the hotel lobby, prepared to make a statement.

"We have paid our daughters' captors the amount they demanded in good faith. We have heard from them disputing the amount and they have not released them. We will not entertain any other communication until we receive solid proof of Amanda and Allison's well-being. Thank you."

The press reporters went into a frenzy. "Alex, does Byron Cook still blame you for his daughters' captivity?"

Sarah took to the microphone. "That is not the least bit important right now."

Another reporter yelled, "Is there a fissure now between your party and the Paris Police?"

"I have no comment on that."

"Sarah, is it true that your husband has returned to the US and is against paying any more ransom?"

"I have no idea where you came up with that!"

"And how is your relationship with Alex's father now?"

Alex took back over. "You asshole!... If you have no more decent questions pertaining to Amanda and Allison's captivity, that will be all."

Eduardo was enraged. Interpol had released a digital photo gathered from the metro station's security camera system of the man who had received the ransom case.

"Burim is getting too damned cute," the strong man expressed to his right-hand man, Marius. "The hat, that hair, and beard. Stupid."

"He claims the Cooks only gave him four million."

"That stinks, Marius. If the banker was going to skimp on the ransom, why an exact million short? Why not just include a half million? Makes no fuckin' sense."

"So you think your nephew is skimming off the top?"

"I don't know. And I got a new message from that damned Laurent wanting to know if I had any private detectives shaking his people down in Paris. I want a meeting set up, Marius. Make it in Cancun."

Burim reviewed the press conference video for a second time. He was reveling in his genius. He had the two girls, a cool five million in cash, and Interpol still had little clue who or where he was, and now Uncle Eduardo wanted a meeting in Cancun. *To promote me no doubt, and deliver our booty... So they want proof, huh? That's easy enough.*

The girls were asleep, awakened by the bright bulb that flashed on. This time two of them stammered down the steps with neither carrying any food or water. They each had a brief thought that perhaps they were being moved. *Or possibly released,* Amanda thought hopefully.

"You will each stand and give a statement," Burim ordered. "Read this to prepare."

Amanda and Allison gathered together and read the few words handwritten down on a single piece of notebook paper. "What bullshit," Allison whispered to her younger sister. "Treated well?... Well fed, my ass... Please pay them in full next time?... What the fuck does that mean?"

"Everyone will know it's all fabricated, Allison. Just give them what they want."

※

The short video went viral on YouTube and all other social media platforms, not to mention being the opening topic of discussion on every broadcast news station in the world. While a final resolution still appeared to be over the horizon, the combined Cook and Moretti families held some sense of relief in at least seeing the girls alive.

Byron and Carolyn Tyler had returned home as he was stung by the apparent failure of securing Amanda and Allison's release despite dishing out a full five million. "The sons-of-bitches are lying, Carolyn! That bundle of cash wasn't a penny short!"

"They're lying? Really, Byron? They kidnapped two young women in broad daylight. Like, do you think lying is even a hesitation for these pricks? The police were right. You should never have agreed to hand them cash with a promise to release your daughters later." Tyler held her tongue on telling him how utterly stupid that was.

"Well, Sarah panicked."

"You and Sarah are divorcing, Byron. She shouldn't be making decisions for you."

"We're still both Allison and Amanda's parents, Carolyn!"

Tyler chose not to further respond, having a passing thought about a future if the two Cook girls were never seen again. She had only a passing acquaintance with Amanda, who seemed like a very nice young woman. Allison was another matter.

The atmosphere in Tony's household was quite tense. Despite Crissy continuously throwing a fit, Tony had committed to drive for the team in the next IndyCar race in St. Louis.

Exasperated, she turned her wrath on Andy, who was sympathetic but his response always came back to the same thing. "We're racers, Crissy."

She then called Alex.

"He's doing what!?"

"Yes, Alex. He's been sneaking down to the shop and playing on that simulator, convincing himself he is ready to drive again. You need to call and talk some sense into his dumb ass!"

Alex knew his sister-in-law was wound up and playing on his own guilt. *Is she suggesting that I go back and drive?* Alex shook his head, knowing he was mentally in no condition to even think about that yet. "I'll call him, Crissy, but"...

"But what, Alex?"

"We are racers, Crissy."

The event in St. Louis was actually held in Madison, Illinois, at Gateway International Raceway, just northeast of downtown with the iconic Arch in the background. Sponsored by one of the metro's largest car dealers, the Bommarito 500 saw last-minute ticket sales skyrocket at the news that Tony Moretti would drive for the first time since his near-fatal accident at Indianapolis.

While not openly gleeful regarding the circumstances, the series brass and broadcast network were benefitting from added attention worldwide to a race that had struggled in attendance and TV ratings the past three years.

British Petroleum stepped up as their Amoco livery on the "5" car was largely replaced with a blatant *Race For Amanda* message. The broadcast crew had arranged for Alex Moretti to appear via satellite in Paris for a short pre-race interview. Tony's misty-eyed brother offered support for the team and his brother while answering questions regarding the latest update on his missing fiancée and her sister.

Crissy had given her husband and father-in-law hell for all she was worth for a couple of days, but once she realized Tony was all in on driving in St. Louis, she got on board and took to her former space on the Amoco-sponsored Moretti pit stand. This would be a 500-kilometer race or 259 laps around the 1.2-mile oval track, an event that Tony had won twice in the past and had three other top-five finishes.

A driver who had to have some assistance getting in and out of his car, Tony felt right at home once strapped in and shared a light moment with the legend A. J. Foyt, who had to comment on how much more comfortable the newer generation cars were, all in good nature, of course.

He had qualified eighth fastest, starting on the outside of the fourth row. Crissy sat on the pit stand with her fingers crossed, shutting her eyes and praying briefly for a safe start. "All right, baby! Make us proud!" She declared to no one in particular.

At the drop of the green flag, Tony had a fast start, moving up to fifth place by the end of the second lap. The broadcast crew would give the "5" car an exponential amount of coverage during the two-plus hour race. At the midway point of the race, there were a mere dozen cars still on the lead lap and the Moretti driver maintained a top five position.

A roving pit reporter approached the Moretti pit stand. "This is Jamie Newman. Here at the pit stand for Tony Moretti's crew, his wife has returned to the IndyCar paddock. Crissy, this is Tony's first time back in a race car since his serious crash at Indy. It was obvious Tony did need help physically just getting in the car. How difficult was the decision for him to race again?"

"For him, not difficult at all. For me, very much so. But he's a Moretti, Jamie. He's a racer."

"Can we expect Tony to return for the remaining four series races?"

"Well, you know he is technically a stand-in for Alex, who is still in Paris. Hopefully, Amanda will be returned to us safely soon and the race teams can get back to normal."

"There you have it. Crissy Moretti is back in the IndyCar pit lane, cheering her husband on under the stress of her brother-in-law's fiancée, Amanda Cook's captivity."

Through a series of caution periods and swift and timely pit stops, Tony found himself in the lead with less than twenty laps remaining as the packed stands roared with every Tony Moretti pass of the flag stand. With the leader running in a fuel-saving mode, the hard-charging Joseph Newgarden, a man with the bit in his teeth and plenty of fuel, was gaining over a second a lap when on lap 253 the caution flag was displayed over debris on the track, triggering a final four lap shootout between the two leaders. In a reversal of Detroit, Tony would throw caution to the wind as the few laps under yellow removed any and all concerns about fuel consumption.

At the drop of the green flag, Tony got the jump on Joseph and held a two-second lead heading into the last turn before the white flag when a lapped car driven by Colin Raeburn came into the banked turn hard and got into the marbles. The backend of the second-tier driver's Dallara gave way and backed hard into the wall. With Newgarden breathing heavily down his neck, Tony stayed low to avoid Raeburn, whose car had bounced off the wall and veered down toward the pitlane retaining barrier, catching the leader hard, literally tearing the rear suspension and transaxle away from the engine, causing the remaining bulk of the chassis to spin violently prior to crashing hard against the inside wall.

Crissy screamed and in a panic got up from her perch on the pit stand and moved down, wanting to jump over the pit wall. Tony's Crew Chief, Gordon Wells, moved to restrain her as Andy quickly acted in concert to embrace her. Such accidents were bad enough without extra personnel running onto the pavement while the safety crew worked to extract the drivers from the wreckage.

In fairly short order, Raeburn got up out of his heavily damaged car and waved to the fans. Tony, however, appeared immobile in what was left of his wounded Dallara when two safety crew members arrived in less than thirty seconds. They were able to extract Tony from the car and the crowd stood and cheered loudly when he stood and waved before being escorted into the safety truck.

Crissy showed up at the infield med center shortly thereafter, rushing in and up to Tony sitting on an examination table. The attending physician stood aside briefly as they embraced.

"Are you okay?"

"Oh yes, at least physically. Mentally I'm bruised. I had it won."

"Is he okay, Doctor?" Crissy asked, wanting assurance.

"I need to fully complete my examination, but so far I see nothing too concerning."

"And what if the damned car would have caught on fire, Tony? You can't even get out of the car without help," she asked him, somewhat angry that question was not asked enough in the first place.

"Oh, sweety. These cars don't catch fire these days like they used to. I don't believe we've had a driver seriously burned in over forty years, right Doc?"

"Don't get me in the middle of this. We have had some serious fires out on the drag strip. But none in here, at least since I've been onboard."

"Well, that's good to know," Tony stated for his bride's satisfaction.

"It's not good enough, Tony. You could have been severely hurt or worse."

"Well, I wasn't, sweety."

"No sugar for you Tony, until I hear your driving career is over, at least until that leg is fully healed and you can walk without a cane and help yourself in and out of these cars."

The physician had completed his work, giving Tony a clean bill of health while the attending nurse looked sheepishly toward Crissy and asked for a selfie with the three of them.

Meanwhile, Alex witnessed the race while stuck in Paris and felt a huge bout of guilt. Tony was standing in for him for the good of the team, and to that extent, the good of the family. His brother could have been seriously re-injured or even killed. For the first time, he began to question his own judgment of remaining in Paris as in the age of instant worldwide communications, wondering whether his being there was helping the cause of freeing Amanda whatsoever.

On the other hand, the race broadcast coverage highlighting Tony's *Race For Amanda* livery on the car was impressive and would play continuously on podcasts and social media reels for weeks.

His call to Tony kept going to voicemail, thus he rang Crissy. "Close call, huh?"

"Oh, Alex, I'm about to ring his neck. He's just upset he didn't win!"

"Let me talk to him."

"Here, Tony. It's Alex," Crissy stated as she handed him her phone.

"Hello little bro."

"Close, but no cigar, Tony."

"Yes, well you know, it happens."

"Your wife doesn't sound happy."

"I know," Tony replied while throwing Crissy a quick smile. But she still loves me. Any news?"

"No, and I need to get out of here before I lose my mind."

"Are you coming home?"

"I don't know, yet. I just need to go somewhere and do something. Anyway, I just wanted to check on you. Give Crissy and the boys my love."

The call was completed and Crissy escorted Tony out of the med center as they made their way toward the team motorhome where he would shower and the two would depart for home.

"You know you're putting Alex on a guilt trip, don't you?"

"I think he should get back behind the wheel, Crissy. His sitting around just waiting for something to break with Amanda can't be good for him."

Despite the late-race accident, Andy was thrilled with the team's performance. Tony would have won and should have won, but racing was racing and Andy knew one had to take the good with the bad. The boost in TV ratings didn't go unnoticed at 16th and Georgetown, and now conversations were plentiful about each team and race promoter reaching out to their sponsors in an effort to display a smaller *Race For Amanda* logo on each car, driver uniforms, and banners at each circuit.

This initiative also didn't go unnoticed at Number Two St. James Market, in London. Brian Fonterra listened with interest on a Webex call as McLaren's Zak Brown shared the experience of IndyCar's race in St. Louis, a weekend event, one that had more than triple the attendance from the previous year, and the race day TV audience was through the roof. The Formula One CEO was quick to take credit for the commercial success of the IndyCar event in St. Louis, pointing out that Tony Moretti was indeed an F1 star now, but all agreed they should do more to better get behind the *Race For Amanda* movement on all fronts.

Although Formula One was the worldwide motorsport leader in TV viewers, Andy had been relatively quiet on the call though humbled to hear the leadership and team principals of Formula One were all solidly behind the suggested initiative in keeping his family, and his still hopeful future daughter-in-law, atop the headlines.

It was also discussed that the strict FIA physical requirement, particularly as it pertained to Tony Moretti, may prevent his taking part in a Formula One race, although Andy's oldest son did compete successfully in a 500-kilometer IndyCar race. Andy was asked if Tony was planning to drive in the upcoming Dutch Grand Prix at Zandvoort, all assuming that Alex would still be in Paris, preoccupied with Amanda's situation.

The Moretti family patriarch considered the great irony of what he was hearing. The power brokers in Formula One, who opposed for years his entry into the sport, now saw economic opportunity in having one of his sons behind the wheel, present circumstances notwithstanding. "Our plans have yet to be finalized for Zandvoort, gentlemen."

Andy knew that Tony would drive in Zandvoort if asked. He also knew that Crissy Moretti would likely go nuclear on both of them if that was the case, especially since the last two times her husband had driven a race car had resulted in horrendous crashes. Adam Herrera had come up with the marketing ploy of putting the *Race For Amanda* livery on the car. He would consult with him on it.

Sarah was now back home in Rock Hill and, like Alex, needed a break from the Paris paparazzi. She greeted her long-lost friend with a smiling embrace. Lisa Williams had sent Sarah a text wanting to see her. Their families had been estranged for many long months since the trial and had rarely even spoken, despite the fact their two oldest children were planning to marry.

"I assume there is no news," Lisa asked with genuine empathy.

"No, nothing. Byron is angry with me over the five million dollars. Those felons took our money and now claim we shorted them."

"Is it possible—"

"No. Byron may be greedy, but he would never endanger our girls by pulling something like that. Now all we can do is wait, and pray."

"Aaron has gotten very distant from us over this," Lisa added with an air of sadness. "Bud had pretty much prohibited he and Allison from marrying over... Well, you know."

"I don't think we should talk about all that right now, Lisa."

"Bud has thought about canceling much of his banking business with Unibank, Sarah."

"That is of little interest to me now, Lisa. I have my own life and Byron has his. I just want to get my daughters back alive now. I don't wish Byron any ill will, I just wish to move on."

"I understand. But this has to have been truly hard on you, Sarah. I mean, after all those years together."

"Yes, it was hard. The betrayal and all. But I have become numb over time to him. He had become such a bitter and vindictive man, wanting to destroy the Moretti family at all costs."

"And now you seem close to them. That must really piss him off."

"I care little about what he thinks. Alex Moretti plans to marry my youngest daughter, Lisa. Throughout all of this, he has been committed to her. A young man like him, a world-famous sports star with handsome Hollywood looks, could have any young woman. But he loves Amanda and he has become like a son to me."

Lisa experienced a quick bout of sadness. *For the longest time, you looked at my sons that way, Sarah.*

"Lisa. Regardless of what happens, and I pray for a happy ending, I will always have a soft spot in my heart for Alex Moretti."

"And what about his father?" Lisa asked seriously.

"Oh, come on, Lisa. Don't tell me you believe all that social media."

"I didn't say that," she replied, now grinning. "But does he have a woman in his life?"

Sarah had always been uncomfortable discussing this topic, but Lisa Williams had always been the one friend in her life with whom she could share anything. "His ex-wife, Sabetha, is living there now."

"Oh, I see. That does add a new twist, doesn't it?"

"I don't think they're sleeping together, Lisa. And I think Andy would like her to return to Europe."

"Do I detect a little wishful thinking on your part?"

"Lisa!"

"Well, you will be single soon. And him? If I were single"...

"He's never looked at me in that way, Lisa. I do believe he's gun-shy after all those months of legal battles with Byron."

"And if he would ask you out?"

"Lisa, that's not going to happen."

"But you're not saying no... He is handsome."

"Lisa, getting into a relationship with another man is the last thing on my mind right now, and that means any man."

"I'm sorry, Sarah. I was just trying to change the subject, if just for a few minutes."

"There's nothing that could get my mind off my two girls. I cry every night thinking about what they must be going through."

⚑✕⚑

Burim pondered his next move, feeling confident in his ability to extract another bounty of cash from the American banker. He had carved out the so-called short million for himself, confident his uncle would be quite pleased when presented with the four million left over.

"You know your uncle better than I do, Burim. But he may not be pleased that you took it upon yourself to handle this," Armend stated.

"Uncle Eduardo will be fine. How many of us would act and bring him such a bounty?... And still have the goods?"

"What do you think our next move will be?"

"I'll demand more cash and if they're foolish enough to hand it over, great. If not, there's always the black market. I know certain individuals who'll pay a robust amount for these two."

Again, Burim. You know your uncle better than I do. "So, when do you plan to return?"

"Should be late Friday, Armend. Until then, you're in charge and I don't want any bullshit problems like what happened with Dominik.

Just make sure our victims remain fresh and if Micah does something stupid, kill the bastard."

※

Adam Herrera accompanied Andy on the flight home, anxious to discuss in detail his meeting with the Van Boden Group.

"I hate to tell you, Andy, but they're getting antsy. Sure, they are all full of empathy regarding Amanda and her sister. But at the end of the day, they are a financial investment corporation and everything eventually comes down to euros and dollars."

"We'll be at Zandvoort with Leland and a second driver. Ian hasn't settled on who yet."

"Andy, I know this is awkward, but they want a Moretti in the car. That performance in Hungary just mesmerized everyone."

"You know Tony's wife is about to divorce him if he gets back behind the wheel," Andy stated, tongue-in-cheek.

"And what about Alex?"

"Alex is still deflated over what happened to Amanda. He's just in no shape mentally, Adam."

"Getting back in the car may be just what he needs. He's a budding Formula One star, Andy."

"I know, Adam. But I also know how he thinks and he would feel guilty as hell. It would be as though he was leaving his post."

"He has to know by now that his being there isn't helping things. On the other hand, hear me out..."

※

Andy's stress meter was pegged on high. His favorite and least favorite daughter-in-law, Crissy, was ragging hard on both him and Tony about the idea of him returning to Europe and driving in a Grand Prix again. His ex-wife was now past visiting and as much as he wished Sabetha would go back home, he knew she had serious problems and was perhaps at risk, so he wasn't going to force the issue, at least yet. After all, Matilde was right. He wasn't at home much during these summer months anyway, and last but not least, the saga of Alex's fiancée and her sister being kidnapped in Paris had his youngest boy in a mental coma.

He fought off the very idea of Amanda's trauma being discussed as a short-term financial windfall for Formula One, IndyCar, and his race teams in general. He thought over Herrera's idea and felt he should discuss it with Sarah. A lunch meeting felt like the right touch.

He suggested a rather surprising choice for an eating establishment, one he felt he knew well but had never been there. She had arrived early and stood up as the two shared a brief embrace.

"I could have met you halfway, Andy. This was certainly an interesting choice."

"I know. I was always curious about this place, but have never been here."

"It's been years for me. It's kind of emotional, us being here. Don't you think?" Sarah asked.

"Indeed. The place has a certain connection."

"Strange as parents looking out there, realizing our children spent the night on a boat here. Were you sneaky like that when you were young, Andy?"

"I didn't have any money to afford a boat like that, Sarah, at least not at that age. So far as the sneaky part, I'll plead the fifth. So, how are you holding up?"

She blinked a couple of times as tears began forming. "I'm trying to be strong for them, Andy. But I fear I may never see my girls again," Sarah replied, nearly breaking down.

Andy held her hand, wanting to avoid saying the wrong thing. Sarah had never let on, but he wondered if she somehow blamed him and the whole sport of motor racing. After all, if he had never met with her husband, had never gained Unibank as a team sponsor, his son would have never met her daughter…

It was almost as if she was reading his mind. "I don't blame Alex, Andy. I don't blame anyone, except those who took them."

Their waitress approached and smiled. "Welcome to Papa Doc's Shore Club," she declared. She took their order without incident.

"Does it seem funny that we could come in here and not be recognized?" Sarah quizzed.

"A bit. I'm kind of glad, though. Byron would explode if he knew I was here with—"

"Andy! What I do or who I do it with is none of Byron's business now."

"All right, I'm sorry."

"Don't be. We've been accused of all kinds of things on social media. I think we deserve to at least have lunch together."

Andy grinned back at her, thinking some ice had been broken in some fashion. "Sarah, what do you think about Alex remaining in Paris?"

"There's little point. I had to have a break from it after a while. The investigation has been moved south to Lyon."

"I think he feels his presence there, along with his talking to those reporters every day, was somehow keeping the pressure on the police. But the reporters are gradually fading away."

"I know, Andy. I just don't want my girls to become this decade's Nataly Holloway."

"Adam Herrera thinks Alex should get back to driving. The *Race For Amanda* livery on Tony's car in St. Louis went over big. My sponsors, and the sport as a whole, are behind a huge campaign to continue that in Formula One. Tony is more than willing to get back in the car again, but his wife, Crissy, is going ballistic over the idea... Alex, on the other hand—"

"It's perfect, Andy!"

He looked stunned.

"What? Did you think I would fault you on it? I saw the delayed coverage of that race in St. Louis. The commentators seemed to talk as much about Amanda and Allison as they did the race action itself. I know Tony's car got more coverage than any other, even before he was leading."

"Yes, Sarah. And in Formula One, multiply that coverage times ten at a minimum. In Europe, the ratings for a Grand Prix rivals the NFL here."

"Okay."

"It will still be his decision, of course."

"Perhaps I should just call him," Sarah offered.

Andy sat there thinking this woman never ceased to amaze him. He found himself beating around the bush and waiting for the right time to suggest that Sarah call Alex, a ploy that would relieve him of whatever guilt he had regarding his station in Paris.

The two concluded lunch and Andy escorted Sarah out to her SUV.

"Sarah, perhaps in a future time when this trauma hopefully ends well, we could go out to dinner, or—-"

"Yes, Andy," Sarah answered, grabbing him around the neck and departing with a brief but emotional kiss. She then got in the Escalade and gave him a short wave before backing out of the parking space and pulling away.

Andy strolled the forty yards to his vehicle, pleased with the way this lunch encounter went. *Hmm,* he thought to himself. *Byron would blow a gasket. But Sarah is right, I guess. It's her business, and Unibank wouldn't ditch Evelyn Stevens next year, even if she was back on board with me.*

Crissy was elated. Tony would be running the Dutch Grand Prix, not as a driver but back as Chief Mechanic for Alex. The whole plan to expand the *Race For Amanda* on all fronts was brilliant so far as she was concerned. BP had stepped up and supported it and even the two-team Mustangs competing in the upcoming NASCAR Firecracker 400 would sport the new livery.

The highlight of the weekend was Sarah being featured in a 30-second spot promoted by BP, issuing a plea for her daughters to be released. At the last minute, they all insisted that Sarah be invited to the Dutch Grand Prix, which she accepted without hesitation.

Alex had all along resisted pressure from Crissy to drive again, which would keep Tony in the pit box. It was the call from Sarah that flipped his switch with her view that his showing up in The Netherlands would likely help Amanda's cause more than being stuck in a Paris hotel waiting for something to happen.

It was almost as if the cadre of reporters had followed him, as the throng gathered in the F1 paddock, cameramen in tow, to get their sound bites in from Alex or anyone else from the Moretti clan.

One reporter was overzealous in putting him on the spot. "Alex, it's been almost four weeks since Amanda Cook and her sister Allison were kidnapped. Does your choosing to get behind the wheel again indicate less hope on your part of the two ever being released?"

Alex hesitated, giving her a hard glare. "I'm not going to dignify such a question with a response."

In short order, Sarah became a media magnet, determined to do her part in keeping Allison and Amanda's plight on the front page. She repeated numerous answers to the same questions. "Have you heard anything from the kidnappers? What is your response to their claim that you and your husband short-changed the bounty by a million US dollars? What would you like to say to your daughters, assuming they're watching the broadcast today?"

Finally isolating themselves at the Moretti Motorsport hospitality area, the team and their guests settled in for the first day's practice. Alex and teammate Geoff Leland finished the session seventh and eighth fastest respectively with both on the hard tire compound.

The team would run soft compound tires in Saturday's qualifying with separate strategies for each driver on Sunday. Leland would start on the hard compound and run at least forty-six of the seventy laps, making one stop for a switch to softs. Sighting his expected speed, Tony planned a two-stop strategy for Alex, starting on soft tires, running the medium compound mid-race, and stopping late for another four softs.

Alex was true to form on Saturday, qualifying a solid fourth, adjacent to the great Louis Hamilton on the second row. Defending series champion, Max Verstappen, and the year's challenger, Lando Norris, shared the front row.

⚑⚑

Allison and Amanda received their second lean serving of food and water late in the afternoon as the replacement grunt said little and retreated back up the steps. This was preceded by another incursion into their dungeon by him and another young gangster they had not seen before, who had finally gathered up and removed the dead body of Dominik Markovic.

With limited daylight remaining before being relegated to full darkness again, Allison tiptoed up the steps, putting her ear to the closed door, listening for anything that may have value.

"I heard two names," she whispered in Amanda's ear. "Armend and Micah. I don't think the one who shot our attacker the other day is still here. At least I didn't hear his voice."

"So, how does this help us?"

"We have to wait until one leaves, Amanda. Then we'll make our move."

The mansion was located in the upscale Zollikon area of Zurich, just east of the lake in the southeast part of the city. The property sat on four acres and had a seven-foot brick wall surrounding the seven thousand square foot three-story mansion. There was a full housekeeping staff who were provided living quarters above the four-car garage, separated from the main structure by a covered brick breezeway connecting.

Fearing his own former agency may track his whereabouts, Arieh had Alon rent a car under an assumed name in Vienna, and the two Israelis and Cotton James traveled to Switzerland.

"There are two full-time bodyguards, including his chauffeur, and at least two German Shepherds on the property that we'll have to take care of," Arieh explained. "The chauffeur normally works from early morning until late afternoon unless Grether and his wife go out to dinner, which is one or two nights during the week, and on Saturday night. He drives the limousine home and back while generally not reporting in on Sunday until noon, as Grether and his wife often spend that afternoon at their country club."

"How do you know all this?" Cotton asked.

"I was about to nail the bastard after a two-week stakeout. Then I was called off over politics. That's when I got out of the Mossad, all after thirty-two years of service."

"So, how do we deal with the lone bodyguard? Do we eliminate him?" Cotton asked while Alon looked on, himself curious about how his brother planned this. In the past ten days, they had eliminated no less than five mob-connected street thugs, all within the realm of self-defense. This time, it appeared different.

Arieh chuckled and reached into his pocket, pulling out some special tranquilizer cartridges. "I'm not that dastardly. These will knock down the dogs for a good six hours, a large adult four. The estate has a power backup system that is housed in the garage, of all places. One of my associates will knock out the power grid immediately upon my cue. Alon will enter the garage through the side entrance and knock out the backup system along with the lead to the phone system, also located there. The on-staff bodyguard will immediately approach through the breezeway to check on it and I will hit him with one of these, which will induce the four-to-five hour nap. We'll then enter the main floor and proceed to have a friendly chat with Herr Grether."

"And what about the house servants?" Cotton asked.

"We'll go in at 0430 hours. They should all still be in bed. If one or two show their faces unexpectedly, we'll just treat them to a nice sleep, too."

"Here's something interesting. The people who are paying the bill have vacated Paris and are now in The Netherlands at a Grand Prix auto race," Cotton stated, showing the two brothers his phone.

"Look at that. *Race For Amanda* all over the side of that Alex Moretti's race car."

"Well," Arieh replied. "I don't know about you fellows, but I'm not a huge race fan and need to get some rest."

⚑✕⚑

Arieh's plan ran like clockwork. Donning black ski masks, the three operatives scaled the wall on the southeast corner, with Alon having to physically help his older weakened brother. The two German Shepherds were put down by Alon within seconds of each other. Grether's main bodyguard noted the abrupt silence of barking and came running through the breezeway toward the garage when he felt a sharp sting in his neck. The former professional wrestler collapsed seconds later before Cotton helped Alon drag his body around behind the garage, laying the two-hundred-fifty-pounder on the ground behind some shrubbery. Cotton then proceeded to search him and retrieved some keys, a loaded Glock pistol, and a cell phone.

The three then entered the main house through the back door, surprising a housemaid who was noisy while stammering around in the dark. Escorting the older woman at gunpoint, she led the three upstairs to the master bedroom at the end of a lengthy corridor, where she herself was subdued with one of Arieh's tranquilizers.

The room was slightly illuminated by moonlight through an open curtained window and Arieh quietly approached the snoring banker's nightstand, reaching under the small lamp shade and flipping the light on before pressing the cold steel barrel of his nine-millimeter pistol against Grether's throat. Alon had silently approached the other side of the king-size bed, placing his hand over the banker's wife's mouth and holding an intimidating large army knife under her chin.

Wide-eyed now, a shocked Grether yelled out, "Who are you!? I keep no cash money here!"

"Just need a little information, Herr Grether. And you will give it to us."

"Information? You're all thieves! Take whatever you can find here and leave us!"

Arieh nodded to Alon, who grabbed Greta Grether by her hair, pulling her upright into a sitting position. The woman, who appeared a good twenty-five years younger than Helmut, stared at the masked intruders as her eyes were filled with terror. "Helmut, please!"

"You are aware of the kidnapping of Amanda and Allison Cook nearly three weeks ago. I want to know who has these young women."

"I am just a banker. I have nothing to do with that!"

"Just a banker, Herr Grether?" Arieh asked menacingly. "A banker who bankrolls every human trafficking syndicate in Europe and beyond. I want to know who has these girls!"

"I told you, I have nothing to do with that!"

Arieh showed little reaction emotionally, but quickly put a nine-millimeter shell into Greta's left thigh, forcing a scream.

"Helmut, what have you done!?" she yelled while desperately clutching her bleeding wound. Both Cotton and Alon looked upon her and then back at Arieh, stunned themselves.

"Your husband has laundered money for the world's worst dealers of human sex slaves. I want names, Herr Grether. I am not a man long for this world, but wish to leave on a high note. And if that means ridding this continent of men like you and his trophy wife in the process, so be it."

"Helmut!" Greta screamed again. "Please!"

"I do not know who captured the Cook girls. I only know it was not Anton Philippe Laurent, and he knows not, either."

"And how do you know Laurent was not behind it?"

"I was paid a visit by the girls' mother and father. I called Philippe immediately afterward. He denied any role in the grab."

"Laurent controls Paris," Arieh pressed. "If not Laurent, then who?"

"You know if I disclose names, we are as good as dead," Grether stated in desperation.

"If we leave without what we need, Herr Grether, neither you nor your lovely wife will see another sunrise."

"You had better believe him, sir," Grether heard the one with the southern American accent. "He does have terminal cancer and flat doesn't give a rat's ass."

"How do I know you won't just kill us if I do disclose what is against a strict Swiss banker's code?"

Arieh didn't hesitate. "You will both be dead for certain if you don't, Herr Grether."

Grether looked at his terrified spouse, upset and ashamed that regardless of how this nightmare would end, she now knew things about her husband that would be very disturbing, *But disturbed is better than dead,* he contemplated. "There are three others who could likely be behind such an act."

"Go on."

"Viktor Agapov mostly operates in Russia, Ukraine, Belarus, and Poland. Fernando Lopez runs the Med. And Eduardo Blaku does business in the Balkan states."

"Which one would be so bold as to pull this right in Anton Philippe Laurent's backyard?"

"I would not suspect any of them would. These bosses do not want to go to war with each other."

"You're lying, Herr Grether," Arieh shouted as he made a scene of re-loading.

"Agapov has no history of operating anywhere beyond the old Iron Curtain. Blaku has relocated to Mexico and I cannot see him leaving something this public to an underboss. That's all I know! Take me if you wish, but Greta has nothing to do with any of this!"

Arieh nodded to his younger brother twice and both shot both Helmut and Greta Grether in their left shoulder using the two remaining tranquilizer cartridges. Alon would wrap up Greta's flesh wound thoroughly and the three would make their way out.

"I really thought you were going to kill them," Cotton stated as they made their way toward their rented car four city blocks away.

"You think so, Cotton?" Arieh replied stoically. "I was never concerned with what you thought. I was only concerned with what they thought."

"So, what did that get us?" Alon asked. In his own mind, the answer was not much.

"We know Agapov never leaves Moscow and has no history of kidnapping or extortion that far out of his theatre. Blaku was wanted by Interpol and fled to Mexico three or four years ago, the world epicenter now for human trafficking. He is under the protection of the cartels who keep the government there from allowing any extradition. That leaves Lopez, and I know he and Laurent are not pen pals. Our next stop will be Cannes."

"We had better lie low before heading out, maybe have one or two of us take the train," Cotton stated.

"No, Grether won't call the police. Police will ask questions. Herr Grether won't want that, especially them questioning his wife."

"He'll have enough in just dealing with her questions," Alon added.

"Indeed, but that's not our problem."

🏁

Burim had departed for Madrid, where his small jet would refuel before taking off for Cancun. Armend was left with Micah to manage their captives for two to three days until his return.

Allison instructed Amanda to be prepared for the right time. Just before dark, Micah brought down a paper plate of food, two small pork sausages, some greasy hash brown potatoes, and a pair of stale oatmeal cookies.

"Micah, what do you do when you're not watching us?" Allison asked.

The grungy-looking tough looked up at her, surprised, no doubt wondering how she knew his name, and mumbled back a reply in a foreign language.

"I'm sorry, Micah. You don't speak English?"

"*Englah?* No."

The three heard the cellar door open and Armend yelled down at Micah, himself hollering in the same tongue. Micah appeared slightly jolted momentarily, shouting back as he displayed a middle finger toward the ceiling and then headed back toward the steps, pausing to give the two girls a slight grin.

Amanda rushed toward her sister. "What is that language, Allison?"

"I don't know. Sounds kinda like Italian. Maybe we're somewhere in Italy. We have to move when just one is here. You know what to do."

"I'm nervous, Allison," Amanda whispered, believing she would be the subject of repercussions if their scheme failed.

"You do want to get out of here, don't you?"

Chapter 8

Breakout Performance

Race day morning in Zandvoort had quite the buzz. The usual festive atmosphere at a Grand Prix had a new dimension as the talk in the paddock was more about Alex Moretti's personal saga than the battle waging for the championship between Red Bull's Max Verstappen, the defending champion, and Lando Norris, an up and coming star with the resurgent McLaren team.

Alex had a distinct air about him as he was still quite cognizant of Amanda, focusing his performance on keeping the world's media keyed on her and Allison, mentally forgoing his past animosities with Amanda's older sister.

Andy was cautiously confident considering Alex's stellar qualifying performance, the best since Moretti Motorsport had entered Formula One.

Tony himself was giddy about it. "I told you, Dad. He's faster than I ever was."

"So long as he can keep it on the pavement," Andy answered, just hoping his youngest son didn't overdrive the car, which was his tendency to do occasionally.

Crissy was in much better spirits with her husband, who still used a cane to walk around, sitting in the pit box directing Alex. She sat beside Sarah, anticipating the start while both were thrilled at the sight of a small plane flying overhead pulling a large *Race For Amanda* banner.

"I want the whole world to know both of my daughters are being held captive," Sarah decried.

"Oh, they do, Sarah. This is the motor racing community and it's all about Alex Moretti and his fiancée."

Allison silently moved back down the steps. "This may be the time, Amanda. I heard a door open and close. I think one of them left. It's about time for our morning ration."

True to form, Micah opened the door a few minutes later, flipped on the cellar light switch, and stammered down the steps toting a paper plate with some biscuits and hard-boiled eggs.

Allison discarded her dingy garments and stood up against the wall nearly naked as if she was attempting to clean herself, prompting a stare from Micah, a young man previously bored with this ongoing babysitting assignment. "What is it, Micah? You haven't seen a naked woman before?"

He sheepishly broke his gaze and stole a glance toward Amanda, who stood nearby wearing her usual fearful expression.

Knowing the thug wasn't understanding a word she said, Allison resorted to using body language, allowing her skimpy panties to drop to the floor, and approached him slowly. Micah seemed to freeze momentarily, mesmerized at the sight of this beautiful and erotic American woman who appeared to want him. As he allowed her to put her arms around his neck to embrace him, he lost track of Amanda, who had possession of one of the cast iron plates from the top of the old stove. She suddenly came in behind him and struck a severe blow to the top of his head. Micah then collapsed to the floor, out cold amid an ugly bleeding wound on his scalp.

"Amanda, quick, grab his phone!" Allison ordered while gathering her clothing.

Amanda found Micah's phone in his hip pocket, a several-year-old Samsung model. "Here."

"See if he has anything else we can use," Allison added while she fingered through the menus on the phone, flustered at everything being in a foreign language.

Amanda found a switchblade knife in Micah's front pants pocket and grabbed his wallet. The two made their way up the steps, hoping the door wasn't locked. Luckily, it wasn't and they found themselves on the first floor of a run-down four-room house, quietly listening to ensure they were alone.

"Let's see if we can find our purses," Amanda stated as the two quickly looked around, luckily retrieving them from the top shelf of a bedroom closet. Both were pleasantly surprised that both of their phones were intact with their other personal items. Unfortunately, as luck would have it, both phones had dead batteries.

"We could hang out here until dark, but that's too long."

"Where will we go?" Amanda asked seriously.

"I don't know. Let me think." Allison replied, grabbing Micah's phone again and finally figuring out how to change the language to English. She opened an app called Poke Locator Map, which displayed a geographic screen with a star in the center, which she assumed must be their location. Quickly zooming the map out, her eyes opened wide as if stunned. "Amanda! According to this, we're in like friggin' Bucharest, Romania!"

"Romania? I'm not even sure where that is."

"It's between Hungary and Greece!" Allison then attempted a direct call, discounting dialing Eric Jordan, *that fucking snake,* and dialed her father instead, with the number "1' country code in front of it. She immediately got a *Call Failed* message. "Damn!" She then tried Aaron and then their mother, Sarah, with the same result. "Here, you try Alex's number while I look around for a weapon."

Amanda tried calling Alex's number but kept getting the same *Call Failed* error. *The SOB probably has no unlimited call plan.* She then had an idea, *WhatsApp!* This was an app that she and Alex had begun to use frequently as their communications would not be logged on her family's phone account. She was thrilled when she heard the call dialing, but the wind in her sails died down when she got his voicemail. *Come on, race man! Answer your phone!*

The starter lights went out and the field all raced toward the first corner. To the dismay of the crowd, McLaren driver Lando Norris attempted a crowded pass on Max Verstappen and the two hit each other, causing Norris' car to spring upward while the Red Bull spun, landing both championship contenders in the gravel trap and out of the race.

Alex stayed right on the tail of Lewis Hamilton's Mercedes and the two remained in concert until the fourth lap. Starting on the hard compound, Lewis was running on a one-stop strategy and gave up the lead to Moretti in the second turn, content to stay within distance of the Moretti car, knowing his soft compound Pirellis would fade and need a stop soon, requiring a second stop eventually.

The crowd stood and went wild when the two leaders sped by the flag stand with Alex Moretti leading by a full two seconds over the series' all-time winningest driver.

"Put down some quick laps, Alex," Tony's voice came in over the headset. "But keep the car in one piece, brother."

Amanda was beside herself as she used the free WhatsApp web-based talk and texting app, dialing Alex multiple times but kept getting a voicemail. Meanwhile, Allison appeared after rummaging through the house and finding an old military-looking rifle in a closet, chagrinned at not coming up with any ammunition for it.

"Do you even know how to work that thing?" Amanda asked while still re-dialing Alex's WhatsApp.

"Hell no, but maybe it will at least scare somebody. Any luck, Amanda?"

"No, but I did leave Alex at least five voicemails and told him we were in Romania."

"Send him a screenshot of a map locator!" Allison ordered.

Amanda pulled the Poke Map Locator app back up and took two screenshots of the screen, the second on max zoom, and re-opened the WhatsApp texting button. *I hope this works!*

She pulled up Alex's number again, preparing to send a new message with the graphic file attached, when the two heard the basement door open and Micah rushed toward them, though still not fully to himself after the blow to his head. Thinking fast, Amanda grabbed a metal kitchen chair and threw it at him. The thug grabbed it, aiming its legs toward her and forcing her into the corner.

"Hey, asshole!" Allison yelled.

Micah then quickly turned and froze at the sight of the older sister aiming the Czechoslovak World War Two rifle at him when Amanda grabbed a hot pot of coffee left on from earlier and smashed it over his head. As the gangster grabbed the top of his scalp with both hands, the previous wound throbbing while his eyes burned from the strong hot coffee, Allison turned the old rifle around and grabbing it by the muzzle end, swung the heavy wooden stock hard against the side of his head repeatedly until he went down to the floor, bleeding profusely and unconscious yet again.

"Do you think he's dead?" Amanda asked fearfully.

"Let's not hang around to find out. Come on, let's get our asses out of here!"

In the spur of the moment, Amanda had dropped his phone on the floor, and quickly reaching down to pick it up, she saw it now had a cracked screen, plus the device had taken its share of the hot coffee to boot. It would no longer even power up. "Oh no!"

"What is it?" Allison asked, trying to catch her breath.

Amanda held up the phone. "This thing is like toast now."

"Let's get the fuck out of here!"

"Wait! Maybe we should head out the back first."

"Good thinking, sister," Allison had to admit.

The back door led out a short way to a worn-down fence with a small gate to an alley. The two agreed it wasn't a good idea to bring the rifle, particularly since it had no bullets, nor did either of them know how to load and shoot it, even if they had. They hovered low behind the fence until confident there were no others about and then headed off to the right.

There were a few wary suspicious eyes on the two from behind closed doors and pulled curtains, suspecting the young women were out of place and knowing why.

Four houses away, an elderly woman was staring out at them through a back window, one who didn't appear friendly or threatening. Allison took a chance and walked up knocking on her back door. The old woman cracked it open to see what these two young women, both who looked alike, could want. They were then confronted with the language barrier when the woman held up a finger as a signal to wait, and shut the door as the nervous Cook sisters stood outside on her doorstep, wondering if they should just stand by or run away before their captors showed up.

The door re-opened and a teenage youth supplanted the older woman, wide-eyed as he turned to speak to the elder and then waved the girls in. The two shared looks briefly before entering a small kitchen while the boy, who turned out to be her grandson, continued their discussion, one which took on the flavor of some sort of dispute. The boy happened to speak some broken English and his grandmother stood aside as he waved the two into their front room, pointing at their TV monitor.

There was live coverage of the Dutch Grand Prix being broadcast in English with Romanian language subtitles. The live feed showed the Mercedes of Lewis Hamilton followed by a white-colored car. The feed changed to focus on the second place car which lit up the female guests like a Christmas tree.

Amanda came to tears as she folded her hands over her face. There was the big *Race For Amanda* painted all over the side of the car and the name Alex Moretti popped up in the subtitles. The announcers kept referencing each team's tire strategy as Hamilton was one of the few competitors starting on the hard compound tires and had yet to pit. Moretti had pitted on lap "24", giving up the lead but now faster and gaining on fresh medium compound tires.

The young man, who had introduced himself as Dorin Aldea, was intrigued as he witnessed the two watch the race. Both of their pictures had been displayed multiple times during the pre-race coverage and he had immediately recognized them. The two sisters had mixed reactions to seeing Alex still in a racecar, but had an emotional uplift when the cameras showed their mother in a special box in the stands beside Crissy Moretti.

Amanda estimated by the lap count and times that the race must have started a little over an hour earlier, prior to her cracking that

Micah character hard over the head with the cast iron stove plate. *Now I know why you're not answering your phone, race man.*

⋙⋘

Hamilton's Mercedes would lead the Moretti as they passed the mid-race point by thirteen seconds, but Alex was gaining rapidly on Lewis, who had yet to stop and was still on the hard compound tires, which lasted longer but were nearly spent. By lap forty the Moretti car had closed to within four seconds. Both would have one more pit stop and each would finish the race on the soft compound tires. Tony was calculating that Hamilton would have to pit no later than lap "48", which would mean twenty-four laps remaining on the "reds" or soft tires. He was planning to pit Alex six laps later, having his brother run only eighteen final laps on his "reds".

Lewis' Mercedes entered pit lane as Alex came out of the last turn and screamed down the main straight, the crowd on its feet to see the *Race For Amanda* livery streak past the flag stand and enter the first turn in the lead. Alex would lead Lewis comfortably as the great champion was still on cold tires and came across the stripe on the following lap ahead of the Mercedes by a full thirteen seconds.

The Moretti's medium tires would eventually fall off themselves and Hamilton was starting to eat into Alex's lead when he pitted for the final time on lap "54". He would relinquish the lead to the Mercedes and the two crossed the stripe on the next lap with Lewis now having what seemed to be a comfortable ten-second lead.

⋙⋘

Amanda and Allison sat together on the old sofa on pins and needles, still nervous they were so close to the place they had spent in that miserable cellar while Amanda watched her man chasing a legend. Dorin's grandmother brought the girls each a cup of hot tea, though the old woman never appeared comfortable with their presence.

Allison managed to ask Dorin if he had a charger for their phones, a request he was all too happy to oblige, taking one of the phones into his bedroom and plugging it in. The two guests jumped when they heard the back door opening again and an older man entered. They could hear a terse conversation ensue from the kitchen as Dorin's mood changed when he left the front room to engage in the tenuous discussion.

"I wonder what's going on?" Amanda asked while her eyes were still glued to the screen.

"I don't know," Allison responded. "But the way the old man keeps looking in here at us, I don't think he's happy about us being here."

The commotion quieted, if a bit, as Dorin's two grandparents sat down to eat. The young man knew the two guests wanted to watch the race, particularly the younger one, and worked to keep things comfortable for the time being.

Alex set the fastest lap of the race as he closed on Hamilton with ten laps remaining. His pace had pushed the leader to the point where the Mercedes' tires were falling off rather badly. The "reds" on the Moretti were also wearing, but having substantially less distance on them was telling the tale.

"Keep up the pressure, Alex. Push him hard while you can," Tony exclaimed. Their testing and calculations concluded the Pirelli soft compound tires would have decent grip for about eighteen to twenty laps unless pushed hard, which Alex was doing and forcing Lewis to defend much more briskly than desired.

"He must be running on imagination by now!" Alex replied.

"Yes, but you know Lewis is a master. If you see an opening, take him, Alex. But bring it home."

With two laps remaining, Hamilton crossed the line a mere two seconds ahead of Moretti, a driver possessed who seemed reminiscent of the late, great Gilles Villeneuve. By the middle of the back circuit, Alex was less than a car length behind and setting up the Mercedes for a run going into the last turn, a place where the worn-out tires would play out the most.

Amanda couldn't contain herself, jumping up and down and screaming, while temporarily oblivious to her surroundings and still dangerous disposition. Allison was the more subdued, of course, ever mindful of the conversation taking place in the family's kitchen, and just how accommodating these local people would end up being toward them. She huddled next to Amanda, encouraging her to tone herself down.

For his part, Dorin was excited himself. Being a rabid Formula One fan, as were many youths in Europe, this opportunity to host the famous Amanda Cook and her near-twin look-alike sister was like a dream come true.

The broadcasters themselves, though bound to be unbiased, could hardly control themselves. As so much of the pre-race show had dwelled on the *Race For Amanda* theme, to have Alex Moretti win would propel their sport to World Cup Soccer class status.

Amanda bit her lip, acknowledging that she should somewhat control herself.

Alex stuck right behind Lewis on the final portion of the twisty circuit, but catching and passing were two different things. Like the Hungaroring, much of the track involved a series of turns making overtaking difficult. Taking the white flag, he knew he had to get by Lewis in the second to last corner, a relatively tight right-hander that required much braking and grip. If the Mercedes could hold off the Moretti coming out of that turn, the last corner heading onto the main straight was a wide sweeping banked turn similar to those at Indianapolis where the powerful Mercedes power plant would kick in and overcome any advantage the Moretti would have on fresher rubber.

Hamilton knew he was cooked as if he attempted to out brake and hold off Alex Moretti, his car would likely careen off onto the run-off terrace between the pavement and catch barrier. Trying his best to hold the inside line, he watched helplessly as Moretti swept up beside him on the outside of the turn, accelerating past the veteran at speed heading into the banked last turn and toward a screaming crowd as he took the checkered flag.

Amanda could hardly control herself as she jumped up and gave Dorin a huge hug, the two dancing around in circles while the grandparents looked on with mixed feelings of concern and amusement. Allison looked on with feigned excitement, disguising disdain for her younger sister's childish behavior.

Dorin was summoned into the kitchen where his grandfather peaked through the curtains out the back window. There was a commotion happening down the alley and a couple of ruffians sporting shotguns were milling around.

Allison told Amanda to turn the sound down as she could tell their hosting family was having a heated conversation. Meanwhile, Amanda watched and listened closely as David Coulthard, a former driver and now Formula One TV personality, approached Alex through the throngs of adoring fans for a word.

"Alex, that was perhaps the most exciting Grand Prix finish I've witnessed in years. It seems you had just the right strategy to win. Congratulations on your first Formula One victory."

"Thank you David and yes, credit my brother, Tony, for calling that one. I think we may have won in Hungary had I better listened to him."

"Alex, the world knows this has been a very traumatizing time for you these past few weeks. How difficult was it to get yourself prepared mentally to drive again, and especially put on such a performance?"

"Well, David. this is all about my fiancée, Amanda, and her sister, keeping their saga on the front page and having the whole world behind the push for their safe release."

"I certainly believe you have accomplished that, Alex. What could Formula One look for at Team Moretti in the near future? Is Tony planning to return to driving soon and could we see both of you as teammates?"

"I don't know. Right now, I just want Amanda back. I want to get married and enjoy life again. And please, if anyone knows anything that would help us get Amanda and her sister back, please call us."

"There you have it. Alex Moretti, our winner of the Dutch Grand Prix, and looking forward to reuniting with his fiancée. Who knows, we could have a preview of the next American world champion, one we haven't seen in nearly half a century when the great Mario Andretti drove for Colin Chapman. Back up to you, Jenson."

The coverage moved on to the racing highlights and the championship battle, including the secondary story about the two top combatants taking each other out on the first turn.

⚑⚑

The grandparents and Dorin all gathered in their front room. Dorin explained in his best English his grandfather's big concern that the two sisters were endangering them. Everyone around feared Eduardo Blaku's *Brigăzi*, even though he had been exiled to Mexico. Now his nephew ran the local operation, and he was a ruthless criminal. The girls could not remain there.

"Could you help us get a taxi to the police station?" Allison asked.

Dorin shook his head vehemently. "You do not want to go to the police. They are part of the mob. The cab company, too."

"Will your grandfather turn us in?" Amanda asked.

"No, my grandfather hates them. My mother got involved with them, just working as a waitress at one of their clubs. They wanted to prostitute her and she refused. She disappeared and we never saw her again. I was four years old. Grandfather believes she was sold on the white slave black market."

"Dorin, I understand the fear of having us here," Allison stated. "Is there somewhere safe we could stay? Now that we have our phones, this will hopefully be over soon."

"Yes, I do know a place. It's a farm on the outskirts of town where my girlfriend from school lives. Her father hates the Blaku mob as much as anyone in Bucharest.

It took nearly two hours for the post-race festivities, including the traditional podium trophy awards followed by yet another ritual, the three drivers dousing each other with champaign as well as their team principals and much of the admiring crowd, at least those who braved being that close to the platform. The many reporters each fought for a quick word with the winner, and Alex used each and every one of these to put out another plug for Amanda.

Some fourteen hundred miles to the southeast, the two sisters sat impatiently for some indication their messages to Alex had gotten through. Allison was disgusted with the whole *Race For Amanda* thing as she had spent her whole life as the dominant sister, visualizing nothing but big things for herself, *CEO* of a large bank or corporation, *Governor* Cook, *Senator* Allison Cook, perhaps even the first female US President. Now she found herself constantly in the shadow of her little sister, her plan to eliminate that problem permanently blowing up in her face.

"Enough of the high fives, people!" Allison yelled at the television. "Hey! We're here!"

"Be patient, Allison. He probably hasn't even gotten to his phone yet."

Dorin informed the two they were welcome to take baths while his grandmother washed their clothing. After dark, he and his grandfather would transport them to their new temporary refuge. Both were elated at this gesture, as the simple thought of a real hot bath was just what the doctor ordered. The sisters' stress level had subsided exponentially over the past couple of hours, a welcome veneer of hope.

Alex showered and prepared to go out to dinner, wanting to forgo the traditional post-race party as a certain sadness kicked in, down that the love of his life was not there to share his first Formula One victory with him. He grabbed his phone to glance at the many expected congratulatory social media messages, including several on *WhatsApp*.

There were five from a single unknown number that he started to blow off as he was used to so many bullshit messages with subjects such as *Amanda is here!* or *I can find the sisters*. But one caught his eye: *Race Man, I'm in Romania!*

No one ever calls me that except... Alex thought quickly and felt a sudden bolt of excitement. He clicked on the message detail, following up by digesting all of the messages from that number that had come in within seconds of each other. He then dialed the number back on *WhatsApp*, getting a message in an unfamiliar language. Still excited, he then made two other calls.

"What do you mean, don't call the police?"

"Byron, the last message stated specifically the local police there cannot be trusted!" Sarah yelled back.

"This is probably a false alarm, Sarah. A con. We should call Interpol and just let them run it down."

"No, Byron! Alex was sure it was Amanda who left these messages!"

"What does he know? With this new artificial intelligence technology, anyone's voice can be duplicated, Sarah. Le Fleur thinks this could be a ploy to just detract law enforcement resources away from Paris."

"We have our own detectives working on this. I don't want to involve the police yet."

"What do you mean, you have your own detectives? What are you talking about, Sarah?"

She immediately regretted her slip of the tongue in telling Charlotte,him that she and Alex had acted alone. "I hired a private detective from Charlotte who is working with someone in Israel to find them."

"From Charlotte?" Byron angrily yelled back. *What would possess this woman to think that any police detective, private or otherwise, from Charlotte, North Carolina, would have a clue about investigating a kidnapping in Paris?* "What is the name of this private detective, Sarah?"

"His name is Eugene James, and don't worry. Alex and I are paying for it."

"Eugene James?" *Eugene James?* Byron thought when it hit him. "Wait, Sarah. Are you talking about a man who goes by Cotton?"

"Yes, do you know him?"

"Do I know him? Do I know him!? He did some pre-trial investigative work for me and it all blew up in my face! Sarah, how could you be so naïve? How much did you pay that imbecile?"

"That's none of your affair, Byron." Sarah recoiled, registering the fact that her soon-to-be ex-husband had gone behind her back months earlier, another of his brazen acts to destroy the Moretti family. "Whatever Cotton James is able to do will be a bonus. I want to give him a couple of days before we involve the police, Byron."

"You're going off half-cocked like this, Sarah, is going to get our daughters killed!" Byron yelled.

She had enough, hung up the phone, and started to break down in tears. *It was Alex who had come up with hiring James in the first place. Was that a mistake?* She regretted even telling Byron about the messages on Alex's phone now. There had admittedly been no other follow-up contact. *Perhaps Byron is right about this being a con.*

It was now late, but Sarah couldn't sleep and needed someone to talk to, someone sympathetic who would listen and advise with reason. She sent Crissy Moretti a text that read, *"Crissy, kindly send me Andy's cell number."*

Alex had played the voicemail messages over and over for his father, and disclosed the fact that he and Sarah had indeed hired a private detective on their own.

"I don't know what to think about it, son, other than it certainly sounds like her."

"That's exactly what I thought, Dad. And my not calling the police?"

"That's your call. That would be the first move normally, but that last message was pretty clear, was it not? But if I were the perpetrators and able to fabricate such a message, the reference to the cops being on the take is exactly what I would include."

Cotton James was getting nervous. Their adventures over the last few weeks had accomplished little in his own mind, and he had burned through most of his upfront retainer money, including some cash he sent Remi to keep her at bay. Furthermore, as thick-skinned as he was, James would flinch at some of Arieh's ruthless techniques, those of a man truly hell-bent on accomplishing their mission, whatever the cost.

The drive from Zurich to Cannes would take seven hours. As the three approached the Italian border just north of Milan, Cotton felt his phone buzz and saw it was Alex Moretti.

"Yes, Mr. Moretti!"

"James, I have received a credible new lead."

"So have we. We're heading down to the French Riviera," Cotton replied, explaining their visit with the Swiss banker, choosing to leave out most of the details.

"I've received some calls from Amanda. I believe they are being held in Romania."

"Amanda actually called you!?"

"That's right, and I'm ticked that I didn't get the calls or messages for hours."

"And she's in Romania? Tell me about it."

Aaron continued an ongoing routine of calling Byron and Sarah every few hours, wanting an update. He finally received a return call from his would-be future father-in-law after leaving multiple messages.

"Moretti got some calls and texts from Amanda, he alleges, claiming she and Allison are in Romania."

"Where in Romania? Can I call Allison?" Aaron responded anxiously.

"I wouldn't get too excited. All indications would lead us to believe our girls are being held somewhere in Paris. Between us and Interpol, we've received hundreds of these so-called hot leads. Since Sarah and Moretti announced the reward was increasing tenfold, these calls have exploded. I relayed the information to Interpol, for whatever good that will do."

"Byron, I wish we had some of our own people on the ground over there."

"We have been in touch with our embassy in Paris, Aaron. I've also reached out to both of our US Senators to see what pressure they could bring to bear. I just learned that Sarah and that damned Alex got together and hired Cotton James, that sleazy private investigator from right here in Charlotte. Ridiculous."

"Cotton James, huh? What a name," Aaron responded.

"I wish we had someone who knows the neighborhood over there, from an international criminal investigative perspective," Byron added. "The people I know in Europe are all financial-related. Now Alex is back to racing cars while the young girl he professes to care about is still missing. These people are just evil," he rambled on, knowing he did have a like-minded ally on the call.

Aaron thought briefly, a young man who felt helpless, stuck in San Diego at his Marine post ever since his fiancée and younger sis had been snatched. "I do have a close friend who's in military intelligence here. He seems to have the means to find out almost anything. Perhaps I should dial him up."

"Nothing to lose, Aaron," Byron exclaimed, having little confidence in the suggestion. *Perhaps it will make you feel better, Aaron, and stop you from calling me every other hour.* Byron did take a moment to reflect on how this young man's father had been his closest friend and customer, a nearly lifelong friendship gone south, all because the Cook family had intersected with the Morettis.

The two disconnected and Byron thought he may send Le Fleur an email, advising him of Cotton James' presence and the likelihood he would be heading to Romania. *Who knows, maybe James can find someone or something that may help Interpol. I doubt it,* he considered but chose to send the email anyway.

Aaron immediately made another call, getting a voicemail prompt to leave a message. "Eric, it's Aaron. I need a huge favor regarding my fiancée, Allison. Call me right away."

⚑⚑

Andy and Adam Herrera left the last of their sponsor contingent, all excited as expected and now making plans for next weekend in Monza.

"I was approached earlier at the party about Alex doing a series of commercials," Adam declared. "I think many assume that I am his agent." *Not that I would mind, of course,* Herrera had as an afterthought.

"What kind of commercials?"

"A vodka brand."

"I don't think he would be up to something like that," Andy discounted it, seeing an intriguing text pop up on his phone.

"How about a late-night drink, Andy? Need a shoulder to cry on. – Sarah."

"We need to discuss Alex and his commercial interests sometime, Andy. He's a star now."

"Not now, Adam. I have some personal business I have to attend to."

<hr>

Burim was disappointed his uncle didn't meet him at the airport, but had him picked up and chauffeured the thirty-plus miles to the place by two very muscular Latino males, neither of whom looked or sounded friendly. His natural mistrust of strangers made for a nervous transfer, particularly since he was carrying such a large duffle bag loaded with cash, one his escorts had inspected, as both were actually looking for weapons.

He began to second-guess his own decision to hand-deliver the large bounty as opposed to a safer and more conventional path in getting the cash into their Swiss bank account. *I want to see the look on Uncle Eduardo's face when he opens the bag*, Burim had considered confidently. The four million would constitute by far the largest single take he had ever been a party to.

He knew his uncle was being protected by the powerful Mexican cartel oligarch, Carlos Cervantes. Burim was on edge, worried that one or two of his chaperones would be tempted to simply kill him and make off with such a massive amount of stash. As they completed the nearly hour-long journey and pulled through the security gate, he concluded the two were motivated by something more powerful than greed,... *extreme fear.*

The historic casa grande was built on a beachfront plot of land several miles north of the old town of Cancun, belonging to Cervantes. He was escorted out to the veranda facing the powdery white sand beach where a single American sat alone. Both were confused and uncomfortable introductions were exchanged.

"You must be Burim Basha... Lieutenant Eric Jordan," he stated and put out his hand.

"Your voice is familiar," Burin replied, while declining the protocol of a handshake. "You are the one who called me down in Budapest."

"Yes, I was just the messenger. Not my call."

"I see," Burim replied, appearing annoyed. "And where is Uncle Eduardo?"

"I was told he would be delayed until this evening."

"That is not good. I need to return to Bucharest very soon."

"Why did you take them to Bucharest?" Jordan asked, surprised and concerned. He was stunned and angry that both Cook sisters were nabbed in Paris after the sanction to grab Allison's younger sister only was called off. He didn't know they were being kept in Romania, a mecca for the human trafficking trade in Europe.

Burim quickly clammed up, refusing to answer while reminding himself that he was not fully informed about what this American was doing in Cancun and what part he was playing. "How do you know my uncle, *Domnule* Jordan?"

Eric was already developing a dislike for the young Romanian's tone. "We've worked together a bit. So, you led the team that grabbed the girls in Paris." It was an assumed statement, not a question. "Why was the oldest sister taken?"

Burim now wore his best smart-ass smirk. "Buy one, get one free. You Americans fuckin' like deals like that, am I right, Lieutenant?"

Jordan was quite worried as he had assumed, like everyone else, the girls were being held somewhere in Paris, and that any reference to Romania was bogus, a revelation he now knew to be quite true. His *pal,* Aaron Williams, advised him that Moretti and the girls' mother had hired their own private investigator, a man from Charlotte. As he waited uncomfortably with Blaku's rogue underboss nephew, any concern that a southern American P.I. could uncover anything of consequence would sink to mere insignificance.

⚑⚑

The beachfront hotel bar was buzzing with activity from the Formula One crowd. She arrived early, took a corner table, and ordered a glass of white wine. Sarah became uncomfortable as a nearby middle-aged male, dressed in expensive clothing and sporting an ample amount of gold jewelry, was making overbearing attempts at flirting with her, all to the point of embarrassment. *Come on, Andy. Where are you?*

The Moretti team principal walked in two minutes later and found her. A waitress quickly appeared and took his order for a Heineken beer. "Sorry, Sarah. Suddenly I have a lot of fans again wanting autographs."

"Oh, that's okay. Thanks for meeting me so late."

"Well, other than the obvious, what's on your mind, Sarah?"

"I got in a terrible argument with Byron."

Andy took a sip of his beer and nodded. "And?"

"He thought we should just call Interpol about the voicemails. Do you think he's right, Andy? I mean, do you think these messages might be fake,... a con?"

"I know there have been a ton of calls with bogus leads, Sarah. But those voicemail messages sure sounded like Amanda."

A young couple walked by at a distance, looking to get a phone snapshot. Andy put up his hand in an attempt to discourage them before waving the two over. "Do you speak English?"

"Oui, Monsieur. I am sorry. It is our first Formula One race and we recognized you both—"

"How about an autograph?" Andy offered. "But no pictures, please."

"Oui, Monsieur." The young Frenchman produced a race ticket, which Andy promptly signed.

"Merci, and Madam Cook?"

"Oh my lord," Sarah reacted blushing. "I didn't know I was so famous." She then signed her name right under Andy's.

The young man took the ticket and thanked them gracefully, when ten seconds later Sarah looked up as another anxious fan's phone flashed.

"How about a walk on the beach, Sarah?" Andy offered, seeing them having any kind of private conversation in the hotel lounge, one overcrowded with out-of-town Formula One fans, was most improbable.

The two discarded their shoes near the outdoor pool and strolled casually down the beach where the lights of Rotterdam could be seen way off in the distance. Despite the late summer season, the North Sea waves were chilly on their feet as the two shifted slightly toward drier sand.

Sarah felt a closeness toward Andy as the two approached a small but lively tiki-style bar. She and Andy chose to stop in and each grabbed two available bar stools, giving the two a pittance of privacy as nearly all the other patrons were locals and paying them little mind.

"Does this Cotton James know his business, Sarah?"

"I hope so, Andy. Me and Alex came to the conclusion we had nothing to lose. Byron never told me he had hired this Cotton James at some point in the past."

Doesn't sound like the Cooks had a very honest and open marriage, Andy thought but chose to keep it to himself. "I think the *Race For Amanda* went over big, wouldn't you say?"

"Yes, and hopefully it will all lead to something positive, for my daughters' sake. What a big day for your race team though, huh?"

"Oh yes. It turned out putting Alex in the car was the right move."

"Yes, but you knew he was good, I mean very good, Andy... I'll have one of those Blue Hawaiian drinks," Sarah informed the barmaid.

Andy ordered himself a draft and offered a toast. "Here's to first victories and finding the girls."

The two glasses jiggled together as the barmaid chimed in. "Congratulations, Andy."

He and Sarah shared a look as the fifty-something-year-old woman smiled. "I remember when you were on your first podium here. It was my first Formula One race... We all had such a crush on him back then," she said to Sarah, smiling.

"I'm sure he was quite dashing back then," Sarah replied with a return smile.

"This place was good to me," Andy added. "I won here the following year."

Sarah stared out toward the dark waves. "Were you and Sabetha together then?'

"No, actually we began dating right afterward... At Monza."

"What happened to you two, Andy?"

"Success, I guess... And failure."

"There had to be more to it than that," Sarah pried expectantly.

"Things started to go south when I left Williams and we moved to a place near my hometown of Genoa, right after I was hired by Ferrari.

Sabetha liked living near London and things were much more quiet in Genoa. Tony was a toddler and I thought Sabetha was a happy mamma, but she missed the attention. I was pressured to spend every waking hour around Maranello, even though input from drivers was discouraged by Abruzzo, the man promoted to Formula One team manager right after I started. It was a three-hour drive one-way, so I spent most of my time during the week there. Those were tough years and I wasn't winning, which I'm sure affected my attitude toward her. She found a rich guy down the coast in Monte Carlo who gave her what she wanted."

"But you almost reconciled a couple of times."

"Ha!" Andy chuckled. "I think we just pretended. It was never that close. I'm not sure I could ever give a woman the time she needs, Sarah."

"I suppose that would all depend on what that woman needs, Andy."

He smiled casually and took another sip of the cold brew. He thought about asking her what she needed but chose to change the subject. "You've been to a few races now, Sarah. How do you like them?"

"Before my daughters were kidnapped, I loved them. Seeing Amanda and Alex together after all they've been through was just magic. I pray it will be that way again someday."

"Are you staying over? For Monza, I mean? I could show you where I grew up."

"Oh, the paparazzi would have a field day with that, Andy."

"Right now, that could be a good thing. The more media buzz, the better. That's what the whole *Race For Amanda* campaign is all about."

The two chatted at length over additional drinks as time escaped them when the barmaid yelled, "Last call."

"I guess we had best be getting back, Sarah," Andy declared as he grabbed his wallet to settle up.

The two now walked hand-in-hand back down the sparsely populated beach, returning to the hotel at just past 1:30 AM, when Andy escorted Sarah to her suite door.

"You can kiss me now, Andy."

"Best suggestion I've had all day."

Eduardo Blaku entered the hacienda well after sundown, annoying both Eric Jordan and his nephew, Burim Basha, which was all by design. The social greetings exchanged seemed to do little to lower the tension.

"So, Burim, you chose to travel all the fucking way to Paris and grab both of these sisters," Eduardo began. "Explain."

Burim could tell his boldness had not impressed his uncle and squirmed a bit before answering. "Armend and Dominik could hardly tell them apart. It was a flash decision. Buy one, get one free."

The young Romanian underboss' effort at injecting humor had fallen flat and for his part, Eric now knew that Eduardo had not ordered Allison's kidnapping, and in fact had apparently not sanctioned the Paris grab at all.

"Should I assume your people in Atlanta have still not taken care of this *Hot Lips* in Charlotte?" Jordan asked, an attempt on his part to assert himself in the conversation.

"They have been recalled. Your *Hot Lips* is of no concern now. Our eliminating her could only lead to more unnecessary investigations with little gain."

"I also assumed we were going to discuss how we may retrieve Allison."

"You assume too much. I received an interesting call just a few hours ago from an old friend of mine in Bucharest," Blaku replied, a statement that made both Burim Basha and Eric Jordan quite confused, if not uneasy. "Lonesku just received a report from Interpol that a lead had come in claiming this Alex Moretti had received voicemails from the Cook sisters, claiming they were in Bucharest. He was also made aware that an independent investigator had been dispatched to Europe from America to find the captive girls."

Burim felt his nerves begin to crawl now. This friend his uncle referred to was none other than the Bucharest Police Chief, Anatolie Lonesku. That line of back channel communication between his uncle and the local police spoke volumes about the assumed level of trust and confidence Blaku had placed in his ambitious and often half-cocked nephew. "Interpol is getting all kinds of these false leads. I think Lonesku has been hitting the bottle too much."

"I see," Eduardo replied. "So Eric, is that why you sent some private fucking cop over there, to free your American lover?"

Jordan had wanted to table the issue of his handing over a hundred grand to Eduardo as a sanction to kidnap Amanda Cook, funds he hoped to retrieve, at least in part as they had gotten their ransom and still had the girls. The conversation had suddenly turned.

"I'll ask you again, Mr. Eric Jordan. Who is this outside investigator?"

Jordan was now squirming. "I believe Sarah Cook and Alex Moretti are paying him. I don't know who it is and didn't take that seriously."

"And when did you learn of this?"

"A close friend of mine, who happens to be Allison Cook's fiancé, got the information from her father and he called me about it earlier today."

"Her fiancé, you say? It would seem your friendship and loyalty is not something one can place trust in," Blaku stated with a blatant verbal jab. "A former American Secretary of State, Henry Kissinger, once said that whatever should be revealed eventually should be revealed immediately. It's disturbing that you didn't make me aware of this little sidebar."

A certain contempt entered Jordan's mind now. He was less than an hour from Tijuana and he and Blaku could have discussed whatever they needed to accomplish without his flying all the way down to Cancun. "I just did confirm it. Can we discuss releasing Allison and get back to the original deal we made? You did get a hundred grand, Eduardo."

"No, I believe the deal has changed, Mr. Jordan." The *Nusa* made a quick nod to his right-hand man, Marius, who put a nine-millimeter slug through the back of the American's skull just off center. Eduardo casually took another puff of his cigar as Eric Jordan fell forward.

As hard and vicious as Burim's facade attempted to present, he froze suddenly as he observed his uncle's poker face, casually lighting his cigar. *The man is so callous, so cold.* The young thug was careful to observe and learn from his uncle, thinking he would be calling all the shots someday.

"So, Burim, you claim this banker screwed us out of a million fucking dollars?"

"Yes, Uncle Eduardo. They gave us four million. Armend and I counted it all three times."

"You waited many days to demand payment which kept the story in the papers longer and then had to make the whole world aware of it on this social media... And you believe this fuckin' banker, a man who is a billionaire, took your threats seriously?"

"Of course. I threatened to kill his daughters. And he did deliver four million."

"Why would a man like that choose to hold back a million? Why would he not split the cache in two with a note stating the other half would be delivered in exchange for his girls? Only a fool would hand over that much cash on a simple recorded promise of getting his daughters back after the fact."

Burin was getting slightly offended by being queried this way. "How the fuck am I to know what's in this American's mind?"

Eduardo sat silent, staring ahead at his estranged sister's son while taking a few more puffs of his cigar, all a ploy to unnerve the overzealous young underboss.

"Trust me, uncle. I will extort more from these people. The son-of-a-bitch will pay dearly for this shortchanging us."

"So, Burim. You left Armend Cazacu in charge while you're away?"

"Yes. He has Micah Dragos with him and backup nearby if needed. The American whores are quite fucking secure, I can assure you."

The soldiers all stiffened and shared glances with each other. While their boss threw around salty language loosely, it was viewed as a blatant sign of disrespect to speak to him this way.

"I would like to speak to this Armend. Get him on the phone."

Burim didn't like this assumed break in protocol. His uncle had always just given him orders and never desired to deal with his underlings. The man was serious, however, and Burim dialed Armend up.

"Armend, tell me how things are going there—"

"Give me the phone," Eduardo ordered, cutting Burim off before he completed his question.

Stunned, the nephew handed his phone over.

"Armend Cazacu, I am told you are in charge. Is that correct?"

The anxious young Romanian thug hesitated. "And who is this?"

"Eduardo Blaku. Now again. My nephew tells me you are in charge there."

The very nervous Cazacu was now fearful. He had left Micah alone earlier that morning while out picking up some basic supplies and returned at noon to find his man dead on the floor in the kitchen, his fears made worse as the two captive girls were now missing. He had called in more help and was scrambling to find them, lest his life depended on it. "Yes, everything is under control."

"Good, very good. Now, I wish to see the goods."

"Excuse me?"

Eduardo gave Burim a strong stare. "Yes! Take your phone, turn on the fucking camera, and show me the two women!"

Armend panicked. Should he admit the captives had escaped, he would be placing Burim in serious danger, not to mention himself.

Eduardo waited impatiently for a few seconds and was then disconnected. "What the fuck!?"

Burim sensed something was bad wrong. He took the phone back from his uncle and re-dialed, repeatedly getting voicemail.

"I'm getting a bad feeling about this, Burim."

"Uncle Eduardo, have one of your men take me back to the airport. I must get to Bucharest on the next flight out and deal with that son-of-a-bitch Armend and take care of things."

Eduardo replayed his unnerving act of just staring and taking more puffs of his cigar. "No, I think you have taken care of enough, nephew." He then retrieved a Beretta pistol from his jacket and fired six shots repeatedly into Burim Basha's torso. The young Romanian stared forward at his uncle in painful and shocking disbelief before it all went blank.

"Marius, I want you to fly to Bucharest and get control of this. Find those sluts quickly and find that missing million dollars."

"Should I plan for some sort of follow-up exchange demand for additional payment?"

"Hell no! It is well past time for this fucking story to fade away. We will sell them on the black market. I know just the right buyer who would pay a fortune for a package like this."

Chapter 9

Bucharest Encounter

The farm was modest in most ways but quite charming for Allison and Amanda compared to what the two had been accustomed to the past few weeks. Dorin's girlfriend, Relia, had pitched the plan to her father, a man who hated the Romanian mafia and the *Nusa,* Eduardo Blaku, personally.

The small two-room house was crowded, with Relia's parents and little brother having to share space with her. Thus, the two house guests would stay in the barn for the night. The next day, Dorin and Relia would stop on the way home from school and purchase a prepaid phone SIM card for the girls to use and call long distance.

Amanda was cautiously optimistic, visualizing their release and reunion with Alex, her mother, and company. Allison looked forward to a path back home herself, but in her own sinful way, lamenting the fact that her despised little sister would be going back with her.

"I'm not sure this Relia's father can be trusted," Allison stated cynically. "He doesn't appear any happier to see us than Dorin's grandpa."

"Be positive, big sister. Would you rather return to that dark, filthy dungeon?"

"No. I just want to get out of this godforsaken place."

"I like still can't believe our phones won't work here. How do these people live without the internet out here? If we ever get back to America, I'm going to kiss the ground."

For once, Allison Cook fully agreed with her younger sister's sentiment.

Eduardo's right-hand man, Marius, arrived just past dawn, angry but not surprised that nothing was in order regarding their captives. The safe house that Burim had used was vacant and his trusted associate, Armend Cazacu, was nowhere to be found.

Word had already spread in the neighborhood regarding the missing sisters, particularly the ramifications of anyone knowing their whereabouts and not immediately contacting the *Brigăzi*, much less harboring them.

After confronting the various mid-level street thugs, Marius reached out to the one source his boss was confident would bear fruit.

"We have seen or heard nothing as of yet, *Domnule* Marius. You will be contacted right away when we do."

"The *Nasu* will expect no less, Captain."

Marius shook his head, not happy with what he was given by their contact in the local police department. He had casually tried to convince Eduardo to let it pass. After all, they were four million US dollars richer, there was little or no evidence their capture could be tied to Tijuana, and the ongoing media exposure could risk future operations.

But his boss had a huge ego and feared wiping his hands of them would show weakness in the eyes of the Cartel, his Mexican partners, and protectors. No, the two young women must be re-captured and sold to the highest bidder through a very exclusive dark web auction, infamously known as *Black Horizon*.

"Leave no stone uncovered, Marius," was Eduardo's last instruction. "Our contraband must be found at all costs."

⚑✕⚑

"Are you out of your mind?"

"I can't stand just sitting around here while doing nothing, Dad. It was really her! I know it... Just a couple of days. I'll be back in Monza by Friday morning, in plenty of time for the first practice session."

"What do you have to go on, Alex? An unknown phone number? You're going into a hostile environment blind, son!"

"I can't go through life always knowing I didn't try."

"If you're a no-show, or show up to Monza late, that won't be good, Alex. Tony will probably insist on being in the car."

"If I leave now, I'll have two full days. Dad."

"What if you're right, Alex? If Amanda and her sister are there, you'll be in the company of some very dangerous actors. You really should let the professionals handle this."

"This is something I have to do, Dad."

Andy stared at his youngest son, knowing he wasn't going to deter his will. Living his whole life in three generations of Morettis racing cars at death speeds, this would be the first time Andy could truly recall a fear of danger. "Well, godspeed then," Andy closed, and the two embraced.

⚑✕⚑

Alon drove at speed on Highway 34 along the south shore of the Danube River in Serbia toward the Djerdap Dam, where they would proceed through the customs and immigration checkpoint and enter Romania. It would be another six hours into Bucharest.

Arieh had an old acquaintance there who he was certain knew the town. Eduardo Blaku had been exiled to Mexico and was still the *Nasu*, but would have an underboss managing his business in Romania. Arieh's man would know about these subordinates, where they could be found, their security, etc.

Cotton looked down at his phone, now buzzing. *Alex Moretti?* "Mr. Moretti, what's on your mind?"

"How many choices do you need?"

Smartass, the Charlotte P.I. felt. "What can I do for you?"

"I'm flying into Bucharest to meet with you."

"You're going to do what?"

"You heard me, James. I want to be there, maybe help."

Perhaps you can bring some cash. That would be the biggest help, Cotton thought, but held his tongue for now. "This kind of work could be hazardous to your health, you know."

"You forget who you're talking to. My occupation is hazardous."

"So I've heard."

"I'm arriving at 4:20 PM and staying at the Novotel City Centre."

"We'll see you before seven," James stated before disconnecting, shaking his head.

"What is it, Cotton?" Arieh asked.

"Alex Moretti is flying into Bucharest to meet with us."

The two Israeli brothers shared concerned looks. "I don't like it. The young man has too much recognition."

"It's his money. We don't have to have him run around with us. Maybe he can set us up with a nice, *and free*, place to stay for a change."

"Just his being in the vicinity will raise awareness, put the local *Brigăzi* on alert. That's exactly what we don't need."

"Maybe we should figure out a way to use this sportsman's celebrity to our advantage," Alon added. He was a man of few words, so when he did speak, his ideas often resonated.

<hr />

One of Marius' men received a tip from a safe house neighbor that two young women had left the previous morning and entered the red-colored house on the back side of the alley. He and two local goons kicked the back door in on Dorin's grandparents' home, threatening the old people at knifepoint.

Leaving a trademark slice across the old man's jaw, Marius was told about the farm where the girls were, the old man claiming it was he himself who drove them there, wanting to protect his grandson.

One of the thugs spoke up as they were leaving. "I know this place and the son-of-a-bitch who owns it. He will be armed and is quite dangerous."

"No problem. We'll just have the police pick them up for us."

<hr />

Cotton and his pair of Israeli mercenaries met Alex at this hotel suite. The three listened intently to the WhatsApp voicemail recordings, while Alex reiterated how and why he felt the messages were authentic.

The four discussed a plan of action when Arieh suddenly became quite animated about something. Pulling his one Ear Pod out of his left ear, he stated, "I caught something on my police scanner app. Two cars are being dispatched to a rural address just outside the metro, regarding two American females being held captive. I have the address."

They approached cautiously forty-five minutes later, parking just past the small gravel lane leading up to the premises. Making their way on foot through the wooded thickets, the four halted at the tree line to observe.

The place was quiet and devoid of any human activity and Alex volunteered to approach the house unarmed while the remaining three trained their weapons in case hostiles appeared. Knocking on the door three times, Alex heard a low moan come from inside, waved his mercenaries forward, and entered to find a man lying bloodied on the floor.

Alon quickly observed the male had two gunshot wounds but was still alive, though barely. He quickly patched his chest wounds as best he could in an effort to slow the bleeding.

Alex began to run around and search the house, frantically looking for signs of Amanda and her sister when minutes later, a noise was heard coming from outside as two teenage kids rode up on bicycles.

"Papa!" The teen female yelled, fearful of the armed men standing in her home. As Arieh attempted to calm the child while she embraced her stricken father, Alex heard the commotion and came running back into the front room.

"Relia, it's him!" Dorin yelled. "It's Alex Moretti!"

The group was all in a confused state momentarily, with none knowing the full extent of previous events. Dorin started to give them a rundown when Relia's father finally came to. "The police came and took the girls. I shot one of the bastards. I am sorry."

"It appears they left you for dead," Arieh stated. "If you have a family doctor, it would be a good time for a house call."

Dorin proceeded to explain the whole episode, starting with Amanda and Allison showing up at his grandparent's home the previous morning, how he arranged to bring them here, and the plan for him and Relia to stop after school and buy them phone SIM cards.

"How would the police finger the girls to this farm?" Cotton asked.

Dorin suddenly felt sick. They must have gotten to his grandparents. "The police and the *Brigăzi* are all in the same here. I am so sorry."

<hr />

The two were again terrified as they sat handcuffed in the back of the small police sedan, heading at speed back into the city. Their feckless attempts at motioning to the many gawking bystanders on the way did nothing to lessen their plight, as the passing crowd would just see two apprehended criminals behind tinted windows being hauled off to jail.

The vehicle pulled up to a metal building in a rundown industrial part of the city and honked one time as a large door opened, allowing the patrol car to pull forward. There they were met by a half dozen rough-looking bearded men, two of whom opened the rear doors and jerked the two captive sisters out, manhandling them to another part of the building where they were each pushed down onto two hard metal chairs.

"You two sluts are getting to be more trouble than you're worth," the one well-dressed male stated. He appeared to be of Latino descent, clean-shaven, and acting with authority. "Fortunately, you will bring *mucho dinero* as a pair. You will both bathe and put on your finest presence. Horea, you will show them."

Both sisters were brought to tears. They were so close to freedom after so many days of hell. They both began to think that perhaps they were never that close at all.

Alex was dropped off in front of the Ministry of Internal Affairs in the Old Town section of Bucharest, which served as police headquarters. He confronted a uniformed policewoman staring at him through thick glass after waiting impatiently behind two others.

She quickly summoned an English-speaking officer who took in the American's information, then directed Alex to wait in the front entrance hall. A full half-hour later an officer approached and introduced himself as Sergeant Coman before guiding him back and into a small office. Unfortunately, no one appeared to recognize him, or if so, none let on.

Before Alex could even speak, the short and stocky built Sergeant asked to see his passport, studying the busy pages for an annoying few minutes. "How may I be of assistance, *Domnule* Moretti?"

"You are aware of Amanda and Allison Cook, two American women who were kidnapped in Paris over three weeks ago?'

"Yes, of course. I've seen the notices put out by Interpol. And it has been all over the media."

"Amanda is my fiancée. She was brought here to Romania and picked up by your police officers, just outside of the city less than two hours ago."

Coman stiffened and leaned back in his chair. "And how do you know this?"

"I just left there! Your officers shot the farmer while Amanda and her sister were taken away to,.. I assume here."

"Would you wait here for a few moments while I look into this?" Coman directed as he got up and left Alex in his small office.

"This was a bad idea, Cotton," Arieh mumbled. "We're wasting time while we should be shaking down the *Brigăzi* right now.

"Since Bucharest is the *Brigăzi's* home turf, don't you think we might be a bit outnumbered?" Cotton hadn't forgotten the brazen act by Arieh at the Grether mansion in Zurich, a man who seemed on a mission to make one last statement on his way out.

"Of course we are. That's why we have to be smart. And this Alex charging into the police headquarters right now is not smart."

After sitting for over an hour, Alex got up and attempted to leave Coman's office in an effort to demand answers, only to find the door locked. He began pounding on the shatterproof glass and yelled, only to have the outside personnel just stare at him.

What is wrong with these people? Alex thought, now exasperated.

Finally, Coman re-approached with two other men in suits who were both let in as Coman then locked the door behind them.

"Mr. Moretti, I am John Rosberg and this is Hans Zelder. We are from the US State Department, sent here from our embassy. You have created quite a stir here."

"State Department?" Alex blurted out. "Do you even know who I am, or why I'm here?"

"Yes, we are quite aware. I am an avid racing fan, myself," Rosberg replied. "But you cannot accuse the police in a foreign nation of attempted murder and kidnapping without causing tremendous anxiety."

"Anxiety!? I don't give a fuck about these—"

"Mr. Moretti,... Alex. If you don't calm down, we cannot help you."

Alex forced himself to lower his tone. "Okay, tell me what you can do for me."

"Our Assistant Ambassador received a call stating that you were here making all kinds of accusations about a shooting at a farm—"

"Listen, John Rosberg. They have my fiancée and her sister. Do you hear me!?"

"Do you have solid evidence of this?"

"This is the police department! They must have a record of calls, dispatches, or something!"

"Unfortunately, their information is limited, Alex. They received a notice from Interpol late yesterday regarding an unsubstantiated call that had come in reporting the missing girls may be in Romania. We have been informed that no evidence exists indicating the missing girls are here."

"You want evidence? I'll get it for you. I have two eyewitnesses."

"Alex, you've come in here and made some serious accusations, thus we were summoned. If you insist on playing some Liam Neeson vigilante on these people, you'll be on your own here."

Alex was emotionally drained. Cotton's Israeli partner was adamant that this was a bad idea. In his own mind, he just couldn't believe a whole police department could be this corrupt, or perhaps he just didn't want to believe it. Amanda was almost back in his arms again, and yet so far.

"If you fellows would kindly have them return my passport, I'll just be on my way."

The two embassy officials escorted Alex back out and onto the street. "Are you certain you'll be all right?" Rosberg asked. "The ambassador would gladly offer you accommodations at the embassy for your stay."

"No, I'll be fine," he replied, holding back on lashing out at the two. "As you stated earlier, Mister Rosberg, I will be on my own."

"Congratulations on winning your first Grand Prix, by the way," Zelder offered in parting.

Alex simply glared back at him. "Yeah."

Alex called Cotton James and was picked up just up the block, shamefully sharing the experience.

"Do you think you were followed?" Arieh asked.

"I don't know why. They all think I'm some sort of nutcase now."

"Just for good measure, how about we take you back to your hotel?"

"No! I want to go wherever you guys go! You want the million bucks, don't you?"

"I'm not sure you have the stomach for this," Arieh stated.

"You guys just tell me how I can help."

"You can help by keeping your head down, at least around us," Cotton claimed. "Your fame places all of us at risk, sir."

Arieh took a call and made the arrangement. "I'm meeting an old associate of mine who can give me some advice. Turn left at the next light, Alon."

"Where are you meeting this associate?"

"At a very public place – the Museum of Communism."

Sarah took the call, anxious for any news. Learning of Alex's experience in Bucharest did little to lift her spirits.

"I have no idea, Sarah," Alex added, exasperated. "The State Department guys said a report had come from Interpol."

"I haven't shared this with anyone,... except—"

"Except who, Sarah?"

"My husband," she replied while closing her eyes and shaking her head. "What are you going to do? Your dad is expecting you to be in Monza by the end of this week."

"I don't know, Sarah. So close,... but so far."

The two had served together all over Europe and much of the Middle East. Arieh had recruited him right after the Americans invaded Iraq and were searching for Saddam Hussein, who was launching Russian-made Scud missiles into Israel in a vain attempt to expand the war.

"How have you been, Yosef?"

"Surviving, sir. And your health?"

"I'm still standing but how long, only God knows. What have you learned?"

"The *Brigăzi's Nasu* is still Eduardo Blaku, but his nephew, Burim Basha, has been running local operations. His base has been the Crystal Club, a strip joint in the red-light district. This is where young women are recruited, manipulated, and perform to the whims of the *Brigăzi*. Those who are uncooperative or poorly performing are sold on the black market.

Basha has been hyperactive in the human trafficking rackets, instilling fear among young women in all areas of Bucharest. Word has it that Basha has become increasingly impatient with his uncle in holding back his efforts to expand the business."

"How difficult is it to get to this Burim Basha?" Arieh asked.

"He always has protection around him. They're always big, ex-wrestler types. How good they are, I do not know."

"And your take on the police?"

"Split in half. Either on the take or passively silent. Every once in a while, a rogue cop will step up and cause the *Brigăzi* some problems. They'll be abruptly found floating in the Dâmbovița River.

"What else can you tell me, Yosef?"

"Only to be very careful, Arieh. This is the human trafficking capital of Europe. The locals fear the *Brigăzi* and will sing like a bird if they see anything."

"Do you have a clue where Basha may have these Cook sisters?"

"It could be any of a thousand places, Arieh."

⛿⛿

"Tell me you didn't call Interpol."
"You're damned right I called them. You had better let me handle this, Sarah. Your emotions are clouding your judgment."
"You stupid fool, Byron Cook! The police just took them! You hear me!? You gave them back to the people who captured them in the first place!... Damn you, Byron Cook! I should never have shared Alex's messages with you in the first place!"
"You're not going to talk to me like that, Sarah."
"I'll speak to you any way I wish! But if we never see our daughters again, I'll have no reason to ever speak with you again, Byron!" Sarah yelled before disconnecting.

⛿⛿

Andy was close to biting his nails after another toxic meeting with Ian Miles. The Formula One team manager demanded that Andy order Tony back behind the wheel as he couldn't deal with Alex's on-again-off-again antics.
"I can't do my job like this, Andy." Miles had stated. "You had no problem with Tony getting back into an IndyCar. That was over two weeks ago. I say he's fit."
"All I can say is I hope Alex shows up in Monza by Friday morning, Ian. Have you ever been through a trauma like this, Ian? We'll just have to make plans for all contingencies."

"I would like a contract extension for next year, Andy. The rest of this season is looking like a disaster and my resume will end up embarrassing me, even if I applied for a bloody London dog catcher job."

"I'm in no mood for that, Ian," Andy replied in half disgust. "We'll discuss that at season's end, just as we have these past two years. I have a call I need to make."

"I believe I should give you my notice then, Andy," Miles stated seriously. "I will serve out through season end and move on."

Andy was stunned. The last thing he needed was to lose his team manager at such a critical moment, but he was never one to react kindly to threats. "I will accept your letter of resignation, Ian. You will make it effective immediately."

Andy was relieved the missed call had come in, one he was glad to return.

"Andy! Thanks for calling me back so fast. I just got into another ugly fight with Byron on the phone. The jerk ass called Interpol about Amanda's messages to Alex. Pardon my language."

Andy was bothered by this news, but not surprised. "I think you should check with Interpol to see if they discovered anything on it, Sarah."

"I just did that. They think I'm hysterical, Andy!... I'm sorry, I know you're busy."

"That's quite all right, Sarah. I'll be back in Genoa by tomorrow evening. In the meantime, I'll call that Captain Le Fleur down there and see what I can find out."

"I don't know what I'd do without you, Andy."

"You're too kind, Sarah. I have to run now. Bye." Andy disconnected. *Don't know what she'd do without me, huh?* Andy thought briefly. With everything going on around him, he was pleased to hear that from her.

Andy called the main number at Interpol in Lyon and when prompted entered Captain Russo's extension, pleased in the current time that he didn't get a voicemail.

"Captain Le Fleur speaking."

"Captain, Andy Moretti. I'm calling to inquire about the status of that Romanian lead on the Amanda and Allison Cook's case."

"Yes, Monsieur Moretti, and congratulations on your victory in Holland. I have sent a notice to the authorities in Bucharest to check it out. Unfortunately, they replied that it was a dead end."

"Okay, and?"

"The Bucharest Police Department reported back on it, Monsieur. Like the hundreds of other leads we have received on this case, it turned out to be nothing."

"My son is confident the messages were authentic, Captain. Perhaps you could send an Interpol team of investigators down there."

"I am sorry, Monsieur. We are not a European version of your FBI who can just show up and usurp the local authorities. Our function is to coordinate these agencies to work together."

"In other words, if any one of your local agencies are corrupted, the chain is only as strong as its weakest link."

"I will send another request down there, Monsieur. That is all I can do at the present."

"All right, Captain. We'll all sleep better at night knowing that." Click.

Andy was now angry. *No wonder Romania doesn't have its own Grand Prix.*

⚑✕⚑

Andy called Adrian Morrison into his office. The thirty-two year old engineer had been on board since the Moretti Formula One team inception and had done yeoman's work. "Adrian, I'm giving you a promotion to Team Manager. Your first task will be to help Ian clean out his desk, devoid of anything sensitive, of course, and escort him from the building. Then load up and head down to Monza. I'll be in Genoa for a couple of days. You know how to get hold of me."

"Uh, sir? Should I change the locks on the doors?" Morrison asked, a bit nervous and overwhelmed over this untimely revelation.

"Yes, Adrian. And it's Andy,... not sir."

⚑✕⚑

Amanda was in tears beside Allison, whose expression was more of disgust. The two were forcibly stripped and held down by multiple goons, while an older, wicked-looking woman shaved them and applied an excessive amount of makeup and red lipstick.

They were then ordered to stand in front of a large white curtain and prepare to be photographed. Both continued to place one hand over their face while the other covered their feminine privacy, which angered their captors.

One of the more vulgar toughs moved to slap Amanda but was stopped.

"No! No fucking marks on the sluts!" Marius ordered. "Just tie their hands above them and be quick. This is taking far too long!"

This was the part of the business that was most stressful, a stakeout. Arieh sat in the rusty-looking old Yugo sedan, watching the joint through a pair of binoculars.

Alon had entered as a typical laborer there, throwing down a generous amount of Romanian Leus to the girls on the well-lit stage who would strip for him and the other patrons. All the while, he observed the overall staff, separating the lounge workers from the bouncers.

At a point when a performance ended and there was a break between strippers, Alon got up and ventured over to the bar, attempting to strike up a conversation with the bartender. "I bet you get a bit put out at all the tips being spent on these whores, huh Comrade?"

The guy grunted, not much for conversation.

Alon was served his beer and left some extra Leus on the bar, which seemed to please the bearded, middle-aged guy. "I bet you all work some long hours, huh? How late does this place stay open?"

"We stay open until 2:00 AM, but I get off at seven."

"Oh? I somehow thought you were Burim Basha."

That actually got a brief smile out of him. "No, just a bartender."

Suddenly the bartender's tone changed as three sharply dressed males walked in, shuffling past the bar and to a door in the back corner where one unlocked it, escorting the one in who looked to be in charge while the third remained standing outside, obviously a mob soldier there to keep unwanted guests out.

"My name is Mihai, not Comrade."

"Very well Mihai, I guess that was him who just walked in then?"

Mihai looked around as he appeared busy wiping down the bar. "No, that was not Basha, and I would not ask too many questions around here."

Alon just smiled and nodded before finishing his beer, then walked out and circled the block before making his way toward the old Yugo, where his older brother waited.

"I thought we had caught Basha, but it was another underboss who just walked in with his two thugs. Their office is in the southeast corner and is kept locked. One of the grunts stands guard outside. The place closes at two but the barkeep gets off at seven."

"What's your take on him?" Arieh asked.

"Not part of the team. The underboss didn't give him the time of day when he walked in. He acted fearful and wouldn't say much."

"I think we should have a talk with him anyway, Alon."

Marius was accustomed to speaking with Eduardo in a very generic language over the phone. "The listing will start in forty minutes at six and end at midnight. Should I set a starting bid?"

"Let's do one point five."

"How many *friends* should I invite?"

"I think two should suffice, don't you?"

"Your expectation?"

Eduardo thought briefly. "What is your gut?"

"I think four mil is possible."

"Let's make it five."

Marius and his boss disconnected. He had set the auction up on the dark website, *Black Horizon,* with invitations sent to a very small and exquisite group of bidders, with one being targeted specifically.

There were two so-called *friends* on the list, which were fake bidders designed to simply run up the price. In the rare instance that such a bid would win, their stock would simply be put on hold and another auction run in two to three weeks. But in this case, Eduardo was confident their targeted bidder would pay whatever it would take, even five million, as this product was perhaps the finest ever offered.

He would stay a bit longer to complete his tasks, which were to profitably dispense of their contraband, assign a new underboss for the local *Brigăzi*, and then take their private jet back to Tijuana.

The man was a smart and vicious operative, but like any human had his weaknesses, and his was opioid narcotics. As supply was never an issue in his line of work, he always had a number of the opium pills in his pocket which he popped regularly. He began to feel the fix and informed the two bodyguards he was ready to depart, anxious that two complimentary prime prostitutes awaited him at his guest quarters in Old Town.

※

Emir Khalid bin Qahtani was the black sheep of the House of Saud, the royal ruling family in Saudi Arabia. Inheriting a vast fortune from his late father, a man close to the former king, Qahtani was shunned by the current Crown Prince, Mohammed bin Salman, and given no position of authority. The emir still, however, enjoyed tremendous wealth and a strong measure of protected immunity.

Qahtani had a well-earned reputation as an international playboy with no limits on what he would spend to satisfy his personal pleasures such as gambling, prostitution, and narcotics.

A less publicized proclivity Qahtani enjoyed was his own personal harem stocked with young women, mostly of Europe origin and notably quite beautiful. The emir had an affection for twins who were forced to act on his erotic desires in unison.

A long time preferred client for the world's dealers in high-end human trafficking, Khalid seemed to have no limit on what he was willing to pay for female contraband of his choosing.

※

"You're making me nervous," Cotton stated.

"Making you nervous? Just your being here tells me you and your band have nothing going on. This sucks, James!"

"My people are trying to identify the gangsters here behind this. Your blowing into Police Headquarters like you're *Dirty Harry* wasn't helpful."

Alex just stared out the window while shaking his head. "Why haven't these bastards called and demanded more money?"

"I wish I knew," Cotton replied as he dialed Arieh's number.

"What?"

"Anything to report?"

"You just asked me that twenty-five minutes ago!" Arieh answered, the tired attitude apparent in his voice.

"Sorry. Our boy here is getting anxious."

"We all are, Cotton. When I have something, I'll call."

※

Andy arrived at the family home in Genoa, a nice but humble abode that he had grown up in. He was greeted warmly by all the women in the family, informing him their special house guest, Sarah, was lying down in the master bedroom.

"She's just mentally exhausted, Andy," Matilde informed. "She's been crying almost non-stop."

"When she wakes up, maybe you should take her for a walk," Crissy added. "Take her into town for some coffee, maybe a drink... Something."

"I'm not sure what I can do to cheer her up. I called that Captain Le Fleur at Interpol earlier. He has no clue."

"Sarah needs a rock, Andy. Like it or not, you're it right now," Crissy declared.

"Oh, he likes it," Matilde observed.

"Oh, Mamma."

"Don't give me that, Oh Mamma, Andy. You're still my baby boy. I know you pretty well."

"So, is it true, Andy?" Crissy asked expectantly. "You and Sarah?"

"See what happens when you women have too much time to chit-chat, Mamma."

"Well, now that we're chit-chatting, Andy, promise me you won't have Tony driving a car at Monza."

"Tony's a grown man, Crissy. You should ask him," Andy replied as he began to search for something in the cupboard. "I fired my Formula One team manager today and Alex is going to Bucharest to play James Bond. I need a drink."

⚑×⚑

Arieh circled the club, seeing a back door that appeared to have been boarded up for ages. "You think that would lead into that office, Alon?"

"It would. Take some work, though."

"There's one security camera on the opposite corner. Do you think it would be monitored after hours?"

"Hard to say, brother. What are you thinking?"

"Not much, yet. It's ten 'til seven. Your bartender should be getting off duty soon.

Mihai left by the front entrance just five minutes after seven and took off on foot two blocks up the street, stopping in at a small market. He left a few moments later carrying a small bag of groceries when an older man approached, shoving a pistol at his neck.

"Get in the car, Mihai. Do as I say and you won't get hurt."

He put up no resistance and was escorted into the back seat of the ragged Yugo.

"How do you know my name?... Wait, I know you." He recognized Alon who was behind the wheel.

"We just need some information, Mihai. That's all," Arieh stated. "Answer all of our questions correctly and you'll be free to go. If not, we will let the *Nusa* know just how friendly you were to us. Understand?"

"I'm just a bartender there. I don't know anything."

"Is Burim Basha the underboss running Bucharest for Blaku?"

"Yes."

See, barkeep. You do know something. "Who showed up earlier with his two bodyguards?" Alon added.

"That was a new guy. Word is that Basha is in trouble and this new guy was sent to fix things."

"Fix what things?"

"I don't know. I just see a lot of anger today. Basha and his right-hand man, Armend Carazo, haven't been around."

"What can you tell us about the *Brigăzi's* relationship with the police?"

"The police do not bother us. The main chief, Lonesku, comes in often and is served with young girls upstairs. I do not believe he pays."

"Upstairs? Is that where these girls are kept?"

"No, they are brought in for business and then escorted out."

"Then where are they kept?"

"I don't know, I swear."

"Bucharest is a mecca for human sex trafficking. Don't bullshit us, Mihai."

"I know that girls and young women are kept in places all over the city. I swear, I have no idea."

"Where does the *Brigăzi* hold auctions to sell their captives?"

"I just tend bar at a gentlemen's club. I know nothing about any auctions," a rattled Mihai answered.

"I start to get this nervous twitch in my trigger finger when I'm around someone who lies to me," Arieh declared fervently. "You're lying to me, Mihai."

"I swear to you, I've never seen any auction here. I have heard that some of the girls were sold online."

"What is the website?"

"I can't say for sure. It is on the dark web."

"You're not giving us anything of value, Mihai," Alon stated. "You had better give that old guy with a pistol something, lest you're a dead man."

The Romanian was sweating, knowing what the *Brigăzi* did with those who were even suspected of disclosing information about them. "I have heard of a site called *Black Horizon*. Just hearsay, though."

"What can you tell us about that office at the club?" Arieh pressed.

"It's an office. I am rarely allowed in there. Basha and his muscle show up every day and spent time in there. Like I told you earlier," Mihai added while addressing Alon. "I don't ask many questions. It is much safer that way.'

"Describe the room for me," Arieh demanded, still having his pistol on the scared bartender's neck."

"It's not large. There is a desk, two chairs, and a leather built-in couch against one wall, along with a closet in one corner."

"Do you have keys to the place?"

"No, none of the regular staff are trusted with keys."

"Who monitors the club security cameras?"

"There is a screen up front. The doorman watches that."

"And after hours?"

"I don't know. I guess it is shut down."

"How often does anyone hang out there after closing time?"

"Never, that I know about. But I could not say for certain."

Arieh and Alon looked at each other as Alon reached into his pocket.

"I've told you all I know."

Arieh grabbed his arms while Alon stuck the needle in his neck. "We just need you to take a long nap for a while, friend."

Alon drove down the street and stopped in front of a vacant building, where he dragged the unconscious bartender out of the car and laid him up against the boarded-up door of what appeared to be an abandoned storefront. Passersby would assume him to be a drunk and simply passed out.

"He could get robbed," Alon said as he drove away.

"Do you think we should have just carried him home and tucked him in? No time for excessive morality, brother," Arieh responded.

"Old guy with a pistol?... Lest you're a dead man? Ha!... You're learning."

Chapter 10
On to Monza

Sarah woke up and greeted Andy, conscious of the way she must have looked.

"I trust you found the place comfortable, Sarah."

"Oh, yes. It's a delightful house."

"I know it's not what you expected. Race drivers didn't make a whole lot of dough back when my father was driving."

"Being rich is measured in many ways, Andy. As tragic as your father's death was, I suppose he went out while living his dream."

"I suppose that's true enough," he replied. *All except the part about my father burning to death while trapped in an overturned race car.*

The two took a stroll together for several street blocks down by the port, where vessels from large cruise ships to small sailboats were moored. The quaint seaside city had a certain charm about it that other well-known cities on the Riviera had lost to traffic, tourism, and inflated prices.

"My father purchased a boat much like that one when I was a boy," Andy said while pointing. "Because of his racing schedule, we seldom used it. I suppose that is why I've yet to buy a boat of my own, probably the only one on Lake Norman with a house on the lake and no boat."

"I could end up with ours in my divorce settlement," Sarah stated half-jokingly. "Not sure Amanda would like that."

"Alex is the boater in our family, Sarah."

Sarah began to well up again. "Andy, I know I'm not very good company right now." She buried her head into his shoulder. "I'm losing hope of ever seeing my daughters again."

"And now Alex has gone off half-cocked to Bucharest, thinking he will parachute in like some Hollywood hero and save them himself." Andy now worried he may never see his youngest again as well. "Never lose hope, Sarah. Miracles do happen in this world."

Back at the hotel, Arieh reached out to Josef about a possible dark website called *Black Horizon*.

"These sites have odd URLs and the nicknames will not appear in any searches, Arieh, I'll check with Tel Aviv and we'll keep looking, but those tend to be very well guarded with a very limited membership. I wish I had better intel."

"Keep me posted, Josef."

At half past 4:00 AM, Arieh and Alon gathered at the rear corner of the club exterior, crowbars in hand, and began to rip open the lumber over the back door, exposing an old lock that Arieh had picked in less than a minute.

Alon ran around to the front of the building and took up station across the street, observing the club entrance while establishing communication with his older brother through their wireless comms.

Arieh entered the office and shined his small light around, flipped on the light switch, and observed the layout. He first opened the small closet in the corner, which was in reality a tall metal cabinet consumed with shelves and having twin doors.

A quick study of the contents revealed nothing of consequence, thus he began to check the desk itself. The main metal drawer had a rudimentary lock on it that he quickly pried open exposing a Ruger 22 caliper pistol. He proceeded to unload the weapon and replace it.

There were numerous paperwork items related to club business such as time cards, liquor invoices, and other files, which Arieh examined piece by piece, looking for anything that could hold a key to Amanda and Allison Cook's whereabouts.

Frustrated, he spied a worn brown jacket laying loosely on a built-in couch. Grabbing the garment to search its pockets, his face lit up as underneath was a notebook computer. This immediately gave Arieh some optimism, thinking about the many times over the years that he had been in on raids of terrorists and other criminal elements. Their computers had almost always produced a treasure trove of data regarding anything from other contacts, to trails of funding, and even specific attack plans.

Coming prepared, he opened the laptop and inserted a large-capacity USB flash drive which included a special app designed to boot up any Windows operating system, identify all passwords, and extract all files while leaving no evidence of entry.

"How are things out front?"

"Dark and clear."

"I found a laptop in here. I'm running the boot app."

"Why don't you just take it, Arieh?"

"It shouldn't take long, brother. At five in the morning, what's the rush?"

Arieh knew there were advantages to grabbing data from a bad actor's computer or phone without them knowing it had been compromised. The perpetrators would be less likely to alter any plans or send out warnings. He watched as the app was taking an exceptionally long time to boot up, taking the time to plant a couple of highly sensitive listening *bugs* that could be monitored.

Minutes seemed like hours for Alon, nervously on watch outside. "What's taking so long, Arieh? It'll be dawn soon."

"I know, should be any minute."

⚑✕⚑

Marius was furious with himself. He had fallen to sleep after being worked over by the two prostitutes, oblivious at the time that Eduardo would want an immediate update on the auction and action plan to deliver the goods to the buyer. He had left the club late, dizzy with the buzz of the pills taking effect, and had carelessly omitted grabbing his notebook computer on the way out.

Mindless of the need to even awake his bodyguards, he drove mercilessly through the streets of Bucharest, parking right in front of the club's main entrance.

"Trouble, Arieh. Someone out front getting ready to unlock the front door and looking like they're in a hurry. I think it's the new underboss I saw earlier. It appears he has no support with him."

Damn, Arieh thought. He quickly flipped the office light switch off and rushed to the so-called closet, barely squeezing in while holding the door shut as best he could from the inside. He could hear the sound of the office's lock, a door opening, and rapid footsteps shuffling around.

It hit the former Mossad operative that he had shut the laptop and placed the old jacket back on top of it, but had left his flash drive plugged in.

Marius first sat down in the desk chair looking around for it. He shuffled for his keys to unlock the top drawer and saw that it was unlocked. *You dumbass, Marius,* he thought, blaming the pills. He then opened the drawer, noticing the pistol. *Something just looks different,* he thought, a man with a naturally suspicious mind. *As if this thing is pointed slightly more forward(?).*

The underboss then looked over toward the couch and recalled that he had left the laptop there under the jacket. He strolled over and lifted the garment, seeing his notebook there with a violet-colored flash drive plugged into the side and blinking. *"What the fuck!?"* Marius yelled and ran back to the desk, withdrawing the pistol from the drawer and frantically looking around before staring at the closet.

As though on cue, Arieh sprung the closet doors open, pointing his own Glock at the mobster who was aiming the .22 Ruger at him. Seeing the interloper as a frail old man, Marius aimed and pulled the trigger multiple times, angry at learning the handgun was empty. Arieh responded by putting a nine-millimeter slug right through the mobster's right kneecap, causing the wounded thug to collapse to the floor, grabbing his knee in pain.

"You have one good knee left, *Mr. Brigăzi*. Where are the girls?"

"Go fuck yourself, Señor."

Arieh placed a second shot through Marius' left elbow as the man shrieked in more pain. "Oh, oh. I missed that knee, but I have seven more tries."

"You're too late, you senile old bastard. They've been sold! How much do you want?"

"You insult me. I'm dying of cancer and could care less how much money Blaku has or how much pain I can cause you. Where are the girls!?"

"You go to hell!"

"You'll beat me to it," Arieh replied and shot a hole in Marius' remaining good knee, just below the kneecap in the Tibia.

The interim underboss screeched in extreme pain. "Qahtani has them now! But you can't touch him! He's protected!" Marius yelled as he quickly took his right hand away from his bleeding knee, grabbed a knife from his sock, and flung the sharp-edged weapon toward his attacker, catching Arieh's upper chest.

Arieh fell forward, clutching his wound and struggling to catch his breath. Despite the pain and blood, Marius crawled along the floor toward the wounded Israeli, reaching for his Glock when he heard a loud crash.

Alon had made his way around to the back of the building and kicked in the door. Seeing the immediate threat, he put three bullets through the underboss' left ear before rushing to his stricken brother's aid.

"What took you so long, brother?" Arieh asked, pulling the blade from his chest and clutching the wound.

"You're hit pretty bad. Let's get you out of here before it's light out and this place gets busy."

"Grab that laptop," Arieh grunted, barely able to speak now. "I didn't want to kill the son-of-a-bitch."

"I see that now," Alon replied, spying the well-placed shots on the dead man's knees. "And your compassion nearly got you killed."

"I did get a name. *Caltony*, or something like that."

Through all the scuffling, the top cushion layer of the couch had been flung to the floor along with the notebook computer, and the special flash drive had been broken in the process. Looking around for the missing pieces, Alon noticed a large blue duffle bag inside the couch frame, quickly unzipping it to throw the laptop inside. He then picked up the bag, surprised by its excessive weight.

Alon's eyes opened wide as he unzipped the bad to find bounds of US hundred dollar bills bundled up inside. He then threw his older brother up over his shoulder while looping the bag up over his other, and made his way through the open door, moving quickly around the building to their car.

There would be plenty of DNA from Arieh's blood on the floor if club management did choose to involve the police, but they would hopefully be long gone by then. At the end of the day, Arieh worried little about Blaku knowing his identity. In fact, knowing his days were numbered, he would take solace in the fact.

⚑✕⚑

Cotton set up a rendezvous at a veterinarian animal clinic on Bucharest's north side. The place opened at 9:00 AM and the four parked outside the place, hoping the vet and staff would arrive early prior to any customers. The hospitals and regular health clinics were being avoided as to not risk reporting to the police.

Alon suggested that Alex tag along, as his celebrity may actually come in handy for a change. He entered first followed by Alon, hoping they would get cooperation without the need for coercion. They were greeted by the owner and his wife, both of whom fortunately spoke some English. She immediately thought the handsome young man looked familiar.

"Doctor, we have my wounded brother here—"

"We are a clinic for animals. You should have gone to a hospital!"

"Doc, we have had an altercation with the *Brigăzi*," Alon stated. "He is here looking for his kidnapped fiancée and we cannot involve the police. Do you understand?" He was prepared to pull his handgun if necessary.

The woman nodded to her husband. "I see. I will do what I can."

While the three waited out front, Cotton pulled up an app on his phone, searching for the name but coming up empty. Alon sent a message to Tel Aviv that Arieh had given him and received a reply in three minutes. *"This sounds like Qahtani, coming from the Qahtan tribe of Arabs dating back centuries from southern Saudi Arabia and Yemen."*

"Like finding a needle in a haystack," Cotton stated in resignation.

Alon's expression lightened as he looked up after reading a follow-up text. "Check this out."

Alex and Cotton together focused on Alon's phone screen. *"The most prominent of this sect is Khalid bin Qahtani, a distant cousin of the House of Saud, known to be an international playboy."*

The two captive young women, each clean and dressed following the degrading and shameful photo shoot, were blindfolded and escorted into some sort of truck or van for transport somewhere.

The ride lasted thirty to forty minutes when they began to hear the sounds of an airport getting closer.

"Maybe we're being released and sent home, Allison," Amanda decried with some wishful thinking.

"Sure, Amanda. That's what the blindfolds are for."

The four all crowded into Alex's hotel suite, down and contemplating their next move after the veterinarian had done yeoman's work in treating and sewing up Arieh's wound. The Israeli looked as though barely alive physically, but the loss of blood hadn't dampened his spirit.

"I can see this Khalid bin Qahtani is all over the internet and Facebook. You name it, he's out there in plain sight! They say I'm world famous now. This son-of-a-bitch is going to get a taste of my celebrity."

"Well, I wouldn't go to the press here, Alex," Cotton stated. "We may never get out of here alive, especially after Arieh and Alon were using their local mob leader's anatomy for target practice."

"The press? I have my own social media. I'm sure Tommy Clarkson or Dale Junior would love to book me on their podcasts. Do you have any idea how many millions of people follow that?"

"Let's see what this might be," Arieh interrupted as he answered a call. "Yes....yes, I see...How long ago was this?...Hmm, interesting...Do me a favor, Noah. Text me that flight and plane info." He then hit the disconnect.

"What Arieh?" Cotton asked, sensing the Israeli had just heard something significant.

"That was our contact in Tel Aviv, stating this Khalid bin Qahtani is a real piece of work, all right, well known for his erotic harem, and he seems to have a thing for twins, namely Caucasian female twins. There have been numerous attempts in the past to take him down, but he has been politically protected. A Gulfstream private jet owned by bin Qahtani arrived early this morning and has just departed from Bucharest Henri Coandă International Airport, bound for Jeddah on Saudi Arabia's Red Sea coast."

Alon quickly pulled up a map on his phone. "With support from the U.S. Government and the King of Jordan, the IDF can intercept that plane while in Jordanian air space and force it to land in Tel Aviv," Alon remarked.

"Is that feasible?" Cotton chimed in.

"The Israeli Defense Forces are capable of anything," Arieh added, "And never lack the will to act."

"So, what then?" Alex asked, still adjusting to this latest news. "Should I call the American Embassy again?"

"I would start with that," Arieh suggested.

"They're scared of their own shadow over there," Alex replied.

"You said you're a celebrity now, Alex," Cotton advised. "Let them know your next call is maybe the BBC, or the Associated Press."

You're smarter than you look, James, Arieh thought. "Better start making the calls, son."

⚑✕⚑

"We believe they have been sold as sex slaves! What in hell do you mean you cannot—"

"You don't understand," Rosberg replied, cutting Alex off. "Khalid bin Qahtani is an emir, a prince in the House of Saud. We cannot have an international incident based on this tale you have come up with—"

"A tale! This is bullshit. I want to speak to the ambassador!"

"I'm afraid she is away at a conference. I will pass a cable to Washington—"

"Pass a cable my ass! You aren't going to do jack shit, Rosberg!"

"Mr. Moretti, you'll have to be patient and wait for our call," the State Department official stated as an angry and frustrated Alex Moretti was steaming.

"I don't want to hear that bullshit! If you don't get on the horn to the White House, or the Pentagon, or somebody important enough to act, I'm calling the BBC and telling them that our government knows exactly where Amanda and her sister are, exactly what it will take to rescue them, and won't lift a damned finger to help them! I have a good friend from the IDF standing right here beside me. If he hasn't received word in fifteen minutes that his pilots have a go, I'm making that call!"

"Wait, Moretti—"

"Fifteen minutes, Rosberg!" Alex added and hung up the phone.

"International incident? What the hell!?" Andy almost yelled.

"This Arieh has his people looking into this Khalid character. If our government or Interpol won't do anything to help us, he says he can organize a mercenary special ops group to go in and rescue them, Dad. If Amanda ends up someplace in Saudi Arabia, it is his belief it will take that and I'm going to be a part of it."

"Oh my god, Alex! Let me send our plane to Bucharest so we can pick you up. You're going to get into deep trouble there."

"I have to think about that, Dad. If there is any chance they are still in Romania, I can't leave."

The two disconnected, as Andy had the dreaded task of updating Sarah, who would yet again break down on his shoulder. He also had the burden of managing the race in Monza with practice starting the following day. All considered, he felt the best thing may be to announce yet again that Moretti Motorsport may have to withdraw from the Italian Grand Prix at Monza.

He knew the world of motorsport would have sympathy for their saga, but also knew the pressure would come from the Formula One brass to have Andy think about selling the team. He would consult with Adam Herrera on it. *You're the public relations expert, Adam. Time to earn your keep.*

The word got all the way up to the Secretary of State, who was interrupted in the middle of an important summit meeting. A call was placed to the Saudi Foreign Minister, who rejected out of hand the notion that Riyadh would give the nod to Israeli fighter jets intercepting a plane owned by a member of the royal family, even expressing offense that the US State Department would even make such a request.

Meanwhile, Andy was now worried stiff that his youngest boy was getting evermore entangled in a very dangerous scenario. He called Alex back to attempt to talk him back from the edge.

"You know, Adam Herrera knows the White House National Security Advisor somehow from their old college days or something. He has a call into him."

"You obviously have more faith in our government than I do, Dad."

Herrera picked up on the first ring, a man sitting on pins and needles, still waiting impatiently for a return call from his old pal, Wayne Tollison. "Yes, Andy?"

"Adam, Alex believes some Saudi prince has bought and paid for Amanda and her sister to add them to his perverted private harem. God help them. I know my son well enough to know that he'll thrust himself into finding her, to the point of getting himself killed!"

"Stand by, Andy. I'll see what I can do."

"Time is of the essence, Adam."

The tension could be cut with a knife. It seemed that Alex's hired trio of mercenary investigators had come so close, but all was being lost.

"What about that laptop?" Alon asked.

Arieh shook his head. "Without that flash drive, I can't get into it."

Meanwhile, Cotton had dug into the contents of the blur duffle bag, wide-eyed with shock, counting the masses of hundred-dollar bills batched together. Cotton finally just dumped the booty out on the carpet, a thought crossing his mind this could be their reward.

Arieh piped in. "That's that million the *Brigăzi* claimed the Cook people shorted them."

The three quickly confirmed there were two hundred batches of fifty one-hundred-dollar bills.

Alex quickly composed himself, not forgetting the problem at hand. "Hey! What about the laptop!? Stop worrying about where that money came from!"

Andy called Alex to inform him that Adam Herrera had reached out to his old pal now serving in the White House, but was not confident in getting any action right away. The administration was involved in serious negotiations regarding a Middle East peace accord and had no appetite for tabling something like this with the Saudi Crown Prince at such a delicate moment in the process.

That's the last thing Alex wanted to hear and he began to go off.

"Wait, Alex!" Andy yelled. "I'm not done. Adam came up with another alternative, one that is quite brilliant, I must say."

He explained the plan to his son, prompting him to stand by with his threat to go public if necessary.

Andy's next call got little result as he was routed to a general corporate consumer voicemail. He then called Brian Fonterra, the acting CEO and President of Formula One.

"What you are suggesting is serious stuff, Andy. I have to think about how to approach this."

"There's no time, Brian! They are the kingdom's national oil company and your biggest sponsor! This will be a public relations disaster for them! I'm telling you, Alex is getting ready to blow the whistle to the world press about this. I can't stop him and as his father, I wouldn't anyway."

Alex continued to pace and kept checking the time. "It's been twenty-five minutes. To hell with it," he declared and dialed the BBC's Leonard York, their world-renowned journalist who had shared phone numbers with Alex in Hungary.

Before Alex heard the second ring, he saw an incoming call from the US Embassy. He thought briefly about sending it to voicemail but chose to cancel his call to York, at least temporarily, and answer. "Yes, Rosberg?"

"Mr. Moretti, this is the US Ambassador to Romania, Amy Kitchen. I wish to inform you the State Department is in close contact with the Saudi Arabian government, attempting to achieve the safe release of your loved ones."

"That's what I heard about the hostages taken by Hamas in Gaza,... a year later."

"Mr. Moretti, I cannot prohibit you from talking to members of the press, but such actions could inhibit our efforts to—"

For a young man who chased thousands of a second for a living, the snail's pace of the US State Department was not reassuring. "Thank you, Miss Ambassador." Alex hung up. "Thanks for nothing."

Abdul Saleh Hassan was the man who managed security for the emir, a kind term for enforcer or enabler. He was paid well and handled all of Khalid bin Qahtani's *personal* affairs such as travel, gambling debts, and prostitution, as well as other entertainment acquisitions, including the purchase and transport of females for his harem.

Hassan had an ideal persona for the job. He was thorough, dedicated, and had no moral code. His boss favored Caucasian twins and these two appeared as such, although one was apparently a bit older. It was custom as a bonus that Hassan would have opportunities to tap into the harem himself, although long after Khalid's appetite for pleasure would diminish on specific females in inventory. This latest pair were stunning in their vanity and Hassan looked upon them with a sinister lust.

The two captives were each seated in comfortable seats but had their hands secured behind them with wire ties, a precaution to avoid trouble. "Where are we going?" Allison asked boldly.

"You will be in your new home soon. I am sorry for the harsh treatment you have received earlier. The emir will be much more accommodating."

"And where is this new home?"

"It is on the sub-continent. That is all you need to know," he replied authoritatively.

"Sorry I asked," Allison responded.

Amanda didn't wish to antagonize the evil-looking Hassan, and thus kept staring out the window and said nothing.

Ziad Al Mansour, the corporation's Executive Marketing Director, had charge of their Formula One sponsorship, a major endeavor on their part since Saudi Arabia and neighboring Qatar, Abu Dhabi, and Bahrain had become heavily invested in the sport over the past twenty years. The call from the Formula One CEO literally shook him up.

"With all due respect, Brian, what you are asking is quite impossible. The Crown Prince would never take the word of the Israelis that these young women were truly onboard that flight. I am sorry."

Fonterra was in a panic, certain that Mansour didn't have a proper grasp of the gravity of what was before them. "Hold for a three-way call, Ziad."

He quickly re-dialed a stored number. "Andy, I have Ziad Al Mansour on the line now. I would like you to explain to him what is about to happen."

"Is he aware of the details of what is going on as we speak, Brian?"

"I think so, but you are welcome to elaborate," Fonterra replied.

"Ziad, because of time constraints I will dispense with any formalities. You are aware that my future daughter-in-law, Amanda Cook, and her sister are being held captive and are on a plane that took off from Bucharest heading to Jeddah, correct?"

"Mr. Moretti, if you cannot substantiate such accusations—"

"Ziad! My son, Alex, is about to paste pictures of Amanda and her sister all over social media, along with the mug of this Saudi emir, not to mention his connection to the Saudi government and their national oil company. That means you, sir! I told Alex to give me fifteen minutes to contact you first!"

Mansour didn't react well. "Brian, please explain to Mr. Moretti the consequences of making such threats that could compromise his team's standing in—"

"Right now, I don't give a damn about any standing, Mansour! This is my family here, life and death. You, sir, will be the one facing consequences!"

Al Mansour, a man wielding a huge checkbook when dealing with anyone connected to Formula One, was unaccustomed to such pressures from Westerners, those who would always bend to his will over their billions of dollars. But he could tell that Andy Moretti, a man with whom he had always enjoyed cordial relations, was serious. *Fonterra is right. This would be an unmitigated disaster for us.* "I will contact Riyadh," he declared before disconnecting himself from the call.

Andy hung on to get Fonterra's comment. "What do you think, Brian?"

"If the Crown Prince does not step in big and release these young women, it will severely cripple Formula One in the Middle East, not to mention the damage to that nation's world standing generally," Fonterra exclaimed, knowing the financial fallout to the sport of Formula One itself would be catastrophic, "The Crown Prince bin Salman always seemed big on image, so we'll see."

"I'll be anxiously awaiting your call back, Brian."

⚑✕⚑

The Foreign Minister was remiss at ever interrupting the Crown Prince, especially during important events such as the king being presented with a tour of the latest Aquarable water park, the kingdom's new world-class tourist attraction.

Mohammed bin Salman was the strong-minded new King of Saudi Arabia, a man known for a certain contempt toward the West but more leery of the kingdom's immediate enemy next door, Iran. He thus understood the need to maintain a certain decorum with other nations.

Since taking power in 2015 from his father, the late King Abdullah bin Abdul Aziz, the new Crown Prince had initiated many controversial policies in Saudi Arabia, including the extremely ambitious Vision 2030 Plan, spending hundreds of billions of dollars on modern cities and world-class tourist attractions designed to upgrade the country's image and world status.

A leader possessing a strong image with piercing eyes, his closest confidants would always hesitate to interrupt bin Salman at inopportune times.

The call from Ziad Mansour seemed most critical and the Foreign Minister pressed the Crown Prince's aid for him to take the call.

⚑✕⚑

Abdul checked the time as he looked out over the Mediterranean Sea below with the coast of Lebanon just off the horizon, content that the flight had neared its halfway point.

He was certain his boss would be quite pleased with his latest acquisition. *At a cost of five point one million, he should be. But what is a million here, a million there to a man like Khalid?*

He thought of his younger days when he was tempted like many of his boyhood friends to become militants and join the great Jihad. He fantasized that since he was so close to Israel, how cool it would be to swoop down and drop a few explosives on the evil infidels. *My gig is much more profitable and enjoyable my friends,* he thought smiling. *And safer.*

He glanced over to the sisters who both avoided his stare. *Such a pair of beauties,* he pondered. *The older one is quite cheeky in her demeanor and likely to give Khalid some problems.*

Hassan recalled one Lithuanian girl a few years back who had bit the emir quite hard on his left arm. Abdul had suggested the young woman immediately be re-sold on a slave auction in an effort to recoup some of her cost, but Khalid was a man who cared little about money and ordered her to be bound in chains and thrown into the Red Sea several miles offshore.

The young one, on the other hand, looked so pure, a lovely girl instilled with fear. *More likely to be more submissive,* he told himself.

⚑✕⚑

Alex was now practically bouncing off the wall with anxiety. "Tell me more about this mercenary plan of yours," he asked Arieh, wondering if he was serious and of the belief that despite his zeal, the man himself would struggle physically taking part in such an operation.

"It's a last resort, of course,... but noble."

Alon had a call come in, informed by his former commanding Colonel that no word had yet come in regarding any intercept order.

"We have a bead on the Gulfstream, Major," the Colonel had told him. "In less than thirty minutes it will be in Saudi air space and we'll have to stand down."

The Crown Prince was very angry. His father had long turned a blind eye to Qahtani's antics, a distant cousin no less. This act, if true, threatened to cause the kingdom tremendous embarrassment. *That fool!*

"You are one hundred percent certain of this?"

"This is what I've been told, Your Excellency. We must not allow the press to get a hold of this."

"Hold the line, Ziad."

Mohammed bin Salman was steamed as he walked around, hands clasped behind his back in deep thought. The last thing he wanted was to owe a favor to the Israelis, particularly when it involved the IDF. He then approached his closest aide. "I want you to get Khalid on the phone, Ahmed."

The aide returned a short time later. "Your Excellency, I'm afraid Khalid is unavailable. His resident informed me that he will try to locate the emir and tell him you called."

The Crown Prince was now furious. "The idiot! Get me in communication with the pilot of his airplane. Now!"

"Yes, Your Excellency. It will take me a bit of time to learn—"

"The Israelis have the details on that flight! Call them if you must! I want contact with that pilot immediately!"

The Moretti team bus and transport trucks rolled into Monza as the team still didn't know the plan for their driver line-up. Tony had discounted his father's plan to withdraw out-of-hand, claiming twice in three races would be a disaster the team could not afford. He had been working on his ability to extract himself from the car within five seconds, which was the FIA standard.

Crissy was still in denial that her husband would even contemplate getting back in a race car after what had happened in St. Louis, holding out dim hope that Alex would show up.

Sarah chose to make the trip to Monza and the four set out for the two-hour trip through the northern Italian countryside with little conversation as the mood was quite dour.

Abbas al Rhumani had been one of three private pilots employed by Khalid bin Qahtani, on his payroll since 2011 and flying the emir, guests, and associates all over Europe and Asia.

The com came in, discounted at first as some sort of practical joke, but when the com persisted, Abbas considered that such a prank on this circuit was extremely unlikely.

"This is HZ213FG768. Over."

The Crown Prince's aide then asked, "Who am I speaking to?"

"This is Captain Rhumani. Who am I speaking to?" The pilot replied with an edge in his voice.

"This is Ahmed El Abadi from the House of Saud Royal Court. You will hold for an important call from Crown Prince Mohammed bin Salman."

"Do you know the penalty for—" al Rhumani could tell the circuit was connected but on hold. He quickly clicked on the intercom button.

"Sayyid Hassan, please come forward to the cockpit immediately."

The security chief was about to fall off for a brief nap and was annoyed at the demand. "What is it, Abbas?"

"You're not going to believe—"

Suddenly a voice came over the com, one that Hassan, along with millions of other Saudis, was quite familiar with. "This is your Crown Prince. Who is in charge?"

Hassan and Rhumani shared quick glances. "This is Captain Rhumani, the pilot."

"Captain, do you have two American women on board your plane?"

Again, Hassan and Rhumani looked at each other, still in a state of shock at this call from the Saudi king and concerned with the question.

"Your Excellency, this is Sayyid Hassan. How may I help you?"

"And who are you, Hassad?"

"I am an assistant to Khalid bi Qahtani, Your Excellency."

"Answer my question! Do you have American women on board!?"

Hassan was in a panic. To deceive the Crown Prince would mean certain severe repercussions, including possible execution. "Yes, Your Excellency."

"And their names are?"

Hassan fidgeted, his hands now shaking as Captain Rhumani looked on nervously.

"It is not a complicated question!"

"They are Allison and Amanda Cook, Your Excellency."

The Crown Prince was now in a near fit of rage. He, of course, was well aware of the media circus surrounding the kidnapping of the American sisters in Paris and their connection to the well-known Moretti race team. But he had hoped this was all a myth regarding any connection to a royal family member from Jeddah, the location of the Formula One Saudi Arabian Grand Prix, of all places.

"You will hold for instructions."

Hassan was near extreme meltdown. Should he contact Khalid immediately and advise him? He pondered for seventeen painful minutes when the Crown Prince returned.

"Captain Rhumani, you will reroute your flight to Tirana, Albania, where you will refuel and proceed to Milan Linate Airport. Sayyid Hassan, you will be met by an executive from Aramco Oil Company, Sayyid Ziad Mansour, who will take immediate custody of the two Americans. They must be unharmed and in excellent condition. You will refuel and fly directly to King Khalid International Airport in Riyadh. Are my instructions clear?"

Hassan and Rhumani shared yet another stare, both of their hearts pulsing now at flank speed. "Yes, Your Excellency."

Alon took an incoming call while the others looked on. They could all tell by the look on his face that something was up, which they all assumed was the IDF given the go-ahead to intercept the plane.

He listened intently while making some notes on some hotel stationary. "Thank you very much, Colonel. This is quite stunning," he added, and disconnected.

"You will not believe this," the retired IDF pilot addressed the group. "Tel Aviv picked up a conversation on the VHF circuit with the Saudi plane. The pilot has been ordered to fly to Milan and release the American women!"

Both Alex and Cotton had looks and were tempted to high-five each other.

Arieh quickly asked, "Ordered by whom?"

"That's the most bizarre part. It was allegedly the Saudi Crown Prince himself."

Alex caught himself, so accustomed to disappointment in this whole sage. "This sounds too good to be true. Let me call the embassy."

Andy's phone rang and his heart skipped a beat when he saw Brian Fonterra's name pop up on the screen. The F1 boss gave him the updated news, assuring him that Ziad Mansour was on his way to the airport in Milan as they spoke and the two disconnected.

Andy looked over at his front passenger. "Sarah, are you ready for some news?"

She looked over at him, fighting back her ongoing bouts of cynicism from so many letdowns. "Please, Andy."

"We're taking a little detour on the way to Monza. We have a stop to make at Milan Linate Airport."

"Is Alex flying back!?" Crissy asked excitedly.

"That's only a part of it..."

Rosberg took Alex's call and discounted the revelation, explaining to Alex they had received no notice that such a resolution had been reached. The mid-level foreign official, along with the entire US State Department, would be embarrassed to learn of what had transpired, mostly from the Israelis, and struggle to admit to having no hand in it.

Meanwhile, Alon took another call as Alex was still talking to Rosberg, holding up a finger and smiling, prompting Alex to quickly dismiss the embassy representative and hang up.

"That was Colonel Kaplan. They have the plane on radar. It just turned and is heading northwest."

Alex received word the Moretti corporate jet had just landed and would be fueled and ready. If he rushed, he just might get to the airport in Bucharest, take off, and arrive in Milan about the same time as the Saudi plane.

"You guys can come along and be part of the celebration," Alex stated to the three. "No airfare."

"I think me and Alon had best lay low and sneak our way out of here. Us showing up and going through airport security right after everything might be a bit much," Arieh stated, thinking they may have been better off silencing the *Brigăzi's* strip club bartender for a longer period of time.

"Then I think I should extend your employment a day or two, gentlemen," Alex spoke as Cotton and his two compatriots raised an eye. "We should get that Dorin kid, his girlfriend, and her pop out of here."

"We'll need a bit more share of your pot, Cotton," Arieh stated.

"No, just bill me separately," Alex stated. "Once they are safe in Israel, we'll make arrangements."

For his part, Cotton was all about accompanying Alex to the airport and getting out of Bucharest as soon as possible. After all, no bartender had seen his mug, and he had seen about all of Romania he cared for. He and his Israeli cohorts shared a look, knowing an issue still lingered that needed to be addressed.

"Alex, what about the reward money?" Cotton asked.

He thought briefly, having not considered it, being so emotionally consumed with Amanda's plight. "Well, Cotton James. There's a million in that bag that technically is stolen money belonging to Sarah Cook and her husband. And then there is that seventy-five grand deposit. And how do you think you'll be able to get that amount of cash through security at the airport?"

Cotton studied momentarily and declared, "I'll just retrace my steps with my pals and get back home by way of Israel."

"So far as that other reward, you and I will discuss that back in the Carolinas, when you bring our new guests with you."

The three mercenaries dropped Alex off at the terminal. Alex smiled and nodded at the three. "Well fellas, I'll be long in your debt. James, call me when you get back in the States."

Amanda noticed a change in Hassan and wondered where they were headed as she felt the plane making a sharp turn. Allison had fallen off to sleep, but she herself was awakened.

The Saudi now had a normal smile as he walked casually to the rear of the cabin and proceeded to remove the wire ties that had bound the American women's hands behind them since the flight had taken off.

"May I get you a drink *an-sata?*" It was the Arab word for Miss.

Amanda looked at him dubiously. "Like, what do you have?"

"I have sodas, coffee, water, or I can mix you a cocktail."

"I'll take a Coke or Pepsi in a can... Unopened, please."

"At your pleasure."

Amanda and Allison shared a look, confused but with just a speck of sudden hope.

The entourage stood on the tarmac while they watched anxiously as the Gulfstream jet landed and taxied to a stop. The side door on the right fuselage opened and flipped downward as the two lone young women looked out, preparing to step downward and hardly believing what was before them.

While security had encouraged the family to wait for the incoming passengers to enter the terminal building, Sarah could not hold back and was left unfettered to run headlong outside and toward the plane.

Amanda almost collapsed from all the time being confined with no exercise, as she and Allison ran forward. Sarah embraced her two girls in a tearful and emotional reunion.

When Sarah disengaged, holding them at arm's length for inspection, Amanda suddenly looked around, seeing the rest of the Moretti family approach along with a few sharply dressed males, one of Arab descent. Following the other welcoming greetings, Amanda asked, "Where is Alex?"

"His plane is arriving from Bucharest in about forty minutes," Andy answered her, checking his phone.

Amanda froze. "Bucharest? He was there?"

"Honey, it's a long story," Sarah declared. "And you two will have your whole lives to share it."

⚑⚑

The Crown Prince had desired that Aramco's marketing executive, Ziad Mansour, make a scene of personally greeting the Cook sisters at the airport and escort them by limousine to reunite with their family, but that was quite impossible as the Morettis and the girls' mother had shown up. Thus, Ziad was content to have a short video of Formula One boss Brian Fonterra and himself greeting all of them.

Sarah noticed Amanda and Crissy Moretti both in tears embracing each other, admitting to herself the two were more like sisters than her own two daughters had ever been. Allison's sinister plan to rid herself of the younger sibling once and for all had failed, but Allison was back safe, in the clear she believed, and still had a new vendetta to wage toward Lieutenant Eric Jordan, the arrogant bastard who was not answering her calls or texts.

The Moretti corporate jet landed and everyone prepared for another emotional reunion. Some foul weather had broken and Amanda looked anxiously through the terminal glass for the twin-engine private jet to roll to a stop. Airport security officials provided little resistance as she ran out the door, her tears mixing with raindrops as Alex stepped down off the plane.

The two embraced on the tarmac, oblivious to the pouring rain. Their lips locked together as if frozen in time as Alex lifted Amanda up off the concrete tarmac and twirled her around.

"I know I look terrible, race man," Amanda said. "I can't wait for us to get somewhere so I can freshen up."

"You look beautiful, babe, just beautiful. Besides, I'm no bargain, either. Haven't shaved in three days."

Amanda smiled up at him, playfully rubbing the scant whiskers on his face. "Why did we come here to this place, anyway?"

"We're in Milan, Italy, a hundred miles from Dad's hometown and just forty miles from Monza."

"Monza? Your next race?" Amanda assumed.

"Three hours ago, that decision was a bit cloudy. I was going to stay in Bucharest until—"

"I had no idea you were there. I just saw you win that race on Sunday!"

"I know. We just missed each other. It's a long story, Amanda. I know you've been through a horrible ordeal. Tony will drive for the team if you just want to go home."

Amanda paused a brief moment to look around. *The whole Moretti family is waiting in the terminal for the two of us to join them. What was that? Mom standing next to Andy, hand-in-hand?*

"I want to see you race at this Monza I have heard so much about. Like, I truly miss everyone in the paddock. I am home now, race man."

JAMES HERBERT HARRISON

Epilogue

The whole experience of captivity and humiliation had traumatized Amanda, to the point of being unable to even discuss the horrid details for several weeks. Alex got in the face of Captain Le Fleur when he pressed her with questions, accusing the Interpol officer of being more of a problem than a solution. A raw nerve was struck when the young racing champion claimed a cancer-stricken Israeli, retired air force pilot, and a redneck private eye from Charlotte, North Carolina, had done more to save Amanda and her sister than the entire European law enforcement apparatus.

In their first evening together in Monza, she acted normal and thrilled to be reunited with her fiancé, but began to break down and come to tears when the two attempted intimacy. Alex was very understanding and simply embraced her all night, hoping her condition would gradually fade away in the coming weeks.

Following a respectable fourth-place finish at the Italian Grand Prix, the Morettis returned home to a near-empty house. Matilde, who had skipped the race and flew back early, announced that Sabetha had departed a few days before, leaving a hand-written letter on her bedspread, thanking Andy and the whole family for their hospitality, joyful the Cook daughters had been recovered safely.

Cotton, Arieh, and Alon took a few days and made contact with the recovering Gabriel Ciobanu, Relia's farmer father, and Dorin Aldea, offering to transport the three and Dorin's grandparents out of the country. The elder couple declined, but the former three accompanied the three mercenaries and departed Bucharest in two small vehicles. They made their way southeast across the border into Bulgaria and to the port city of Balchik, where a ship voyage was arranged for transport to Tel Aviv. Ciobanu and the two teens would emigrate to America following a lengthy process in acquiring work visas sponsored by Moretti Motorsport, Inc.

The Levy brothers would each get their three hundred grand while Cotton retained the remainder, a nice take even less the expenses. On his own flight home, he again considered bringing up the *other* million-dollar reward to Alex and his future mother-in-law, but thought better of it, accepting the bounty in hand as the reward.

Taking the high road, Sarah had contacted her divorce attorney, instructing her to include the missing million in her settlement, an admittance on her part that agreeing to exchange the huge ransom and trust the captors to release the girls after the fact was a mistake. The other four million appeared to be *Gone With the Wind*, at best a battle to be fought another day.

Following an emotional homecoming at the airport in Milan, Allison wanted no part of going to Monza and caught the next flight home to Charlotte. Aaron and Byron met her at Douglas International with her dad's mistress, Carolyn Tyler, who feigned happiness in greeting her.

On the ride south to Rock Hill, Aaron would describe how distraught he was during her captivity and the agony of getting a leave from duty.

Oh, you poor child, Allison thought disdainfully.

He also explained how he had asked his close friend, Eric Jordan, to get the naval intelligence apparatus involved in trying to locate them.

"So, what do you think Jordan accomplished?" Allison would ask cynically, informed by her fiancé that his trusted fellow serviceman had taken a few days off to vacation in Cancun, yet to return. A week later, the US Navy would report Lieutenant Eric Jordan AWOL and missing.

Byron began to engage in a long and fruitless process through the FBI attempting to retrieve his five million dollars, enduring more grief when Carolyn Tyler insisted that lost ransom should be split with Sarah as a part of his divorce settlement.

As a large portion of his personal wealth was tied directly to Unibank stock, Byron and his attorney engaged in a scheme to delay the final divorce settlement until fourth-quarter earnings were posted, expecting the stock to take a hit upon news of the Williams car dealership empire pulling the plug on their banking business.

This plan all went amiss when Lisa Williams, anxious to mend fences between the two families, pressured her husband to hold off and Bud's post-Thanksgiving announcement in kind had actually given Unibank's stock price a nominal increase.

Andy Moretti's racing enterprise would finish the season on high notes, with Alex finishing in the top five in three more F1 races, including a podium appearance in the last event in Qatar. The combination of performance and publicity had Moretti Motorsport flooded with sponsorship inquiries. Their main two, British Petroleum and Van Boden Financial, were feeling very good locked into their next two years with the team.

Their next season looked promising as the possibility of Moretti Motorsport's F1 squad could feature both Tony and Alex Moretti on the grid, spurring a friendly family dispute about who would be number one.

The budding romance between Andy and Sarah was in full view of the public now, as the two were constantly seen together. There was even talk of Sarah moving up north to Lake Norman, with a quite serious condition. "I'm still a traditional southern girl, Andy. I'll need a ring first."

Allison's grand plan to have her despised sister disappear had backfired, while at the same time giving her a dose of her own medicine. She would smile to herself in her own sinister way, however. After all, she had escaped scrutiny and had lived to fight another day.

The news that Aaron's father had lightened up, indicating the Williams and Cook families may restore their relationship, gave Allison some new optimism. She would marry Aaron and have access to all of his wealth to accompany her own, despite having to wait another two and a half years to tap into much of it.

Although British racing star Evelyn Stevens and Allison's sister Amanda Cook were still the motorsport world's media darlings, Allison herself had garnered her fair share of attention over their captivity, and she would play it up for all it's worth with appearances, book deals, and possibly a gig as a racing commentator. At the end of the day, it appeared she had stepped in manure and came out smelling like a rose.

Allison's confident reflections drew a pause, however, when she had an email notice pop up on her phone.

So glad you're back and in one piece, Allison Cook. I need another fifty grand. You have two weeks... *Hot Lips*

Afterword

Racer's Fiancée was written as a purely fictional novel with some *authenticity* with actual teams, events, places, and true-life individuals from the international world of motor racing. While several well-known drivers and teams are noted in the plot for effect, the Moretti racing family and the Moretti Motorsport teams are 100% fictional, with any apparent or relative similarity to actual characters and/or teams purely coincidental.

Dale Earnhardt Jr does have a very popular podcast on YouTube featuring mostly guests from the NASCAR world, and there are numerous podcasts featuring news and commentary about Formula One. I get much of my racing opinion commentary on the domestic front from the David Land and Marshall Pruitt podcasts, featured on YouTube, great sources for updated behind-the-scenes information about the sport and IndyCar in particular. As a purist, I am still partial to publications such as Motorsport and Racer magazines, both of which have popular websites related to the world of motor racing.

As I am a huge fan of motorsports (as you can tell), I wish to give a special shout-out to some who inspired the Moretti Racing Family Saga series. I've always been a huge Andretti fan and I for one take it as an affront to all American racing fans that Formula One has challenged Michael Andretti's quest to enter F1. Hopefully, by the time most readers get to this page, the challenge will be old news and the Cadillac-powered Andretti F1 car will be well on its way toward the grid.

Look for the sequel to Racer's Fiancée, the next chapter in the Moretti Racing Family Saga, in Racing Champion, planned for release in late Autumn, 2025.

Your reviews would be most appreciated at the origin of purchase and/or visit my website at www.jamesherbertharrison.com where you may check out my blogs and sign up for my newsletter.

About the author

James Herbert Harrison, a native of Cape Girardeau, Missouri, has lived and worked throughout the continental United States as a businessman and industrial equipment/software sales representative. He currently resides in Olathe, Kansas, with his wife, Maryna, and their teenage son. James has an older son who lives in Cape Girardeau, as well as two older stepchildren. The family are proud members of Lenexa Baptist Church in Lenexa, Kansas.

James' pedigree as a writer began years earlier with the publishing of his first novel. *Quest For Power*, a political thriller to be re-released as *The Programmer*. *Miracle From Ukraine*, a totally different departure in genre, was inspired by the real-life saga of James and Maryna having experienced many of the actual events in the story.

A lifelong motor racing enthusiast and avid collector of motorsport memorabilia, James is often found in warm weather on Table Rock Lake when not attending a major motorsports event. Fans are welcome to reach out at jamesherbertharrison@gmail.com or find James on the various social media apps.

Printed in Great Britain
by Amazon